THE SU
F

SARA FRASER

The Summer of
the Fancy Man

WARNER BOOKS

A *Warner* Book

First published in Great Britain by
Little, Brown and Company in 1993

This edition published by Warner in 1994
Reprinted 1994

A CIP catalogue record for this book
is available from the British Library.

ISBN 0 7515 0364 9

Printed in England by Clays Ltd, St Ives plc

Warner Books
A Division of
Little, Brown and Company (UK) Limited
Brettenham House
Lancaster Place
London WC2E 7EN

Introduction

It was during the summer of 1902 that the fancy man returned from the war. Three women, each one in her own way a prisoner, each one a victim, each one bereft of hope, would come to know him, and that knowing would irrevocably change their lives. For the rest of her days each woman would keep locked in her heart the memory of that fateful summer of the fancy man.

Chapter One

Redditch, Worcestershire. June, 1902.

Cleopatra Dolton was woken by the slamming of the front door and for a few moments lay staring dazedly upwards, her mind still filled with the images of her broken dreams. The bedroom was very dark, the heavy curtains that shrouded its window blocking out the moonlight that silvered the world outside. Wakefulness came with a rush as she heard the heavy stumblings of her husband's unsteady progress up the stairs and her full lips curled in disgust as his hands came clumsily fumbling for the brass knob of the bedroom door, and his hoarse breathing and muttered curses betrayed his drunkenness.

Pale gaslight from the landing wall lamp suddenly bathed her face as the bedroom door was pushed open and in the doorway the bulky body of Arthur Dolton was a black silhouette against its glare.

'Am you awake?' His tone was loud and aggressive and the woman knew from bitter experience that to feign slumber would only aggravate his drunken temper and provoke a violent outburst.

She pushed herself upright and faced him, the long thick plait of her black hair hanging down across the full breasts that thrust against her white nightshift.

He belched loudly, and, even across the distance that separated them, Cleopatra Dolton could smell the fumes of beer, whisky and tobacco, and the rank acridity of stale sweat.

'Why warn't you downstairs waiting for me?' he

demanded angrily. 'I wants a bite to ate when I gets home, and summat to drink.'

For a brief moment an angry retort rose in her mind, but conscious of her sleeping children in the next bedroom she quelled the impulse to give voice to it, and instead forced herself to answer meekly.

'I'm sorry Arthur, but I took a queer turn earlier on, and I had to lie down for a while. I fell asleep, that's why I wasn't downstairs when you came in.'

He made no answer, only stood swaying, his breath rasping in his throat.

'I'll go down now and make you some supper,' the woman offered, and thrusting aside the bedclothes she swung her legs to the floor. As she moved, the friction of the cloth caused her nightshift to ride up high on her rounded white thighs, and the man's bleared gaze shifted to her exposed legs and his voice thickened as he told her, 'Youm a good looking 'ooman still, aren't you wife?'

A familiar sensation of dismay and dread swept over her, and keeping her head down she stood and quickly freed the folds of the nightshift so that the hem fell to her ankles.

He still blocked the doorway and she asked him, 'Let me by please?'

He grinned, and came towards her. 'I doon't want any supper now, Cleo. I'se just seen summat else I'd sooner have.'

A sense of mounting desperation caused her low pitched voice to rise slightly. 'But it'll not take me long to cook you something, Arthur.'

He reached for her and his hands grasped the thin cloth of her nightshift and he tugged it roughly upwards over her wide shapely hips.

'Gerrit off!' he ordered harshly. 'And get back on that bloody bed.'

'But I'm not feeling well!' she protested despairingly.

'Gerrit off, I tell you!' He was shouting now, and wrenching viciously at the nightshift. 'Youm me lawful wife, and you'll gi' me me rights.'

Knowing that any further resistance on her part would

8

only cost her a savage beating, and would not save her from sexual congress, Cleopatra Dolton did as she was bid, and lifted her nightshift over her head, then lay naked upon the bed.

Her husband made no attempt to close the bedroom door, and feasted his eyes upon her body, pale in the gaslight, as he tore his own clothing from him and threw it to the floor.

Cleopatra kept her eyes closed, and shuddered visibly as his grossly fat belly crushed down upon her flesh, and his big hands cruelly mauled her breasts. His mouth smothered her own, and she felt sickened by his slobbering lips. He entered her with brutal urgency, grunting and gasping as he rutted, and the sweat that poured from his hairy flabby body trickled down her sides and added to the repulsion she was experiencing.

Mercifully her ordeal was soon ended, as with strangled gasps and groans he reached his climax and slumped suddenly down upon her. Then he rolled over and without another word relapsed into drink-sodden, snoring, sleep.

Moving cautiously so as not to disturb and perhaps rouse him to wakefulness, Cleopatra collected her daytime clothing and went downstairs and into the scullery at the rear of the house. There, by the gentle illumination of the moonlight that shone through its window, she used carbolic soap and cold fresh water from the tap above the big shallow stone sink to lather and wash her body and intimate parts and to cleanse every trace of her husband's sweat and smell from her. She dried herself on a large length of rough towelling, rubbing hard until her skin glowed and tingled, and then, still naked, went into the moonlit kitchen and sat by the black iron cooking range where the banked-up fire still emitted heat.

With her fingers she gently explored the bruises Arthur Dolton's brutal hands had left on her tender flesh and the intimate inner soreness that the savage coupling had inflicted upon her. Although bitter resentment seethed in her mind, she shed no tears of self-pity or grief. All such tears had long since been shed. Instead she dressed herself

9

in her undershift and pulled on her long stockings and drawers, then the layers of petticoats and the stays that, despite the fact she had borne several children, were hardly needed because her waist was still almost as slender as a young girl. She buttoned her high-ankled boots and lastly donned the dark dress with its high collar and long puffed sleeves, and a long white apron.

Using a wooden spill to take a light from the fire, she lit one of the burners of the gas stove and set a kettle of water to boil. She then took spoonfuls of tea from the caddy and savoured the scent of the dark leaves as she tipped them into the ornately decorated teapot. These mundane tasks soothed her, easing somewhat the savage resentment against her husband that seethed in her mind.

When the tea had been made she poured herself a cupful and added milk, then sat by the range fire and sipped its steaming fragrance, and allowing herself the indulgence of her favourite daydream, imagined a future that by some unforeseen miracle would be free of her husband.

'I hate you, Arthur Dolton,' she told him in her mind. 'I hate and despise you, and every single day of my life, I pray for your death.'

Her dark eyes glowed with a fierce passion and the sheer intensity of her emotion caused shivers of excitement to course through her being.

'I'll dance on your grave the day you are put down into it, Arthur Dolton,' she whispered sibilantly. 'That I swear on my children's lives . . . I'll dance on your grave . . .'

Chapter Two

'Please father, drink this. Dr Pierce expressly instructed me that you were to take a draught four times daily.'

Miriam Josceleyne bent over the blanket-swathed figure sitting in the great leather armchair to hold the small glass tumbler to his shrunken mouth, but from under the huddle of blankets his claw-like hand shot out and struck it away. The purple liquid splashed into the woman's thin face and down the front of her white blouse. The shock of impact caused her to jerk back and cry out softly, and the blanketed figure emitted a wheezy jeering laugh.

Tears brimmed in Miriam Josceleyne's faded eyes and turning away she hurried from the room, the jeering laughter jarring through her head as she closed the door and stood in the shadowed corridor gulping the stale musty air into her lungs, fighting to bring her overstrained nerves under control, and to slow the frantic pounding of her heart.

When she had calmed a little and the thudding of her heart had slowed she went into her own bedroom further along the corridor and stared at her reflection in the full length mirror that stood to one side of the window. The purple stains imparted a grotesque clown-like appearance to her sallow face, and sighing heavily she unbuttoned the soiled white blouse and placed it into the hamper beneath the window, then went to the marble-topped wash-stand and poured water from the big jug into the bowl and washed her face and hands. As she was doing so her father's cracked voice echoed along the corridor as he shouted peevishly.

'Miriam? Miriam, where are you? It's time for my

medicine! Miriam? Miriam? Miriam? Where are you? Miriam? I want my medicine! I want it!'

He continued to shout while she took a clean blouse from a drawer and put it on. Then she drew a long breath and told herself, 'He's old and ill, he cannot help the way he behaves. He's old and ill.'

In her father's room she forced herself to smile at his skull-like face and to ignore the querulous abuse he hurled at her. Once more she measured out a draught of the purple medicine into the small glass tumbler, breathing a silent prayer of thanks as this time he sucked it greedily into his toothless mouth, the tendons in his shrivelled, grey-whiskered throat standing out like cords and his glottal jumping up and down in an unnerving manner as he noisily swallowed, then belched loudly.

Miriam rearranged the blankets around his bony shoulders and told him, 'I have to go out today for a little while, Father.'

His deep-sunk rheumy eyes glared suspiciously. 'Go out? What do you mean, go out? Where? Where do you have to go?'

'I must speak with Franklin, Father,' she told him quietly.

'Speak with Franklin? What the devil for? What business have you got with your brother? Are the pair of you plotting against me? Is that it?'

'No, Father, of course we are not plotting against you.' Miriam Josceleyne could feel the familiar tightening in her head as her father's spittle sprayed and his cracked grating voice drilled into her ears. 'I merely want to consult with Franklin about the new servant girl.'

'New servant girl?' he challenged furiously. 'What are you blabbering about, you fool? What has Franklin got to do with a new servant girl? What's the matter with the girl we have? What's wrong with her?'

'Nothing, Father.' Miriam's fingernails bit into the skin of her palms as she fought to keep herself from screaming into his face. 'Nothing is wrong with her, but she's left our employment, Father. Don't you remember? I've told you every day for a week now that Iris has left us.'

'You've told me nothing at all, girl!' He screeched, and his clawed hands came flailing towards her face, causing her to jump back in sudden fright.

'Damn you! You're the same sort of damned fool that your mother was! Useless! You're nothing but a lazy, useless fool!'

Miriam Josceleyne fled from the room and down the stairs to the ground floor of the big house, and his howls and execrations followed her. In the front parlour, crammed with sombre heavy Victorian furniture, its walls covered with the portraits and sepia photographs of sombre heavy Josceleyne forefathers, she went to stand by the bow window and stare through the net curtains at the sunlit scene outside.

The window looked westwards across Church Green, a large open triangle of land surrounded by buildings which was the virtual hub from which the town radiated in all directions. Church Green formed the northern point of the town centre and, from the apex of its triangle, the main road to the city of Birmingham, some fifteen miles distant, rolled down Fish Hill. Church Green itself was divided into two separate portions. The northern apex, which Miriam Josceleyne was now staring over, being a recreation garden for the townsfolk to sit or stroll in, complete with lawns, flowerbeds, an ornamental fountain and a bandstand, and a larger southern portion which was occupied by the mighty-spired Church of St Stephen, surrounded by its churchyard, gravestones and massive elm trees.

Now a smile touched Miriam Josceleyne's lips as she saw a trio of small, ragged, barefoot urchins clamber over the low decorative iron railings of the garden and begin to splash around in the water of the small pool beneath the fountain. Her smile broadened as their shrieks of delight came faintly to her ears, and then she frowned as a helmeted police constable appeared and chased the urchins away. Sighing in sympathy she turned away from the window, and decided that it was time she visited her elder brother to seek his advice concerning a new servant girl.

13

The imposing dark red-brick structure of the Metropolitan Bank of England and Wales stood on Church Green West, on the opposite side of the open triangle to the Josceleyne house. Franklin Hubert Josceleyne was its branch manager, and considered himself a man of great consequence in the Needle District. In his early forties, he was well below average height and, self-consciously resentful of that fact, he compensated for it by strutting arrogantly and acting overbearingly towards his professional and social inferiors. An attribute which led the unkind wags of the town to give him the nickname, the short-arsed rooster. He wore a full beard and the obligatory black frock-coat. Both these articles only emphasised his lack of height.

Now, as he strutted up and down in front of Miriam in his opulent office, she thought of his nickname and was forced to stare hard at the floor with her head downcast while she struggled to suppress the wild desire to giggle which had suddenly overwhelmed her.

'I am fast losing all patience with your father, Miriam,' he blustered angrily. 'Indeed I am. Your father is becoming an intolerable burden to me.'

Miriam forbore from pointing out that Hector Josceleyne was her brother's father also.

'What was the reason this last girl gave for leaving your employment?' Franklin Josceleyne demanded.

Miriam coughed nervously, holding her lace-edged handkerchief to her lips, and a blush rose from her throat and began to colour her sallow face.

Her brother came to a standstill and turned to face her, rocking backwards and forwards upon his heels, his hands clutching the lapels of his coat, he hissed impatiently.

'Well, sister, I'm awaiting your answer?'

Miriam's embarrassment became an acute agony, and the blush was now a flaming glow.

The man's expression mirrored the contempt he had always felt for this timid weakling of a sister and, like many bullies of his type, the knowledge that she was afraid of him only served to whet his appetite to inflict more pain and humiliation upon her defenceless head.

14

'Far be it from me to cause you any distress, Miriam, or to offend your sense of modesty. I realise that you cannot help being an old maid,' he told her with a scathing sarcasm, then raised his voice and almost shouted, 'but I'm damned if I'll allow your mealy-mouthed cowardice to prevent me from ascertaining the truth of the matter. Now you will tell me the reason for the girl leaving your employment, and you will tell me this instant. Do you hear me, Miriam? This instant!'

Near to tears with shame, and twisting the handkerchief between her fingers she stuttered, 'F,f,father behaved b,b,b,badly towards her.'

'How? How did he behave badly?' Franklin Josceleyne hectored unmercifully. 'I demand to know how?'

Miriam drew a long shuddering breath, then blurted out, 'He insulted her both mentally and physically.'

'In what way?' Her brother was ruthless.

'He t,t,t,tried to molest her person.'

By now Miriam Josceleyne's agitation was such that the lace edging of the handkerchief was beginning to tear as her fingers tugged at it.

'To molest her person?' her brother exclaimed incredulously.

Miriam nodded, then gulped out hurriedly. 'She told me that he had repeatedly attempted to fondle her breasts, and other parts of her body, and that he had offered her money if she would perform certain indecent acts upon his person.' From somewhere deep within her being a sudden spurt of courage rose, and with a flash of spirit she asserted, 'There, you know it all now, and this is not the first time it has happened. Father behaved in the same shameful manner towards the girl before Iris as well. I'll not submit to any more of your badgerings about his behaviour. The fault is not mine, although I feel the shame of it.'

She began to weep noisily, burying her head in her hands.

The man looked down at his sister's frail shoulders heaving, and a fleeting sense of shame and pity touched him. He patted her shoulder telling her gruffly,

'There now, it's over. Control yourself. I'll not press you further.'

Another aspect suddenly caused him concern, and his face twitched worriedly as he asked his sister in a gentler tone.

'Tell me, Miriam, I have to know. Does anyone else know of these occurences?' He paused, then added hurriedly. 'Apart from yourself and the girls in question, that is?'

Miriam Josceleyne shook her head. 'No one, and both girls have sworn to me that they'll never speak of it to a living soul.' Again a rare flash of spirit asserted itself, and she told him, 'They promised for my sake, Brother Franklin, because they told me that I had been a good mistress to them, and were it not for father, they would have wished to stay with me for all their lives.'

Relief showed in Franklin Josceleyne's eyes, but his inbred snobbery caused him to grumble aloud, 'It's a pretty thing, is it not, when a family of our position in this town must be beholden to grubby little serving girls. Grateful that slum-rats will hold their tongues.'

He resumed pacing up and down, his thoughts rampaging as he mulled over what his sister had told him, and the facts so enraged him that at one point he burst out, 'Damn father! It were better he should have died before bringing this disgrace upon the family name.'

Miriam quite suddenly felt strangely calm, and the flush that had coloured her sallow cheeks was now visibly ebbing. She was able to ask her brother in an even tone.

'Father is still with us, Franklin, and therefore, what's to be done about him? If I obtain the services of another girl, then what is to prevent him from behaving in this manner again?'

Her brother came to a halt and regarded her with a frown. 'Why, you must exert a greater degree of vigilance, sister. You must ensure that it cannot happen again.'

To her own amazement Miriam found that she was able to argue quite daringly with her feared brother. 'But how can I ensure that? I cannot spend twenty-four hours of every day with father. And even if I could do so, there

16

would come a time when I must of necessity fall asleep. What would there be to prevent him molesting another girl then?'

The man shrugged. 'Well then, if that's the case you must do without a servant, and look to the house and to father by yourself.'

Miriam Josceleyne's new-found courage abruptly deserted her, and once more agitated nerves caused her fingers to twist and tug the handkerchief.

'But Franklin, I cannot carry the burden by myself,' she protested weakly. 'Can you not do something to help me?'

She visibly flinched when he suddenly stormed at her, 'What in Heaven's name do you expect from me? Do you not consider that I also am over-burdened with the responsibilities of my own family, and my position in the bank? Why is it always I who is expected to shoulder the burdens of the family? To assume the responsibilities and direct the affairs of all of you? You are twenty-eight years of age, sister. A woman of mature years. Thanks to me your financial position is secure, and so is father's. All I ask of you in return is that you care for him in his last years. God only knows he'll not live too much longer, will he?' He paused for a moment or two, and a gleam of cruelty shone in his small eyes. 'After all, Miriam, what else have you to look forward to in life, other than the company of father? I doubt that you'll ever marry. You're an old maid now, and hardly what a man seeking a wife is looking for. A man wants a young and lively woman, who has something to offer him, not a shrivelled stick like you.'

The words appeared to affect Miriam Josceleyne like physical blows, and she flinched and huddled defensively, her sallow face once more flaming with shame and embarrassment.

Franklin Josceleyne stared down at her frail bowed figure and downcast head and experienced a savage satisfaction of victory. Knowing that she would now dutifully accede to anything he might direct.

'I myself shall go to Ludford's, this very morning, and shall engage a suitable person to assist you. Now, you'd best get back to father, I've many pressing matters to attend to.'

He seated himself behnd his large desk and busied himself in riffling through a sheaf of papers and, as timidly as a mouse, Miriam Josceleyne rose and went silently from the room.

Outside, on the street, she gusted a long shuddering sigh and glanced about her almost furtively, dreading that she might see someone who would expect her to greet them, or at the very least exchange a bow of acknowledgement. As always after an interview with her older brother, Miriam Josceleyne's almost non-existent self-confidence was eroded to vanishing point, and even the thought of meeting an acquaintance created a frisson of fear that she would commit some social gaffe which would embarrass her beyond endurance.

She lowered her head and with eyes firmly fixed on the ground scurried around the railinged churchyard and headed back towards her home.

'Miss Josceleyne?'

The sound of her name being called caused her to catch her breath and very reluctantly she slowed her steps, and then came to a halt as a man stepped in front of her.

The plump-featured, clean-shaven, shabbily-suited, bowler-hatted man was aged thirty but looked forty. He had been standing in a doorway beneath a sign which proclaimed in sadly weathered gold lettering, 'For artificial teeth of exquisite shape and beauty enquire inside. Mr James Whitehead – Dentist. Fees within reach of all classes.'

James Whitehead smiled at her, displaying a set of ill-fitting artificial teeth, the appearance of which were sadly at variance with the boast of his advertisement.

'How are you, Miss Josceleyne?'

'I'm well, I thank you, Mr Whitehead,' she told him stiffly, and glanced nervously in the direction of the Metropolitan Bank.

'You've not been in church these last two weeks, Miss Josceleyne. I was becoming concerned that you might be ill.' He stared at her face, which despite its sallow paleness and shadowed faded eyes still showed traces of the pretty girl she had once been.

18

'I have not been ill, Mr Whitehead.' She was uneasy, and gave the impression of desiring to flee.

With a pathetic eagerness to detain her with him, the man asked hurriedly, 'Will I have the pleasure of seeing you at church this coming Sunday, Miss Josceleyne?'

Again she glanced nervously towards the Metropolitan Bank and side-stepped in overt agitation.

'I must go, Mr Whitehead.'

She looked at him and saw the disappointment upon his face, and not wishing to hurt his feelings, explained quickly, 'My father is not well, Mr Whitehead. I cannot leave him alone for too long. I must go.'

'Will you be at church this Sunday, Miss Josceleyne?' he questioned anxiously.

'Yes, well, I may be.' She was already moving past him, drawing her skirt aside so that it would not touch him. 'That is . . . I really don't know Mr Whitehead. Goodbye.'

She hurried on, blushing hotly, and the man stared sadly after her, with an expression of longing suffusing his plump face.

Chapter Three

Winston Farr sat at the table in the odorous cramped room and scowled at the beautiful face of his daughter Emma, seated facing him across the greasy thick wooden surface. The eighteen-year-old girl scowled defiantly back at him, provoking him to growl threateningly, 'I shall wipe that bloody look off your face wi' me fist in a minute, our Emma.'

'You do that!' she defied him. 'You give me some marks, and then see me goo to the police office with 'um.'

'You fuckin' bitch!' The shirt-sleeved, collarless man rose to his feet with fists clenched, and from behind him his slatternly wife begged.

'No Feyther, doon't. It 'ull only bring trouble on your own yed. You knows that well enough by now. You knows what happened the last time you give her a tanning.'

Her warning made him hesitate, and while he stood undecided, a flurry of knocking came on the door which opened directly onto the street outside.

The older woman rushed to open it, and the small boy standing on the doorstep gabbled breathlessly.

'Our chimbley's took fire and me mam says can Mr Farr come straight away and see to it? Straight away, me mam says!'

'Wheer does you live, my duck?' the woman asked him.

'Fourteen Lodge Road. Can Mr Farr come straight away, me mam says.'

'All right my duck, you goo and tell your mam that Mr Farr is coming along directly.' Amy Farr assured the child, and turned to her husband, still standing glaring at his daughter.

20

'You'd best get down theer straight away, Feyther, or next time theer's a chimblcy fire then Old Noakes 'ull get the job.'

Winston Farr grudgingly accepted what the woman told him, and pulled a pair of hobnailed boots onto his filthy bare feet. From the cubby hole beneath the stairs he took his dirt-blackened jacket and bowler hat, and his chimney-sweeping equipment of extendable brushes, rods and scrapers, with several hessian sacks. Loose soot was dislodged from the various articles and spread out across the floor and the nearest surrounds, but made no appreciable difference to the grimy state of the room.

As he went through the door Winston Farr growled over his shoulder, 'I'll sort you out when I gets back, our Emma.'

'No you'll not,' she flashed back cheekily, 'for I'll not be here by then.'

Furiously he swung round, and his wife bodily pushed him out into the street. 'Leave it Feyther, leave it for now. Get down to Lodge Road and make sure o' that bit o' work. God knows we needs the money bad enough.'

Cursing loudly he stamped off along the street, and with an expression of exasperation on her worn, lined features Amy Farr told her daughter, 'You should be shamed o' yourself, our Emma, cheeking your feyther so. You'd oughta show him more respect.'

'Bugger him!' The girl's small white even teeth bared in a fierce grin. 'Just because you'se bin his bloody doormat for years, it doon't mean that I'se got to be the same. Bugger the old sod!'

'You wicked little cow!' her mother burst out indignantly. 'He's bin a good feyther to you. He's always treated you the best of all the kids.'

Emma tossed her thick cloud of chestnut coloured hair so that it settled in long burnished waves, framing her oval face, and despite her anger with her daughter, Amy Farr was yet again filled with a sense of awed amazement that she had ever managed to produce such a beautiful creature from her womb. For neither she or her husband had ever possessed any physical beauty.

21

The girl stretched her arms wide and yawned, then drew a deep breath which filled her lungs and caused her pert rounded breasts to push against the thin fabric of her cream coloured blouse. Her mother's look of worried exasperation became tinged with an admiring puzzlement. She thought it a virtual miracle that despite the dirt and slovenliness that had surrounded her upbringing, Emma Farr's own physical appearance always radiated a clean freshness.

Of course, the girl had been in service ever since she was little more than a child, and was accustomed to households where cleanliness was the norm, and physical tidiness was obligatory. But Amy Farr was forced to acknowledge even that explanation could not fully account for her daughter's fastidious attention to her appearance and personal hygiene.

'Well, I hope your fether's temper 'ull be cooled by the time he gets back,' Amy Farr said now. 'Or you might well find yourself with a sore face, my wench.'

Emma Farr rose to her feet, and smoothed her long neat skirt down over her slender rounded hips. 'It doon't matter to me what state the old sod's temper 'ull be in, Mam. I'll not be here to suffer it.'

Her mother's face showed instant concern. 'Wheer am you gooing, our Emma?'

'I'm gooing to see Aunt Bella, and find another place. Christ knows I'm sick to death o' being a servant, but I'd sooner do that than stay here at me dad's beck and call, and having to put up wi' his bloody moods.'

Amy Farr was forced to concede the point. 'Yes, it might be for the best iffen you did that, my wench. You and your dad 'ull never agree, not iffen you both lives to be a thousand. But you'll come and let me know how you gets on wun't you?' she entreated anxiously, 'because youm still me daughter, wicked wilful though you may be, and your feyther loves you in his own way.'

The younger woman softened. 'I knows you both loves me, Mam. And I loves both o' you. But I wants to goo me own way in life. I wants more from it than you'se ever got from it, Mam. And God knows, I doon't want to spend any

22

more time here in the bloody Silver Street. I'se seen all that I wants to o' this slum.'

Mrs Bella Ludford, widow of the late Charles Ludford, and sole proprietress of Ludford's Servant Agency, Unicorn Hill, Redditch, bore a striking resemblance to the lately deceased Queen Victoria, and like that monarch she gloried in her widowhood. Her gown was black, her jewellery was jet, her shawl was black, and even the handkerchief that she had tucked into the wrist of her sleeve was the same funereal colour. Now her hanging jowls quivered and shook as she berated the young woman standing facing her across the tall narrow counter that, apart from a solitary wooden wall bench, comprised the sole furnishings of the Application Office of the Agency.

'What the bloody 'ell as you bin adoing this time, our Emma? This last 'un makes it the third place that you'se bloody walked out on, aren't it? What the bleedin' 'ell does you expect me to do for you this time? I carn't find a place in a God fearing, respectable family for a wench that aren't brought a character from her last situation can I?'

Suddenly she hushed as the outer door was pushed open, causing the bell hanging above it to jangle loudly. Bella Ludford's manner changed dramatically, and coming from behind the counter she gushed, 'Why Mr Josceleyne. Sir, this is an honour. Will you please be so kind as to step into my office, sir?'

The bank manager nodded a curt acceptance of the invitation, and once she had opened the door and ushered him into her private sanctum, Bella Ludford hissed to her niece, 'You wait for me, girl, and be quiet.'

Within twenty minutes Emma Farr had been called into the inner office, and had been offered and accepted the post of General Servant to Mr Hector and Miss Miriam Josceleyne, at Cotswold House, Church Green East, Redditch. She was to commence her duties that very day. Wages to be eighteen pounds per annum, with full board and bed, and uniforms supplied. Every Wednesday evening free, and alternate Sundays. On those free

23

Sundays she was to attend Divine Service at least once, but was permitted the church or chapel of her choice.

When Franklin Josceleyne had departed, Emma questioned her aunt.

'What did you tell him about me not having brought a character from me last place, Auntie Bella?'

'He warn't that bothered, Emma.' Her aunt answered with an assumed casualness.

The girl, whose innate shrewdness had been honed by the harshness of her years in the slums, grinned knowingly, and challenged.

'Come on now, Aunt. Let's have the truth on it, shall we? You're not talking to some thick-yedded yokel wench from off the farm now you know. What's the snag with the job?'

Bella Ludford tapped the side of her bulbous nose with a pudgy beringed finger. 'There's nothing wrong wi' the job, girl. You should have learned by now not to poke your nose into the affairs o' your betters.'

Emma chuckled scornfully. 'Bugger that for a game o' soldiers! Come now, tell me, or I'll not goo to the bloody house, and that won't make you look so wonderful in Mr High-and-Mighty Franklin Josceleyne's eyes, 'ull it, if he gets let down like that.' She paused to evaluate the effect of her threat, and then went on. 'So you tell me now, why did the last maid leave theer, and why aren't Franklin Josceleyne concerned about me having a character?'

Bella Ludford accepted defeat with good grace, and chuckled lewdly, before explaining. 'I'se heard a whisper that it's because of the old man, Mr Hector, that the last two girls left theer. He keeps on pestering the maids to give him a bit o' you know what. But theer's no call for you to worry about him. From what I'm told, the old bugger is as weak as a babby.' She peered shrewdly at her niece. 'I knows that you'll be able to deal with his nonsense without any trouble, our Emma.'

The younger woman laughed gaily. 'I was just thinking of that old saying, Aunt. About the definition of a Silver Street virgin.'

The old woman cackled raucously with delight. 'I knows it, our Emma. It's a girl who can run faster than her

24

feyther and brothers.'

'Just so, Aunt.' Emma Farr's bold black eyes twinkled merrily, and she winked broadly. 'I was always a good runner. It 'ull take more than a doddering old bugger like Mr Hector to catch me, and that's a fact.'

Chapter Four

Station Master William Mann donned his frock-coat and top hat and came out from his office beneath the roofed section of the platform as the noon train from Birmingham arrived at Redditch station. The oily dark-red locomotive rolled past his tall portly figure hissing jets of steam from its boiler and belching clouds of black and grey grit-laden smoke from its tall funnel, while a long line of carriages clanked and clattered behind it.

Tommy Hands, an eager young porter, bustled self-importantly along the platform screeching at the top of his high-pitched voice, 'Redditch, Redditch, Redditch, next stops Studley, Alcester, Evesham, Ashford. Redditch, Redditch, Redditch.'

William Mann winced slightly as the youth's screech neared him, but forbore to remonstrate, not wishing to dampen the youngster's enthusiasm for his new profession.

From his waistcoat pocket the station master drew a large pocket watch and checked the time, nodding in satisfaction at the realisation that the train having arrived a couple of minutes early could not fail to depart from Redditch station precisely on schedule.

'Sir, sir, look theer!' Tommy Hands' thin features glowed with excitement. 'Look at that soldier. What regiment is he, sir?'

The station master stared in the direction of the porter's pointing arm. From the carriage directly behind the engine a solitary passenger had alighted onto the platform. Mann squinted his eyes to see more clearly but the smoke from the funnel was being blown by a skittish

26

breeze to form a shifting veil in between himself and the khaki-clad figure.

'Does you reckon he's bin out in South Africa fighting them Boers, Mister Mann, sir?' An expression of hero-worship mingled with envy was dawning in Tommy Hands' face. 'I wish I could ha' gone for a soldier and had a goo at them bloody Boers.'

'Mind your language, Hands,' the station master admonished sternly, then softened slightly. 'If he has bin out theer, then he's come back too late for the celebrations, aren't he? The peace was signed two weeks since.'

By now several more passengers had left the carriages and were making their way towards the station exit, and, turning his attention towards them, William Mann nodded in lordly fashion to those he knew and bowed respectfully to one man who was a local factory owner. From the luggage van of the train the guard shouted for a porter to come and unload a large travelling trunk, and the station master ordered Tommy Hands.'

'Goo and take care o' that, boy.'

'I'd like to take it with me immediately, Mr Mann.'

It was the soldier who had spoken, and William Mann blinked at him in surprise and exclaimed: 'My oath! I never saw you coming.'

The soldier grinned, disclosing good white teeth, and indicated the billowing clouds of funnel smoke.

'This gives good cover.'

Mann stared at him curiously. About six feet in height, the soldier was wearing a dashing slouch hat with a turned-up side brim and a plume of black feathers in the puggree. A Sam Browne belt crossed with a bandolier on his broad chest and he wore a holstered pistol and ammunition pouch on the right side of his waistbelt. His cavalry breeches were met at the knee by polished riding boots with steel spurs on their heels. His face and hands were deeply sun-bronzed, and his body in the close-fitting khaki tunic looked lithe and muscular. His dark brown hair and moustache were neatly trimmed, and, although not handsome in the conventional sense, his hard features with their clear blue eyes were attractive to look upon.

Unaccountably there came into the station master's mind a visual remembrance of a picture he had once seen in a book.

'You looks just like that bloody pirate in the face, doon't you?' he thought.

Again the soldier grinned easily at him. 'Have you remembered me yet then, Mr Mann?'

A trifle disconcerted the older man frowned. 'Should I?'

The soldier nodded. 'Oh yes. I used to live next door to you in Izods Yard.'

'God Strewth!' Sudden recognition caused William Mann's jaw to momentarily gape. 'Youm young Johnny Purvis, aren't you!'

The younger man laughed and acknowledged, 'That's me, only not so young any more.'

'Well, I'll be buggered!' The station master was still amazed. 'The last time I heard about you was when you'd gone for a soldier. That must be ...' He paused, screwing up his eyes in the effort of remembrance. 'Let me think now. That must be more nor ten years since.' He stared hard at his companion. 'I can remember your Mam atelling me that you'd bin sent out to India. O'course, that warn't so long arter you'd took the shilling was it, because her's bin dead for a good few years, aren't her.'

Sadness clouded the other man's eyes.

'Yes, it's more than eight years since she died.'

'Has you bin fighting the Boers, mister?' Tommy Hands had brought the loaded four-wheeled trolley back from the luggage van, and was staring at the dashing figure before him with open hero-worship.

Johnny Purvis nodded and grinned. 'That's right, son. For the last couple of years, anyway.'

'Strewth!' The youngster's eyes shone.

'Am you still in the army, Johnny?' William Mann wanted to know. The other man shook his head, causing the black feathered plume to wave slightly. 'I'm all but finished with it now. I've got my discharge leave, and then I'm done. I'm back home to stay now, Mr Mann.'

'There's bin a few changes in the town since you left it,' the station master told him. 'A lot o' the old buildings pulled down, and new 'uns put in their place.'

'Does the Unicorn still stand?' Purvis asked.

'It does. And it still serves good ale.'

'That'll do for starters then.' Purvis grinned at Tommy Hands. 'Can you bring my trunk up there, son?' He raised his eyebrows in silent interrogation at the station master, who nodded assent.

'That's settled then.' Purvis touched the thong of the riding crop he carried to the brim of his hat in salute. 'Nice to have met you again, Mr Mann, no doubt we'll see each other around the town now that I'm back.'

He walked through the entrance hall, and Tommy Hands wheeled the trolley after him, trying to walk tall and imitate the swagger of his new-found hero.

From the booking office a weedy bespectacled clerk came to stand by the station master and stare after the disappearing khaki back.

'Who's that then, Mr Mann?'

'Johnny Purvis.'

The clerk sucked reflectively at his decayed front teeth, then remarked, 'I was at school the same time as a kid called Johnny Purvis. He used to live in one o' them yards up Front Hill.'

'That's him,' the station master confirmed.

'He used to be a real wild bugger,' the clerk remembered. 'Always in trouble wi' the teachers. Went for a redcoat in the end if I remembers rightly.'

'That he did,' Mann nodded. 'But he's finished with the army now from what he's just told me. He's come back here for good he reckons.'

Again the clerk noisily sucked his front teeth, then shook his head disparagingly. 'He went for a redcoat because he was a ne'er-do-well like they all am. He should stay on in the army wi' the rest on 'um. That's the only place for buggers like him.' He paused, then added spitefully, 'Or in bloody jail.'

The railway station was situated at the bottom of the steep Unicorn Hill, named after the inn of that name which stood almost on its brow, just before it joined the flat plateau on which the centre of the town was built. Before

29

he had climbed many yards, Tommy Hands was panting and straining with the effort of pulling the trolley and its heavy load. An ever-lengthening distance ahead of him, Johnny Purvis strolled easily upwards, tapping the thong of his riding crop against his polished boot, and despite his hard toil, Tommy Hands was immensely gratified to see the effect that the sight of his new-found hero was having on the scattering of loungers and passers-by along the roadway, who stared avidly and exchanged comments on this exotically uniformed stranger.

Johnny Purvis had almost reached the entrance to the courtyard of the Unicorn Inn when a large garishly-painted wooden sign nailed to a wall took his eye. He halted to read the words.

> Rest Driver, rest on this steep hill.
> Dumb beasts pray use with all goodwill.
> Goad not, scourge not with thonged whips.
> Let not one curse escape your lips.
> God sees and hears.

He chuckled wryly and instantly turned to stare down the steep incline to where the slightly built youth was struggling, bent almost double, to painfully drag the trolley upwards.

'Hold there, son,' he called, and retraced his steps to grasp the handle of the trolley and pull it up the hill behind him with an ease that denoted great strength and fitness.

In the courtyard of the inn he chuckled again as he saw the sweat streaming down the youth's red face, but there was no malice in his amusement.

'Here, this is for you.' He handed a silver florin coin to Tommy Hands, whose eyes widened at the sight of such largesse. 'Have you time to take a drink, son? The treat is on me.'

Tommy Hands was sorely tempted to accept, but then the thought of William Mann's wrath, should he find out that one of his porters had been drinking during working hours, forced him to decline the invitation regretfully.

'As you please. Maybe we'll share a jar or two on some other occasion.' Johnny Purvis responded pleasantly.

Tommy Hands' reluctant return down the hill with the empty trolley was cheered, however, by the reflected glory he had gained, as several loungers stopped him to ask who the stranger was, and where he had come from.

'That's Mr John Purvis,' the youth informed them self-importantly. 'He's just come back from fighting them Boers. Killed hundreds on 'um, so he did. Told me all about it, and wanted me to stay and drink with him. But I got to get back to the station. Mr Mann needs me to be theer to look arter things when the two o'clock from Ashford comes in . . .'

A flight of stone steps led up from the courtyard into the taproom of the Unicorn, and Johnny Purvis could hear the hubbub of talk and laughter coming from inside it. He stepped into the smoky room, being forced to duck under the low lintel of the doorway. At his entrance all eyes swung towards him, and the talk and laughter hushed suddenly so that his footsteps and the clinking of his spurs were the only sounds that broke the silence as he walked to the bar which dominated one end of the long room.

From behind the bar Thomas Hyde, the shirt-sleeved, aproned landlord greeted the newcomer, eyeing his uniform curiously. 'Arternoon. What's your pleasure?'

'I'll try a glass of your ale,' Purvis told him, and tossed a gold sovereign onto the bar top. 'Have one yourself,' he invited.

He seemed unaware of the curious stares of the other customers, and the continuing hiatus in the conversations, and he lifted the foam-topped glass to his lips and drained it, then set it down on the counter.

'That's good ale,' he congratulated. 'I'll take another.'

The landlord refilled the big glass, and then held up the drink that the soldier had bought him.

'Here's good health to you.'

Johnny Purvis nodded acknowledgement. 'Cheers.'

Hyde gulped the dark liquid noisily, then wiped the froth from his moustache with the back of his hand, and asked, 'Bin at the war, has you Mister?'

Johnny Purvis nodded. 'Yes, I've had a couple of years of it.'

The landlord indicated the uniform. 'What regiment is that then, Mounted Yeomanry?'

Purvis shook his head. 'No, it's the North Cape Scouts. We were irregular cavalry.'

'North Cape Scouts?' another man questioned curiously. 'Where am they from?'

'We were raised in the Cape Colony,' Purvis explained. 'But the lads came from all over. Australia, Canada, Natal, Cape Colony itself, and from here at home.'

'Did you see much fighting?' a second man wanted to know, and Johnny Purvis hesitated before telling him quietly, 'More than I wanted to.'

'What does you mean – more than you wanted to?' the same man asked.

Purvis grinned ruefully. 'Well, I can't answer for the other lads, but, speaking for myself, I've never enjoyed getting shot at. It used to put the fear o' Christ up me.'

After a couple of seconds silence, a roar of laughter came from his listeners and, as if his answer had broken some invisible barrier, men now pushed forward to shake his hand and to offer him drinks and to ply him with questions about the war and his part in it.

'I knows who you am now,' an elderly man exclaimed. 'Youm Old Ezra Purvis's youngest lad, aren't you? From up Izods Yard.'

'That's right,' Johnny Purvis nodded. 'Is my Dad still alive? We never got on you know and when I took the shilling he swore he'd never speak to me again and disowned me, and I've not had word about him since my Mam died, although I wrote to him quite a few times.'

'Ah, Old Ezra's still alive, and still up in Izods Yard,' the elderly man informed him, and grinned toothlessly. 'But he's still a miserable old sod. He 'udden't give a blind man the time even if he owned two watches, 'ud Old Ezra.'

The talk and the laughter went on, and the drink flowed, and Johnny Purvis's blue eyes glowed with pleasure, and the happiness of homecoming bubbled through him.

32

One man stood aloof from the throng around the soldier. A big man with a sweaty red face, a straw boater tipped back on his sandy hair, a high winged collar cutting into his thick neck and a blue suit covering his bulky body. Arthur Dolton had been sitting holding court among the drinkers in the taproom until the advent of Johnny Purvis, and now his fat face was morose with resentment at this newcomer who had become the centre of admiring attention.

'What does you reckon to them Boers as fighting men then, Johnny?' Thomas Hyde asked during a momentary lull in the laughter and talk.

Purvis pondered for a couple of moments, then answered thoughtfully, 'They're probably the finest fighting men in the world.'

This answer provoked some doubtful frowns among his listeners, and one young man protested, 'How can they be, when we'se just give 'um a hammering? You can't tell me that they'm braver than our chaps.'

Johnny Purvis's smile disappeared, and his expression became serious. 'I didn't say that they were braver than us, mate. What I said is that I think they're the finest all-round fighting men in the world today.'

Seeing the puzzlement in the faces around him, he tried to clarify his statement. 'Look, what I mean is, man for man they more than matched us. At least until we began to learn from them what modern war is all about. They could shoot and ride better than us. They could march all day and night and still be ready to fight, and go for weeks on a diet of biltong and water. They could ambush us and knock over our men and be up and away before we could even realise what was happening. Their generals made ours look like donkeys. They ran rings round Buller and Gatacre and the rest of our generals. Those old fools seemed to think that we were still fighting the Battle of Waterloo.'

'They didn't run rings around Roberts though, did they my buck?' It was Arthur Dolton who challenged the soldier, and his manner was deliberately offensive. 'Roberts soon raised the old Union Jack over Pretoria, didn't he, ne'er mind what your opinion might have been on him. He couldn't have paid you too much attention, could he?'

'That he did, Arthur. He soon chased 'um back home.'

'Ahr, that's right. Old Bobs showed the buggers what it was all about, didn't he?' A couple of Dolton's cronies supported him.

Johnny Purvis's blue eyes regarded the bulky-bodied Arthur Dolton warily, recognising the aggression burgeoning within the man.

'Roberts took Pretoria, but the Boers went on fighting for two more years,' he pointed out, trying to keep his tone neutral because he did not wish to mar his homecoming with dispute. 'And Kitchener needed more than a quarter of a million men and unlimited resources to bring them to the peace table.'

'That's as maybe, but they was already beaten. There might have been a few on 'um still wandering about. But Roberts had hammered 'um. All you lot had to do then was to mop 'um up. Bloody irregular cavalry you was, warn't you?' the big man observed scathingly. 'You lot didn't have to do any real fighting, did you? From what the papers said, you was only used as scout patrols and suchlike.'

Sharp memories scythed through Johnny Purvis's mind. Memories of the hardships, the bloodshed, the bitter fighting he and his comrades had endured during those long years of savage guerrilla warfare. Memories came also of that period before he had obtained a transfer to the irregular cavalry. When he had fought as an infantryman in the bloody defeats of Stormberg and Spion Kop.

Taking the soldier's silence as a token of impotence to reply, Arthur Dolton laughed jeeringly, 'Theer's a few chaps in this town who was in South Africa when the real fighting was being done, my buck. I should advise you to have a few words wi' them afore you begins shouting off your mouth about what heroes you irregulars was.' Pursing up his liver-coloured lips he spat contemptuously into the spittoon at his feet. 'For my money you bloody irregulars warn't worth a damn when theer was real fighting to be done.'

A murmer of protest greeted his words, and Thomas Hyde remonstrated, 'Now then, Arthur, that's not the way to talk. This chap's bin out theer, arter all.'

'Which is a sight farther than you'se ever bin, Arthur,' the elderly man pointed out.

The big man's fists balled and he growled menacingly, 'What does you mean by that, Harry Chambers?'

Johnny Purvis had no fear of Arthur Dolton, big and bulky though the man might be. He saw the gross belly and the rolls of fat beneath the other man's chin, and knew without any doubt that should it come to a physical confrontation he could master him. But he was saddened at how the pleasant atmosphere that had existed in the room had now been soured, and he had no desire to be the cause of violence erupting among the company.

'I've got to go.' He spoke directly to Arthur Dolton, and met the big man's threatening glare with level eyes. 'I expect we'll meet again some time. Maybe we can continue this discussion then. Goodbye all.'

With that he walked out of the room and descended the stone steps to the courtyard. There were two down-at-heel men sitting on the bottom step, and he asked, 'Do you want to earn a couple of bob, lads?'

When they readily assented he indicated his trunk. 'Carry that up Front Hill to the Plough and Harrow for me then.'

He walked from the yard followed by the men, and up in the taproom Arthur Dolton jeered to his cronies.

'I put that bloody hero in his place, didn't I lads?'

Those that were afraid of his violence agreed vociferously, but others kept their own counsel, and longed for the day to come when this bully would be put in his place.

Chapter Five

Cleopatra Dolton caught sight of her reflection in the long mirror displayed for sale in the shop window, and was pleased with what she saw. The dark-blue figure-hugging bolero jacket and skirt flattered her body, and perched on her piled dark hair the flowered toque with its whispy veil was both jaunty and demure at the same time. Because of the hot sunshine she carried her silken parasol opened above her head to gain some protection from the sun's rays and with her left hand gathered her skirts so that the flared hems did not drag in the dust of the pavement. At the central crossroads, on the south-western edge of St Stephen's churchyard she halted for a moment and glanced down towards the Unicorn Inn, then turned southwards along Evesham Street, one of the town's main shopping thoroughfares.

Along its length several delivery vans were parked, and a couple of carriers' carts drawn by sweating horses trundled slowly along. There were few pedestrians. Most housewives had done their shopping earlier in the day, and at this hour of the afternoon most children were at school and most adults in their workplaces.

There was a butcher's shop standing near to the end of the street where it joined Front Hill, rows of dressed carcasses of sheep and pigs hanging down above its open front, and flies swarming among the trays piled high with joints and cuts of varying types that filled its display windows. A highset signboard running the length of the entire frontage proclaimed it to be the Redditch Meat Company. It was one of three butchers' shops in the district owned by Arthur Dolton.

'Here she comes, the Queen of Egypt,' Ozzie Clarke, head butcher, nodded towards the oncoming woman, and his assistant, Walter Spires, came from the chopping block in the rear of the shop to stand and stare also.

'Bloody 'ell!' The assistant licked his lips. 'Her's looking toothsome today, aren't her? Gawd Strewth!' His hand moved to cup his genitals. 'I'd love to give her what for.'

'You and me both, Walter,' Ozzie Clarke grinned lasciviously. 'You and me both.'

When Cleopatra Dolton came into the shop both men were busy at the chopping block. She stood just inside the door for a few seconds until with assumed surprise Ozzie Clarke looked up at her.

'Why, Mrs Dolton, I ne'er 'eard you come in.' He was young, tall, well built and personable, and Cleopatra could understand why he had the reputation of being something of a ladies' man in the town.

Now he laid aside his cleaver and wiping his greasy hands on his striped blue apron, came smilingly towards her, his straw boater at a rakish angle on his curly brown hair. From the chopping block the older, uglier Walter Spires slyly regarded the couple.

'What can I do for you, ma'am?' Ozzie Clarke's manner was deferential, but the expression in his eyes was boldly admiring as he stared down at his employer's wife, his gaze momentarily flicking across her thrusting breasts.

The woman smiled up at him, enjoying the reaction that her proximity aroused in a young attractive man. Enjoying also the knowledge that she held power over him, because if he should overstep the bounds of propriety a single word from her to her very jealous husband would ensure Ozzie Clarke's instant dismissal from his employment, and almost certainly a physical beating from the formidable Arthur Dolton to go with it.

'Do you know where my husband is?' Even as she asked that question, Cleopatra Dolton knew what the answer would be.

'I believe he'll be down at the Unicorn, ma'am. He went to see Tommy Hyde about next week's order.'

The woman made no immediate reply, only remained

with her large dark eyes dwelling on the young man's handsome face. Not for the first time she was wondering what sort of lover he was, and speculating on the number of women who already knew the answer to that question.

For his part Ozzie Clarke was mentally stripping the bolero jacket, high-necked blouse and long skirt from her body, and imagining how she would look laying naked on a bed, arms outstretched and thighs parted to receive him.

She said something, and so deeply enmeshed was he in his vivid mental pictures that he did not comprehend her words.

'Clarke?' she questioned sharply, and he started slightly.

'I'm sorry, ma'am. I didn't quite catch what you said.'

He saw her full moist lips part in a fleeting, knowing smile, and the tip of her pink tongue showed momentarily. Then she repeated, 'Will you send some beefsteaks to the house?'

Behind the wisp of veil her dark eyes seemed to hold invitation, and he experienced a sudden surging in his loins. His face remained impassive however, as he told her.

'Of course I will ma'am. I'll cut and trim them myself.'

She smiled warmly at him. 'Many thanks, Clarke.'

Seeing that smile, Ozzie Clarke, not for the first time, wondered if there might be a possibility of entering upon a different type of relationship with the wife of his employer. His reputation as a ladies' man was well deserved, and he had enjoyed several illicit affairs with married women in the town. Now he decided to risk exploring that possibility.

'If you wish ma'am, I could bring them round to the house myself in half an hour,' he smiled charmingly. 'I'd not like you to have to wait any longer for them than needful.'

Instantly her dark eyes became frosty. 'We still employ an errand boy at this shop, do we not, Clarke?' she asked coldly.

Cursing himself for his error of judgement, Ozzie Clarke managed to keep his smile fixed on his face. 'Yes, ma'am. We do indeed.'

'Then let him deliver them. My husband does not employ you to act as an errand boy, Clarke.'

'You bloody cow!' he thought, but betrayed not the

slightest sign of his internal feelings, as he touched the brim of his straw boater and smiled.

'Certainly ma'am. The boy will have them at your house directly.'

Cleopatra Dolton turned and left the shop, and Ozzie Clarke's eyes dwelt on her firm rounded buttocks and swaying hips as she walked away down Evesham Street.

A snort of smothered laughter sounded from behind him and he swung round to meet Walter Spires' grinning regard.

'What's so funny?' Clarke demanded, then abruptly laughed himself, and, picking up a piece of meat from the tray beside him, hurled it at the other man's head. 'Don't you take the piss out o' me, you old bastard! You'll be laughing the other side o' your face the day I gets between the Queen of Egypt's legs, wunt you?'

The other man snorted again with laughter. 'You got more chance o' shaggin' the Queen of England than you 'as o' shaggin' the Queen of Egypt, Ozzie Clarke. I'll lay odds to that.'

Ozzie Clarke chuckled and turned for a final look at the now distant figure of Cleopatra Dolton, then murmured almost to himself, 'You never know what might happen, Walt. You never know . . .'

Cleopatra Dolton smiled with a satisfaction tinged with cruelty as she made her way towards the crossroads.

'What stupid fools you men are,' she told herself. 'Like dogs on heat. A woman has only to smile at you, and you think that you can bed her.'

She was conscious that from behind some of the shop windows other men stared hungrily at her as she passed. From the time she had been a schoolgirl Cleopatra Dolton had been fully aware of the effect her face and body had on men. It had always given her a sense of power, but she was an intelligent woman and she had long since realised that the very same power she could exert over men could rebound on herself with dire consequences.

She frowned now as certain memories came flooding back to torment and anger her. 'Dear God, if only I had the physical strength of a man, there's none of them would ever get the better of me then.'

She thrust the unwelcome memories from her, and mentally shrugged.

'I'll never have the physical strength to match them, but I can always be more cunning than them, and find other ways to beat them.'

Her smile now was contemptuous. 'You are all pigs, you men. All of you.'

She was now only a few steps from the crossroads and she halted to look into the window of a bookshop. An avid reader, she had always sought and found escape from the tedious or unpleasant realities of her life in books, absorbing volumes of history, and travel, and the classic novels with a never flagging appetite. After a few moments browsing she stepped back from the window and in doing so collided with a passer-by.

The impact caused her to stumble sideways and she would have fallen but a strong hand grasped her elbow and steadied her.

'I do apologise, ma'am.'

The slouch-hatted, khaki-uniformed soldier stared at her with concern. 'You're not hurt, I trust?'

She shook her head. 'No, I'm not hurt. Only startled.'

'I'm relieved to hear that.' Johnny Purvis smiled, and releasing her arm he lifted his riding crop in salute. 'Again my apologies, ma'am. Good day to you.'

He strode on along the pavement, his spurs ringing musically, and two shabby men came past her to follow him, carrying a large leather-bound trunk between them.

Cleopatra stood for a moment, still unsettled by the encounter. She stared after the tall khaki figure, and thought briefly how exotic the plumed slouch hat appeared against the humdrum everyday backdrop of Evesham Street. Then, dismissing the incident from her mind, she walked to the crossroads and went eastwards along the market place.

She walked proudly, head held high, seemingly oblivious to the people she passed on the road, and when occasionally a man or woman greeted her, she only nodded a fleeting acknowledgement and momentarily quickened her pace as if to discourage any attempt to halt her.

Some fifty yards from the easternmost edge of the Church Green the road forked left and right, to become Alcester and Red Lion Streets respectively, and Cleopatra Dolton went along the latter. It was a street of small noisy factories, mean terraced cottages built beneath road level, and shabby-fronted public houses. The Red Lion Inn stood midway along the street on the right, and flanking its grimy red brick walls was an archway leading to a long narrow winding alley of fetid hovels known as Silver Street. One of the worst slums in the town.

As she came abreast of the archway, Cleopatra Dolton slowed and halted. Her head turned slowly as if by duress, and her breathing quickened as she stared along the alley's filth-strewn cobbles, the rank stench emanating from its confines filling her nostrils. Cleopatra Dolton knew every inch of that alley. She knew its scald-headed, ricket-legged children, its brutalised men, its haggard women. She knew its drunken brawls, its screams of pain, its cries of anguish. She knew its bitterness, its hopelessness, its despair, its gutter-devil of defiant rebellion. Because Cleopatra Dolton had been born in one of its hovels, dragged half dead from the womb of her dying mother, while her father lay in swinish drunken helplessness upon the same heap of stinking bloody rags that served as a childbed.

Suddenly her breath caught in her throat, and her eyes widened as if she could not credit what they saw. From one of the fetid hovels a young woman had stepped into the alley, and was now picking her way through the filth towards the archway entrance. The white dress that she wore shimmered in the sunlight creating a glow of pristine purity against the dinginess, and as she came nearer the clear bloom of her complexion and the glossiness of her neatly piled chestnut hair beneath the wide-brimmed straw hat created a sense of wonderment in Cleopatra Dolton's mind.

As the young woman came under the archway Cleopatra Dolton was aware of bold black eyes, and the scent of clean linen and young fresh flesh, and the cloth-wrapped bundle the young woman carried brushed against her skirts. Cleopatra Dolton mumbled an apology and stepped back to allow the other a clear passage, and the young woman's white teeth glistened as she smiled, but she uttered no words and went on without a backward glance towards the town centre.

The older woman stood staring after her, and an eerie sense that she had somehow travelled backwards in time assailed her.

'I wore a white dress on the day I left this foul place,' she recalled, as the memory vividly assailed her. 'And I carried my few belongings in a cloth, just like that girl is doing.' A sudden rush of emotion caused tears to brim in her eyes, and in her mind she called after the young woman, 'I hope you are escaping from here, and I hope that you'll find more happiness than I ever did after I'd escaped.'

Cleopatra Dolton slowly walked away from the archway with the sad realisation that she could never really escape from Silver Street; it travelled with her.

Chapter Six

Emma Farr's heart was light as she went past the well-dressed woman at Red Lion Arch and walked towards the town centre. She passed behind the dark grey mass of St Stephen's Church and along Church Green East until she reached Cotswold House opposite the recreation garden. She stood outside the tall spiked iron railings and examined the large house. It was double-fronted with a pillared portico and tall bow windows on the ground floor. All the front windows were veiled with net curtains, behind which hung dark drapes, drawn now against the rays of the afternoon sun, giving the house a funereal aspect.

'All it needs is a crape wreath hung on the bloody door knocker and you'd think they had a corpse laying inside.' Emma hated curtains drawn to exclude the sunlight and a sense of misgiving rose within her; for a brief moment she was tempted to turn on her heels and go back to Silver Street. Then she remembered her morning dispute with her father, and shrugged resignedly.

'If I goes back, then more than likely I'll end the day with a thick lip. Might as well gi' this place a twirl, now that I'm here.'

She transferred her cloth bundle from one hand to the other and moved away from the front gate towards the tradesmen's entrance at the left-hand end of the railings. The hinges squealed as she pushed it open and walked to the door at the side of the house. She tugged the bell-pull several times in quick succession and listened with satisfaction to the noisy jangling.

'That'll fetch you a bit rapid.'

43

Allowing a few seconds to elapse Emma again tugged the bell-pull, and this time did not release the handle, but kept on creating a noisy jangling, until the door swung open and a hoarse breathy female voice scolded.

"Ull you give over making such a din! I aren't got the speed o' lightning. Youm making rattle enough to wake the dead.' It was an elderly fat woman, wearing a voluminous white apron with an old-fashioned floppy mob-cap pulled low on her frizzy hair.

She peered curiously at the girl in the white dress and questioned, 'Be you the new wench?'

'I am. My name's Emma Farr. I'll bet that you're the cook here, aren't you? Well, I've been engaged as the upstairs maid, but I don't mind giving you a hand in the kitchen if you wants me to,' Emma told her, quite unabashed by the other's scolding tone.

The fat woman stared hard into her black eyes, and then said huffily, 'Youm a saucy 'un, you am. I can tell that just be looking at you. Yes, I am the cook here, and you calls me, Mrs Elwood.'

Emma grinned, and for a moment resembled the cheeky urchin she had once been. 'And you've got a heart o' gold. I can tell that just by looking at you.'

The fat woman scowled suspiciously, but Emma's engaging grin did not falter, and after a moment the other woman could not help but chuckle amusedly.

'You saucy little cat. Well, doon't stand theer all day, wench,' she jerked her head. 'Come on along wi' me. You can put your stuff in your room, and then Miss Miriam 'ull want to see you.'

She waddled heavily along the corridors and up the stairs and along the landings of the big house, and Emma dutifully followed. The air inside the house smelt musty and stale, and the young woman frowned briefly. In her experience such staleness usually denoted the absence of other servants to help share the cleaning chores.

Emma was also possessed of an acute intuition and she sensed an atmosphere of oppressive sombreness pervading the house, which could not be totally attributed to the dark woodwork and sober wallpapering.

The servants' quarters were on the topmost floor of the house, and consisted of two tiny rooms directly beneath the roof.

'This is yourn,' Mrs Elwood told her.

Emma briefly scanned her new home. It had white-washed walls, and a single iron bedstead on which rested a straw-filled palliasse, folded sheets and blankets and a pillow. There was a small battered chest of drawers beneath the dormered window with a cracked fly-spattered mirror atop of it, and nails driven into the walls and door served as clothes hangers.

'This was Iris's room, her that youm come in place on, and young Charlotte the scullery maid used to be next door,' Mrs Elwood informed. 'Charlotte left afore Iris did.'

'Do you live in?' Emma wanted to know, and the fat woman shook her head.

'Not I. I'se got a cottage down Easemore Lane theer, just round the corner from here. Next to Cresswell's, the undertakers. Me 'usband works for 'um, and Tommy Cresswell lets us have the cottage rent free.' The woman chuckled wryly. 'Mind you, considering the state on it, it should ha' bin pulled down years ago. Still, beggars carn't be choosers, can they.'

Emma Farr's grin was rueful as she agreed. 'That's the truest thing I've heard said this week, Mrs Elwood.'

Miriam Josceleyne was sitting in the front parlour, its heavy drapes now drawn back sufficiently to admit some daylight, and when Emma Farr was ushered into the room she instructed quietly, 'Stand over there, girl, so I may see you clearly.'

The sunlight lancing through the gap in the drapes was filled with shimmering motes of dust which swirled and danced as the young girl moved through them. She stood facing Miriam Josceleyne, and the older woman experienced a sense of dread as her eyes noted the shapely curves beneath the pristine freshness of the white dress, the clear bloom of skin and glossiness of rich chestnut hair.

'You're too beautiful,' she thought. 'Father will never be able to control himself.' Aloud she asked, 'Where do you come from, girl. What family are you?'

45

'If you please, ma'am, me dad's Winston Farr, the chimney sweep. We live in Silver Street.'

'Good Lord!' Miriam Josceleyne could not help but exclaim softly in surprise that such a radiant beauty could have come from such dismal surroundings. It took a moment or two for her to digest that answer, and then she asked curiously. 'Have you lived long in Silver Street?'

'I was born and bred theer, ma'am.'

'Good Lord!' The older woman murmured once more, and then went on to question the girl about her previous experience in service, but in reality paid little heed to the answers, knowing that whatever she herself might think the fact that her brother Franklin had engaged this new servant meant that she would have to accept the girl at face value.

As Emma answered the questions, altering the facts of her previous service as and when it suited her, she in her turn studied her new mistress.

In the small world of the town the urchins from the poorer quarters often roamed the streets and inevitably came to know by sight and name many of its richer and socially superior inhabitants. In contrast the children of the self-styled 'superior' classes were trained to ignore their social inferiors who, they came to believe, were on this earth solely to cater to the manifold needs of their 'betters' and who remained for the most part an anonymous mass, distinguished by their dirty smelliness and raucous ignorance.

So, although Emma had known Miriam Josceleyne by sight and name for many years, Miriam Josceleyne had no recollection of ever having seen her.

Emma could remember her new mistress as a teenage girl, possessed of a sweet prettiness of face and figure. Now she mentally contrasted that visual image with the frail, thin, sallow-complexioned woman sitting before her, whose manner, despite her station in life, was timid and hesitant. Emma judged silently with some contempt. 'Bugger me, if you aren't turned into a real old maid, Miriam Josceleyne. A real old stick.'

The questioning ceased and her new mistress smiled,

46

displaying good teeth, and for a brief instant she resembled the pretty girl she had once been.

'Very well, my dear. I shall call you Emma, and you may address me as Miss Miriam. You may now go and help Mrs Elwood in the kitchen. She will instruct you as to your early morning duties for tomorrow, and after breakfast I myself shall continue your instruction. Mrs Elwood will give you your uniforms, and you will have ample time this evening to alter them to fit.'

Emma bobbed a curtsey. 'Very well, Miss Miriam.'

She turned to leave the room, but Miriam Josceleyne halted her.

'Oh, one moment, Emma. There is one point, I am unsure whether my brother has told you.'

Emma waited obediently.

We do not allow our servants to have any followers Emma.'

Although the girl knew exactly what her new mistress meant, her imp of devilment caused her to stare with wide eyes and ask in innocent bewilderment.

'What do you mean, Miss Miriam? Followers?'

A faint flush began to colour Miriam Josceleyne's cheeks. 'I mean males, Emma. That is, male friends.'

Emma's black eyes danced mischievously. 'Not even my friends from Sunday School, Miss Miriam?' she asked.

The older woman's faded eyes blinked hard, and her confusion caused her cheeks to blush more hotly. 'Well –' she began, then hesitated, 'well –'

'Only you see Miss Miriam, my friends from the chapel Sunday School are all mixed like.' Emma's face was a picture of pure innocence. 'There are girls and boys, you see. And we all meet together after Sunday School for Bible study.'

'What chapel do you attend, Emma?' Miriam Josceleyne sought for time in which to decide this knotty problem, and desperately wished that her brother Franklin were here to advise her.

'The Primitive Methodist up at Headless Cross, ma'am.' Emma lied without a moment's hesitation. Knowing that staunch Church of England adherents like the Josceleyne

47

family would be unlikely to have an intimate knowledge of the congregation of such a socially lowly sect.

Miriam Josceleyne sighed in desperation, her thoughts becoming an increasing confusion, then nodded. 'Oh very well, Emma, you may mix with your male friends at the Sunday School, but there are to be no male friends other than those, and you are not to spend time in their company in any locality other than the chapel.'

'Yes ma'am,' Emma accepted dutifully. 'Thank you, ma'am.'

With relief Miriam Josceleyne ended the interview. 'You may go to Mrs Elwood now, Emma.'

As she closed the door behind her, Emma Farr could hardly keep from laughing aloud at her new mistress's unworldliness. Then, unexpectedly a pang of sympathy pierced her. 'God Strewth! What an awful dull life you must have led, Miriam Josceleyne. I 'udden't want to be in your shoes, for all your money and fine big house. I truly 'udden't.'

Miriam Josceleyne sat motionless for some minutes after the girl had left her. She had not been dissatisfied with Emma Farr's manner, and wholeheartedly approved of her obvious physical cleanliness, but the fact of the girl's beauty disturbed her greatly.

Her father couldn't keep his hands off ugly, unkempt Charlotte and surly fat Iris. She dreaded to think how he would react to this gorgeous creature. She frowned resentfully. Surely Franklin should have considered more carefully before he engaged the girl. He should have sought for an older plainer woman.

A loud thumping came from above her head, and tiny flakes of plaster fell from the ceiling. Miriam Josceleyne sighed heavily, and rose to go upstairs in answer to her father's summons.

Down in the kitchen Emma found Mrs Elwood sitting at the large table. A big pot of fresh-brewed tea, bread and butter, and a plum cake were laid out on its well-scrubbed surface, and the fat woman invited, 'Come on and sit down, my wench. It's tay-time for us.'

Emma was possessed of a healthy appetite and ate and

drank heartily, relishing the fresh bread and butter, the sweet richness of the cake and the strong flavoured tea.

The two women talked and Emma found that the cook had been a schoolfriend of her mother, and that they had many acquaintances in common. An easy sense of companionship and a mutual liking quickly grew, and by the time the meal was finished Emma knew that she had found a friend and ally in the older woman.

Mrs Elwood went from the kitchen to return some minutes later, her arms piled high with clothing.

'Here you am, my duck. These am your uniforms. There's some for the rough work, and some arternoon and evening fancies.'

There were both print and black dresses, and a variety of aprons, ranging from bibbed coarse canvas-backed, to frilled linen, as well as several small linen caps with long streamers attached to their rear.

'You sort out what you needs, my duck,' the fat woman instructed, 'and I'll goo on getting a bite o' supper ready for Miss Miriam and the old man. Elwood's gone to Brummagem today to visit wi' his brother, so he'll not be back 'til tomorrow. I'll be able to stay on for a while tonight and gi' you a hand wi' altering them dresses.'

Emma was not very enthusiastic about wearing clothes that other girls had worn before her, and the other woman noted this, and reassured her, 'They'm all spotless clane, my duck, and you'll not need to wear 'um for long iffen Miss Miriam takes a liking for you and thinks that you'll be staying. Her's got a good heart, and her 'ull buy you all new if you gives satisfaction. Her's a real kind mistress, so her is. But too soft for her own good, if you gets my meaning.'

'How about the old man, Mr Hector?' Emma queried.

The other woman stared questioningly, and her manner became defensive. 'What does you mean, how about him?'

Emma decided to speak plainly. 'Well, Mrs Elwood, to tell you the truth I've already been told a few things concerning him that I'm not too happy about. So I'd like you to tell me about him. I think I've a right to know, haven't I?'

The fat woman grimaced unhappily, and shrugged her massive shoulders. Her loyalty and liking for Miriam Josceleyne making her hesitant to answer. Then she sighed. 'Yes, you've a right to know, girl. Truth to tell Mr Hector has gone a bit doolally-tap. He was always a proper Christian gentleman, but arter his missis died last year he went a bit funny in his yed. He leads Miss Miriam a terrible dance, so he does.'

'He leads the maids a terrible dance as well, from what I've been told,' Emma said forthrightly. 'Tries to make free with 'um, doon't he?'

Mrs Elwood nodded. 'Ahr, that's so, my duck.' Then suddenly her mood lightened and she chuckled. 'But the poor old sod carn't do any harm, girl. His willie is shrivelled to naught, and he aren't got the strength of a gnat. A fine strong girl like you 'ull be able to handle him easily enough.'

Emma's black eyes twinkled mischievously. 'Just so, Mrs Elwood, just so. I'll be able to handle him all right. Now can you tell me what else is expected of me?'

Later that night, when the cook had gone to her own home, Emma went upstairs to her room. The gaslighting had not been extended to the attics so Emma unpacked and arranged her belongings by candlelight. This done, she blew out the candle and sat on the head of her bed so that she could lean against the window-sill and stare out through the open casement.

The recreation garden, and the roadways that bounded it were used by the youth of the town as their meeting place. The locals called it the Monkey Run, and on a fine warm night such as this, groups of youths and girls walked round and round, eyeing each other, exchanging banter, seeking romance and adventure.

Emma smiled to herself as she watched this parade. Several huge globed gas lamps created pools of pale light and the shadowy figures became clearly visible as they entered those pools. Emma recognised several of the youths and girls and watched with an avid interest the interplay between them. Some of those that passed had considerable physical attractions, but Emma felt no envy for those girls who had acquired handsome followers. With a touch of smugness she knew that she could take her pick from the local youths and young men, but they held no interest for her as potential husbands. In her heart of hearts she was a romantic and she wanted a figure of romance as a mate. She found the local men too commonplace, too limited in their life-styles, and their very familiarity of experience and background to herself robbed them of any appeal for her.

She yawned and stretched and stood up to begin undressing for bed. Then she saw a tall solitary figure entering the pool of lamplight directly across the road from Cotswold House. He was a soldier, wearing a plumed slouch hat, and his riding boots and leather belting glistened as the lamplight played upon them. Emma stared hard, and experienced a sudden surge of interest. She could not see the soldier's face because the broad brim of his hat cast it into shadow, but she followed his swaggering figure with her eyes until the darkness swallowed it up.

Chapter Seven

'This is Emma, Father. She will give you your breakfast this morning.'

Emma stood at Miriam Josceleyne's side holding the tray on which there was a large bowl of hot milk with bread broken into it.

Lying in bed, Hector Josceleyne's shrivelled figure was hardly discernible beneath the thick layering of blankets and coverlets, and his waxen-skinned bald head reminded Emma of a skull she had seen displayed at the fair.

His rheumy eyes opened and blinked several times and he coughed phlegm and dribbled it from the side of his shrunken mouth.

'Oh, Father,' Miriam Josceleyne sighed, and used her handkerchief to wipe away the waste matter, then lifted the old man upwards and pushed pillows behind his back to keep him upright.

Fully awake now the rheumed eyes gleamed as they fastened onto the young woman's face, and his mouth opened as he looked her up and down.

'Who are you?' he demanded, and Emma was startled by the loudness of the cracked voice issuing from such a wasted looking body.

'I have already told you, Father. This is Emma, our new maid,' Miriam Josceleyne informed him, then flinched bodily as he screeched at her.

'You told me nothing, you stupid bitch! Nothing!'

Emma saw the embarrassment and fear mingled in the older woman's faded eyes, and quickly intervened.

'I'm Emma Farr, Mr Josceleyne. I've come to help Miss Miriam to look arter you.' To the woman she said, 'I'll feed him, Miss Miriam. Why don't you go down and eat your own breakfast before it gets cold.'

'Will you be all right?' Miriam Josceleyne asked her anxiously, and Emma smiled and nodded.

'Oh yes, Miss Miriam. I'll be fine. You go along now.'

Her mistress hesitated, reluctant to leave the young girl alone.

'That's right, go on downstairs, you stupid woman! You're not wanted here. Go away!' the old man screeched.

'I'll be all right, Miss Miriam,' Emma assured her confidently, and her mistress went slowly out of the room.

Miriam Josceleyne closed the door behind her, then leaned back against its panelling, straining to hear what was happening in the room, her heart thumping in fearful anticipation.

Emma placed the four-legged bed table over the old man's thighs, and put the tray upon it.

'There you are then, Mr Hector,' she told him, and pushed the silver spoon into his clawed hand. 'Come on now, eat it all up. That's lovely bread and milk that is, and I've put plenty of sugar on it, just as Mrs Elwood said you liked it.'

He stared at her with open lust, his eyes devouring her shapely body. Letting the spoon drop onto the coverlet he beckoned.

'Come here, girl. I want to whisper to you.'

Emma momentarily debated with herself the wisdom of approaching him, then decided she might as well get it over and done with and went to him.

He gripped her slender wrist with a surprising strength and pulled her down towards him.

'Come closer. Come closer, girl,' he urged pantingly, his sour breath filling her nostrils as she bent her head towards his lips.

His free hand shot out from beneath the coverlet and clutched the back of her head.

'Give me a kiss,' he tried to crush his mouth against her own and Emma was filled with a wild desire to laugh.

'Don't tease. Don't tease you little bitch,' he snarled angrily as she resisted his downward pull.

53

Emma felt for the large bowl of hot bread and milk and lifting it poured its contents over his head.

He screamed out in shock and released her, clawing with both hands at the soggy mess that streamed down his face.

Emma's laughter pealed out as Miriam Josceleyne came rushing back into the room.

Her eyes widened as she saw her father, and she stared wildly at Emma, who, almost helpless with laughter, could only shake her head as she struggled to control herself.

'You bitch! You bloody bitch!' Hector Josceleyne screeched, and struck out wildly at the laughing girl. His furious lunge unbalanced him, and he toppled sideways to hang over the edge of the bed and Emma went into fresh paroxysms of laughter, tears streaming from her eyes.

Miriam Josceleyne was torn between shame, and an almost uncontrollable urge to scream with laughter herself and when Hector Josceleyne's furious struggles to right himself ended in his falling completely out of the bed to lie on the floor with his stick-like legs waving in the air, she dissolved into helpless mirth, and for the first time in many many long years laughed until her sides ached and the tears ran from her own eyes.

It was the furious jangling of the front door bell that finally penetrated her consciousness and brought her abruptly back to reality.

'Oh my goodness!' Her hand went to her mouth and she stared apprehensively at Emma Farr. 'I'd quite forgotten!'

'Forgot what, Miss Miriam?' A smile still wreathed Emma Farr's lips, and she had to summon all her willpower to subdue her laughter.

'It must be the Reverend MacDonald. He sent word yesterday that he would be calling to talk with father.' She clasped her hands together, fingers tugging and kneading in distraction. 'What am I to do? What am I to do?'

All laughter had gone from her, and she was again the timid nervous woman of normality.

Emma was equal to the challenge. 'You stay here Miss Miriam with Mr Hector. I'll go down and answer the door. Now you stay here, until I come back.'

54

Before the older woman could make any reply Emma was out of the room and hurrying down the stairs.

On the front portico the Reverend Mosse MacDonald M.A., heard the hurrying footsteps clicking across the parquet floor of the entrance hall and frowned. He had been waiting here for at least three minutes, continually tugging the bell-pull, and he resented being kept waiting. He was the senior curate to the Reverend Canon Horace Newton, the Vicar of Redditch, and as such was a person of some importance in the Needle District. A large-bodied florid-faced man who wore a full beard to add dignity to his twenty-eight years, Mosse MacDonald was ambitious to rise in his chosen profession, and to further that ambition he assiduously cultivated those parishioners who were possessed of wealth and standing in the town.

Emma opened the door. 'Yes sir?'

The cleric's eyes, magnified by his pince-nez, regarded the beautiful girl with some surprise.

'You're new here, aren't you?' he questioned. His speech, from which he had carefuly eradicated any trace of his Scottish origins, fluted in the sing-song tones favoured by the Anglican clergy.

'Yes sir,' Emma replied, her eyes examining the top-hatted, frock-coated man before her.

The cleric went to move into the hallway, but the girl stayed where she was, and he was forced to halt. He frowned slightly.

'Do you know who I am, girl?'

Emma smiled winningly. 'Indeed I do, sir. You'll be the Reverend MacDonald, come to call on Mr Hector, won't you sir?'

'Indeed I am he,' Mosse MacDonald confirmed loftily, and again would have moved forwards but Emma remained blocking his way, and his frown deepened.

'Your mistress is expecting me girl,' he stated irritably.

'Oh I know that sir,' Emma beamed at him. 'But Miss Miriam sends her apologies, and asks that you'll excuse her this morning. Her and Mr Hector have both took a bug, sir, and are in their beds. She thinks the bug might be catching, sir.'

The curate was mortally afraid of any infectious illness and involuntarily took a backwards pace.

Emma's shrewd brain instantly intuited the impression her news had made on the man, and now she pressed.

'I'm going to send for the doctor if Miss Miriam and Mr Hector doon't look any better by noonday, sir.' She smothered a fit of coughing, and gasped, 'Beg pardon, sir. It looks as if I've took the bug as well, I've bin coughin' and splutterin' all morning, so I have.'

Mosse MacDonald had seen and heard enough. 'Convey my sympathies to your master and mistress, girl,' he ordered. 'And inform Miss Miriam that I will call upon her at a later date. Tell her that she will be in both my thoughts and my prayers until then.'

He turned and walked majestically away, and Emma stuck out her tongue at his back, then closed the door and returned upstairs.

In her absence Miriam Josceleyne had managed to get the old man into his armchair, and while doing so he had spitefully pulled at her hair and struck her with his fists, and now she appeared in a sad state with her face puffed and reddened by the blows, her hair hanging in tangled tendrils and her eyes swollen with tears.

Emma guessed what had been happening, and regarded her mistress with a mingling of sympathy and contempt.

'Bugger me, if you aren't a pitiful cratur!' she thought, but aloud said briskly, 'I told the gentleman that you and Mr Hector were took badly with a bug, Miss Miriam. He told me to tell you that he'd call on another occasion, and until then he'd be thinking about and praying for you.'

'Oh Emma!' the older woman exclaimed in shocked protest. 'How could you lie like that, and to a clergyman?'

Emma chuckled richly, 'Oh it's just as easy to lie to a parson as to lie to anybody else, Miss Miriam. We couldn't have him coming up here to see Mr Hector like this, could we now?'

Her smile broadened as she regarded the old man's skull-like head still smeared with the remnants of bread and milk.

He snarled at her, 'You bitch. You wicked bitch,' and

shook his fist threateningly, causing Miriam Josceleyne to gulp back a sob.

Emma moved towards him. 'We're going to have to get you cleaned up, Mr Hector. Give you a good wash, and change your nightshirt.'

Miriam Josceleyne stared at the younger woman in disbelieving horror.

'Mrs Elwood's husband always comes in to wash and change my father, Emma. It would not be seemly for a female to do so.'

'Don't you worry your head about that, Miss Miriam,' the young girl told her airily. 'I used to wash and change my old grandad when I was still only a bit of a kid. Mr Hector's got nothing that I aren't seen before.'

She regarded her mistress with open sympathy. 'Look Miss Miriam, Mr Elwood's in Brummagem today. It's hard to say when he'll get back here. We can't leave Mr Hector all messy like this, can we now?' She paused, then suggested softly, 'Why don't you go and lie down for a bit, Miss Miriam? You're all upset, aren't you? By the time you've rested, I'll have everything sorted here.'

She gently ushered the other woman from the room, ignoring the screeching execrations of the old man, and half led, half pushed her into her own bedroom, where she coaxed her to lie down on the bed.

'Don't you worry about a thing now, Miss Miriam,' Emma smiled reassuringly. 'By the time you wakes up, everything 'ull be ship shape and Bristol fashion.'

As trustingly as a small child, Miriam Josceleyne nodded and closed her eyes. For a moment or two Emma remained staring down at the thin sallow features on the lace-edged pillow.

'By Christ, youm naught but a weak, nerve-ridden, pathetic cratur, Miriam Josceleyne. You 'udden't last five minutes in Silver Street, 'ud you?' Emma thought with a mingled pity and contempt. 'Maybe it's your menfolk has made you like this, but I'm buggered if I'd ever let any man get me into this state. I'd bloody well swing for him first, that I swear.'

She went quietly from the room, easing the door shut

57

behind her. Then grinned, and walked briskly back to where Hector Josceleyne was still mouthing threats and abuse in his screeching voice.

Emma closed the door and advanced to stand over him, arms akimbo, fists resting on her hips.

'Shut your foul mouth, you old bastard!' she suddenly hissed menacingly, and sheer shock made him fall silent and stare uncertainly up at her.

'That's better.' Emma's face metamorphosed into a ferocious mask. 'Now you listen to me.' From her apron pocket she produced a long-bladed pair of scissors, which she brandished before his eyes, causing him to pull back fearfully. 'Theer's nobody can hear you now, you old bastard. Miss Miriam's sleeping, and Mrs Elwood's not come to work yet, so theer's only you and me. I'm going to wash and change you now and if you makes so much as a bloody murmur, then I'm going to shove these straight through you.'

She pounced on him and grabbed the front of his nightshirt in one hand. He screeched out in fright and she shook him bodily.

'Hold your bloody rattle, or I'll bloody stab you!'

He subsided into a fearful, harsh-panting, cowering posture, and after a moment Emma released him, and stepped back.

'Right then, Mr Hector. I see that we understands each other, doon't we?' She smiled grimly and asked him, 'So then, are you going to behave and be a good boy wi' me in future?'

He glared at her with fear and hatred, but slowly nodded his head.

'Good!' Emma exclaimed, then added softly. 'But remember now, I'm not here to put up with your nonsense. I'll look arter you properly, and I'll look arter Miss Miriam, and you'll find me trustworthy, but if ever you gets up to your old tricks with me again, I'll bloody well swing for you. And that's not a threat, it's a promise. Does you understand me?'

She waited expectantly and once again he grudgingly nodded his assent.

'Right then,' Emma told him briskly. 'Now you can stay in your chair while I goes down and gets the water hot to bath you with. Don't you go making any noise and waking Miss Miriam up.'

Humming to herself she went downstairs. 'Well, I've won that battle with the evil old bugger,' she thought, then grinned, 'but I reckon it's going to be a long war.'

Chapter Eight

The Plough and Harrow Hotel stood on the point where the Front and Back Hills merged to become the southward Mount Pleasant. It was a large square three-storied building with extensive stabling and a yard at its rear, and it resembled a Georgian manor house in appearance.

Johnny Purvis had rented a room there. He rose early on the day following his homecoming and for a while stood staring out of the large window, westwards across the hilly heavily-wooded countryside. To his right Front Hill's red-brick terraces sloped sharply downwards towards the town centre, and to his left the slightly more elaborate terraces topping the long high ridge of Mount Pleasant rose in a gentle incline to run through the outlying districts of Headless Cross and Crabbs Cross. At one time separate hamlets, these were now joined by an umbilical cord of bricks and mortar to their newly acquired parent town.

The man briefly wondered at the basic incongruity of his birthplace. The centre of Redditch was built on a flat plateau on the northern spur of a long ridge of high land which ran from the Birmingham Plateau in the north, southwards to the edges of the Vale of Evesham. North and west of the town centre the land fell steeply to the valley of the River Arrow, eastwards its fall was more gradual to that same valley, but south of the town centre the land rose sharply in a long high ridgeway which periodically widened and narrowed, and which the locals fervently but erroneously believed constituted the highest land between England and far-off Russia. Among the more credulous it was an article of faith that the bitterly cold easterly winds of winter blew directly into Redditch from Siberia.

But for Johnny Purvis the incongruousness of his birthplace was not its geographical peculiarities, but the fact that despite being set deep in the heart of the lush farming acreage of the Worcestershire/Warwickshire border, and away from the main trading routes of the country, it was nevertheless a town of industry and far flung commerce. It was the undisputed world centre for the manufacture of needles and fishing tackle. Within its confines other light and heavy engineering industries flourished also, and factories, workshops and mills abounded. Extremes of wealth and poverty, fastidiousness and filth, knowledge and ignorance coexisted among its red-brick streets, alleys and courts, and it was possessed of a turbulent and violent history.

A sense of burgeoning excitement and anticipation caused Johnny Purvis's heart to beat faster as he turned from the window. Today he had much to do, and he was eager to begin.

His return to Izods Yard created tumultuous uproar, and from its two facing rows of mean cottages, neighbours who had known him as a youth shouted greetings and came hurrying to shake his hand. Johnny was both touched and pleased by their welcome. Izods Yard was a dwelling place of the respectable poor, a stronghold of Chapel goers, and he remembered with amusement how many of those who now clamoured around him had once accused him of bringing the Yard into disrepute by 'going for a redcoat'.

Inwardly he smiled wryly and thought, 'At least the war has served to raise we soldiers up in people's estimation.'

'Has you come to see your dad, Johnny?' asked a shawl-wrapped woman wearing a man's flat cap on her grey head.

'Yes, I was hoping to catch him before he went to work,' he told her.

'Old Ezra aren't doing a deal o' work these days, Johnny. He aren't too good. Took a bad turn last winter, he did, and he aren't able to get about much now.' The woman

61

shook her head gloomily. 'It's just as well that you'se come now because I doon't hink he's got much longer on this earth.'

Concerned by her words, Johnny Purvis broke free of his welcomers and went to the cottage at the far end of the yard. As he stood outside its shabby warped door a host of memories assailed him, and a sharp pain of sadness pierced his being as he thought of his dead mother, whom he had loved so dearly. For a brief instant he wanted to turn away from the door. There had never been any closeness between him and his grim, God-fearing father. Johnny had wanted to love his father and as a boy had tried to please him and to draw closer to him, but the man had never seemed to reciprocate his feelings, and had always remained cold and distant towards his son.

The neighbours grouped together midway along the yard, watching the tall khaki-uniformed figure with curious eyes and whispering together, wondering why he was delaying so. Johnny glanced briefly towards them, then drew a long breath and rapped on the door with the handle of his riding crop.

It was a stranger who opened the warped panels and peered suspiciously out: a bent-backed, white-haired, shrivelled-featured old man. Johnny Purvis stared in dismay, trying to discover some physical resemblance to the erect strong-bodied father he had known. He swallowed hard, and greeted quietly, 'Hello Dad, it's Johnny . . . I've come home.'

The palsied old head lifted and it was Ezra Purvis's eyes that met Johnny's and the younger man silently prayed that he would find a welcome in them.

For long moments the two men stood locked in a silent regard, then Ezra Purvis's mouth opened to disclose blackened stubs of teeth and Johnny saw tears brim in the red-rimmed eyes. The old man beckoned and croaked hoarsely, 'Come in, Son.'

A flood of emotion brought tears to the younger man's eyes also and he had to swallow hard to relieve the choking constriction in his throat as he stepped through the low doorway into the sparsely furnished, spotlessly clean room.

Inside the room the old man faced him, one trembling hand resting on the table top to support himself, and Johnny wanted to go to him, and to clasp the frail body in his arms, and to tell his father that despite all their bitter quarrels of the past he had always, and still did, love him dearly. But he held himself in check. Knowing that such a gesture would be an alien thing in the austere, emotionally repressed, hard-living world that his father had always dwelt in.

Ezra Purvis's eyes were still the hard clear blue of the man he had once been as he examined his son closely and in silence. When he finally spoke his voice still held traces of the strength and confidence it had always exuded.

'When you left here you was still only a boy, John. But you'se come back a man. Set yourself down.' He indicated a straight-backed wooden chair, one of four set around the white-scrubbed deal table. 'I'll make us a cup o' tay.'

He shuffled painfully out into the minute scullery that comprised the only other room on the ground floor of the small cottage, and Johnny removed his hat and set it on the table, then let his eyes move slowly around the cramped confines. Apart from the table and chairs there were no other furnishings except for a shelf beneath the window on which were ranged a massive leather-bound Bible, books of sermons and theological writings that his father had constantly pored over, and several small hand-embroidered samplers bearing biblical quotations hanging framed on the walls.

Johnny smiled sadly, remembering how when his mother had been alive, she had filled this austere room with wild flowers and herbs, and on the mantelshelf above the black-iron firegrate and oven she had kept her treasured collection of knick-knacks and souvenirs of day trips to Malvern, Evesham and Stratford. The mantelshelf was bare now, not even a clock standing on it, and Johnny stared at the empty space and pondered the fate of those knick-knacks.

'They'm all upstairs – on the shelf facing me bed.' Ezra Purvis spoke from the scullery doorway and Johnny was startled by the old man's uncanny percipience. 'I moved

63

'um up theer arter your mam was took from me. So's I can look at 'um last thing at night, and fust thing in the morning, and bring her clear to me mind.'

Again Johnny was forced to swallow hard to dispel the lump that his father's words brought to his throat.

It took the old man several shuffling journeys back and forth to the scullery to bring out the cups, saucers, milk, sugar and teapot.

'Does you want summat to ate, John? I'se got a bit o' bacon I can fry for you?'

'No thanks, Dad. I've already eaten.' The younger man found that he was pervaded by a curiously sweet sadness as he sat opposite his father and slowly sipped his tea. Covertly he studied the old man, noting the clean collar, the neatly knotted tie, the threadbare, but well-brushed jacket and trousers, and the sheen of cracked but polished boots. He admired the way his father, despite his obvious bodily afflictions, was nevertheless shaved and washed, his thin white hair brushed neatly.

In his turn Ezra Purvis was covertly studying his youngest son and secretly glorying in the fine-looking man he had become.

For almost an hour they sat in silence and imperceptibly a feeling of warmth and companionship developed in the small room and with this a secret inner healing of old wounds and a softening of bitterness.

At length they began to talk in slow easy exchanges and Ezra Purvis told his son about his much older brothers and sisters, now all married and gone out to Australia, Canada and America. In return Johnny Purvis told his father about his soldiering in India, Egypt, the Sudan and South Africa. They talked about the woman who had been wife and mother to them and found that they were able to smile in happy recollection of her and that memories of her had become joyous, now that time had muted the grief of loss.

'Do you still preach, Dad?' Johnny asked.

'No, not now. I can't get about like I used to, John. To tell you the truth, I'se lost patience wi' ranting and raving from pulpits.'

His rheumy blue eyes suddenly held amusement, and

Johnny Purvis felt a shock of surprise at this display of levity from a parent who had been a hellfire and brimstone Christian.

The old man noticed that surprise and chuckled throatily. 'Oh I've changed while you'se bin away, son,' he declared. 'I've become a real sinner in the eyes o' the Chapel.'

'How's that, father?' Johnny was very curious.

'Well, I've come to the conclusion that what happens between a man and his God should be a very private thing. Not summat to be shouted from the rooftops.' He paused ruminatively, then continued. 'And I think I've become a sight more tolerant than I used to be, son.'

'I'm glad to hear that,' Johnny answered with a degree of irony. Remembering all the conflicts that his father's intolerance had created in the past.

'So, youm back home to stay now, are you?' Ezra Purvis asked. 'What sort of work am you thinking o' doing?'

Johnny shrugged. 'I haven't made my mind up about work yet, Father. There's plenty of time for me to do that after I've settled and bought a house.'

The old man frowned quizzically. 'And how 'ull you live while youm making your mind up? What 'ull you use for money? How can you afford to buy a house? Soldiering has never paid any good wages to my knowledge, has it? Or am you the only one whose ever bin known to make your fortune out of being a soldier?'

A slow grin spread across the younger man's features and after a while he nodded. 'Yes, you could say that, Father. I did make my fortune out of being a soldier.'

The grin broadened as he saw the wonderment in his father's eyes, and he laughed softly, and told him.

'You'll never know want again, Father. And neither shall I. I've come back home a rich man.'

His laughter stilled, and very seriously he repeated, 'Yes, Father, it's true what I'm telling you. But it must remain a secret between you and me for the time being. I've come home a rich man . . .'

Chapter Nine

The Dolton family home was a large Regency house on the lower slopes of Red Lane, the westerly continuation of Unicorn Hill. It had considerable pretensions to elegance with decorative verandas and upper balconies of ornate ironwork and a large front lawn shaded by two immense elm trees. There were several other large houses of the town's gentlefolk in its vicinity and the area had an opulent, almost rural air, notwithstanding that less than a hundred yards distant were slum streets and factories and the grimy railway station and goods' yard.

During the long hot summer afternoons it was the custom of the ladies who belonged to the town's social elite to pay calls on each other. Sometimes merely to leave their calling cards, sometimes to take tea and exchange gossip. If accompanied by their menfolk they might even exert themselves in a game of croquet or lawn tennis. Expensive carriages and horseflesh were frequent sights in Red Lane, as the gentlefolk from other parts of the town called on their fellows who lived there.

Arthur Dolton had bought the large house some years previously and had expected to gain acceptance in the favoured circle of the town's self-regarded elite by virtue of his increasing wealth, but no carriages ever entered his driveway and no expensively printed calling cards ever found their way onto the silver salver kept on its table in the hallway. To his bitter chagrin he had discovered that his ownership of three butchers' shops and an elegant house were not sufficient to gain him and his wife admittance into the circle of 'at homes', social calls, musical evenings and dinner parties.

In the intricate grading system of class, Arthur Dolton was considered to be near to the bottom of the ladder of social desirability. His uneducated accent and lack of social graces did not really matter too much. Some of the older needle manufacturers and factory owners in the district were men who had risen from very lowly origins and gloried in that fact. But they were in commerce, and Arthur Dolton was in trade and a bloody brutish trade at that. Therefore he could never be ranked as a gentleman.

The irony of the situation was lost on Arthur Dolton, who was unable to laugh at the ridiculous pettiness of such snobbery. He only knew and bitterly resented, that the middle-class professional or businessman, even though they might be merely a bank or insurance or ledger clerk, were considered to be higher in the town's social order than he, despite the fact that he was much wealthier than most of them.

Of course there were some shopkeepers in the town who were admitted to the elite circles. But these were mostly related to the accepted families, or were influential laymen in the Anglican Church, or had acquired considerable landholdings and property ownerships which could entitle them to be considered as very minor landed gentry.

Arthur Dolton frequently brooded about his exclusion from the circles he hungered to be accepted into, and, unwilling to countenance the real reasons for that exclusion, would seek elsewhere for a scapegoat. Inevitably that scapegoat was his wife, Cleopatra.

It was four o'clock in the afternoon and Arthur Dolton had been drinking in various public houses around the town centre since ten o'clock that morning. His mood had progressively worsened as the day wore on and the alcohol he had swilled copiously had taken effect. Twice he had attempted to pick quarrels with other drinkers, but both men had been afraid of his reputation for violence and had meekly accepted his insults. Now he stood in the doorway of the Royal George, a small public house near to the central crossroads, and morosely eyed the quiet Evesham Street.

Some distance away he spotted one of his sycophantic

drinking cronies and shouted loudly, 'Reggie, does you want a drink?'

The man realised that Dolton was half drunk, and from long experience could recognise the aggressive mood of the butcher.

'Sorry Arthur, carn't stop now. I'se got urgent business to see to.' He waved and made a quick evasion down a side entry.

Dolton's lips mouthed a curse, and then he shrugged, 'I might as well goo on home then. Theer aren't no fun to be got up here. Like a bloody cemetery, aren't it?'

The sun beat down strongly and by the time Dolton had walked to the railway station bridge sweat was trickling from beneath the band of his bowler hat and his high starched collar was wilting and wet. A train was passing beneath the bridge and clouds of smoke billowed, carrying red-hot smuts, some of which landed on Arthur Dolton's flushed face, causing him to curse at the specks of sharp pain.

On the front veranda of his neighbour's house he could see a collection of ladies in flowered hats and expensive gowns. They were sipping tea and eating cakes while watching a game of croquet being played on the wide front lawn between laughing blazer-clad men, and young girls in flimsy summer silks. He knew some of the gathering by name and knew that they patronised his shops so he halted to stand and stare at their play for some moments, hoping for even a fleeting recognition and greeting.

'Good afternoon,' he called. 'It's just the weather for that game, aren't it?'

They coolly ignored him, not even deigning to glance in his direction, and his temper became evil.

'You stuck-up bastards!' he thought. 'I might just as well be a bit of dirt for all the notice you takes of me.'

He wanted to bawl out insults, but retained a sufficient sense of self-interest to restrain himself. He knew well that he could not afford to make enemies of these gentlefolk, not if he wished his various shops to continue to prosper. Cursing them under his breath he went on and into his own house.

For a while he stood in the big entrance hallway with its massive oak hat stands and side tables. There was no sound to be heard except the ticking of the great grandfather clock which stood beside the door. Arthur Dolton scowled suspiciously, and muttered, 'What's they up to?'

He employed three house servants, comprising two maids and a cook, and of his three children, he would have expected the youngest at least to be at home at this hour, although the two elder sons might still be at their school. Then there was his wife. Surely with all those people in the house he would be able to hear at least one of them moving around.

'They'm up to summat,' he decided, and his large hands clenched into fists. 'And if I catches any on 'um doing what they shouldn't, then it'll goo hard with 'um.'

Stealthily he began to prowl through the house. The drawing room with its profusion of spindly chairs, small tables and cabinets smothered in ornaments and photo frames, and its ebony grand piano. The dining room, dominated by its huge mahogany table, chairs, sideboard, gleaming dully against the dark-red wallpaper. The study, with its wall shelves packed with books that he had never opened. The kitchen, a myriad of burnished pots, pans and a great shiny steel and black-leaded range, facing a modern gas cooker.

He could see through the open kitchen door into the adjoining scullery and that too was empty. Dolton frowned in puzzlement, and was about to turn to go along the passage and upstairs, when he heard his wife's rich throaty laughter sounding faintly from the rear garden.

Cautiously he moved to the scullery window from where he could see the length of the rear ground. It comprised a large vegetable plot, some herb and flower beds, and at the end a small orchard containing apple, pear, cherry and plum trees. The man's liver-coloured lips parted and he bared his tobacco-stained teeth in a savage snarl. Seated on the grass under the blossoming trees were his wife, his three sons, the three women servants and the elderly gardener. Between them there was spread a cloth strewn with the remains of a picnic meal. For a while he watched them talking and laughing, the women and man taking drinks from bottles of ale and the three young boys sharing bottles of lemonade.

Dolton's bile rose as he thought on the scene at his neighbours' house and the way he had been so humiliatingly snubbed.

'It's all the fault of my bloody missus! Theer's Ida Huins next door entertaining the cream o' the town and here's my bleedin' missus sitting drinking and ateing wi' the bloody servants. No wonder nobody comes calling on the bloody cow. No wonder we doon't get invited into the best houses. That's what I gets for marrying a bloody slum-rat. Nobody with any standing in the town wants to be seen mixing with her.'

He slammed through the door into the paved back yard and started towards the happy group.

Cleopatra Dolton was the first to see her husband and the laughter died on her lips. Momentarily her heart quailed, then she mustered her considerable courage and quickly instructed, 'Milly, take the children to the study. Doll, help Mrs Danks to clear this up and you get back to work Fred.'

She rose and went towards the oncoming man, while they all scurried to obey her. When she halted to face her husband she forced a smile.

'You're home early, Arthur. I didn't expect to see you until this evening.'

He scowled and gestured to where the women were hurriedly clearing the remnants of the picnic. 'That's plain to see, aren't it, that you warn't expecting me. What the bloody hell does you think youm doing here?'

Although afraid of her husband, Cleopatra Dolton would never give him the satisfaction of displaying that fear, and now she challenged boldly.

'What do you mean, what are we doing? You can see, can't you?'

'Oh yes, my lady, oh yes,' he spat out savagely. 'I can see all right. While other folk are entertaining in the proper manner, youm out here swilling and gutsing with the bloody servants. It's no wonder that nobody ever calls on you, is it.'

Her dark eyes fired angrily. 'Oh we're going to have this again, are we? You're going to blaggard me because we're not invited to Lord and Lady Muck's garden parties.'

'It's your fault that we aren't,' he shouted, then became aware of the servants' eyes fixed upon him and of his frightened children scurrying past with averted bowed heads. He was uncaring of their fear, but he did not wish his words being spread to the houses of his neighbours by gossiping servants.

'You come on upstairs,' he growled. 'We'll settle this in private.'

Cleopatra wanted with all her heart to disobey him. But she knew that if she did so it would only make matters worse. So dutifully she walked with downcast head behind him.

In the bedroom he swung on her and bawled. 'What the bleedin' hell does you think youm doing, gutsing and swilling with the bleedin' servants?'

She held her head high, trying to keep up her courage by fuelling her own hot temper with resentment of this unjust treatment.

'It's Andrew's birthday.' She referred to their youngest son. 'He's four years old today, or have you forgotten? I gave him a little picnic party as a treat for him. There was no harm in that surely?'

'Doon't you take that tone with me,' her husband hissed warningly, 'or you knows what you'll get.'

'I know that all right,' she uttered with a bitter despair. 'It's what I've been getting ever since the day I wed you, isn't it?'

'And it's what you deserves.' He regarded this beautiful woman with an expression akin to hatred. 'I ought never to have married you. You came from scum and that's what you am yourself. Nothing but scum!'

The woman stared down at the carpeted floor, her stomach churning and nausea sweeping over her so that her olive skin became sheened with a clammy sweat.

Arthur Dolton's eyes gleamed with an insane cruelty and he seemed to relish the words he spat against her bowed head. 'No wonder no decent 'oomen in this town 'ull have anything to do with you. They knows what scum

71

you are. Your own father babbied you, didn't he? He was shagging you for bloody years, warn't he? And you enjoyed it, didn't you? How did you feel when he was on top o' you? You liked him to shag you, didn't you? You loved having his prick inside you night arter night arter night.'

Cleopatra's stomach heaved sickeningly, as his voice battered her, the words seeming to become solid entities that rooted and swelled inside her skull, agonising pain lanced through her head and suddenly something snapped within her mind and she screamed and hurled herself at the man, hands hooked, fingers clawing at his mouth in frantic effort to close it and choke off the foul obscenities.

He roared with savage laughter as she hurled herself forwards, his fists thudded into her face and body like great hammers and she was beaten to the floor to lie groaning and half senseless. Panting heavily he stared down at her and his eyes dwelt on her heaving breasts. Suddenly his mouth dried and a raging lust swept over him. He fumbled at his trousers and dropped them to his knees, then straddled her to rip her bodice open and maul and bite her white pulsing breasts. He snatched at her skirts and tore her undergarments from her hips. She tried to fight him off, but he pinioned her hands to the floor above her head with one hand and gripped her soft throat with the other, squeezing mercilessly while she frantically heaved and twisted in futile effort to escape from beneath his bulk. Grunting gutturally like some enraged beast he released her throat and guiding his manhood with his free hand, drove himself into her. Cleopatra sobbed helplessly, and stopped struggling, and her body sagged to lie in abject surrender while his gross hips and belly pounded down upon her flesh.

In the study the three young boys sat on the floor at the skirts of Milly, the maidservant. The eldest boy, ten-year-old Simon, stared with frightened eyes at the entrance of Mrs Danks, the cook.

'Where's my mother, Mrs Danks? Is she crying again?'

The woman glanced meaningfully at the maidservant, then smiled kindly at the boy's white strained face.

'Now doon't you moither your yed about yur mam, my

72

duck. Her and your dad am having a quiet little talk upstairs. They'll both be down later. But in the meantime your mam wants you three to goo out for a walk with Milly.'

As they preceded the maid through the front door she whispered to the cook, 'What's going on upstairs then?'

The cook frowned and grimaced sympathetically. 'The bastard's giving the poor cow what for again. I 'udden't blame her if she poisoned the sod. I know I 'ud, if he was my man. Bad bastard that he is. Keep them kids out for at least a couple of hours. It'll give the poor cow a chance to put herself to rights afore they comes back.'

When the boys and Milly had gone, Mrs Danks went into the drawing room, directly beneath the bedroom of her master and mistress. She stood listening to the noises that came from above and shook her head in pity.

Chapter Ten

'BUNEGAR'S TROUSERS DOWN AGAIN' the huge-lettered, garish placard declared, and Johnny Purvis smiled as he read it, and the sign beneath it:

F.Bunegar and Son.
The Working Man's Tailor.
Suits to measure.
No Fit – No Pay.

The shop adjoined the Crown Inn on the very top of Fish Hill. Now, in the heat of the afternoon, its front windows were opened wide and the immensely fat Fred Bunegar and his equally fat son, Billy, were sitting crosslegged on a raised platform in the shop window, busily plying their needles.

Johnny Purvis grinned to see them, and thought how closely they resembled the fat twins of the nursery rhyme. He moved up to the open window and greeted them.

'Hello Fred, how's business?'

Two fat faces beamed at him and the elder chortled happily.

'It just proves the truth of the old saying, that bad pennies always turns up again, doon't it?' He turned his rolls of chins towards his son. 'Does you know who this gallant warrior is, our Billy?'

'O' course I does, our Dad,' his son chortled. 'It's Johnny Purvis, aren't it? We went to the same school, didn't we Johnny?'

'We did that, Billy,' Purvis confirmed with a smile. 'And we were both drummer boys in the Volunteer Corps, weren't we?'

'Ahr, that we was.' It was Billy Bunegar's turn to confirm. 'But it looks like youm a bloody general now, Johnny. That looks like an officer's rig to me.'

'I'm only a lieutenant in the Irregular Cavalry, Billy, and I shan't be that for much longer.'

'I heard you was come back from the war, Johnny. Has you bin to see your old dad?' the old Bunegar wanted to know, 'only if I recollects rightly, you and him didn't always see eye to eye, did you?'

'I've just left him. I think we'll be better friends from now on.' Johnny Purvis abruptly changed the subject. 'Can you do a rush order for me, Fred?'

'Ahr, I should think so, mate,' the fat man asserted confidently. 'What is it you wants? A suit? I can do you a nice three piece for a guinea.'

'I want three suits to start with; a blazer, a hacking jacket and breeches, a cycling suit, an Ulster, shirts, cuffs, fronts, collars and ties. I want a complete wardrobe, Fred. But I want only the best cloth and your best workmanship.' As an afterthought he added. 'I'll need a morning coat and a topper, and maybe a frock-coat as well.'

The fat man puffed out his cheeks like great pink balloons, and exclaimed in shocked surprise, 'That'll come very dear, Johnny.' A trace of doubt entered his eyes, small in their puffy layers of fat. 'If you wants the very best of cloth, then you could be talking six or seven guineas for a suit and more for your frock and morning outfits.' He paused, breathing stertorously, as he mentally reckoned the cost of a whole wardrobe. Then frowned doubtfully. 'I'd have to buy in a deal of cloth, Johnny. I doon't keep too much o' the dearer sorts by me these days.'

Johnny Purvis smiled reassuringly, and from the pouch on his waistbelt he pulled a small money sack which clunked heavily when he tossed it onto the wooden platform.

'There's sixty sovereigns in there, Fred. That should do to be getting on with. I'd like to see some samples of cloth to choose from. How soon can you have them?'

Fred Bunegar's pink face shone with delight. 'You can call tomorrow, Johnny. I'll have 'um here for you by then.'

75

'Good,' the soldier nodded. 'I've got to go up to Brummagem tomorrow, so I might be late in calling. Are you still living over the shop?'

'I am. You call whenever it's convenient, me old mate. I'll wait in for you.'

As the dashing figure moved away from the shop front the younger Bunegar sighed and remarked enviously, 'I wish I'd have gone to the war now, Dad. I'd like to be wearing a uniform like he's got.'

His father laughed uproariously, and scoffed, 'Doon't talk so bloody sarft, our Billy. You heard him say that he was in the bloody cavalry, didn't you? Wheer 'ud they have bin able to find a bloody horse wi' a back strong enough to bear you?'

Johnny Purvis sauntered along the tree-shaded Church Green West, admiring the long façade of the recently constructed Smallwood Hospital, which had replaced the old cottages that he could remember. Next to the hospital was the tall-spired, high-gabled, grandiosely structured and named, Literary and Scientific Institute. It stood on the corner of Church Road, a short thoroughfare which contained the police station, the Post Office, and the big public hall. It also contained in some old houses various solicitors, auctioneers, and insurance offices. It was to one of these auctioneers and estate agents that Johnny Purvis now went.

He only stayed inside for a short time, and then came back into the street and headed briskly towards Cotswold House on the opposite side of the recreation garden.

'My name's John Purvis, I'd like to speak with Mr Hector Josceleyne please.'

Emma Farr thought that the soldier resembled a character from some romantic novel, with his plumed hat, bright medal ribbons, gleaming leather and spurred riding boots.

'Could you wait here for a moment, sir?' she invited him into the hallway. 'I'll go and speak with the mistress.'

She smiled and left him, her small high-heeled boots clicking across the highly polished parquet flooring.

Johnny Purvis stared appreciatively after her trim

76

figure, thinking how attractive she looked in the neat black dress, lace-frilled bibbed white apron and the dainty, long-streamered lace cap perched on her high-piled chestnut hair.

'I'll bet you break all the errand boys' hearts,' he thought.

After a short interval the pretty maid reappeared in the hallway.

'Miss Miriam Josceleyne will see you, sir.'

'Thank you.' He smiled, and removed his hat, and she took both hat and riding crop from his hands and laid them on the hall table. Close to him Emma was sensually aware of his masculine scent. A compound of cologne water, leather, tobacco and clean flesh and linen. She found his hard-etched, sun-bronzed features extremely attractive, and wondered how his lips and thick moustache would feel against her skin. Then she coloured slightly as she realised that while she had been staring at his mouth, his startlingly blue eyes had been regarding her with a quizzical amusement. Momentarily disconcerted, she flustered, 'Will you come this way, mister,' and led him towards the rear of the hall to the drawing room.

At this hour of the day with the sun in the east, the room was shadowed and gloomy, and the sallow-faced, frail-looking woman standing before the fireplace in her dark grey dress appeared equally devoid of any colour or warmth.

Johnny Purvis smiled and half bowed. 'Thank you for receiving me, Miss Josceleyne. My name is John Purvis.'

Miriam Josceleyne coughed nervously, and asked hesitantly, 'Do I address you by your army rank, er, er, Mr Purvis?'

He shook his head. 'No ma'am. That isn't necessary. I'm all but finished with that nonsense now and shall very soon be a civilian once again.'

His easy manner seemed to instil a degree of confidence in her and she smiled in return, and for a brief instant Johnny Purvis saw the pretty girl she had once been.

'Please,' she indicated an armchair by the fireside, 'won't you sit down, Mr Purvis.'

'Thank you, ma'am.' He seated himself and she took the

77

opposite armchair, perching on the very edge of its seat, as if prepared to flee.

'My father, Mr Hector Josceleyne, is indisposed at this present time, Mr Purvis, but perhaps I can be of assistance?'

Her soft, tremulous voice was in keeping with her subdued appearance and timid manner, and the man found to his own surprise that she invoked a protective instinct in him.

'Perhaps you can, Miss Josceleyne,' he smiled warmly. 'I have been at the offices of Neasom and White in Church Road, making enquiries as to house properties for sale in the town. Mr Neasom's head clerk informed me that your father had a property in Mount Pleasant that he wished to sell.'

Miriam Josceleyne hesitated before replying. 'He must be referring to Grange House, Mr Purvis. It lies back from the roadway some distance past the Woodland Cottage Inn.'

'The very place, ma'am,' Johnny Purvis confirmed.

Part of the reason for her hesitance now became apparent. 'But I'm not sure if the property is still for sale, Mr Purvis.'

Seeing his look of puzzlement, Miriam Josceleyne became acutely embarrassed, and to her own chagrin she felt a hot flush spreading from her throat to her cheeks. Stammering slightly, she tried to explain.

'You see, Mr Purvis, it was my father who put the house on the market, but he has been ill for some time now, and ... and ...' She hesitated and her blush deepened. Mortified by her own inability to explain the situation with a confident fluency, Miriam Josceleyne became perilously close to tears. Her fingers intertwined and knotted on her lap. Johnny Purvis sensed her mounting distress and hastened to soothe her.

'Please Miss Josceleyne, there is no need for explanation,' he said gently. 'It's obvious that Mr Neasom's clerk informed me wrongly as to the situation concerning the property.' He rose to his feet. 'I'm sorry for intruding upon you, Miss Josceleyne.'

Again he smiled at her, and in startled shock at her own reactions, Miriam Josceleyne suddenly realised how personable she found him. With equal shock she heard herself stammering, 'I'll speak with my father, Mr Purvis, and find out his present feelings on the matter of selling Grange House. Perhaps you could call on me later this week, and I'll be able to clarify the situation for you.'

His pleasure at this was immediately apparent. 'That's very kind of you, ma'am. I'll most certainly call on you again.' He paused, as if debating with himself, then went on impulsively, 'You see, Miss Josceleyne, I was born and bred here in Redditch, and for some reason, which I myself cannot account for, I have always wanted to live in Grange House. Even as a small boy, I would stand and stare at the house and would imagine myself being its owner. It has always exerted a peculiar fascination over me.' He shrugged with smiling self-deprecation. 'I don't doubt but that sounds very strange to you, ma'am. I must confess it sound somewhat bizarre to myself also.'

Her faded green eyes fixed on him with a pleased amazement, and quite abruptly her timid manner metamorphosed into an enthusiastic assertiveness. 'But it does not sound so to me, Mr Purvis. I know exactly how you feel. I myself when a child would so stand and stare at Grange House. It was a veritable palace of romance to me. I could always imagine it to be a place of wonderful and romantic happenings. Indeed, it still fills me with such emotions, even now, after all these years.'

It was Johnny Purvis's turn to be surprised at this abrupt metamorphosis in the woman's manner. His surprise showed momentarily in his expression which instantly reversed Miriam Josceleyne's transformation as mortified self-consciousness flooded over her and drove her back into her customary fearful introversion.

She sat stiffly, with head bowed, and her hands twisting together on her lap, and the man realised that he should leave her to herself.

He thanked her once more, and with a fleeting smile of what he fancied to be gratitude Miriam Josceleyne tugged the bell-pull to summon Emma Farr.

'Please show Mr Purvis out, Emma,' she stammered, and her cheeks flamed once again, as he smiled and half-bowed in farewell.

Emma Farr had been waiting with ever-increasing impatience to see this romantic stranger at close quarters once again. Curiosity about him had consumed her, and as soon as she had ushered him into the drawing room she had run down to the kitchen and badgered Mrs Elwood with questions.

When she had heard his name, the cook had pursed her lips and thought deeply, then nodded. 'Ahr, he'll be old Ezra Purvis's youngest, I'll be bound – young Johnny. Went for a soldier years ago. Fair broke his mam's 'eart, if did, when the young bugger took the shilling. Lived in Izods Yard, the family did. I reckon his old dad still lives up theer now.'

Sudden puzzlement caused Mrs Elwood to frown doubtfully. 'But what's Johnny Purvis want to come here for? I mean to say, he aren't the Josceleynes' class, is he, even if he has become an officer, like you says he is. And fancy him coming ringing at the front door as bold as brass?' She sniffed indignantly. 'The cheeky bugger! Him being made an officer counts for nothing in this town, does it, because his family has always bin poor folk, and other folks knows that he was born and bred up in Izods Yard. He aren't entitled to come ringing at gentlefolks' front doors. He ought to have used the side door like the rest on us has to. He's getting above his station in life by the sounds on it, I'll declare. Oh the Purvis family has always bin respectable enough, I'll grant you that, and very religious, but poor, not carriage class like the Josceleynes.' She tutted disparagingly. 'I doon't know what the world's coming to these days, I'm sure I doon't. People used to know their rightful place when I was a girl. But everything seems to be turned upside down these modern days, doon't it?'

Despite her normal aversion to the men of her own social class, Emma was paradoxically pleased to find out that Johnny Purvis came from lowly origins. It was knowing this that emboldened her to smile flirtatiously at

80

him when she handed him his slouch hat and riding crop from the hall table.

'I think your uniform's very becoming, Mr Purvis.'

He looked closely at her, surprised by such forwardness from a maidservant.

Her black eyes danced and she met his searching look without any trace of shyness.

Johnny Purvis found her gamine-like confidence immensely appealing and thought her quite beautiful. Now he returned her compliment.

'And I think that your uniform is very becoming also, Emma.'

She bobbed a mock curtsey. 'Why thank you, Mr Purvis, sir.'

Her eyes twinkled with such infectious mischievous gaiety that he could not help but chuckle as he walked down the flagged pathway to the front gate.

At the gate he turned to look back at the girl standing framed in the doorway watching him, and smiling he lifted his riding crop in salute. She giggled delightedly, then blew him a kiss and in a swirl of skirt and petticoats disappeared inside the house. He remained for a couple of seconds gazing at the closed door, then shook his head in wry wonderment and walked away still smiling, quite charmed by their brief encounter.

Chapter Eleven

Saul Shibco carefully examined the unbroken wax seal on the large travel-stained envelope, then broke it and extracted the several sheets of notepaper contained within. He read the letter in silence, then sighed heavily and, refolding the sheets of notepaper, placed them on the desk before him.

On the opposite side of the desk Johnny Purvis waited patiently, sitting at his ease in the comfortable leather chair, his slouch hat held on his lap, his booted legs crossed.

Johnny judged the other man to be in his early thirties, and smiled inwardly as he considered how Shibco's physical appearance was so totally different from the popular stereotyped image of Jewish men. Saul Shibco was a big blond Anglo-Saxon in appearance, and now when he looked up at Johnny and began to talk, his accent was that of a well-educated Midlander.

'Firstly, I want to thank you for bringing my brother's final letter back to me, Lieutenant Purvis. Tell me, were you with him when he died?'

'Yes, I was,' Johnny confirmed quietly. 'If it is any comfort to you, his death was instantaneous. He neither knew nor suffered anything.'

'Thank God for that,' the other breathed gratefully. 'It is a relief to know that David died cleanly and quickly.'

Johnny Purvis's memory flashed back to that dusty track in the distant Transvaal and once again he heard the sharp crack of the Boer rifle and the simultaneous dull thud of impact, and he saw David Shibco's head explode in a shower of blood, bone and flesh as the dumdum bullet shattered it. Aloud he said to the other man, 'Yes, it was indeed quick and clean, Mr Shibco.'

Saul Shibco touched the sheaf of notepaper with his well-manicured fingers. 'According to his previous letters, you and David were very close friends, Lieutenant Purvis. He mentioned you often, and with much gratitude for your support of him when others were hostile towards him because of his religion.'

Johnny pondered briefly, before replying, 'We became good friends only after he had served in my troop for several months, Mr Shibco. My initial support for him was no more, and no less than I offered to any of my men who were being victimised or bullied by their fellow soldiers.'

A grim smile briefly quirked his lips. 'In the early days following the formation of the North Cape Scouts there was a necessity among the troopers to establish a pecking order, so to speak, Mr Shibco. Particularly since we had such a diverse variety of men from all over the Empire within our ranks. I did not intervene to save David from taking his lumps with the rest of them. He would not have thanked me for doing that. It was only when a couple of the men began to display an unjust prejudice against David because of his religion, that I intervened.'

Again with a grim smile he added, 'To be truthful, Mr Shibco, in other circumstances I doubt if I would have made any intervention. I considered that David was old enough and big enough to fight his own battles. But, because of the mixture of nationalities in my troop, a virtual Foreign Legion almost, I wanted with me only those men who would judge their comrades solely on their merits as soldiers. David was a very good soldier, and those two who persecuted him were bad soldiers. Once they were dealt with, then the rest of the troop accepted your brother fully as one of their own, and that was because of his own merit as a soldier, Mr Shibco, not because I wished them to do so.'

Saul Shibco nodded. 'I appreciate your forthrightness, Lieutenant Purvis. In fact, you are exactly as David said you were. Almost brutally honest and plain-spoken. It was one of the aspects of your character that he admired greatly.'

He leaned forwards across the desk and cupped his

hands as if in invitation. 'Lieutenant Purvis, is there any way that I can be of service to you? Forgive my rudeness in asking you this, but I know that soldiers do not earn a great deal. Is there any service I can render you in this way? Any business in which you would like to buy an interest, now that you are finishing with the army? Please do not take offence at my offer. I am truly desperate to try and find some way in which to demonstrate my gratitude towards you for all the kindness you showed towards my brother. He truly regarded you as his dearest friend, Lieutenant Purvis.'

Johnny shook his head in a smiling refusal, then a thought struck him.

'There is one service you could do for me, Mr Shibco.'

'Name it. Please name it,' the other man urged.

From his waistbelt Johnny took a small pouch made of soft leather and emptied its contents on the desk.

'These are my spoils of war, Mr Shibco,' he said quietly. 'Do you know a reputable dealer who will give me a fair price for them? Could you act as my agent in the matter?'

Shibco stirred the small stones with the tip of one finger, and they flashed and glittered in the sunlight. After a couple of moments he looked up at the soldier and grinned wryly.

'And there I was offering you financial assistance, Lieutenant Purvis. I'm no expert, but in my judgement these diamonds are worth a great deal of money. In fact, when they have been sold you will be in the position of being able to buy and sell me many times over.

'I know a very good man who will dispose of these for you. But perhaps in your own interest, you might prefer first to obtain valuations from other dealers and find out what prices they would be prepared to offer you? There are several here in Birmingham who are reputable.'

It was Purvis's turn to grin wryly. 'Mr Shibco, I looted these diamonds from a dead Boer. Looting is a Court Martial offence in the British Army. I can't risk hawking them around the Birmingham jewellery district and perhaps having to answer awkward questions concerning their origin.'

Shibco's blond head nodded. 'I quite understand, Lieutenant Purvis.' He winked broadly. 'In my opinion soldiers are entitled to their spoils of war. After all, they have risked their lives to gain them. You may leave the matter with me. I shall ensure that you get a good price for them.' He grinned jokingly. 'I shall not charge you any commission for acting as your agent.'

He rose and collected the diamonds back into their pouch, then taking a key from his waistcoat pocket he opened a large safe standing against the wall and deposited the pouch inside it. Before closing and locking the door he lifted another pouch from its interior, and handed it to Johnny Purvis.

'There are two hundred sovereigns to be going on with, Lieutenant Purvis.'

Johnny took the pouch. 'Many thanks, Mr Shibco. But please, I wish you to take a commission on the deal. I'm in no position to sell them myself after all.'

The big Jew held up his hands in a gesture of refusal. 'Absolutely not. I will not take a penny, Lieutenant Purvis. You were a friend to my brother when he most needed a friend. Please allow me to repay some of that kindness that you showed to him. Those are my terms, and I will only act for you if you accept them. Please, allow me to do this service for you. Please.'

Recognising Shibco's obduracy in this matter, Johnny Purvis grinned, and shook the other man's hand in acceptance.

Chapter Twelve

Preparations to celebrate the Coronation Day of King Edward VII had been ongoing for many months in Redditch and district, and the news of the King's sudden illness which would mean the temporary postponement of his Coronation had created great concern to those who formed the Coronation Celebration Committee. The Reverend Mosse MacDonald was one of the leading lights of this committee and now, as he sat and took tea with Miriam Josceleyne and some other ladies in the drawing room at Cotswold House, he was voicing his dismay at considerable length.

'. . . and of course, dear ladies, the greatest concern at this particular moment is the wastage of the food we have collected to feed the poor. In this hot weather it just will not keep.'

He adjusted his pince-nez to examine the assortment of cream cakes and fruit tarts on the double-tiered silver cake-stand in the middle of the table.

'Please try the eclairs, Reverend MacDonald,' Miriam Josceleyne invited politely.

'Yes do try them, Reverend MacDonald, they are particularly good,' Mrs Amanda Allcock, wife of the town's leading fishing tackle manufacturer urged, and graciously congratulated Miriam Josceleyne. 'You possess a very good cook in Mrs Elwood, Miriam, my dear. She has the lightest touch with pastries, I do declare.'

The clergyman frowned doubtfully. He had already demolished two platters of salmon and cucumber sandwiches and several assorted savouries, and he knew that he would pay for his greed with a bout of indigestion.

Nevertheless the eclairs did look very appealing and his tooth was very sweet. In a spurt of rash daring he decided to risk the possibility of added discomfort and he took several eclairs in quick succession and disposed of them with noisy, lip-smacking relish, while Miriam Josceleyne watched him with an ambiguous expression in her eyes. While not a hairshirt Christian herself, she vaguely felt that the clergy should set an example of restraint when it came to the satisfaction of bodily appetites, and Mosse MacDonald's shameless gluttony offended her sensibilities.

Her gaze flickered around the table resting briefly on each of her guests in turn. Mrs Amanda Allcock and Miss Julia Playfair, both good and estimable women who did a great deal of charity work; Mrs Ida Huins, the town's leading hostess and an arbiter of social standings; the Reverend MacDonald; Mrs Violet Milward, daughter-in-law of the lately deceased Colonel Victor Milward, the doyen of the needle manufacturers; Mrs Beatrice Kendrick, widow of the town's leading solicitor.

It was a very select gathering, and testimony to the high standing of the Josceleyne family within the community. To have been able to attract such notables to her fortnightly 'at home' made Miriam Josceleyne the envy of many women whose own 'at home' could never hope to be so honoured with the presence of such illustrious figures.

But Miriam Josceleyne was forced to admit to herself that she found them tedious company, and inwardly she was counting the minutes until their departure. In the privacy of her thoughts she constantly wished that she had the courage to choose her own companions, and to drop out of the eternal mind-numbing rounds of social calls, tea parties and 'at homes'.

The Reverend MacDonald, uncomfortably full and fearing that his overstrained digestive tract might grossly and shamefully betray him, suddenly remembered a mission of mercy that he must immediately depart upon, and made his farewells.

Emma Farr was rung for to escort the Reverend to the front door and her appearance in the room created much covert interest among the ladies. Such beauty in a servant was rare.

Once the solitary male had departed, the ladies breathed secret sighs of relief. It was hard to enjoy a really good gossip in the presence of a clergyman.

As always, it was Amanda Allcock who had the first titbits to relate. Owing to her constant charity work she roamed in wider fields among the town's population than her companions, and so tended to garner more recent information about what was happening in the town.

Despite her inner boredom, Miriam Josceleyne was forced to admit that at times the items of gossip stirred her own interest also. She listened as intently as the rest when Amanda Allcock's plump features smiled archly and she said, 'I really cannot understand why the Reverend did not see fit to inform us that a decision has already been taken by the Coronation Celebration Committee to carry on with the celebrations regardless.'

She paused, and, satisfied with the impact her news created, continued, 'Yes, Willy Woodfield himself told me of it. Apparently our dear King has indicated that he wishes his subjects to indulge themselves regardless of his own unfortunate illness. His Majesty understands the effort and expense that has been expended upon the preparations and does not wish the poor to suffer any loss of pleasure.'

Once this item had been dealt with, it was Miss Playfair's turn. It always afforded amusement to Miriam Josceleyne to see how even in the retailing of gossip certain unwritten laws of procedure were strictly adhered to. Miss Playfair was a satellite of Mrs Allcock and as such would never offer any item of news until her leader had spoken first. She also acted in the capacity of information-forager for the elder woman, and now, in that capacity, she asked Miriam Josceleyne, 'Where did you find your new maid, Miss Josceleyne? She is a very dainty and pretty creature, is she not?'

'She comes from Silver Street, Miss Playfair. Her father is Winston Farr, the chimney sweep,' Miriam informed them, and smiled inwardly with wry amusement at the shocked glances her companions exchanged.

'A sweep's daughter! And from Silver Street, no less. Well I would never have believed it!' Amanda Allcock exclaimed, then questioned with an air of incredulity, 'And do you find her satisfactory?'

'Eminently so,' Miriam informed gravely.

Further glances were exchanged, and eyebrows lifted, and unspoken, yet clearly understood comments passed.

Miriam found herself resenting her companions' silent disparagement of the girl, but lacked the self-confidence to assert firmly that Emma was proving to be an excellent maid, and remained silent herself.

There was a brief hiatus in the conversation, then Ida Huins decided it was time to establish her supremacy as the purveyor of really juicy titbits.

'My neighbour has been behaving brutishly again, I regret to say.'

All eyes brightened, and breaths were bated in anticipation. Ida Huins' neighbours, the Doltons, were a constant source of fascination.

'Yes, I was entertaining the Ladies of the Guild and that awful man came along the road, obviously the worse for drink, and endeavoured to hold a conversation with some of the younger ladies and gentlemen who were playing croquet. Of course they cut him.'

Nods of approval were given, but no one attempted to speak. They knew from past experience of the spokes-woman that the best was yet to come.

'Arthur Dolton walked away with a face like thunder and from what my housekeeper has told me, behaved quite abominably in his own house.'

Faces were rapt, and bodies leaned closer, heads tilted slightly to hear more clearly as Ida Huins, with consummate mastery of the craft of story-telling, lowered her voice to almost a conspiratorial whisper.

'Apparently after shouting the foullest insults he physically dragged his wife up to their bedroom, and after beating her unmercifully, then proceeded to abuse her body in the vilest manner, whilst his children were sobbing with fear and distress on the very landing outside the bedroom door.'

Audible gasps of indrawn breath punctuated the utter silence and the ladies' expressions were a panorama of horror, excitement and gratification. Ida Huins went on to give more graphic details culled from the highly coloured account given to her housekeeper by Milly, the Doltons' maid and embellished in turn by the Huins' housekeeper, and so completely were her listeners drawn into her story, that none of them heard the front door bell jangling.

The story ended, and the listeners sat back in their chairs, still held silent and enthralled by what they had heard.

'If you please, ma'am,' Emma Farr broke the spell. 'It's Mr Purvis come to see you. He says he has an appointment with you.'

'Whom did you say, Emma?' Miriam had been so horrifiedly engrossed by the awful story that at first she could hardly comprehend what her maid had announced.

'It's Mr Purvis come to see you, ma'am,' Emma repeated.

'Mr Purvis,' Miriam Josceleyne murmured, and then could have wept as she felt the heat of a blush begin its inexorable progress from her throat to her cheeks.

The knowledge that avid eyes were noting that hot flush and eyebrows were being raised in silent query across the table added to her mortification, and when in the doorway behind Emma the tall khaki-clad figure appeared Miriam Josceleyne could only beg for sudden death to release her.

'Good afternoon, Miss Josceleyne, ladies.' Johnny Purvis seemed quite unaware of the minor sensation his appearance had created around the table, as he apologised with complete easiness of manner, 'I beg your forgiveness for intruding upon you in this manner, Miss Josceleyne. I expected you to be alone.'

Thoughts raced, and conclusions were arrived at almost instantaneously, as the women's eyes devoured this newcomer, and noted their hostess's embarrassment and confusion.

Miriam Josceleyne was agonisingly aware of her guests' thought patterns, and with a rising sense of panic she lost her head completely, and standing up blurted without thinking, 'Show Mr Purvis into the front parlour, Emma. I'll speak with him privately.'

She could not bring herself to look into Johnny Purvis's eyes, and he frowned slightly in puzzlement at her strange attitude, and lack of courtesy.

The avid eyes around the table took full note of this interplay and lips twitched in gratification.

'Well, it just goes to show, doesn't it,' Ida Huins thought with a surge of malicious pleasure. 'You can never really know anyone, can you? This must be her secret lover. Why else should she be so embarrassed? What a sly cat she is. Here we all were thinking her to be a dried-up old maid, and all the time she was having a relationship with this colonial.'

Similar conclusions were also being reached by her fellow guests, and when Johnny Purvis half-bowed and apologised once again for disturbing them, before retreating to the front parlour, they all stared at him without any attempt to conceal their raging curiosity.

Miriam Josceleyne was fighting a desperate inner battle and her ever-deepening flush betrayed this agitation. She briefly debated with herself whether she should explain why he had come. She assumed it was her own invitation concerning Grange House that had brought him here. But a covert glance at the faces surrounding her brought the realisation that any attempt at explanation would only titillate their lewd fancies still further. Anger at herself helped her through the next few minutes.

'Please excuse me,' she stammered in apology. 'I have urgent business matters to discuss with the gentleman.'

They accepted their curtailed visit with good grace and made their various farewells. Eager to congregate elsewhere as soon as humanly possible and debate this exciting happening.

In a flurry of flowered hats and feathered bonnets, a swishing of skirts and flourish of parasols the ladies departed, leaving Miriam Josceleyne standing alone in the drawing room.

She remained motionless for long minutes while an

91

inner conflict raged within her mind. One part of her being longed to see and talk with Johnny Purvis, the other part was quite simply terrified of doing so. The dichotomy created a chaotic confusion in her thoughts, and she was quite unable to understand the motivation for either of these reactions.

'I hardly know the man,' she muttered, as her fingers entwined and tugged and twisted. 'He is nothing more than a casual acquaintance to me. Why am I feeling like this? Why? Why?'

'Are you all right, Miss Miriam?' Emma Farr was staring at her with concern.

Nervous strain made Miriam Josceleyne snap at the girl. 'All right? Of course I'm all right! Why do you ask me that?'

Emma frowned resentfully and answered with a touch of surliness, 'Well, the gentleman is still waiting in the parlour, ma'am. Shall I tell him you'll see him, or what?'

The woman shook her head irritably. 'Oh tell him . . . tell him . . . No! Wait!' She went to the writing table beneath the window and taking pen and paper hurriedly wrote a note. She took the silver shaker of fine drying powder across the wet ink, then blew off the sediments and folded the sheet of paper.

'Here, give this to Mr Purvis and give him my apologies for not being able to receive him. Tell him I am suddenly afflicted with a headache.'

Her irritation sparked once more as the girl stared at her puzzledly. 'Here, girl. Take it.' She thrust the folded sheet into Emma's hand. 'Will you do as I bid?'

Emma tossed her head haughtily and flounced from the room. Miriam Josceleyne stared after her with dismay. 'Dear God, am I going mad?' she murmured, and her faded eyes brimmed with tears. 'What is the matter with me? Dear God, what is the matter with me?'

In the front parlour Johnny Purvis scanned the rows of small neat handwriting and shrugged, then folded the paper and tucked it into his tunic pocket. He smiled at Emma Farr.

'Please convey my condolences to your mistress for her sudden affliction.'

The bold black eyes twinkled at him, as if she were repressing inner laughter. 'Oh yes, Mr Purvis, I'll do that for you.'

She walked before him to the front door, and he found himself gazing appreciatively at her curvaceous hips and slender waist. Johnny Purvis was a hot-blooded man and there had been several women in his life. But he was also a man who preferred love to lust, and therefore he tried to control his promiscuous urges.

As she handed him his slouch hat, leather gloves and riding crop the girl asked, 'Will you be in Redditch for the Coronation celebrations, Mr Purvis?'

'I thought the Coronation had been put back because old Teddy is ill?' he queried.

'That's as maybe, but I was listening at the door to what the ladies was saying, and Mrs Allcock said that the celebrations are still going to be held in the town here.'

'Well then, I'm bound to be here for them, aren't I, Emma?' Johnny grinned. 'After all, I'm back home to stay now.'

'I'm ever so pleased to hear that, Mr Purvis,' she told him, and her black eyes were soft with invitation. 'I shall have a half-day holiday. You never know but that we might run into each other when the celebrations are going on.'

For a brief instant Johnny Purvis was tempted to accept the unspoken invitation in her eyes, and ask her to meet him. Then a warning voice echoed in his mind. 'Hold hard now, Johnny. This is just a young girl you're talking to. Luscious though she may be. She's just a young maidservant who doesn't really know what she's about.'

Reluctantly he put temptation from him, and only smiled pleasantly, and wished her goodbye.

Emma Farr stood admiring his confident swaggering gait as he traversed the pathway separating the recreation garden from the churchyard. She thought him wonderfully attractive, and her heartbeat quickened as she imagined how it would feel to be close locked in his arms, naked body pressed to naked body, mouth crushed to mouth.

'Emma? Emma, wheer am you?' Mrs Elwood's shout sounded from behind her and with a final look and a sigh of longing, the girl turned back into the house.

'Is her still with him then?' the cook asked when the girl came into the kitchen.

'Still with who?' Emma answered absently, her thoughts still engrossed with Johnny Purvis.

Mrs Elwood snorted impatiently, ''Ull you get your yed out o' the bloody clouds, my wench! I asked you if Miss Miriam was still with her fancy man?'

Emma came back to reality. 'Fancy man?' She stared questioningly. 'What am you on about, Mrs Elwood? Who's Miss Miriam's fancy man?'

'Why Johnny Purvis o' course.' The fat woman chuckled lewdly. 'The poor silly cratur's bin mooning about the house ever since her met him.' She winked knowingly. 'When you'se seen as much o' life as I 'as, my wench, you'll recognise the signs plain enough. From the minute her clapped her eyes on him he become her fancy man. I could tell it right off.'

Emma stared incredulously. 'But Miss Miriam's an old maid. She'd never have a fancy man.'

The older woman's small eyes gleamed salaciously. 'Doon't talk so sarft, my wench. It's the old maids that am the worst for it. Doon't you think that Miss Miriam doon't lie in her bed night arter night hungering for the feel of a man between her legs?'

Emma Farr could not even begin to imagine her timid, nerve-wracked, almost sexless mistress ever having hungered for a man's loving.

'It's you that's talking sarft, Mrs Elwood,' she giggled. 'Why, I reckon Miss Miriam 'ud die o' fright if a man even saw her knee.' Her giggle became a peal of laughter. 'If a man dropped his trousers in front of her, why then I reckon she'd just explode into little pieces.'

The cook laughed with her, then reaffirmed, 'Well, just mark my words. I knows the signs well enough. Old maid or no old maid, our Miss Miriam has finally found herself a fancy man. If you knew her as well as I does, you'd have noted the changes in her since her met Johnny Purvis.'

Emma thought hard for a moment, then frowned uncertainly. 'Mind you, she was acting real queer just now. She 'udden't goo into the parlour to talk with him. I had to take him a note instead. After he read it, he left straight off.'

'What did the note say?' the cook asked curiously.

Emma felt vexed with herself. 'I never read it. More fool me! I wish I had now.'

A sudden pang of jealousy struck into her. 'Johnny Purvis 'ud never want to make love to an old maid like Miss Miriam. She's nothing but a dried-up stick. A fine man like him wants somebody who's young and pretty, and who's got some life in her.'

The cook's eyes were shrewd with understanding as she regarded the young girl.

'Took a liking for him yourself, has you, my wench? Wants him for your own fancy man, does you?' she baited.

Emma Farr tossed her head indignantly. 'Not me! He's too old for me! He must be well over thirty I should reckon.'

Mrs Elwood chuckled lewdly, and said, 'Well, theer's many a good tune played on an old fiddle, my duck.'

Emma's momentary show of indignation dissolved into a giggle, and her eyes danced as she nodded, 'That's true enough, Mrs Elwood. It's true as well that I 'udden't mind being the fiddler using Johnny Purvis's bow.'

The older woman cackled with delight. 'You shameless little cat!' She shrieked with laughter and threw her apron up over her fat red face in mock shocked modesty.

On the bottom step of the Metropolitan Bank of England and Wales, Johnny Purvis extracted the note from his tunic pocket and re-read it.

Dear Mr Purvis,

All future negotiations concerning the sale of Grange House to yourself will be dealt with by my brother, Mr Franklin Josceleyne, manager of the Metropolitan Bank of England and Wales. He will be available for consultation at his office during the normal business hours.

Yours sincerely,

Miriam Josceleyne

Johnny Purvis grinned wryly and shook his head. 'What a strange creature she is,' he thought. 'Yet there's something very appealing about her, for all her nonsense. She does bring out a certain protective instinct in me, I must admit.'

Inside the bank, dark-coated bespectacled clerks perching on high stools, bent industriously over ledgers, stared at the soldier with great interest. Behind the vast mahogany counter a young man smiled in welcome. 'Yes sir, how can I help you?'

Johnny returned the smile. 'I'd like to see Mr Franklin Josceleyne please. My name is Purvis, John Purvis.'

'On what business might I enquire, sir?' the young man asked politely.

'It's a personal matter,' Johnny told him pleasantly, 'but I believe he'll recognise my name.'

'Yes sir. Could you wait here for a moment please?'

He disappeared into the inner sanctum, walking with a noticeable limp, to return in a few seconds.

'Mr Franklin is engaged at the moment, sir. But if you would care to wait, he will see you as soon as possible. If you cannot wait, then I'll be happy to arrange a future appointment for you.'

'I'll wait,' Johnny told him.

'Would you care to take a seat, sir?'

'No thank you, I'll stand.'

'As you please, sir.' The young clerk's eyes were moving constantly up and down Johnny's uniform and Johnny regarded him with some amusement. The young man suddenly became aware of this and smiled.

'I was wondering what regiment you're in, sir?'

'The North Cape Horse.'

'Oh yes, irregular cavalry. I was in the Imperial Yeomanry myself.'

'Were you now?' Johnny was instantly interested. 'Did you see much action?'

'A little, but after Paardeburg I was invalided home.' He tapped his leg with his fingers. 'My horse went down and I didn't get out from under her quickly enough.'

'Well, at least you got home safely,' Johnny commiserated. 'There's a lot of chaps who didn't.'

'That's true enough.' The young man's thin pleasant face suddenly became wistful. 'But I miss the life, you know. The bank's all right I suppose, but I find it very dull after South Africa.'

'You're bound to,' Johnny agreed. 'What's your name?'

'Foley Field.' The young man grinned somewhat shamefacedly. 'Don't ask me where my parents found my Christian name from. I've never been able to find that out for myself even.'

They laughed together and Johnny Purvis found himself liking the other man. In a way he reminded him of the close friend he had lost in the Transvaal, David Shibco.

They talked easily for some time, reminiscing about the war and then the bell on the counter rang and Foley Field grimaced good-humouredly.

'His Majesty summons you, Mr Purvis.'

'I've enjoyed our talk,' Johnny told him. 'I hope we'll meet to share a few jars some other time.'

'Yes, that would be good,' Foley Field agreed enthusiastically. 'I'll look forward to that.'

Then he showed Johnny into the office of Franklin Josceleyne.

Within a very few minutes Johnny decided that he thoroughly disliked this bumptious arrogant little man, but he forced himself to smile pleasantly while they discussed details. The price that the bank manager was asking for Grange House was well above its true market value and Johnny knew this fact well. However, he so hungered to own the house that he was not disposed to haggle for any length of time and eventually they closed the deal for only slightly less than the bank manager's original demand. When Johnny Purvis left Franklin Josceleyne's office and waved in friendly farewell to Foley Fields, he was to all intents and purposes the owner of Grange House.

Chapter Thirteen

It was the twenty-sixth day of June, and although King Edward VII was prevented by an attack of appendicitis from celebrating his Coronation Day, his loyal subjects prepared to celebrate it all the same.

At seven o'clock in the morning the bells of St Stephen's Church rang out the Royal peal, and the fitful breeze carried the sound over the dew-sodden rooftops of the town.

While the sonorous chimes echoed above their heads, the members of the Redditch Town Band mustered at the kiosk in the recreation garden on Church Green, under the command of bandmaster Spenser. A crowd of excited children, some of them carrying their breakfast wedges of bread in grubby hands, gathered to watch the bandsmen. The men were resplendent in red frogged tunics, white crossbelts and peaked caps; they seated themselves beneath the kiosk's golden weathercock, set up their music stands and tested their instruments.

The last echoes of the bells wafted away on the breeze, and Phillip Spenser tapped his baton. 'Right then, lads. Let's wake the town up, shall we.'

The band struck up the rousing chords of 'Rule Britannia' and the urchins cheered and capered wildly around the kiosk.

Emma Farr came into Hector Josceleyne's bedroom, her dainty nose wrinkling with distaste at the smell which emanated from the open commode at the side of the old man's bed.

Hector Josceleyne was awake, sitting up in bed propped by his pillows and his rheumy eyes gleamed with spiteful satisfaction as he saw the girl's reaction to the stench.

She ignored him and crossing to the window pulled back the heavy drapes, reaching under the net curtain to open the casement wide, bringing a rush of fresh chill morning air sweeping through the room.

'Damn and blast you, you bitch! I'll catch my death of cold!' he screeched furiously.

'Good!' Emma snapped, and slammed shut the commode's lid. 'If you dies then I won't have to put up with your stink any more, will I?'

The brassy music sounded loudly through the open window and Hector Josceleyne scowled. 'What's that rattle? What's happening out there?'

'You know well enough what's happening,' Emma told him shortly. 'It's Coronation Day, and you'll be coming to church later with me and Miss Miriam.'

'I'm too ill to move,' he declared sulkily, and Emma could not help but grin in amusement, because he so resembled a grumpy ancient gnome, with his old-fashioned tasselled nightcap pulled low on his head, his nose almost meeting his chin as he clamped his toothless jaws together in a mulish obstinacy.

To her own astonishment Emma had become perversely fond of the old man, despite her constantly referring to him in her conversations with Mrs Elwood as, 'that old devil'.

Now she warned him, 'You'll come to church, even if I have to drag you there by your willie, you old devil!'

'Don't you talk to me in that way, you saucy slum-rat!' he screeched, and shook his claw-like fist at her.

She stood at his bedside, hands on hips, arms akimbo and laughingly teased him, 'Come on then, if you want to fight! Come on then!'

She stepped closer and he struck futile blows at her which she parried with ease. Then suddenly she grabbed him and wrestled him down onto his back and pinioned him so that he was helpless.

While he cursed and spat at her she laughed down into his face, and cheekily stuck out her tongue to torment him further.

99

His feeble strength gave out and he relapsed, gasping for breath, and Emma released him and straightened her rumpled dress and apron, then asked in a gentler tone, 'Do you want some breakfast now?'

He closed his eyes and refused to answer, and she chuckled.

'All right then. But you'll be hungry later on, and I'll not offer you anything else until dinnertime.'

His eyes opened, and like a sulky child he grimaced and nodded.

'That's a good boy.' She patted his sunken cheek. 'But first I'll get rid o' this stink.'

Pinching her nostrils between finger and thumb she opened the lid of the commode and lifted out the foul smelling pail.

'You stay quiet now and listen to the band until I come back,' Emma instructed.

The old eyes hungrily dwelt on her body as she left the room and the briefest suggestion of a smile twisted the lipless mouth. For in his degenerating brain, Hector Josceleyne had in his twisted way become as perversely fond of Emma Farr as she was of him.

Miriam Josceleyne was sitting at her dressing table, staring at her reflection in its large mirror. Despondently she touched her sallow cheeks, and the dark puffy shadows beneath her faded green eyes.

'Just look at me,' she thought in sad despair. 'I'm twenty-eight years of age, and I look nearer forty-eight.'

With her fingers she unbraided and loosened the long thick plait of mousy hair which hung nearly to her hips. It was lustreless and felt dry and stiff to the touch. Beneath her thick flannel nightshift only the slightest of mounds betrayed her breasts, and when she lifted her head her throat looked wrinkled and scrawny.

From the drawer of the dressing table she took a photograph framed in brown leather. A pretty young girl smiled out to her from that brown leather frame. Her hair was fair and glossy, her body sweetly curved beneath the white dress, and despite the stiff formality of the posed portrait the vibrant, humorous, hopeful spirit of that young girl shone through.

'What became of you?' Miriam Josceleyne stared with a puzzled sadness at the girl she had once been. 'Where did you go to? When did you leave me?'

Without conscious volition her thoughts suddenly pictured Johnny Purvis and she whispered, 'I wish you could have seen me as I used to be. You might have loved me then.'

A yearning swept over her, a hungering that burgeoned with a strength that she could neither deny nor contest. But that overpowering surge of emotion carried with it also the bitter conviction that her hungers could never be satisfied, and she buried her head in her hands and sobbed, 'It's too late. Too late! Too late!'

Chapter Fourteen

At half past eight in the morning the Reverend Mosse MacDonald left his house midway down Fish Hill and walked majestically up the steep slope towards Church Green. He was going to adminster Holy Communion at the church at nine o'clock. Despite the knowledge that he would be in complete charge of the proceedings, Mosse MacDonald was not happy. In fact his mood was definitely sour, and could not be sweetened by the fine freshness of the morning, or the lively music coming from the kiosk.

The reason for his present mood was the fact that the main service of this Coronation Day was to be held later this morning at eleven o'clock. Every notable in the town would attend, and it would be a once-in-a-lifetime opportunity for the presiding clergyman to preach a sermon which would resound down through the ages and live on in the memories of those present. Mosse MacDonald scowled. His superior, the Reverend Canon Horace Newton was to preside at the main Divine Service at eleven o'clock and would be preaching the sermon.

'Selfish old pig! I'm his senior curate. He should have had the grace to stand aside and let me preach the sermon,' Mosse MacDonald muttered behind his beard with most un-Christian rancour. 'He should have retired years since. He's in his dotage. It's men like him who hold back the careers of men like me.'

Mosse MacDonald bitterly resented the fact that, although still considered a very young man in a clerical context, he had not advanced further up the hierarchical ladder of the Anglican Church. Not without some justification he blamed what he considered to be the painfully slow progress of his career on his lack of personal wealth and family influence.

'If only I had money,' he thought longingly. 'If only I had some family influence in this town. It would make all the difference.'

He reached the top of the hill and was forced to stand for a moment or two to allow the night-soil cart to pass before him on the roadway. He hurriedly pulled out his lavender-scented handkerchief and crammed it to his nose and mouth to block out the vile smell of the cart's contents and its attendants. Three unshaven, brutish looking men whose battered shapeless hats, filthy clothing and great hobnailed boots appeared to have been soaked in the contents of the privies and middens that they had been emptying throughout the night hours.

The encounter left him feeling more than a little nauseous and he silently bewailed his hard lot as he continued on towards the church.

'This is no life for me. Having to get out of my bed at the crack of dawn to administer the sacrament to a few old women. If I were vicar, I'd have my own curates to do it for me. I need money and family influence.'

He passed by Cotswold House and thought about its inhabitants.

'Miriam Josceleyne would make an ideal wife for a clergyman in many respects. She's not really to my taste as a bedfellow, I admit. But then, a man cannot expect perfection in all he seeks for, can he?'

His footsteps slowed perceptibly, as the idea of Miriam Josceleyne as a wife struck him more forcefully.

'Her father would be a terrible nuisance, but he surely cannot live much longer. Her brother is an interfering, bombastic, arrogant clod. But if she was my wife, then I would have control of her financial affairs, would I not? Franklin Josceleyne would just have to keep his nose out of it. Mind you, with all his faults, Franklin is not such a bad fellow, and he has a deal of influence in the town, has he not? A man could do much worse than have him as brother-in-law.'

Mosse MacDonald's sour mood sweetened considerably.

'Yes, maybe I'll see how the land lies in that direction. I'm sure Franklin would not take the idea of my marrying his sister amiss, and it's common knowledge that she obeys him in all things. If he was agreeable to the match, then it's as good as made. I'd kill two birds with the one stone, wouldn't I? I'd gain both money, and family influence.'

His mind now made up, the cleric strode out briskly towards the church, and cheerfully acknowledged the salutation of the bandmaster as he passed the kiosk with a lifting of his top hat, instead of the normal brief condescending nod he vouchsafed to his social inferiors.

Chapter Fifteen

'Will you take us to see the lights this evening, Mother?' Simon Dolton pleaded. 'Please say that you'll take us.'

Cleopatra Dolton smiled at her eldest son, and her dark eyes moved along the breakfast table to meet the beseeching gaze of eight-year-old James and little Andrew.

'Well, I'll have to ask your father.' She saw the disappointment clouding their faces and added quickly, 'But I'm sure that he'll give his permission. Now, have you all finished?'

They nodded in unison, and she told them, 'Very well then, you may leave the table.'

'Can we go out to play, Mother?' Simon asked.

'You can play in the orchard, but don't make a great noise.'

She kissed each of them in turn as they came to her and her heart welled with the love she had for them.

Alone in the dining room she sat toying with the edge of the white linen tablecloth, her thoughts dwelling upon her marriage. She had been twenty-five years old when she married Arthur Dolton eleven years ago. She had not loved, or even particularly liked the man, but marrying him had been a way of escape from a life that had become intolerable.

Now she grimaced and caught her full lower lip between her white teeth. Her marriage was fast becoming equally intolerable. Arthur Dolton's drunken brutality was worsening and his physical assaults upon her were recurring with an accelerating frequency. She gusted a long shuddering sigh. What was in some ways harder to bear than the physical pain was the mental anguish of knowing that her husband's behaviour was now beginning to adversely affect her eldest son, who was reaching an age when he could understand what was happening between his parents.

'No wonder he's so thin and nervous,' the woman thought sadly. 'Next it will be James's turn to begin to understand, then he'll be harmed by it too.'

Miserably she mentally revisited the years of her childhood. When her mother had died giving birth to her, there had been older children of the marriage. One by one they had died and by her eighth birthday there had only been herself and her father left in the fetid slum hovel. In fairness to him, he had not been a violent man towards his family. But he was a hopeless drunkard, whose drinking habits had rendered him unfit to continue his trade of bricklaying and he had eked out a miserable living as a scavenger.

Cleopatra Dolton's dark eyes clouded as she relived the progress of her incestuous relationship with her father. As a child she had never known the kisses and caresses of a loving parent and neither had many of her contemporaries in the slum alleys of the town. So, during her ninth year, when her father had first taken her into his bed, she had not understood that his feverishly seeking hands were not fondling her as a loving parent, and that those other acts he made her perform upon him were wickedly unnatural between father and daughter.

Inevitably he progressed to having full sexual intercourse with her, and, at fifteen years of age, she had given birth to a stillborn child. Puerperal fever had set in and for long months she had hovered between life and death in the workhouse infirmary at the nearby town of Bromsgrove. Her father died during an attack of delirium tremens while Cleopatra was in the infirmary, leaving the orphaned girl alone in the world.

Her mental and bodily sufferings had paradoxically wrought a startling change for the better in her physical appearance and the plain, woefully undernourished, acned girl who had entered the infirmary, was metamorphosed into a young woman of considerable beauty.

Other changes had been wrought within her as well. During her time in the infirmary she had been introduced to the world of books by some of the charitable visitors to the workhouse. Cleopatra had begun to read voraciously, absorbing any book she could lay her hands on. Her latent intelligence, never before having been given the opportunity to flower, now did so, and she took immense pleasure and satisfaction from the discovery that she possessed an agile and retentive mind.

Upon her discharge from the infirmary, the young girl returned to the only world she had known, the hovels of Silver Street. She found work in a needle factory and by dint of exercising the utmost stringency was able to rent a room and support herself upon her meagre earnings.

Her beauty attracted many men to pursue her and at times the young girl would accept an invitation to walk out with one or other that she found attractive. But always, when a man attempted to kiss or caress her, she would repulse him. She found that their eager searching hands brought back the acute memories of her father's abuse of her and she regarded them with the same disgust that she had conceived for him.

There were many nights when Cleopatra would lie in her bed, wracked by her natural desires, tormented by self-loathing as she remembered the times when with her own father she had experienced fleeting spasms of sexual ecstacy. Then, hating her body for what it demanded from her, she would satisfy her own needs, and her hands would momentarily become her father's hands and her fingers his thrusting manhood, and she would writhe and moan and at last cry out in tortured pleasure, and collapse into bitter sobs of self-disgust.

The years passed, and Cleopatra continued to work and read and dream of one day escaping from her bondage of poverty. Many men continued to pursue her, and she took a perverse delight in arousing and tormenting their desires, then in rejecting them with a harsh contempt. Some of her suitors reacted violently to this treatment, and there were times when the young woman found herself under physical assault, and was lucky to escape with no more than bruises, or cut and swollen lips. She was capable of taking an objective viewpoint of herself, and she realised before too long that her cavalier treatment of men would at some point inevitably embroil her in a situation that might lead to serious harm or even death befalling her.

Her desire also to escape from the drudgery of factory work and the poverty of Silver Street was now becoming overwhelming. She assessed her situation and her chances of altering her life for the better, and realised that the only chance of doing so lay in finding a wealthy husband.

This was something that was much easier to realise than to achieve. There were few secrets in a small town and Cleopatra was well aware of the fact that many people knew that as a young girl she had given birth to a stillborn child. What had remained a secret however was the identity of that child's father. Bitterly ashamed as she was of her incestuous relationship, Cleopatra had steadfastly refused ever to disclose what had happened between herself and her father, and although there were those among her neighbours, wise in the ways of their small world, who could surmise that her own father had impregnated her, no one knew for certain that this was the case.

To give birth to an illegitimate child was considered a terrible stigma among the respectable elements of the town's population. But in the slums the unfortunate woman who did so was not condemned with the same virulence. The brutal realities of life that beset the poor from birth until death tended to make them more accepting and tolerant of young women's peccadillos. Therefore a young woman as beautiful as Cleopatra would experience little difficulty in finding men of her own class willing to marry her. But to marry into poverty was the last thing that Cleopatra wanted, not even if she found a poor man that she could love. So she took stock of her assets, to consider what she had to offer a wealthy man.

These assets were quite considerable. A beautiful face and a voluptuous body; intelligence and a varied fund of knowledge garnered from her voracious reading; an ability to wear what clothing she could afford with style and elegance; a personal fastidiousness in hygiene and a voice from which she had endeavoured to erase the raucous accents and tone of the slums. She had eradicated most of the tell-tale impediments of her class and retained sufficient gutter-devil to give her an aggressive self-confidence. The main obstacle to her succeeding in her aim as she saw it was her age. Twenty-five was not young and with every passing year opportunities would lessen. Therefore, she had no more time to waste. She must make haste and ensnare the first wealthy man that she could find.

Sitting now at the breakfast table, Cleopatra smiled bitterly. That man had been Arthur Dolton.

She shook her head regretfully. Certainly she had escaped from poverty. But the emotional and physical price she had paid, and was still paying, constituted a very hard bargain.

She heard the clumping of boots on the staircase and frowned.

'So, you've dragged yourself out of your bed at last, have you, you drunken pig.' Hatred for the man lanced through her, but she managed to keep silent, her expression impassive and neutral, as Arthur Dolton came into the room.

He didn't look at her, but instead went to the large sideboard and lifted the lids of the bain-maries ranged along its length. He heaped a plate with bacon, kidneys, sausages and grilled tomatoes, and seating himself at the table, began to shovel the food into his capacious mouth with every appearance of gusto.

He ate like a voracious animal, slurping, grunting, smacking his lips noisily, and Cleopatra closed her eyes to shut out the unappealing sight of him, but the sounds of his eating could not be shut out and her repulsion shuddered through her.

'Wheer's the boys?' he questioned, and she was forced to open her eyes and answer him.

'They're in the orchard.'

He grunted acknowledgement, then stared hard at her face, noting the bruises his fists had left there.

109

She kept her gaze fixed on the table before her, and he scowled and with a hint of defensiveness in his tone, told her, 'It was your own bloody fault. You drives me to it.'

Cleopatra felt anger start to seethe within her. Arthur Dolton always did this. Always! Every time he beat or raped her he would, when eventually he became sober, blame her for what had happened. Knowing its futility she still could not help but follow the familiar pattern of their conflicts, and accused, 'You blame me?' She lifted her hand to point at her bruised features. 'You blame me for these? What did I do to deserve this? And what did I do to deserve what else you did to me?'

For a moment he made no reply, then he blustered, 'I only slapped you because you had a goo at me. If I hadn't of knocked you down, you'd have had the bloody eyes out o' me yed.'

'Really? Is that the way of it?' Her anger made her uncaring of consequence. 'And how about what followed? What had I done to deserve that?'

He stared with what appeared to be genuine puzzlement. 'What do you mean, how about what followed? I'se got the right to have you whenever I wants you. Youm my lawful wife.'

'Yes, I'm your lawful wife, not some prostitute that you've paid to let you use her like she was a dumb brute beast.'

His resentment at his own sense of guilt caused him to shout bullyingly, 'You might just as well be a bloody prostitute for all the time I spends in your bed. It's you who insists on sleeping in a separate room, aren't it? It's no bloody wonder that a man gets driven beyond endurance at times.'

'And you've driven me beyond endurance this time,' she hissed at him venomously. 'I'm going to leave you, Arthur Dolton. I just can't stand any more of your treatment.'

Even as she voiced it, she knew it was an empty threat. Where could she go with three young boys? How could she support them? With all her heart she wanted to run away from this man, but she knew that by fathering three children upon her, he had imprisoned her as securely as if he had locked her into the deepest dungeon in the land. She could never leave her children, and if by some miracle she was able to run away taking the three boys with her, then all that they would have to look forward to would be utter destitution. They were not tough hardy children, all three were weak and delicate in health. She would only be taking them to their possible deaths.

For a while he only stared silently at her, then his liver lips parted and his yellow teeth gleamed in a mocking smile. 'Gooing to leave me, am you?' he jeered openly. 'Goo on then. Leave! But the boys stays here with me. And you goes with nothing! Goo on back to wheer I took you from if you wants to. Goo on back to the bloody slums. But you'll go back with nothing! Nothing!'

He stood up, and grinned triumphantly down at her. She sat with her face flaming with impotent temper directed mainly at herself, for having voiced the empty threat. She remained motionless while he slammed out of the room.

Some short time later she heard him leave the house, and only then remembered that she had not asked his permission to take the boys up into the town centre that evening. Her lips set into a hard stubborn line.

'I'll take them anyway, and be damned to him.'

She knew that if she did so, and he came to know of it while he was in one of his drunken aggressive moods, then she would receive a beating for doing so. But she refused to let that prospect deter her.

'I'll take them up to see the lights this evening, and be damned to him.'

Chapter Sixteen

At ten o'clock that morning the civilian soldiers of the 4th Battery of the 1st Worcestershire Royal Garrison Artillery Volunteers mustered at their drill ground in Easemore Lane and marched up to the Church Green, led by their mounted officers and senior NCOs. Their blue uniforms, red striped overalls and red and blue side caps made a fine show, and people came from their houses, drawn by the beating of the drums, and cheered the men as they swung past, while a myriad of children capered excitedly at the sides of the serried ranks.

At the same hour the Volunteer Rifle Corps in their dark green uniforms and black leather accoutrements mustered at their drill hall in Ipsley Street and marched along Red Lion Street towards the town centre. The shrilling of their fifes likewise brought men and women to cheer their passing and a horde of small urchins to ape their marching.

Both units of Volunteers took station around the churchyard and the green, and kept the roads and church entrance clear for the worshippers to arrive at the church.

At half past ten the majestic chords of the organ resounded from within the church, and the carriages bearing the worshippers began to arrive at the church gates.

Eager crowds of onlookers pressed against the stop lines of the Volunteers to see and comment upon the display of shining coachwork, fine horseflesh and splendid clothing, as each individual group of the town's elite halted at the gilt-topped, scrolled iron gates and stepped down from their equipages.

Hemmings, Milwards, Bartleets, Youngs, Neasoms, Playfairs, Treadgolds, Woodfields, Allcocks, Terrys, Morralls, Shrimptons, Chillingworths, Holyoakes; each family's representatives vying with their peers to present the most opulent and impressive spectacle as they gravely paraded into the church and took their pews.

Even on this day the careful gradations of class and position were rigidly adhered to. People greeting their social equals vocally, exchanging silent bows with those slightly beneath them, nodding brusquely to those further down the social scale and ignoring completely the lower orders of humanity.

Outside Cotswold House stood Franklin Josceleyne's hired carriage and pair. It's driver, more accustomed to funerals than festivities, waiting glumly in threadbare black morning coat and black-cockaded top hat as he held the horses' heads.

In the drawing room of Cotswold House a heated altercation was raging between the bank manager and his father.

'It is preposterous, Father! I've never heard the like of it!'

Franklin Josceleyne strutted up and down in front of his aged parent, who was sitting on a straight-backed chair, propping himself upright on his gold-nobbed walking stick, his black frock-coat hanging upon his shrivelled body, and his shiny top hat looking comically over-large on his bald skull-like head.

To one side of the old man's chair stood Mrs Franklin Josceleyne and her two teenaged daughters, all three of them tall and massively fat in their multi-frilled, over-ornamented gowns of black satin, their wide brimmed hats topped with huge plumes of purple feathers.

On the opposite side of the chair, Miriam Josceleyne, hands twisting agitatedly together, was a muted greyness of severely cut jacket and skirt and dark-veiled plain bonnet. By the door, Emma Farr, presented a radiantly pretty picture in comparison with the other women. She wore her white dress, and perched on her high-piled chestnut hair a dainty toque with a wispy veil set off her

113

fresh colouring to perfection. Her black eyes danced with an inner amusement as she watched and listened.

Franklin Josceleyne came to a standstill and bending towards his parent demanded irascibly, 'Have you considered what people will say?'

The wizened features wore an expression of mule-like stubborness, and the lipless mouth remained firmly closed.

The bank manager snorted impatiently, and scowling fiercely, turned on his sister. 'Don't just stand there, woman. Try and make him see sense, will you.'

Miriam flushed and stammered and her fingers tugged and twisted against each other. 'B,B,But where is the harm in it, B, Brother Franklin?'

The little man stared at her as if he could not believe the evidence of his hearing. 'The harm in it?' He shook his head in mock-bemusement. 'The harm in it? Are you really so stupid, Miriam? Are you really so lacking in any sense of propriety?'

Her eyes suddenly blurred with tears and with a disgusted exclamation, her brother ordered, 'For God's sake control yourself, woman!' He glared at her for a long moment, then with an air of exerting upon himself an iron control, he gritted out in slow cadence, 'If we are seen to have a servant girl standing beside us in our family pew, sharing it with us as though she were an equal, then we shall be rendered a laughing stock in this town.' He paused and glared interrogatively at the woman, as if expecting her to reply. Then, when she only continued to twine her hands in silent agitation, he exhaled impatiently, and shouted, 'Damn it all, Miriam, have you so completely lost all respect for our family's position and standing in this town?'

'Hold your tongue, boy!' It was Hector Josceleyne who answered him, and his voice sounded strong and forceful enough to cause his son to stare at him in astonishment.

'The girl comes to church because I want her there to help me. That is an end to it. I'll hear no more whining from you. Remember, I am still head of this family.' A warning note entered his tone, 'And a last will and testament can always be altered, can it not?'

Emma Farr stared in shocked surprise at the old man, as

did all those others present in the room. The silence engendered by the old man's statement lasted for some seconds and Emma kept her gaze modestly downwards, aware that Franklin Josceleyne's eyes were constantly switching from her to the old man, in suspicious unspoken questioning.

The bank manager's thoughts were racing. The family's wealth was still owned by his father, although he, Franklin, dealt with the administration of the various funds and properties, and despite the old man's increasing senility, he could still, in a period of lucidity, procure witnesses to testify to his capability and legally alter his will. Hector Josceleyne had always been a harsh and tyrannical father towards his children, and Franklin Josceleyne knew that the old man was perfectly capable of carrying out his present veiled threat to cut him, Franklin, out of his will completely, if he should be angered sufficiently.

Again Franklin Josceleyne eyed the new maidservant suspiciously, but now there was a newborn wariness in his regard. She was a good-looking girl and had a body that would tempt a saint. It would not be the first time that a clever young woman had succeeded in enticing a senile doting old fool to marry her and to leave her his fortune.

The bank manager reluctantly decided to accept a temporary defeat. 'Very well then, Father. If it is your wish that she does so, then the servant girl may accompany us to church.'

He shot a glance of angry loathing at Emma Farr's downcast head and followed it with a stare of utter contempt directed at his sister.

'We had best be on our way,' he snapped curtly.

He offered his arm to his father, but the old man rejected the proffered aid with an impatient snort. 'Emma will help me. Not you. The further you keep your miserable ugly face away from me, the better I shall be pleased.'

Franklin Josceleyne's complexion suffused with a dull red fury at this insulting rebuff, and he glared at the women as if daring them to display any sign of having witnessed his humiliation.

When their carriage drew up at the church gates the contrast in the physical attractions of the women created something of a stir among the watchers, and one youth exclaimed incredulously to his friend, 'That's Emma Farr, that is! Her dad and mam lives next door to me. Fuck me! Look at her, 'ull you! Riding like one o' the fuckin' toffs in a fuckin' carriage and pair!'

Several other of the watchers recognised Emma, and another youth shouted, 'Wheer's your dad then, Emma, couldn't he leave the chimbleys?'

Miriam saw her brother's expression of glowering fury, and her heart quailed. Emma grinned openly at the youth and waved her hand in reply, then stepped down from the carriage and helped old Hector Josceleyne to descend.

Two small girls, dressed in dirty pinafore dresses and broken boots, their hair tangled masses around their grubby faces, called to Emma. 'Emma? Emma? It's us.' They babbled excitedly, 'You looks ever so posh, Emma. Is that your carriage? Is it, Emma? Can you give us a ride in it?'

Emma saw them and smiled broadly. 'Hello Elly, Hello Marty, can't stop now, kids. I'll come and see you later and bring you some sweets.'

Franklin Josceleyne physically pushed his wife and daughters to hurry them into the church, and his expression was murderous as he snarled, 'Miriam, get your father inside and be quick about it!'

The church was almost completely filled and for once in his life Franklin Josceleyne hated the fact that his family pew was in a prominent position almost at the very front of the seating.

As befitted the head of the family, Hector Josceleyne went first, shuffling with a painful slowness and leaning heavily upon the arm of Emma Farr. The couple were followed by the blushing, quailing Miriam, and then the three monolithic figures of Mrs Josceleyne and daughters. Franklin Josceleyne brought up the rear forcing himself to keep his face impassive, as he noted the raised eyebrows and heard the whispered exchanges provoked by his familial progress down the aisle.

116

He acknowledged the bows and nods of greeting that came his way, but inwardly cringed at what was to come when the identity of Emma Farr had been spread through the congregation. He could quite happily have murdered his father for spoiling what would otherwise have been an eminently successful and satisfactory social occasion for him. Even the mighty Hemmings, and Milwards, deigned to bow quite deeply in reply to his own respectful greetings, a gratifyingly public testimonial to his own personal standing in the town.

When the family were all seated, Franklin distinctly heard a woman to his rear ask in a penetrating whisper, 'Who is that girl with the Josceleynes? Is she a relative?'

Another woman answered, and this time Franklin Josceleyne realised that he was meant to hear.

'No my dear. It's a servant girl. Comes from Silver Street, I do believe.'

He sat with clenched fists, staring rigidly to his front, and the dull flush on his neck and cheeks became almost purple, so great was his murderous fury when the first woman said acidly, 'Isn't it sad to see respected old families demeaning themselves so. I wonder at the gall of it. Introducing servant girls into our society with such brazeness of manner.'

'I quite agree, my dear. It's a disgrace! But then, that family is no longer what it used to be, is it? I've heard talk.'

Emma Farr also clearly heard the whispered exchange. But she only smiled mischievously and answered under her breath, 'Bollocks to you as well, you nasty old cats!'

She found that she was enjoying this novel experience of sitting among the cream of local society, and in a vantage point from where she could clearly see the whole of the proceedings of the clerics, their acolytes, and the choristers. She even listened with interest to the prayers of intercession offered by the stately old Reverend Canon Newton for the recovery to health of King Edward VII. But when the old gentleman went on to express the profound depths of anxiety and sadness that he and his listeners were suffering as a result of their monarch's illness, and all around her expensively dressed over-fed women ostentatiously dabbed their eyes with silken handkerchiefs, wiping away non-existent tears, while their menfolk assumed expressions of grieving concern, Emma experienced a burgeoning of scornful anger.

'There's little kids in Silver Street who've never known what a full belly or a decent suit of clothes feels like, and they sickens and dies because of the filth they'm forced to live in, and here's you lot of bloody hypocrites making out that youm all upset because that fat-bellied old bastard in London has got an ache in his guts. All he's ever done all his life is to enjoy himself and live off the fat of the land and get between the legs of other men's wives.'

Emma Farr was not an admirer of the monarchy and aristocracy of her country and had only contempt for those among her own class who professed to love their King. But once the sermon had been preached and the local Choral Society joined forces with the choir, the young girl's normal cheeky good humour reasserted itself, and she listened with immense pleasure to the massed voices raised in tuneful chorus.

Chapter Seventeen

'But it's a bloody holiday, Johnny!' Fred Bunegar's fat face wore an aggrieved expression. 'I'll be the only silly sod working on this day while everybody else is out having a good time.'

'You promised me that the first suit would be ready three days since,' Johnny Purvis said firmly. 'If you didn't worship St Monday and St Tuesday, then I wouldn't need to be here today, would I?'

The fat man's lips pursed petulantly. 'I warn't well last Monday and Tuesday, that's why I couldn't get the job done.'

'You weren't well because you were blind drunk on Friday, Saturday and Sunday, my buck.'

'That's true, Johnny. He was as drunk as a bob-owler,' Billy Bunegar put in, and met his father's angry glare with a nonchalant shrug. 'It's no use you screwing your face up at me, our Dad. It's the bloody truth, and you knows it is.'

It was a few minutes past noon and the three men were in the living room above the Bunegars' shop. Through the open window they could hear the strains of music from the kiosk where the Redditch Town Band was giving a further programme, and the murmurous voices of the crowds parading around the recreation garden and the Church Green.

'Mind you, Johnny, if I had a uniform like yourn, then I'd be wearing it for the rest o' me life,' Billy Bunegar grinned enviously. 'I bet all the girls gives you the glad-eye when they sees you, doon't they?'

Johnny chuckled. 'I can't say that I've noticed any of them giving me a glad-eye, Billy. Although I'm proud to wear this uniform, it's been more than ten years since I put on the Queen's coat; I'm more than ready to wear my own coat now. I'd like to begin to feel how it is to be a civilian again.'

Fred Bunegar gusted a long, drawn out sigh, and with a whine of self-pity in his voice offered, 'I'll tell you what, Johnny. If our Billy 'ull give me a hand wi' it, I can have your dark blue suit ready for you by five o'clock this arternoon.'

'That aren't fair, our Dad,' his son protested vigorously. 'I was working on Monday and Tuesday while you was lying in bed.'

Johnny grinned at the younger man and rattled the coins in his pouch. 'Do it as a favour to me, Billy,' he coaxed. 'And I'll see that you won't lose by it.'

Billy Bunegar was unconvinced. 'Ahr, but then this bugger 'ud want a share on it.'

His father swore heartily, but seeing the obstinacy on his son's face, grudgingly assured him, 'If Johnny sees his way clear to giving you a few bob extra for your trouble, our Billy, then you can keep whatever he gives you.'

'Does you swear to that, our Dad?' Billy demanded.

'I'se just told you, aren't I?' the older man exclaimed aggrievedly.

'Then swear on the Bible.'

'I'll swear on your fuckin' yed in a minute, you young bleeder!' Fred Bunegar bawled, and cuffed his son's head hard. 'Now come on down to the shop and let's get it done with.' He grinned good humouredly at his son's bellow of protest and told Johnny Purvis, 'You come at any time after five this arternoon, Johnny, and it'll be waiting for you. That's a promise, that is.'

Outside once more, Johnny Purvis stood for some time looking at the scene before him. The broad promenade of Church Green West was a festive parade of men, women and children dressed in their best clothes. The men in top hats, bowler hats, flat caps and straw boaters, frock-coats, morning coats, suits, brightly striped blazers and white duck trousers. Young women wore figure hugging bolero jackets and hip hugging skirts which they

120

lifted from the dust to display temptingly slender ankles, and froths of lacy petticoats. Matrons were majestic in satin overcoats and feather boas and broad beflowered and feathered hats. Schoolboys shouted excitedly in gangs or walked glumly behind their parents, stiff and hot in Eton collars, small peaked caps and knickerbocker suits, while their sisters followed demurely in their white pinafore dresses, narrow brimmed straw hats topping their long waist-length, bowed and beribboned hair. Tiny children were sedate in velveteen suits and sashes, or rakish and dashing in wide collared sailor rigs, and Jack Tar hats complete with the ribboned names of ships.

Gaily coloured strings of bunting and flags hung from the façades of the buildings and were strung between the branches of the trees in company with thousands of Japanese lanterns and strings of the new electric light bulbs, which were to be lit that evening. Huge banners blessing Edward VII and proclaiming the town's love and loyalty had been stretched across the wide expanse of parade and road itself, and among the crowds, hawkers festooned with masses of small union flags did a brisk trade.

Johnny took his watch from his breeches pocket and glanced at its wide face. Almost half past twelve. He debated where he should go now. Then his name was called and Foley Field, wearing a straw boater and garishly coloured striped blazer above white duck trousers, came up to him smiling. 'Well now, Mr Purvis, how are you?'

'I'm in fine fettle,' Johnny grinned. 'And the name is Johnny.'

They exchanged a brief handshake and Foley Field asked, 'Are you alone, Johnny?'

'I am, and if you are, then let's join forces.'

'An excellent idea,' the young man concurred enthusiastically. 'I was thinking of watching the Volunteers fire the Royal salute? Would you like to go there?'

'Wherever,' Johnny agreed easily and the two men walked slowly away from the shopfront.

They crossed the top of Fish Hill and went down Easemore Lane towards the Victoria Recreation Ground.

121

Many other people were heading for the same venue and Johnny's uniform attracted interested stares, while his fine physique and hard-etched features brought not a few inviting glances from the females among the crowds.

As the two men entered the field the first thuds of the guns firing percussed the air. The men looked at each other.

'Brings back memories, doesn't it?' Foley Field grinned.

There were two long-barrelled howitzers positioned in echelon with ammunition carts and limbers, and the blue uniformed civilian artillery men performed the intricate gun drills with a professional alacrity.

'They've been well instructed by the looks of them,' Johnny observed. His companion nodded towards a ramrod straight figure, wearing the dress uniform of a regular artillery man, standing some distance from the guns with a pace stick under his arm and a ball-topped helmet on his cropped head. 'That's because Sergeant-Major Fogg is a stickler for discipline. He's the gunnery instructor seconded here from the regulars. He's not been here long. By coincidence his old battery was attached to my regiment for a time out in South Africa. In actual fact I met him at the Modder River crossing.'

Johnny studied the regular soldier, noting the tough features, the taut stance of the lean hard body, the row of campaign ribbons on the broad chest, and quite suddenly an unexpected nostalgia assailed him. A yearning like a homesickness for the sounds and smells of the barracks and the mess, and the company of fighting men.

Foley Field looked at his new friend's face and intuitively understood what Johnny Purvis was feeling at this moment. 'You miss it, don't you, Johnny. You miss the army.'

It was statement, not question, and Johnny nodded slowly, curiously reluctant to accept the truth, yet unable to deny it. 'Yes, I miss it, Foley. Yet, there were times during my service that I hated the army and I'd have deserted like a shot if I'd had money enough to get me to America or some other country out of reach of the laws of England.' He smiled ruefully. 'Here I am standing watching Volunteers firing blanks from their guns and it's making me homesick for the bloody army. It's madness, isn't it?'

'No, it's not,' Foley Field shook his head emphatically. 'I was only a yeoman cavalryman, just like one of these lads really, not a regular, but a civilian volunteer. But I find that I miss the life and I only served for a comparatively short time on active duty. You soldiered for more than ten years, didn't you, Johnny? It's a great slice out of your life. You're bound to miss those comrades and scenes that you knew.'

'But I want to be free of it, Foley,' Johnny Purvis stated with heartfelt passion. 'I never again want to have to obey orders, or to jump when I'm told to. I want to be my own master from now on. I've had more than enough of serving masters. I want no more of it.'

He fell silent, but in his mind a voice persisted, 'You'll never be free of the army, John Purvis. You've marched behind the band, with bayonets fixed and colours flying, and every time you hear the beating of the drums and the shrilling of the fifes your heart will fill with yearning. You'll never be free of the army for as long as you live. You'll never be free from the tunes of glory!'

When the firing ceased the crowds cheered and dispersed in search of fresh entertainment. At some of the hotels and inns of the town hundreds of old people and the poor were being served with a free celebratory dinner of roast beef and plum pudding, and Johnny Purvis and Foley Field made their way to the Royal Hotel in the market place on the south side of the churchyard and bought their own dinner of beefsteak sandwiches and good ale. Replete, they decided to make their way to the Red Lane musketry ranges where a Volunteer and Open Sports were to take place.

Many hundreds of their fellow townspeople had made that same decision and once again the two men walked surrounded by good-humoured crowds down Unicorn Hill and up and over the hilly slopes of Red Lane, to where the open musketry ranges, bounded to the west and south by the green Pitcheroak and Foxlydiate Woods, were already being filled by eager onlookers and contestants.

Arthur Dolton had spent the morning drinking in the

town centre public houses, but most of his usual drinking cronies were spending this Coronation Day with their families, and eventually, tiring of his own company, he decided that he would spend some time with his own family and take them, as a special treat, to see the Volunteer Sports.

The family walked to the sports ground, Simon and James, the eldest boys neat in their school caps, Eton collars and knickerbocker suits and little Andrew in white sailor blouse and a wide-brimmed straw hat with HMS *Britannia* lettered in gold on the blue hatband.

Cleopatra Dolton wore a pale yellow gown with long puffed sleeves and a wide-brimmed summer hat decorated by flowers. A veil tied down beneath her chin hid her bruised face from curious eyes and her yellow parasol shaded her head from the hot rays of the sun. Despite the simplicity and lack of ornament of her dress, men still stared hungrily at her full breasts pushing out the tight-fitting bodice and her slender waist and richly curving hips.

Arthur Dolton himself was wearing his normal thick serge dark blue suit with high winged collar and diamond stickpinned cravat. His sole concession to the heat of the day was the straw boater tilted back on his sandy hair and his face was flushed and sweaty.

Marquees, tents and stalls had been erected around the edges of the open ranges, some to serve as changing rooms for the contestants, others as hospitality tents for the two Volunteers Corps, others for beer and refreshments. Flags fluttered everywhere and the band of the Artillery Volunteers was playing a selection of military, patriotic and light opera tunes. Some showmen had set up swinging boats and roundabouts, coconut and hoop-la stalls. Hordes of children were riding wooden horses on carousels and screaming with fearful delight as the swingboats rose higher and higher. Young men and girls strolled around in search of romance and flirted shamelessly in front of the disapproving frowns of their elders. Men brought out brimming frothing glasses from the ale tents while their womenfolk and children drank ginger beer and lemonade and ate brandysnaps and hokeypokey ice creams. The young bloods of the Volunteer Corps twirled their moustaches, swaggered and preened in the full glory of their regimentals. The more kindly among them condescended to allow small admiring boys to hold their bayonets in grubby paws and try on their smart forage-caps.

Johnny Purvis and Foley Field went to watch the heats of the sprint and hurdle races and wholeheartedly applauded the efforts of the panting, sweating athletes in their tight-fitting jerseys and long drawers.

Through a megaphone a steward called for all contestants in the mile race to muster at the starting point. This was one of the high spots of the sports. An open entry with money prizes to be won, it attracted a great deal of interest from the spectators. A large crowd quickly gathered around the starting line.

While waiting for the race to begin, Johnny saw a wistfulness in Foley Field's expression as the other man stared at the runners limbering up and stretching.

'Did you used to be a runner Foley?' he questioned curiously.

The man nodded, and a fleeting sadness crossed his thin face. 'Yes, I was the champion miler for Worcestershire and Warwickshire before the war.' He made the statement with no hint of braggadocio, merely as a matter of fact.

'Good God!' Johnny was impressed. 'Can you not run at all now?'

'Not really,' Foley Field shook his head. 'I can walk all right and even trot a little but my running days are over now. I've tried building this up again,' he tapped the thigh of his injured leg, 'but it's still too weak.'

'How bist, Foley?' A tall well-built young man with thick curly brown hair greeted them. He was wearing the tight-fitting jersey and long drawers of a contestant and beneath the thin material his muscles writhed and bulged as he moved.

'Hello Ozzie,' Foley Field spoke warmly. 'Are you running today?'

'I am that,' Ozzie Clarke grinned in self-deprecation.

125

'But I'll tell you now, Foley, that if you was entering, then I 'udden't bother to run.' His eyes swung to Johnny Purvis, and he said, 'I doon't know how well you knows Foley, mate, but I can tell you that before he went off to the wars, he was the finest miler that this town ever saw.'

Johnny Purvis liked the friendly open manner of the man, and now he smiled and held out his hand. 'My name's John Purvis, and I'll take your word about Foley's running.'

The other man took the proffered hand. 'I'm Oswald Clarke, John, but everybody calls me Ozzie. I've seen you walking around the town these last days and I wondered who you was.' He grinned. 'To tell you the truth I've bin feeling jealous about how all the women bin looking at your uniform.'

Johnny laughed easily. 'Well, after today they'll not be looking at it any more, Ozzie, because I'll be back in civilian clothing.'

'Ozzie? Ozzie Clarke?' a voice bellowed, and the young man grimaced resentfully.

'Jesus Christ! I thought I was getting a day away from this bleeder.' He winked at the other men and explained, 'It's my boss, Arthur Dolton. I'll have to be civil to him. If I'm not, then I'll be out of a job.'

Johnny Purvis watched Arthur Dolton bulling his way through the crowd. He recognised him for the loud-mouthed bully he had encountered on the day of his homecoming and the dislike he had felt for the man then now burgeoned afresh as he saw how Dolton thrust people from his path with an arrogant brutality of manner. His gaze moved beyond Dolton to the shapely woman in yellow who followed him, with three small boys trailing miserably behind her. Recollection flickered in Johnny's mind, and then he remembered how he had physically collided with her outside the bookshop.

Ozzie Clarke had seen where Purvis's eyes travelled and he chuckled and informed in a low voice, 'She's a beauty, aren't she? That's the Queen of Egypt, that is. Cleopatra Dolton. It's the bugger's missis. Why she ever married that pig, I'll never know.'

Johnny smiled at the nickname. 'I'll bet she curses the day she was named Cleopatra.'

'Oh it aren't just for her name that she's called that,' Ozzie Clarke explained. 'When you sees her close up you'll see that she looks like a gyppo. All dark and foreign looking.'

Johnny could not help but continue to stare at the oncoming woman. Admiring her graceful, sensual walk and the tempting curves of her body. His eyes slid to her husband; he compared Arthur Dolton's unappealing grossness with his wife's physical attractions and was forced to shrug mentally in wonderment at women's perverse tastes in men.

'Am you gooing to win, Ozzie?' Arthur Dolton had reached them.

'I think so, Mr Dolton.' The young man grinned confidently, then looked over the other man's shoulder and nodded politely, 'How d'you do, Mrs Dolton.'

'Hello Clarke,' Cleopatra greeted in her low-pitched throaty voice.

Johnny Purvis was aware that her dark eyes were studying him and he half-bowed politely. 'Good afternoon, ma'am.'

She nodded. 'Good afternoon, Mr?'

'This is Mr John Purvis, and Mr Foley Field,' Ozzie Clarke introduced them. 'You'll know Foley already won't you, Mr Dolton?'

'Yes, I knows Foley all right.' Arthur Dolton's expression was surly. 'And I'se met the soldier boy before.' He made a show of turning his back on the two men and drawing Ozzie Clarke to one side.

'Now then, Ozzie, I'se bet a lot of money on you winning this race, so you'd better not let me down, if you knows what's good for you.'

His tone was aggressively hectoring, but Ozzie Clarke only grinned and shrugged his broad shoulders. 'I'll do me best, Mr Dolton. I've bet on meself winning, after all.'

'Now listen to me, I'se bin checking on the others. Young Barclay from Astwood Bank is going to try and take an early. . .' Arthur Dolton talked volubly, and Ozzie

127

eyes held the shadow of resentment, but he kept a grin fixed on his face. Foley Field's thin pleasant features had also clouded with annoyance at Arthur Dolton's deliberate rudeness, and Johnny's own sense of repulsion for the man had deepened.

'Never mind him,' he told himself now. 'The day's too pleasant to let an ignorant pig like Arthur Dolton spoil it for you.'

He smiled at the three boys who were staring at him with wide-eyed admiration. 'Are you enjoying the sports, lads?'

'Yes, thank you, sir,' the eldest boy answered timidly, then drew a deep breath as if gathering courage, and asked hesitantly, 'If you please, sir, is that a real gun?' He indicated the holstered weapon at Johnny's side.

'Yes it is,' Johnny told him. 'Would you like to see it?'

'Oh yes please, sir,' the boy assented eagerly and the smaller boys' faces mirrored their brother's excitement.

Johnny unholstered the pistol and held it on his open palm for them to see it clearly. 'It's a Mauser 7.63 millimetre calibre, with a ten shot magazine, and it's got almost the same velocity as a rifle.'

He extracted the magazine and checked that the chamber was empty, then let the boys handle the pistol and aim it. Their eyes shone with thrilled pleasure, and they bombarded him with questions about the war that he tried to answer as honestly as he could. At last their mother told them to hand back the weapon, and with a grudging reluctance they did so. As Johnny refitted the magazine and returned the pistol to its highly polished wooden holster, Simon Dolton asked gravely, 'Please, sir, do you think that I might be able to see it again sometime? And could you tell me some more about the war?'

Johnny smiled at him. 'Certainly you may see it again, and we can talk about the war. That's if your mother doesn't object.'

He glanced enquiringly at the veiled woman, who had been standing silently watching the boys, her lips curved in a smile of pleasure at their pleasure.

'I think that I can permit that, Mr Purvis,' she told him.

The veil shadowed her face, but as she moved her head

128

to meet Johnny Purvis's questing look, by a trick of the light her features showed clearly through the gauze-like material and Johnny could see the swollen discolouration of bruises around her mouth and eye. A fleeting frown creased his forehead. She saw that momentary expression and, as if embarrassed, dropped her head and spoke sharply to the boys who had recommenced their eager questioning of Johnny.

'Come now, stop your pestering. Let the gentleman have some peace from your questions.'

Abashed, the boys shuffled their feet and dropped their heads in a gesture exactly like their mother's and Johnny spoke quickly to ease the mood of tension that had so suddenly been engendered. 'Please, Mrs Dolton, I'm enjoying talking with them. Please don't be too hard on them.'

Arthur Dolton had been taking note of the exchange, and now his half-drunken surliness erupted into anger, fuelled by his resentment at his sons' open admiration of the soldier. 'We'll do what we please with our own children, Purvis. So you just mind your own business.'

'Arthur, don't!' Cleopatra Dolton protested instantly and her husband rounded on her viciously.

'Hold your bloody tongue woman! It's your bloody fault in the fust place, letting the silly young buggers be sucked in by a bloody toy soldier's tales.'

Johnny Purvis's own hot temper threatened to flame, but he kept a grip on himself.

He silently signalled to Foley Field with a tilt of his head and said to Ozzie Clarke, 'We'll have to leave you now, Ozzie. Good luck in the race.'

Ozzie Clarke nodded understandingly. 'Thanks John, I'm pleased to have met you.'

'Mrs Dolton, boys.' Johnny nodded farewell and turned to walk away and Arthur Dolton jeered.

'That's right, toy soldier, you goo off and find some other stupid idiots to stuff wi' your bloody lies.'

Johnny swung about and his face was murderous. In another split second he would have attacked Arthur Dolton with the controlled ferocity and ruthless deadly skills engendered by a hundred savage brawls. Then he saw the frightened faces of the three boys and the frantic shaking of Cleopatra Dolton's head as she silently beseeched him, and he forced back the ravening lust to destroy the other man.

'Tell me, Dolton,' he gritted out the words, 'did you say that you had bet a lot of money on this mile race?'

Arthur Dolton had himself been shocked and a little frightened by the sudden transfiguration he had seen in John Purvis when the man had swung about to face him. Now the blustering bully reasserted itself in him and he sneered arrogantly, 'Why do you ask, soldier boy? Do you fancy laying a bet against my runner? Have you got a man to beat him?'

Johnny glanced at Foley Field, who gave a warning shake of the head, then looked across at Ozzie Clarke, who shrugged and grimaced as if to point out his own impotency to do anything other than win the race for Arthur Dolton. He was aware of Cleopatra Dolton's dark eyes boring into him, but he would not meet them. Instead he smiled grimly, and told Arthur Dolton, 'That's right, Dolton. I'm wanting to lay a bet against your runner. I've got a man to beat him. Will you match me?'

The man's white-coated tongue ran slowly across his liver lips as if savouring the taste of them and his yellowed teeth gleamed as he sneered, 'How much can you afford to lose, soldier boy?'

'As much as you're willing to bet,' Johnny answered curtly.

By now the people about them were taking note of what was being said, word quickly spread and more and more people clustered around the group listening eagerly.

Dolton looked about him, glorying in being at the centre of attention, making a great show of considering what Johnny Purvis had said. Then he grinned confidently and said loudly so that all around could hear him, 'I doon't want to be too hard on you, soldier boy, I knows you army chaps doon't earn much money. So what do you say to twenty sovereigns?'

He preened in satisfaction at the exclamations of awed

130

excitement that came from the listeners as they heard the huge sum which represented several months' wages for many of them. Then Dolton sneered triumphantly at Johnny Purvis, 'Or is that too much for you to match, soldier boy?'

Johnny exalted inwardly. Only that morning a special messenger had arrived from Saul Shibco in Birmingham with an instalment on the sale of some of his diamonds. Secreted in his room at the Plough and Harrow Hotel he had more than five hundred gold sovereigns.

Now he appeared to hesitate as if made nervous by the challenge, deliberately prolonging his silence to entice Arthur Dolton into jeering, 'Too much is it? I thought it might be. It's amazing how soon a fine-feathered cockerel like you shows a white 'un, when he meets up with a real fighting cock, aren't it?'

Johnny waited until every eye had been turned upon himself, and then shook his head and uttered a contemptuous snort. 'I thought you meant that we'd make a real bet, Dolton, not a little pitch and toss wager. Phew, I've lost more than that on a Crown and Anchor board in a barrack canteen. Let's make it a hundred sovereigns shall we?'

Dolton's mouth gaped in astonishment and the spectators erupted into a storm of applause.

It was Johnny's turn to sneer openly. 'Well, Dolton? I'm waiting. Or is it too much for you? I know you butcher boys don't earn much money.'

Laughter at his sally sounded from the crowd and Dolton flushed with anger.

'All right!' he snarled. 'All right, smart arse! I'll take the bet.'

Johnny turned to the crowd, and asked them, 'Have you all witnessed that? One hundred sovereigns is the wager, to be paid over to the winner tomorrow morning.' He thought for a moment, then grinned. 'To be paid over in the taproom at the Unicorn.' He raised his eyebrows in silent interrogation at Dolton and the butcher nodded surly agreement. 'That's all right by me.'

Now that the first shock of wagering such a massive

amount was passing, Arthur Dolton was starting to take pleasure from the sensation it was causing, and he was certain that he held the winning card in having Ozzie Clarke as his runner. There was no one in the town who stood a chance of beating him.

'Right then, soldier boy,' his customary arrogance returned in full measure. 'Everybody knows who my runner is – Ozzie Clarke. Who's your man?'

'I am,' Johnny told him quietly.

The butcher's red meaty face showed surprise. 'Youm running yourself?'

'That's what I've just said, isn't it?' Johnny turned to Foley Field. 'Do you know of anybody who can loan me a running kit and spikes?'

His friend looked doubtful. 'There's some who'd lend them to you, Johnny, but I doubt we'll be able to find one before the race is started.' He nodded towards the start line where the stewards were shouting for the contestants to take position. 'They'll be off in a few seconds.'

'No matter,' Johnny grinned. He quickly stripped off his belts, tunic, boots and stockings and stood wearing only his breeches and white vest.

Foley Field looked doubtfully down at Purvis's bare feet. 'You're going to be sadly disadvantaged without spikes Johnny.'

'No matter,' Johnny grinned again. 'I'm well accustomed to running barefoot.'

'Take your places now!' the steward bellowed through his megaphone. 'The race will start in ten seconds.'

Johnny pushed through the excited, close-packed spectators, and as he passed by Cleopatra Dolton momentarily gazed into her dark eyes. Behind her veil he saw her white teeth gleam briefly, and heard her low throaty whisper, 'Beat him, Mr Purvis. Beat him.'

He stared in shock, but could not delay any longer, and joined the other nine entrants.

He found himself between Ozzie Clarke, and the tall skinny youth from Astwood Bank, young Barclay.

Ozzie Clarke grinned and winked. 'I'm only sorry that you made that bet with Dolton, Johnny. Knowing that you've got to pay that bastard 'ull take most of the pleasure for me out of winning this race.'

Johnny returned the wink and grin. 'I just hope he doesn't give you the sack for losing it.'

'On your marks! Steady!' the starter bellowed, and lifted high his starting pistol.

Johnny drew a deep breath and put all else from his thoughts but the race ahead.

The starting pistol cracked loudly, and the runners surged forwards, as a roar of cheering came from the spectators.

Foley Field, arms piled high with Johnny Purvis's clothing, boots and accoutrements, studied the contestants anxiously as they streamed away around the circular course. His experienced eyes noted that his new friend ran with a fluid loping pace, feet skimming the ground, arms held loose and low to conserve energy. Foley smiled with considerable relief. 'You look as though you know something about the game, anyway, Johnny.'

On the first circuit of the track a short stocky runner took the lead, punching his way forwards as if battling with an invisible adversary, and Foley dismissed him almost immediately as a potential winner. In second place on the stocky man's heels Ozzie Clarke was running smoothly, and behind him at some five yards distance young Barclay and Johnny Purvis ran shoulder to shoulder.

Four circuits would total a mile and by the time the second circuit had been completed only four runners were in any real contention. The short stocky man had dropped back to the rear and now Ozzie Clarke led, closely followed by young Barclay, Johnny Purvis and a young Rifle Volunteer, in that order. The rest of the field were bunched more than twenty yards behind the leaders.

Cleopatra Dolton's lips parted slightly as she watched Johnny Purvis come pounding past her for the third circuit. His white vest was patched with dark spreading sweat stains and his feet were dirty from the track. She saw the muscles of his lean powerful torso writhing beneath the thin tight-fitting cloth and the expression of dogged determination etched in the hard-set features and found herself visualising his nakedness and a sudden hunger of sexual desire assailed her. 'If I ever was to take a fancy man then it would be someone like you, John Purvis,' she thought.

He went swiftly onwards and the rear runners obscured her view of him. Her eyes went sideways to where her husband was bawling encouragement to Ozzie Clarke. She stared at his flabby sweaty red face, the thick wet liver lips, the huge paunch spilling down over his trouser top, bulging out his waistcoat and jacket, and she experienced an acute self-disgust.

'How did I ever willingly share his bed?' she asked herself bitterly. 'How could I have lain there night after night while he slobbered on me?' Her self-disgust intensified to almost self-loathing. 'I'm worse than a prostitute. I couldn't help what my dad did to me, but I knew well what I was about when I got this bastard to marry me. I knew well what he'd expect from me. Christ above! I'm nothing but a filthy whore to have let this bastard use me like he has done for the past eleven years. I should be hating and despising myself as much as I hate him and despise him.'

Her sullen glare switched back to the runners, now on the opposite side of the circuit, and with every atom of her being she silently urged, 'Beat him for me, Johnny Purvis. Beat him for me! For my sake beat the filthy rotten bastard!'

The steward jangled his big brass handbell to signal the final circuit, and the spectators roared encouragement as the runners pounded past them.

Johnny was feeling an ever-increasing confidence. He had been worried that the turf underfoot would not provide good traction for his bare feet, but the hot sun had ensured that the close-cut grasses were dry and gave good purchase. During the third circuit the Rifle Volunteer had overtaken him, and Johnny had not attempted to dispute it. He could hear the man's rasping, labouring breath, and see the head beginning to roll, and knew that the Volunteer had used up his reserves of strength.

He himself was breathing easily enough and his muscles,

although tired, still had plenty of spring in them. The heat of the day had proven beneficial to his chances also. He was acclimatised to far stronger intensities of heat than this, and knew that the high temperatures would adversely affect the other runners to a greater degree than himself. He saw that both Ozzie Clarke and young Barclay's running kits were saturated with sweat, and surmised that at this particular point in the race the unaccustomed heat would be weakening them rapidly. Not knowing what sort of finishing sprint either man was capable of, Johnny decided that his best chance lay in launching his attack at a greater distance from the finishing post than they would be expecting.

He heard the bell jangling and summoning every ounce of courage and strength he exploded forwards. He was aware of the Volunteer's eyes wide in shock as he surged past him, and heard the roar of the crowd rising to a crescendo as he drew closer to young Barclay. The tall thin man risked a backward glance and Johnny saw his frown as he drew alongside. The other man rose to his challenge and quickened his own pace to match Johnny stride for stride. Shoulder to shoulder they overtook Ozzie Clarke on the last bend and, although he bravely tried to raise a sprint, his energy was all but used up and he could only grit his teeth and doggedly plug on behind the pair.

Johnny's breathing was now a choking gasping and his tall thin opponent was running with mouth wide, arms pumping maniacally as if the air before him had become a solid entity to be battered through. Ahead Johnny could see the broad bright tape of the finish fluttering and the screaming of the crowd was a cacophony in his ears. His leg muscles felt as if they were on fire and rapid thuddings of agonising pain threatened to split his skull. He sensed his opponent suddenly disappear from his shoulder and the wild elation of victory blotted out all agonies of lungs and muscles. Only yards to the tape. Only yards to triumph. Then an excited yapping dog jumped out at him and the furry body collided with his legs. Johnny tumbled forwards and felt the white-hot shafts of pain as young Barclay's spikes punched into his leg, a crushing impact came on the back of his head and fiery-speckled darkness engulfed him.

The cold water splashing onto his face and head brought him to his senses and he tried to push himself upright, but hands pressed him back.

'Take it slowly, Johnny,' Foley Field was staring down at him, his thin features anxious. 'You've had a hard bang on your head.'

Johnny hissed softly at the throbbing pain and gingerly felt the back of his head. His fingers came away red and sticky with blood. Full consciousness had now returned, and he asked, 'What hit me?'

'Young Barclay's head,' Foley Field told him. 'He's over there.'

Johnny tentatively turned his own head so that he could see where the other man was lying, surrounded by people, with men crouching to minister to him.

Johnny frowned anxiously. 'Is he all right?'

'Yes, he'll recover,' Foley Field grinned wryly. 'He's got just as hard a head as you.'

Johnny grimaced as the throbbing pain of his injured leg added its quota to his general discomfort, and he raised himself to look down at the bleeding punctures in his calf muscle.

'I felt the spikes go in after the dog tripped me. I suppose young Barclay fell over me didn't he?'

Foley nodded confirmation. 'He had no chance of avoiding you, Johnny.'

'I'm sorry for what happened, Johnny,' Ozzie Clarke came to crouch by Johnny's side.

Johnny forced a grin. 'It was just one of those accidents, Ozzie. Did you go on to win?'

The other man nodded somewhat shamefacedly. 'I crossed the line fust. But I can't really say that I won, even though I did cross the line fust. You would have won if the dog hadn't fetched you down. In fact, I've already told the stewards that I won't accept the prize money or the trophy. I've asked them to divide the money between you and young Barclay. You ought to get the trophy by rights, because you was in the lead and only had a few yards to goo. He'd never have caught you.'

Johnny shook his head, and winced as the movement sent a sharp pain lancing through it. 'No Ozzie. You must take both the money and the trophy. The race is won by whoever crosses that finishing line first and it doesn't matter what causes the other runners to fail.'

Ozzie Clarke's handsome features were troubled. 'Listen to me, Johnny. If I was to do what you says, then Arthur Dolton could claim the money you bet him. You would have won that race if that bloody dog hadn't ha' tripped you. You and young Barclay must make an official objection to the result. The stewards am willing to allow any objection you makes to stand. They'se already as good as told me that. Then the bet can be counted as void.'

Johnny Purvis pondered briefly, then slowly shook his head. 'No Ozzie, I appreciate your good sportsmanship and I thank you for it, but as far as I'm concerned the result stands.' He smiled ruefully. 'Although it hurts me to do it, I'll pay Dolton the bet.'

Foley Field regarded him quizzically. 'I think that you're being rather too noble about this, Johnny. After all, Dolton is not the sort of chap that deserves to be given any sort of favour. You may be certain that if positions were reversed he would most certainly take full advantage of any opportunity to avoid paying you.'

Johnny held his friend's stare and explained quietly, 'I'm not being noble at all, Foley. I'm paying the man because I dislike him so much.'

Both of his listeners were puzzled by this apparent paradox and their expressions showed how they felt.

'I'm paying him because I couldn't bear to be beholden to him in any way whatsoever,' Johnny went on. 'So the result stands and Ozzie is the winner as far as I'm concerned. I'll make no objection to the stewards.'

Both men saw the stubbornness in his expression, and realised that nothing they could say would alter his decision.

'All right, mate, have it your way. But I think youm sarft for giving him anything at all. He 'udden't do the same for you, that's for sure.'

137

Ozzie Clarke patted Johnny's shoulder and rose to his feet.

'Do you want me to give you a hand to get dressed and home?' he questioned.

Johnny shook his head. 'No, I'll be fine now, thanks Ozzie. Maybe I'll see you later up in the town.'

By now the men around young Barclay had finished bandaging his split forehead and they came to Johnny, to wash and dress his wounds.

While they were doing so, the crowd of spectators began to lose interest in the proceedings and gradually dispersed to watch the other ongoing events. Arthur Dolton came to stand looking down at Johnny and jeered triumphantly.

'Theer then, soldier boy, didn't I tell you that my runner 'ud have the beating of you. I'll be expecting you in the Unicorn tap at twelve noon sharp tomorrow.'

Without looking at him Johnny nodded and replied curtly, 'I'll be there.'

'You'd better be,' the butcher told him aggressively. 'And make sure you brings the full money with you as well. We doon't like welshers in this town.'

Foley Field flushed with anger and would have risen to confront Dolton, but Johnny clamped his hand upon his friend's arm, and kept him kneeling by his side. 'Leave it, Foley,' he hissed. 'Leave it!'

Dolton emitted a jeering laugh and swaggered away.

'I'd like to smash his face,' Foley Fields gritted angrily, but Johnny Purvis only smiled grimly and shook his head. 'I know you would Foley, but you're just going to have to wait your turn. I think I deserve to be the first to have that pleasure, don't you?'

Chapter Eighteen

The great day continued with an amalgamated schools procession parading around the centre of the town. More than four thousand excited children, each carrying a small union flag took part, and their demonstration of loyalty culminated with them massing around St Stephen's church to sing the national anthem. Then it was the turn of their elders. Led by the Artillery and Town bands the portly dignified members of the County and Urban District Councils solemnly headed a long procession of the town fire brigade, detachments of Volunteers, deputations from the Masonic Lodges and Friendly Societies, decorated floats and drays from the various manufacturers, and last but not least the members of the Coronation Celebration Committee. While up at the top of Mount Pleasant on the wild open space known as The Soudan another unofficial sports and games meeting took place, with local boxers sparring, wrestlers grappling, and strong men grunting as they vied with each other to lift the greater weight.

Nightfall brought no diminution in the general merrymaking as the vast crowds swirled through the principal streets of the town to view the illuminations. Such wonders of light and colour had never been seen before in the Needle District. Thousands of coloured lamps and Japanese lanterns glowed in the Church Green's trees and shrubbery. Illuminated devices, flags and bunting decorated the fronts of inns, business premises, factories, houses and shops. The kiosk, the fountain and three huge triumphal arches were ablaze with electric light, and the whole spectacle resembled some modern day fairyland.

Cleopatra Dolton had taken advantage of her husband's good humour after winning his bet to obtain his permission to bring her three sons to see the illuminations and now the four of them wandered through the crowded streets, the boys' faces mirroring their awed delight in what they saw.

She was happy because Arthur Dolton was ensconced in the Unicorn Inn with his cronies. Had he been with them her boys would have been too intimidated by their fear of him to express their delight and wonder at this feast of light and colour.

Her own thoughts continually strayed back to that afternoon, to the mile race she had witnessed. Again and again the visual image of Johnny Purvis's lean muscularity and hard-etched features came into her mind. Even as she condemned herself for thinking about him, she could not help staring at the faces that eddied about her, hoping that one of them might be his.

When Purvis had been brought down by the dog and injured, she had experienced bitter dismay; her first impulse had been to rush to where he lay. But during the long harsh years of her marriage, Cleopatra Dolton had learned to control her reactions and display impassive features to the world, so she had stood in apparent indifference while the spectators had noisily reacted to the incident.

'Look Mother! Look there!' James pointed to the front of the Royal Hotel in the market place where a huge portrait of the King and Queen had been framed with coloured electric light bulbs, which flashed on and off so that their faces continually appeared and disappeared.

'May we go closer, Mother? May we?' the boy pleaded, and she smiled and nodded. 'Of course.' She scanned the thickness of the shifting crowds admiring the device and warned, 'We must all keep very close together or you'll get lost in the crowd.'

She held Andrew by his hand and ushered the two older

140

boys in front of her as they threaded their way through the noisy good-natured concourse. The four of them reached a vantage point on the opposite side of the roadway to the Royal Hotel and stood gazing up at the flashing lights.

To the side of the hotel's front doorway a small troupe of painted and spangled clowns began turning cartwheels upon the pavement, blowing trumpets, beating drums and inviting the swarming children to gather close around them.

'Can we go, Mother?' Simon begged. James and little Andrew added their pleas so that she could not find the heart to deny them. 'Here, you'd best have these to give to the clowns when they make their collection.' She handed each of the boys some pennies. 'Stay together, the three of you. I'll wait here.'

Faces shining with the thrill of their adventure, the three of them scampered across the road and were swallowed up in the swarm of children clamouring around the clowns.

Cleopatra stood smiling at the scene, pervaded by a wistful regret that she had never known such magical moments during her own bitterly harsh childhood.

'Good evening, Mrs Dolton.'

Cleopatra's breath caught in her throat as she turned her head to encounter Johnny Purvis's smiling face and she inwardly berated herself for the sudden pounding of her heartbeat. 'Dear Christ, I'm reacting to this man like some infatuated, addle-headed girl.'

A sudden anger directed at Johnny Purvis for having this effect upon her caused her to snap curtly at him, 'You've startled me, Mr Purvis, sneaking up on me like that.'

'I'm sorry, Mrs Dolton. I didn't mean to startle you.'

The coloured lights flashing on and off struck answering gleams of colour from his eyes, and Cleopatra's breathing quickened in a flustered nervousness. She saw that he was wearing a civilian suit, and the street was so brightly illuminated that she could see every detail of what he wore, and could not help but admire his elegant appearance, and the dashing tilt of his curly brimmed bowler hat.

She remained silent, her thoughts and feelings jangled and confused. She had never been affected in this way by

141

any man she had previously met, and she could not understand why Johnny Purvis should create such discomposure in her mind. 'He's not that handsome!' she told herself angrily. 'And I'm a respectable married woman with three children. Who does he think he is, to come up and address me without so much as a by your leave?'

Johnny lifted his hat politely. 'Goodnight, Mrs Dolton.'

As he went to turn away from her, a sudden overwhelming impulse to detain him caused her to blurt out, 'I'm sorry about your accident, Mr Purvis.'

He halted and for a moment regarded her with puzzlement. Then he realized that she was referring to the race that afternoon. 'Oh that.' He smiled and shrugged his broad shoulders. 'It wasn't serious. But I thank you for your concern.' He fell silent for a moment, then chuckled, 'In fact I think the poor dog suffered more from it than I or young Barclay did.'

Quite abruptly Cleopatra Dolton's heart lightened and her earlier confusion left her as she accepted the attraction John Purvis exerted upon her. She also chuckled, and said, 'Judging by the way the poor thing yelped, I'm sure it would agree with you.'

There came a sudden commotion among the crowd just in front of them as a brawl erupted and a man came staggering backwards to cannon against Cleopatra Dolton. The impact caused her to stumble sideways and Johnny Purvis grabbed and held her close to steady her, then moved her away some yards, interposing his body between her and the brawl.

She was instantly aware of his masculine smell compounded of tobacco, cologne water, clean flesh and fresh linen. Although his grip was firm it was not painful and she could feel the taut muscular body pressed close against her as they moved.

The brawl lasted only seconds, and then the crowd grabbed the young men and hustled them away.

Cleopatra stayed quiescent, enjoying the exciting proximity to this man who attracted her so powerfully; regret invaded her as he finally released her and stepped away.

'It's all over now, Mrs Dolton. Forgive me for taking

hold of you in that manner, but I wanted to shield you from harm.'

'I'm grateful to you for it, Mr Purvis,' she told him quietly, and through the wispy veil her dark eyes locked on his, and Johnny could sense the warmth of her regard.

'Mother? Mother?' her eldest son's high-pitched voice held a note of panic as he came searching for her and she smiled at Johnny Purvis. 'I must go to my children.'

The man nodded and stared at her gravely for a long drawn out moment, then said quietly, 'I hope that we'll meet again, Mrs Dolton.'

She nodded. 'I too, Mr Purvis.'

'Mother? Mother?' the boy's voice was nearer now and Cleopatra turned to call, 'Simon, I'm over here.'

When she looked back towards Johnny Purvis, he had gone, and a momentary wave of desolation swept over her.

As he threaded his way through the dense crowds, Johnny tried to clarify his thoughts about what had just happened. He himself had been powerfully affected by Cleopatra Dolton. When he had held her close a wave of sexual desire had coursed through him, and the urge to crush her to him and kiss her mouth had been so strong that it had taken an immense effort on his part to resist it.

He grinned wryly to himself. 'It's because you haven't been with a woman for a long time, my buck. That's why you felt so randy all of a sudden. And she's a luscious piece. She'd tempt a saint. That's the only reason you felt the urge so strongly.'

But even as he tried to rationalise his emotions, a nagging disquiet persisted. It had not been solely sexual lust which had dominated him, but something far stronger and more pervasive.

'You're bloody mad!' he castigated himself furiously. 'You're just randy, that's all. Just bloody randy!'

The crowds began to close in on him unbearably and he thirsted to break free of their confinement. He decided to take a walk where he could be alone with his thoughts away from the noise and the bustle.

On the bottom slope of Front Hill there were two rival

143

displays. On the western side the District Council Offices were ablaze with clusters of electric lights. Facing the Council Offices, the Gas Company offices showed off their own brand of illumination. Hundreds of hissing jets entrapped within fancy glass globes of a myriad different colourings.

'It 'ull never take the place o' gas, Emma, never!' Albert Bott stated emphatically, and stared with an open contempt at the electric lighting, which was flickering alarmingly. 'Just look at it. It's forever breaking down. What can you do with it apart from getting a second rate light? Nothing! Nothing at all! With the gas, you gets lights, and heat, you can cook with it, and warm up your water. You can do nearly anything you wants with it. Choose how much light or heat you wants. And them new gas mantles am marvellous. I'se got 'um fitted on all my lights at home. You must come and see 'um, Emma. I'se got 'um in . . .'

Emma Farr could hardly keep from yawning with boredom as the young man talked on and on and on, and she sneaked glances from side to side, yearning fancifully for a romantic dream hero to come galloping down the hill on a white horse and snatch her up to transport her to some glamorous faraway place.

' . . . I had a bit of a job to fit the kitchen for me mam's new gas stove, but what I did in the end was to . . .' Albert Bott's jaws moved ceaselessly, and Emma wondered if it were possible for the joints to eventually overheat and seize up.

Because of the lighting she could see her reflection in the panes of window glass, and she smiled as she saw how smart she looked in her bolero jacket, tight-hipped skirt and narrow-brimmed straw boater tilted down on her high-piled mass of glossy hair towards her broad forehead. Then her smile became a sigh, as she looked at Albert Bott's earnest, boyish features beneath his flat peaked cap.

'Why do I keep company with this gas fitter's mate?' she silently asked herself, and her eyes went down and up, taking in his high stiff collar and narrow tie. His jacket,

144

and waistcoat and trousers of different colours and materials, and worst of all in her view, his great clumping boots. Highly polished and gleaming in the lamplight, but still unmistakably, great clumping hobnailed boots.

'Why do I keep company with him?' she asked herself again, 'when he bores me stiff, like he does?'

Even as she pondered the question the doors of the True Briton public house opened and a raucous group of youths spilled out onto the pavement, some of them singing at the tops of their voices:

> Goodbye Dolly I must leaaaavvvee youuuuu,
> Though it breaks me heart to goooooo.
> Something tells me I am neeeeeeded,
> At the front to fight the foooooooe.

Emma watched them staggering and bawling along the roadway, noting their caps worn at rakish angles on the sides of their oiled hair; the white mufflers tied loosely around their collarless throats; their baggy unpressed trousers and dirty footwear; the still-lighted cigarettes that, to show their utter disregard of pain, they stuck behind their ears; she heard the curses and foulness of their speech, and knew why she was keeping company with Albert Bott. 'At least he never shows me up in public, like those hooligans would. And he never hits me, or tries to take money from me.'

Emma knew too many young girls of her own class who kept company with young men like those she was now watching, and knew just how badly many of them were treated by their boyfriends.

'I'll never stand for that,' she assured herself now. 'Theer's no man going to treat me like dirt, that's for sure. I'd bloody swing for any bugger who tried to treat me bad.'

'Does you want to come back home for a cup of tea, Emma? Only me mam 'ud like to see you I know, and I told her that we might pop in on her for an hour or so?'

The young man stared beseechingly at her, and Emma was reminded of a puppy she used to own who had stared at her with the same expression of slavish devotion.

Irritation flashed, and in a moment of cruelty she sneered, 'Oh that'll be exciting, won't it. Sitting taking tea with your mam, while everybody else in the town is out having a good time.'

She saw the hurt look on his clean-shaven face, and shame mingled with the irritation. 'Oh all right then,' she sighed impatiently. 'But I'm not stopping long.'

Instantly he beamed at her and reached for her hand, but she snatched her own hand away from his seeking fingers, and snapped petulantly, 'Don't maul me about, Albert.'

His family home was up on Mount Pleasant, and side by side they began to walk up Front Hill. As they did, Albert talked constantly. 'I'm going to be out of me time next month, Emma. I'll be a fully qualified tradesman then, and Mr Hawker says that if I keeps on the way I've bin doing with me work, then he'll put me on the big jobs just as soon as he can. That means I'll be counted as a senior fitter, Emma.'

'How thrilling,' she murmured sarcastically, then immediately felt ashamed of herself once more. 'I'm sorry, Albert. I doon't mean to be nasty to you.' She grimaced. 'I'm just out of sorts today, that's all. It's nothing to do with you. It's just my mood.'

'That's all right, love. I should have realised how you was feeling. It's my fault for being so selfish and only talking about meself. I should have more consideration for you.'

There was something pathetic in his eagerness to excuse her own rudeness, and inwardly Emma screamed at him, 'For Christ's sake tell me to sod off, won't you, Albert. Tell me what a miserable bitch I am. Don't be so bloody mealy-mouthed all the time. Be a man, not a bloody doormat.'

'O' course, once I'm a senior fitter, then me money 'ull be better, Emma. I could afford to get wed then, that's if we was careful with our spending.'

She was not really paying attention to what he said, and only nodded absently in reply.

Albert took her nod to be one of agreement and he

laughed elatedly. 'We can live with me mam arter we'em wed, Emma. She's more than willing to let us have the front room to ourselves. And it 'ull be cheaper for us to start off like that, won't it? We'll be able to save money and perhaps even buy a house of our own some day.' He looked longingly at her. 'What do you think to that, love?'

Immersed in her own thoughts, and far away from reality, Emma again nodded absently.

By now they were on Mount Pleasant itself, with the long terraces of tall houses stretching ahead of them. The road was almost deserted, except for a solitary pedestrian coming up from the town behind them creating a dark blob against the glow of the occasional gas lamps.

Albert halted outside the centre house of one of the long terraces.

'Here we are then, love.' He pointed to the light shining through the coloured glass overframe of the front door. 'Look, me mam's left the light on in the hallway for us. I'll bet she's got the kettle boiling already.'

Emma regarded the light with a distinct lack of enthusiasm. She had visited Albert's mother before and knew what awaited her.

Mrs Bott worshipped her only son and made no secret of the fact that she considered a girl from Silver Street to be a bad match for him.

Emma remained at a standstill outside the gate of the minute front garden and Albert had reached the door when he suddenly realised that she was not following.

'What's up, Emma?' he asked anxiously.

Emma made no reply, and as if seeking a way of escape glanced from side to side along the roadway. The oncoming pedestrian passed under the gas lamp some twenty yards further down the road, and Emma drew in her breath with a sharp hiss. Even though the man was dressed in civilian clothes with a tall curly brimmed bowler hat shadowing his features, she could have sworn it was Johnny Purvis. He walked with a military bearing, his metal tipped cane ringing smartly on the pavement although he limped slightly.

'Emma, am you all right?' Albert Bott left the door and

147

came to her, but she was so intent upon the approaching man that she didn't even hear the question.

The man was now only a matter of some ten yards distant from her, and although the slight limp of his gait puzzled her, nevertheless she was sure that it was John Purvis.

Albert Bott stared puzzledly at her, and then his eyes also switched to the man. 'Does you know him, Emma?' he asked sharply, as jealousy pricked him.

Emma ignored him, and abruptly asked loudly, 'Is that you, Mr Purvis?'

Johnny Purvis halted in surprise, and peered through the gloom at the couple, and then recognised Emma Farr.

'Hello Emma,' he greeted, and smiled. 'I wondered who it was for a moment.'

He walked up to her and again halted, leaning slightly on his cane to rest his injured leg which was throbbing painfully.

'Why aren't you down town celebrating, Mr Purvis?' Emma asked grinning cheekily. 'I'd have thought you'd have been dancing with the ladies on the Church Green.'

He chuckled, amused by her gamine-like air. 'Well, I might well have been, Emma, but I had a slight accident this afternoon, and I don't really feel like dancing just now.'

He became aware that the young man was glowering at him, and shrewdly surmised the reason for the sour look.

'Been leading you a dance has she?' he thought sympathetically, and aloud said, 'Well, goodnight to you both.' He politely lifted his hat then walked on.

Emma stood staring after him, and called, 'Goodnight, Mr Purvis. Hope to see you again soon.'

Johnny Purvis half turned and lifted his cane in acknowledgement, before continuing on his way.

Albert Bott's demon of jealousy was now raging. 'Who's he, and how does you know him?' he demanded harshly.

Emma's gutter-devil was instantly roused by his tone. 'What business is that of yours, Albert Bott?' she challenged.

'It is my business when the girl I'm engaged to talks to

other men,' he stated angrily, and Emma stared at him incredulously.

'The girl youm engaged to? And who might that be?' she demanded to know, and it was the young man's turn to stare incredulously.

'Why you, o' course.'

'Me?' Emma's voice rose. 'That's the first I've heard about it, Albert Bott.'

His fresh face was a rapid kaleidoscope of differing emotions; disbelief, anger, puzzlement in a rapid succession.

'But we'se just been talking about getting married, ain't we?' he said. 'And you was agreeable to it.'

Emma mentally compared him with the elegant appearance of Johnny Purvis, contrasting their personalities and their manner. As she did so all the darker crueller side of her nature rose to the surface, and she spat out venomously, 'I'll never be agreeable to marrying you, Albert Bott. Your mam makes it plain that she thinks I'm beneath your family because I'm from Silver Street. Well you can tell the old bitch from me, that if and when I gets married, then my husband 'ull be a real man, who's seen and done things and has travelled the world. He won't be a bleeding gas fitter's mate, who's never gone more than a bloody mile from his mam's apron strings. I never wants to see you again, nor your bloody mam neither.'

With that parting shaft she gathered her skirts up in both hands and ran down Mount Pleasant with all the speed that her lithe body was capable of, leaving Albert Bott standing by the gate staring after her in miserable bewilderment.

Chapter Nineteen

Approximately halfway up Mount Pleasant where, behind the terraced houses and a long factory façade, the high ridge fell away eastwards, Grange House stood on the wooded hillside overlooking Arrow Valley. A long driveway wound from the house and debouched onto Mount Pleasant between a row of houses and the factory. Two huge spreading chestnut trees stood like sentinels on each side of the driveway entrance and the driveway itself was lined along its length with densely packed shrubs and trees whose tangled leaves and branches had been allowed to grow wild and unchecked across the narrow unmetalled track, creating the impression of a long dark green tunnel that had no end.

As a small boy Johnny Purvis had been fascinated by this green tunnel, which to him had seemed a mysterious pathway that led to strange romantic places peopled with legendary creatures. He would sometimes stand for hours peering along its length, hoping for some glimpse of those same creatures, but too timid to venture beneath its overhanging branches.

Then, on his ninth birthday, he had gathered all his courage and had entered the dark tunnel. With a pounding heart he had crept further and further along its leaf-shrouded dankness, following its winding path until he feared that he had gone from his own familiar world into another place unknown to man. The smell of decaying wood and moulding leaves permeated the air and no sound penetrated the thick dense undergrowth, so an unnatural hushed stillness surrounded him. Sudden dread assailed him, he wanted to turn and run, but, small boy though he was, he steeled himself to go on, instinctively realising that he was facing some sort of test which, although he could not understand its import, was of crucial importance in his life.

On and on he went, losing all track of time. Then abruptly, bright warm sunlight splashed upon his head and there before him on open grassland was an ancient, tall-chimneyed, greystone house, with small arrow-slitted turrets, mossy tiles, dormered windows and latticed panes set deep in its weathered sides. The boy's lips parted in wonder and delight. In that moment he somehow knew with absolute certainty that some day in the far future, this house would become his home.

Now, in the freshness of the early morning, as Johnny Purvis walked along the winding driveway towards Grange House, he smiled as he remembered that small boy. His fingers went into his jacket pocket to touch and hold the great iron key which would open the doors of the house that he had now come to claim as his own.

As on that long ago day, the bright warm sunlight abruptly splashed onto his head, and there before him was the house, looking exactly the same as when he had first seen it.

Beyond its grey walls the wooded hillside stretched downwards into the rich fecund meadows of the Arrow Valley. Johnny's gaze roamed across their green expanse and his lungs filled with the fresh pure air. There were no gardens surrounding the house, only the green-sward: some hundred square yards bounded by the woodlands, and a large, oval, gravel forecourt before the arch of the great iron-studded front door.

His shoes crunched the pinkish-grey pebbles of the forecourt and quite suddenly his instincts, honed by the long years of guerilla warfare, told him that someone was watching him. He swung round, his eyes searching the ground and the facing woodland, and saw a slight figure in a grey dress and straw boater hat standing some fifty yards distant against the treeline.

For a moment or two he remained motionless, studying the figure. Then, despite the distance separating them, he knew without any doubt who the figure was, and he waved and shouted in invitation, 'Miss Josceleyne, please come here.'

He began to walk towards the woman and after he had taken some twenty paces she in her turn advanced towards him.

When they met Miriam Josceleyne's sallow cheeks were flushed, and her hands twined and twisted together nervously. Her faded eyes only met his for brief moments, then slid away as if unable to sustain their regard, and she whispered hesitantly, 'What must you think of me Mr Purvis, finding me here like this and at this hour of the morning?'

He smiled with a wry amusement. 'Why, I think you are very sensible to be taking a walk on such a pleasant morning, Miss Josceleyne.' He waved his arm towards the house. 'Where could you find a more beautiful view than this one?' He paused and waited, and her green eyes came timidly to meet his own. He smiled and invited softly, 'Please, Miss Josceleyne, would you be very kind and show me over the house? I've not yet been inside it, you see.'

Flustered she shook her head, causing loose tendrils of her mousy hair to fall against her cheeks. 'Oh I could not, Mr Purvis.'

He frowned in puzzlement. 'But why not, Miss Josceleyne?'

Colour burned in her cheeks. 'It would not be proper, Mr Purvis.'

Johnny found her confusion sweetly appealing and could not resist teasing gently. 'I don't understand, Miss Josceleyne. How would it not be proper?'

Her hands twisted and tugged against each other as she drew a long tremulous breath. 'Because a lady should not be alone with a gentleman in such circumstances, Mr Purvis.'

He chuckled warmly. 'But since I *am* a gentleman, Miss Josceleyne, then no lady has anything to fear from me, has she?'

Miriam Josceleyne's emotions were a maelstrom of conflicting urges. One part of her being clamoured to

152

accompany this man whom she found so personable. The other part of her being was screaming at her to leave this place this instant and to behave with the propriety expected of a gentlewoman of her standing and social position.

'Come now, Miss Josceleyne. Please do not desert me in my hour of need,' he coaxed lightheartedly. 'If needs be I can swear myself to secrecy and no one but we two shall ever know that you have accompanied me on a tour of my new home.' He grinned at her. 'Do you know, if you refuse me in this, Miss Josceleyne, I shall begin to believe that you consider me to be one of the brutal and licentious soldiery.'

Her blush deepened, but then her lips curved and she giggled. 'I hardly think you to be that, Mr Purvis.'

'Well then, prove it by coming and showing me around the house,' he beseeched, and the vital young girl that she once had been abruptly resurrected herself. Miriam Josceleyne heard her own voice saying, 'Very well then, Mr Purvis. But I cannot stay for very long.'

As they walked side by side towards the house Miriam Josceleyne was very conscious of Johnny Purvis's masculinity. Everything about him was so very different to the men that she had lived her life with. Although she knew that he originated from a social class far below her own, she found herself able to accept him as a true gentleman. She kept on sneaking sidewards glances at his sun-bronzed hard-etched profile, and her heart thudded almost painfully. Although he now wore a dark-blue suit and curly brimmed bowler hat, her visual imagination persisted in super-imposing the romantic plumed slouch hat and the gleaming leather accoutrements and khaki uniform that she had first seen him wearing.

She was able also, with an ever-increasing ease, to acknowledge and accept the fact that what had brought her walking along the woodland paths to this house so early in this morning was the secret hope that she might encounter him in just such a manner as this.

At the door, as she watched him insert and turn the great iron key and heard the squeal of the rusted lock, her

153

personal dichotomy again asserted itself, twin personalities assailing each other with accusatory charge, and countering defiance. 'You're behaving shamelessly, Miriam Josceleyne . . . So, what if I am? . . . You're a stupid old maid! . . . Only because I've been forced to become such . . . How dare you throw yourself at this man? You're behaving like a trollop! . . . I'm not throwing myself at him and I'm not behaving like a trollop . . . You should be ashamed of yourself . . . Well I'm not. I've done nothing to be ashamed of . . . What if your brother comes to hear of this? What will he say? . . . I don't care if he does hear of this. He can say what he damn well chooses! I really couldn't care less for his opinion of me, or for anyone else's opinion either!'

She smiled triumphantly as her carping opponent went toppling into defeat, and then came back to reality to find John Purvis staring at her questioningly. 'Did you say something, Miss Josceleyne?'

'Oh my God!' she thought in mortified dismay, 'I must have been thinking out loud.' She blushed furiously, and then to her own amazement she heard herself laugh gaily, and answer, 'I was probably talking to myself, Mr Purvis. It's a habit we old maids tend to get into.'

He laughed softly, and his eyes were warm as he told her, 'You're not an old maid, Miss Josceleyne. Believe me, you are not.'

Then he led the way into the house.

The interior was as unusual and archaic as the outer façade. Big empty high-vaulted rooms on the ground floor, whose stone flags echoed hollowly beneath their feet. On the upper floors there was one large dormitory, surrounded by a myriad of small cramped cells, haphazardly spaced on erratic levels, joined by winding stairways and narrow corridors.

There were no gas or electric fittings and the water supply was a long-handled upright pump outside the back door in the stabled courtyard. A brick-built privy, standing some yards to the rear of the stables, provided for personal offices. For cooking purposes there was a big rusty iron range and in each of the ground floor rooms ingled hearths with iron firebaskets, dogs and spitjacks.

154

Miriam Josceleyne stared doubtfully at her companion's impassive features as they went from dusty room to dusty room, and at length she asked him, 'Don't you find it very primitive, Mr Purvis? I cannot help but wonder if you are not disappointed with this house?'

'Disappointed?' For the first time since they had entered the house, Johnny Purvis spoke, then smiled broadly, and with almost boyish enthusiasm told her, 'I love the place, Miss Josceleyne. It's everything I ever dreamed it could be. Tell me now, what do you know of its history? I can remember hearing tales about it being a home for the monks when Bordesley Abbey was abandoned, and other stories as well, but I don't know how true those stories were.'

As Miriam Josceleyne related what she knew of the history of Grange House, her faded green eyes began to glow lucently, her sallow features became animated with pleasure and tinged with a rosy colour. Johnny Purvis saw in her face the pretty young girl she had once been and a liking for her burgeoned ever stronger within him, as her passion for the house communicated itself to him, and in turn fired his own vivid imagination.

'My great-grandmother's family have been in this district since the Norman Conquest, Mr Purvis. When I was a very small girl she would tell me stories about this house that had been told to her by her own grandmother when she was a child. She said that the house was originally a grange farm of Bordesley Abbey where several of the monks lived together with the lay brothers who tended the sheep. But when the black death came so many monks died at the Abbey itself that this house was abandoned by them and only a couple of lay brothers stayed on here.

'In about 1361 a very wicked man named John de Acton was appointed Abbot of Bordesley. He used his office to defraud the Abbey of its property and wealth and he lived a life of debauchery. He took possession of this house for himself and installed his mistress here. It was said that until John de Acton had met this mistress he had been a God-fearing, virtuous man. It was this woman who had made him wicked. She was supposedly a very beautiful foreign woman who had been brought back to this area by a Crusader returning from the Holy Land. She ran away from the Crusader and sought refuge at Bordesley Abbey. That is how John de Acton met her. The local people said that she was a witch and that she had enslaved him by magic. They called her the Saracen Witch. She was supposed to have very dark skin, long black hair and eyes like deep shining black pools. The local people believed that if a man looked into her eyes then she could draw his soul from him and make him her slave.'

Johnny Purvis listened fascinated by the story. The ruins of Bordesley Abbey were situated on the north side of the town, on the flat land at the bottom of Fish Hill. As a small boy he had walked across the Abbey Meadows exploring the mysterious grass-covered mounds and hummocks which covered the remains of the buildings. He kept his eyes fixed on Miriam Josceleyne's face and marvelled at the change in her as she related these local legends. There was no trace of her usual timidity or self-consciousness, only animated happy confidence. He increasingly thought how charming she was and was surprised at his ever-strengthening attraction towards her.

'Of course, eventually the Chapter General of the Cistercian Order investigated John de Acton and he was deposed from his office. But he stole the great seal of the Abbey and went to London where he used the seal to obtain money on false pretences from the Lombards. He was arrested, but escaped and returned here.

'As you'll know, Mr Purvis, all this area in those days formed part of the Forest of Feckenham; outlaws and masterless men could hide deep in the woods. The story is that while John de Acton was in London the Saracen Witch had used her powers to recruit a band of outlaws who used this house as their headquarters. When John de Acton returned here, the witch persuaded him to lead her band of outlaws in an attack upon Bordesley Abbey. She wanted him to plunder all its treasures, and bring them to her. Anyway, he did lead an attack, but was beaten off, and again taken prisoner. The Sheriff of Worcester then led a band of soldiers to hunt down the outlaws, and most of them were captured and hanged.'

'And the Saracen Witch? What happened to her?' Johnny Purvis was enthralled by the story.

Miriam Josceleyne's green eyes were shining and her lips curved in a dreamy smile, so engrossed was she in her memories.

'My great-grandmother said that the witch took refuge in this house and the sheriff's soldiers surrounded it. The day was wild and stormy, and it was said that the winds screamed among the branches of the trees like lost souls in torment. The sheriff rode up to the door and hammered upon it with his mace, then his men shouted for him to come back to them. The witch had climbed out onto the roof. The soldiers could see her standing on the very top of the gable with her long black cloak streaming out from her shoulders as the wind took it. The sheriff summoned her to surrender and ordered his archers to make ready to fire at her. Again the sheriff warned her to surrender, but she only made cabalistic signs towards him and he became afraid that he would be bewitched, so he ordered the archers to shoot at her.'

Miriam Josceleyne's voice sounded curiously strained and her expression was distant, as if she were far away from this room. Far away in the depths of time, back in that moment when the witch had defied the Sheriff of Worcester.

'The arrows flew through the air, and the soldiers shouted as they saw the shafts bury themselves in the witch's breast. She screamed and fell and her body came hurtling down, but as it thudded onto the forecourt there came a terrible roaring clap of thunder and a bolt of lightning which struck the ground in front of the house and flashed so brilliantly that it blinded the men's eyes for several seconds. When they could see again, they found that there was no sign of the witch's body. She had disappeared. The sheriff forced the soldiers to search the house and all the surrounding woods, but they found not a single trace of the witch.'

Johnny Purvis found that he had been holding his breath in anticipation and now he gusted out a long sigh.

'What happened then?' he asked quietly.

Miriam Josceleyne shook her head slightly, as if to clear it, and blinked at him as if she had just awoken from sleep.

'The witch was never seen nor heard of again. This house, believed to be cursed, a place of witchcraft, apparently was left to fall into ruin. The local people were too afraid to come near it, believing that the witch haunted it. It remained abandoned until my great-grandmother's forefather took it over after the Civil War and repaired it.' She smiled a trifle grimly. 'He was a supporter of Oliver Cromwell and had been an Ironside trooper. He feared neither man, ghost nor witch.'

'And did the ghost of this Saracen Witch ever appear?' Johnny Purvis questioned eagerly.

Miriam Josceleyne smiled with a hint of ambiguity, and teased him, 'Are you afraid of ghosts, Mr Purvis?'

He chuckled. 'No, Miss Josceleyne, I'm not afraid of ghosts. But then, since I've never seen one, I can't really claim to be completely unafraid of them, can I? Who knows how I might react if I was to meet the Saracen Witch one dark night.'

'Well if you should do so, Mr Purvis, take care that you don't look deeply into her eyes, or she might well enslave you as she enslaved John de Acton.'

An unbidden visual image of Cleopatra Dolton's dark eyes suddenly invaded Johnny Purvis's mind, and he remembered the powerful effect she had had on him during that brief interlude outside the Royal Hotel.

'Perhaps I've already met the Saracen Witch,' he smiled at the fanciful thought, then frowned as the next instant he remembered that he was due to meet Arthur Dolton at twelve noon.

He took out his watch and glanced at its ornate face. It was now half past eleven. It was with a considerable reluctance that he told Miriam Josceleyne, 'Unfortunately I've an appointment at noon in the town centre, Miss Josceleyne. Sadly I can't remain here any longer.'

Instantly all the radiant self-confidence that she had been exhibiting fled from her, her green eyes lost their lustre and once again she was the familiar nervous, timid

158

creature that he knew.

'I'm sorry, I've been rambling on so, Mr Purvis. Whatever can you think of me? I quite forgot myself, telling those silly stories.'

He saw with concern how her hands again entwined and tugged and twisted in agitation and he hastened to try to recapture the previous sense of easy camaraderie that had briefly existed between them. 'Please Miss Josceleyne, I've thoroughly enjoyed your company. I've a great wish to hear more about the history of this house and of your family. I'm very interested in what you've been telling me. Really I am.'

She forced a fleeting smile and Johnny felt impelled to ask her, 'Could we meet again, Miss Josceleyne? I'd love to talk with you at greater length.'

Her lips twitched, her sallow cheeks flamed and dropping her head she mumbled, 'I must go, Mr Purvis. My father will be expecting me.'

Before he could say anything more to her, she had scurried out of the house. By the time he reacted and followed, her frail slender figure was hastening across the green-sward towards the treeline.

He sighed heavily, and shook his head, afraid that if he went after her, he would only cause her distress. So, locking the great iron-studded door behind him, he made his own way towards the green tunnelled driveway that led out onto Mount Pleasant.

As Miriam Josceleyne hurried across the close-cropped turf, her thoughts were whirling giddily. One instant she felt embarrassment and shame that she had allowed herself not only to come here in hope of seeing Johnny Purvis, but worse, had spent a considerable time alone with him. The next instant she would feel elated and happy that she had done so.

She neared the treeline and unconsciously slowed her pace, half-hoping, half-dreading that she would hear him calling her, perhaps even find that he was coming after her. A deliciously fearful tremor shivered through her at that thought and she could not resist glancing behind to see if he was indeed in pursuit.

The green-sward was empty. Acute disappointment lanced through Miriam Josceleyne and she halted and turned about, her eyes searching hungrily for him. She spotted his tall upright figure disappearing into the dark tunnel of the driveway and her anger flashed.

'He did not care enough even to call after me!' she thought indignantly. 'And I've risked my good name and reputation for him!'

Then the ridiculousness of her reaction struck home to her and she could not help but smile in self-derision. 'What an idiotic fool you are, Miriam Josceleyne. The man asked if he might see you again, did he not? All you could do was to blush and stammer like a half-wit and run away from him. You're twenty-eight years old, my girl, not eight, it's high time that you took charge of yourself.'

She walked slowly onwards and entered the cool sun-dappled shades of the woodland. As she wandered along the narrow tracks she slowly began to realise that strange new powerful undercurrents were beginning to surge through her being. She found that for the first time in many long years, perhaps for the first time ever, she was suddenly able to view herself and her life with a controlled objectivity. She found also that she disliked and despised what she was viewing.

Enthralled by this new-found ability to make judgements with such a degree of ruthless self-veracity, Miriam Josceleyne was prepared to explore it to the very limits of its capacity. For the first time she dared to bring into the light memories that she had kept deliberately buried. Recalling how, when she had been still only a nineteen-year-old girl, her mother had taken to her bed as an invalid and stayed there, becoming daily more self-pitying, querulous and tyrannical, in her ever-increasing physical and emotional demands upon her family.

Miriam's lips quirked in a mirthless bitter smile. Her father and her brother had withdrawn almost immediately from any attempt to share the burden of caring for the sick woman; that burden had fallen solely upon her, Miriam's, shoulders.

Her father had also demanded that she assume her

mother's position as the keeper of his house. Unfortunately for Miriam, Hector Josceleyne had always been something of a domestic tyrant. Harsh and unyielding in his demands for near perfection from those that he dominated, his meanness had precluded him from obtaining the extra help that his wife's long illness had made necessary. So a seemingly endless procession of overworked and underpaid servants had either left or been dismissed. For long periods of time the young woman had been forced to cope alone with all the menial tasks of the house, as well as nursing her sick mother and acting as her father and brother's virtual handmaiden.

The old familiar sense of guilt assailed Miriam Josceleyne as she remembered how the love she had once had for her parents had been slowly eroded through those long years. But now, in the grip of this strange new mood, she was able to justify and condone that lost love.

'From the day she took to her bed, until the day she died, my mother treated me as if I were her personal slave. My father did the same. And still does. As for Franklin . . .' She frowned scornfully. 'Franklin has always placed his own needs and desires in the forefront, the devil take anybody else. My parents nagged me into my consciousness of family loyalty and the duty and obligations I owed to them, to all the family. When it came to it, I was the only one of all our family who ever showed that loyalty, or acted dutifully, or honoured those obligations.'

The track in front of her forked into different directions, one of which would bring her up onto Mount Pleasant, the other down into the lower road leading to the village of Studley. Miriam knew that in the village there would be an ox-roast and a fair taking place, as in Redditch itself. An impulse to take the fork which led to Studley village overcame her, as she remembered a day in her childhood when her nursemaid had taken her to a Mop Fair in the village. She had marvelled at the jugglers and tumblers, cheapjacks and gypsies, ridden on a gaily painted wooden horse, eaten sweet oily ginger snaps and drunk tart lemonade.

'How I'd love to do that again.' Nostalgia and longing

161

welled up in her and she stood at the fork, undecided which direction to take.

'I should really go back home and see if Emma and Mrs Elwood need any help with Father.' She smiled as she thought of Emma Farr. During the brief time the girl had been at Cotswold House, Miriam had conceived a real affection and admiration for her. 'Emma doesn't need help with Father. She controls him better than I or anyone else ever did, or could. In all truth, I have to admit that she and Mrs Elwood don't need me at all, so there is really no call for me to go back home on their account. But Mrs Allcock's 'at home' this afternoon. She will expect me to attend.'

Miriam's brow furrowed resentfully. 'I don't want to spend such a lovely afternoon sitting with her and her cronies, tearing other people's characters to shreds.'

Engrained habits and attitudes died hard and she still hesitated. 'If I don't go, then they will expect an explanation from me for my absence. They might well think that I'm deliberately avoiding their society.' The next instant she tossed her head defiantly. 'Well let them think what they choose. Because I really could not care less.'

She began to marvel at herself. 'What has happened to me? Why have I suddenly begun to entertain all these wild thoughts? Have I gone mad?'

Then the visual image of Johnny Purvis's smiling face entered her mind and she fancied she could hear his warm chuckle in her ears.

'It is you that's happened to me, isn't it, John Purvis,' she murmured that abrupt realisation aloud. 'All these thoughts and feelings have been inside me seeking an outlet for years, but I've always suppressed them, haven't I? But you have come into my life, and you have acted like a catalyst upon me!'

She smiled wonderingly, 'Well, I don't know what the future holds, or whether you have any further part to play in my life, John Purvis. I do know that no matter what happens, my meeting you has been a marvellous thing for me. I don't know if these new feelings I have will last, but while they do, I'm going to enjoy them to the full.'

Lightheartedly singing to herself, Miriam Josceleyne

took the path towards Studley Village without any more doubts or hesitations.

Chapter Twenty

Franklin Josceleyne's position with the Metropolitan Bank
of England and Wales carried many advantages, not least
among them being the occupancy of a rent-free house
adjoining the bank's business premises on Church Green
West.

It was here that the Reverend Mosse MacDonald, M.A.,
called on the morning following the Coronation Day.

Franklin Josceleyne received his visitor in the over-
furnished drawing room, and apologised for the absence
of his wife and daughters, who were visiting friends some
miles distant.

'Please, Mr Josceleyne, say not a word,' the clergyman
said unctuously. 'I am disappointed not to see them, of
course, but the matter I am here to talk with you about is
of a rather delicate nature and I prefer that we should be
alone while discussing it.'

The bank manager's already sour mood instantly
worsened. 'Does this matter you speak of concern the
presence of a servant girl in my family's pew yesterday
morning, Reverend?' he snapped curtly.

He was still furious with his father and sister for
insisting that Emma Farr should accompany the famiy to
church and bitterly chagrined at what he considered to be
his own loss of face among the town's polite society as a
result of their action. Consequently he was in no mood to
be taken to task about the incident by a mere curate. No
matter how senior that curate might be in the local church
hierarchy.

The other man's plump florid features registered
surprise at Franklin Josceleyne's tone. But having regard

for his own interests he forbore from taking offence, and now spoke mollifyingly. 'Goodness me no, Mr Josceleyne. Speaking personally I greatly admire what you did yesterday in allowing a servant to share your pew. I thought it to be an act of truly Christian charity. In fact I said as much to Reverend Canon Newton and he agreed with that sentiment wholeheartedly.'

'Did he now?' Franklin Josceleyne's mood lightened immediately. The wealthy Reverend Canon Newton was a highly valued customer of the bank and one of the doyens of local society.

Mosse MacDonald sensed the good impression he had made and decided to build on that foundation, even if in the construction he should be forced to use untruths. 'Indeed he did, Mr Josceleyne. He went on to state quite emphatically that it was a great pity that certain others among the leading citizens of this community could not have acted in a like manner to yourself.'

He paused and gave the impression that he was judiciously considering his next words, then gestured with his hands as if making an irrevocable decision. Lowering his voice as if not wanting to risk being overheard, he leaned conspiratorially towards the other man and went on, 'In the strictest confidence, between ourselves, Mr Josceleyne, I may tell you that the Reverend Canon Newton holds your good self in the highest respect and admiration, and imparted to me that in his opinion our congregation is sadly lacking in truly Christian gentlemen such as yourself.'

Again he paused momentarily to evaluate the effect of his words and, satisfied with what he saw, finished, 'Man to man, Mr Josceleyne, I will tell you frankly that I concurred most heartily with the Reverend Canon Newton's views on that subject.'

With becoming modesty, Franklin Josceleyne murmured self-deprecatingly, 'I'm but a miserable sinner, Reverend MacDonald, who is trying to live life according to the tenets of our Saviour.'

By now he was beginning to congratulate himself for having allowed Emma Farr to share the family pew and was deeply gratified by what his visitor had told him. Viewing the clergyman benevolently, he invited, 'Please sit down, Reverend MacDonald, and let me offer you some refreshment.'

Waving aside the other man's feeble protests he rang for the maidservant and, when she appeared, ordered her to bring tea and sandwiches for the visitor.

When Mosse MacDonald had satisfied his appetite, Franklin Josceleyne asked, 'Now what is it you wish to talk with me about, Reverend?'

When seeking to advance his own interests, Mosse MacDonald was never shy.

'I will speak frankly and openly to you, Mr Josceleyne. The matter which brings me here concerns your sister, Miss Miriam Josceleyne.'

'Indeed?' The bank manager frowned doubtfully, his mind instantly racing, as he wondered what his despised old maid of a sister could have done to warrant himself being called upon by a clergyman.

Mosse MacDonald radiated a manly open-hearted sincerity. 'I will not beat around the bush, Mr Josceleyne, but will speak as one gentleman to another, as Christian brother to Christian brother. Although I have known Miss Miriam for only scant years and have only exchanged with her the commonplaces of social intercourse, yet there has developed within my heart the most sincere and profound attachment towards her. In brief, Mr Josceleyne, I have come to love your sister and I desire more than anything else in this world to make her my wife; to join with her in the bond of Holy matrimony. I am here Mr Josceleyne to seek your permission that I may ask for Miss Miriam's hand in marriage.'

For a brief moment Franklin Josceleyne's jaw dangled in utter amazement, and he was unable to formulate any reply.

Mosse MacDonald moved quickly to forestall one objection which he conceived might be made by the bank manager. 'Of course, at this moment in time, Mr Josceleyne, I am merely the senior curate to Reverend Canon Newton, but I have a good relationship with the

166

Windsor-Clives. The family has intimated to me that, should I get married, then they have a benefice in Shropshire which they would be most happy to bestow upon me, the stipend of which would be considerably in excess of my present income, and perfectly adequate to support a wife in the manner befitting a gentlewoman.'

Franklin Josceleyne's first shock of amazement had passed, and now his brain was working with its customary shrewdness. Automatically disbelieving in the existence of any lucrative benefice in Shropshire, his initial impulse was to send this fortune hunter packing, but he restrained it. Just lately his sister had been behaving very strangely, displaying uncharacteristic flashes of resentment against his strictures. Flashes of resentment that on occasion almost verged into open rebelliousness. The bank manager was now wondering if that behaviour had anything to do with this man in front of him. Could she know that the clergyman was professing himself to be in love with her? Unthinkable though it might be, could she be harbouring tender feelings for Mosse MacDonald? Franklin Josceleyne decided to tread warily.

He smiled warmly. 'I am deeply gratified that someone whom I hold in the utmost respect, and have such high regard for should wish to wed my sister Miriam, Reverend MacDonald. Might I enquire if she has told you whether or not she returns your feelings for her?'

Mosse MacDonald also smiled warmly, and his manner became grotesquely arch. 'In as many words, Mr Josceleyne, no, she has not. A lady as pure and modest as Miss Miriam would hardly declare such intimate feelings openly. But when a man is in love, then he can recognise whether or not the object of his devotion returns his feelings. I sincerely believe that in this case the lady in question is not averse to myself.'

The bank manager steepled his fingers before him and rested his chin upon their points and closed his eyes as if deep in thought. That Miriam should get married at this time in her life was the last thing that he had ever expected to happen. Of course, during the preceding years there had been on occasion some man or other who had paid attention to Miriam. But she had been younger then, and still pretty.

At that time he would not have objected to Miriam getting married to a suitable applicant. He had been devoting himself to what he had fondly hoped would prove a glittering career in the banking world and his sister's personal hopes and dreams had been of little importance and even less interest to him. But now, he knew that he had reached his own personal pinnacle in his career and would progress no further than this managership of a provincial branch. His dreams of gaining a fortune had proven to be false ones. Consequently the family wealth had become a matter of supreme importance to him. He had assumed that he would always remain in control of it, because when his father died, Miriam, being an old maid would remain under his dominance, so continue to rely completely upon himself to administer their joint inheritances.

Now, sitting here with closed eyes, Franklin Josceleyne felt for a few moments as though the very foundations of his world were shifting and cracking beneath him. But one determination remained solid. Miriam must not be allowed to marry this fat, pompous glutton sitting before him, or anyone else. He opened his eyes and smiled at the clergyman.

'Please forgive me. I was impelled to pray for our Lord's guidance.'

'I am delighted to hear that, Mr Josceleyne, I also prayed for long hours and beseeched His help and guidance before coming to see you this morning,' Mosse MacDonald informed fulsomely, and waited with an expectant air.

Franklin Josceleyne sighed hard and slowly shook his head. 'You do our family a great honour, Reverend MacDonald. I am frankly somewhat overcome by what you have told me.'

Inwardly the clergyman shouted, 'Get on with it, you damned pompous fool. Give me your blessing and let's have done with this damned nonsense!' Outwardly, he gravely nodded his head in acknowledgement of the other man's words, and stated softly, 'If I should receive your consent and your blessing, Mr Josceleyne, then the honour is done to me.'

By now the bank manager had managed to formulate a plan of action. 'Of course you have my permission to ask for my sister's hand in marriage, Reverend MacDonald.'

He paused to watch the beaming smile of triumph spread across the other man's features, then went on, 'I know that I can rely upon your concurrence with the request that I am forced to make of you at this moment. As one gentleman to another, as Christian brother to Christian brother.'

Mosse MacDonald nodded vigorousy, causing his long full beard to ripple in a wavelike motion. 'Anything Mr Josceleyne. You may ask of me anything, and it shall be granted.'

'Thank you.' Franklin Josceleyne inclined his own head in gracious acceptance. 'My request is merely that you postpone speaking to my sister concerning this matter, until such time as my poor afflicted father's present indisposition has resolved itself.' Sadness creased his forehead. 'Whether it be for the better, or for the worse it will not be long delayed in either aspect, I do assure you, Reverend. Doctor Pierce has told me in the strictest confidence, that the matter is very near to resolution.'

Mosse MacDonald was both elated and disappointed, but he graciously acceded to the request and the two men parted wih an outward show of mutual warm regard and fervent protestations of Christian brotherhood.

Alone once more, Franklin Josceleyne permitted himself a brief moment of congratulation for the way he had handled such a tricky situation and succeeded in gaining valuable time. He decided that he must immediately ascertain exactly how his sister felt about Mosse Mac-Donald. He rang for the maidservant and when she appeared told her curtly, 'I'm going out. If there should be any urgent need of me, I may be found at Cotswold House.'

Mosse MacDonald's satisfaction with the interview was short-lived. As he walked ponderously back towards his house a sudden suspicion that he had somehow been bamboozled by the bank manager entered his mind. 'Why should he have asked me to wait until his father's illness took its course? The old man is merely going senile. He isn't ill in any life-threatening sense, is he? Only suffering the usual afflictions of old age. It could be years before any resolution of his condition is reached. How could any doctor be sure in his diagnosis as to an early resolution of the old man's condition?'

The cleric frowned with resentment. 'Josceleyne is playing games with me. He doesn't wish me to marry his sister.'

Another train of thought overlaid his resentment. 'Perhaps he doesn't wish me to marry her because he's afraid that when I do so I shall gain control of her money. That means that he must know the contents of his father's will. Miriam must be receiving an equal inheritance to himself when the old man dies.'

A hopeful elation rose within him. 'Maybe she is to have everything: all the property and all the money. Perhaps Franklin Josceleyne knows that and because of it is fobbing me off with his cock and bull tales about his father. He's trying to gain time to persuade his father to change his will in his favour. I've been barking up the wrong tree by making my approaches to her brother. It's directly to Miriam Josceleyne herself that I should be paying my attentions. Legally neither her brother nor her father can exert any control over her actions. So the sooner I marry her, the better.'

The fact that Miriam Josceleyne herself might not wish to marry him did not even occur to Mosse MacDonald. He believed that an old maid such as she would gladly jump at any chance of a suitable marriage, particularly to such a man as himself. Mosse MacDonald possessed an overweening personal vanity. Flattered and fawned upon by the matrons of the congregation; a social lion in the drawing rooms of the elite among the town's society, he regarded himself as a great catch, and was confident that Miriam Josceleyne would be both honoured and delighted by his proposal.

'She's a bit skinny for my taste,' he accepted. His sexual

appetites were aroused by more meaty women. 'But I'm a lusty fellow, and I don't doubt but that I shall enjoy bedding her well enough. Why at times, she looks quite appealing, I must admit. We'll do well enough in that department, I'm sure.'

For a moment or two he toyed with the idea of calling at Cotswold House immediately on the pretext of visiting old Hector Josceleyne. But at the thought of the tasty luncheon his cook would have prepared, the call of his belly overcame that of his heart. 'I'll call on Miriam later this afternoon.'

He smiled in anticipation as he passed by Cotswold House and went on down Fish Hill.

Chapter Twenty-One

As Emma Farr mounted the stairs, heavily laden with a large bucket of hot water, scrubbing brush, washcloths and broom, she could hear the thumping of the old man's stick as he banged it on the floor of his room. Laying down her burdens outside his door she opened it and went in.

'What's yov .naking all this rattle for?' she demanded.

'Is it time for my bath, Emma? It must be time for my bath,' Hector Josceleyne questioned impatiently.

With an equal impatience the girl told him, 'Will you give over werritin' me. I've got to finish cleaning Miss Miriam's room before I can bath you, and anyway, Mrs Elwood is very busy so you'll just have to wait until we'se both got time to do it.'

He petulantly thumped the arm of his chair. 'Why does that old hag always have to help you to bathe me? I only want you to do it.'

Emma grinned cheekily down at him, 'Oh yes, and we know why, doon't we?'

Huddled in his voluminous dressing gown from which his claw-like rope-veined hands, scrawny neck and bald head protruded, the old man irresistibly reminded Emma of an ancient tortoise, and she chuckled at the thought.

'What are you laughing about, you saucy little bitch?' he shouted angrily, and waved his stick in threat. 'I'll lay this about your shoulders if you don't show more respect.'

She put her hands on her hips and laughed aloud. She made a pretty picture in her gingham dress covered by a long coarse apron, her head covered by a floppy mob-cap from which strands of her glossy chestnut hair had

172

escaped to dangle against her cheeks and soft rounded throat.

The old man's tongue kept darting serpent-like from his lipless mouth and his rheumy eyes filled with lust as they fixed on her pert high breasts. 'I'd give you money, Emma, lots of it, if you were kinder to me.' His head wavered on its stalk of unshaven throat.

Emma's imp of mischief roused instantly. Widening her eyes in mock innocence she said, 'But I am kind to you already, Mr Hector, so why would you want to give me money? What for?'

'For being nice to me, Emma. For doing what I ask you,' he panted urgently, as his demon of lust mercilessly drove him.

'What is it you want to ask me to do for you, Mr Hector?' She tormented him by moving closer, undulating her hips and thrusting out her breasts tantalisingly. 'You'll have to explain what you mean, because I'm only an ignorant servant girl, and I doon't understand things.'

He tried to rise from the chair to grab hold of her, but today his rheumatic joints were stiff and sore and he groaned in pain and relapsed back into the depths of the chair.

Emma waggled her forefinger and remonstrated, 'There you see, you naughty boy. You know that your rheumatics are bad today, and still you try and walk around. It serves you right, that does.'

He cursed her irritably, then ordered, 'Come here to me girl. I'm the master of this house, and you'll do as I order you.'

'Oh no I shan't, you dirty old devil!' Abruptly her mood became petulant. 'I'm not coming near you so that you can try and maul me about. In fact, I've a good mind to pack my traps and leave this house for good. I'm sick and tired of your bloody nonsense.'

Real dread shafted through his degenerating brain. 'No Emma! No, don't go. I don't want you to leave me.'

She frowned, and turning flounced out of the room, slamming the door closed behind her.

The old man shouted after her, 'Don't go, Emma. Don't

173

leave me ' Then he started to thump his stick down against the floor with all the strength he could exert. 'Come back, Emma. Please come back!'

Emma stood outside the door, giggling to herself as his shouts echoed through the house. Then she heard the jangling of the front door bell, followed almost immediately by the sound of that door opening and closing, and the clack of footsteps across the parquet flooring of the hallway.

She ran to the head of the stairs and peered down, to find the angry face of Franklin Josceleyne glaring up at her from below.

'What the devil is going on up there?' he demanded. 'Why is my father making such a noise?'

'If you please, sir, he's just having one of his turns,' Emma told him, struggling to keep from smiling as Hector Josceleyne's cracked bellowings reached a crescendo.

'Come down here, girl. I cannot hear what you're saying with that din going on,' Franklin Josceleyne ordered and Emma hastened to obey.

'Where is my sister?' the man wanted to know.

'If you please, sir, she's gone out.'

'Where?'

'I don't know, sir.'

'At what time is she returning?'

'I don't know, sir.'

Franklin Josceleyne's expression was thunderous. 'At what time did she leave here?'

'I don't know, sir.'

'You don't know?' The man was incredulous.

'No, sir. But it must have been very early. Because when I went to wake her up this morning, she'd already gone.'

Emma felt a fit of giggling rising dangerously close to the surface as the little man began to stamp up and down the hallway in a tantrum, and she thought how closely his strutting resembled that of his nickname, the short-arsed rooster.

'Damn and blast the woman! Damn and blast her! Where the devil is she? She can never be found when I need to speak with her. Where the devil has the fool gone to?'

The thumping and bellowing from the old man's room

redoubled its fury and suddenly Franklin Josceleyne threw back his head and bawled at the ceiling, 'And you can stop making that noise, you stupid old fool!'

His shout brought fat Mrs Elwood rushing from the kitchen, calling out in an alarmed voice, 'What's the marrer? Has summat bad happened? What's the marrer?'

And Emma's suppressed glee erupted and she was forced to turn away, her shoulders heaving, and her hands pressed against her mouth in a futile effort to smother her laughter.

Franklin Josceleyne crashed out of the house, and from overhead the thumping and bellowing went on and on and Mrs Elwood stood staring in complete stupefaction at Emma, enquiring plaintively over and over again, 'What's the marrer? Has summat bad happened? What's the marrer?'

But Emma could only lean helplessly against the wall and laugh until her sides ached.

Slowly she calmed and wiped the tears from her eyes with the edge of her long apron. Overhead the old man's thumping and shouting had now ceased and, glancing at Mrs Elwood, Emma winked and jerked her head upwards. 'I hope he hasn't gone and bust a blood vessel.'

The other woman regarded her with mingled amusement and admiration. 'I dunno as how you dare carry on like you does, girl. But I'se got to hand it to you, you aren't bin here a month yet and already you'se got the old bugger eating out of your hands, and Miss Miriam as well, come to that. She thinks the sun shines out of your arse.'

'Well, if she does, she hasn't shown her gratitude by raising me wages yet, has she?' Emma observed dryly.

Mrs Elwood chuckled lewdly. 'I reckon you doon't need any raise in wages from her, my wench. I reckon youm making a fortune out on old Hector.'

Emma regarded her with shrewd eyes. 'Oh yes, what makes you think that, Mrs Elwood?'

The older woman winked broadly, but said nothing, and Emma felt a stirring of irritation. 'Come on, speak out what's in your mind,' she demanded tartly. 'Never mind just winking.'

'Wellll,' the fat face grinned broadly, 'I'se been here a good length o' time now, Emma, and youm the fust servant that the old man has ever took to church wi' him. You must have a powerful hold on the old sod, for him to do summat like that. Especially when his own son was dead set agen it.' She nodded wisely. 'I reckon you could do yourself a power o' good if you was to box a bit clever, my wench.'

'If you thinks that I'd let the old bugger make free with me for a few bob, then youm wrong, Mrs Elwood,' Emma spoke without any rancour. A girl born and bred in the Redditch slums inevitably came to view life realistically. She had personal knowledge of all too many cases where servant girls permitted their male employers to take sexual liberties in return for a few shillings, or a small present.

Mrs Elwood raised her hands defensively. 'No, me wench, youm taking me the wrong way. I knows you well enough to know that you 'udden't do such. You'se got too much about you for that. But, a girl wi' your looks, and your brains, can do very well for herself, iffen she boxes clever.'

Emma puffed out her breath with exasperation. 'Bugger me, but youm gooing the long way round, aren't you, Mrs Elwood. I wish you'd just speak plain.'

'All right!' Mrs Elwood nodded agreement. 'I 'ull spake plain. I'se bin watching you wi' the old man, and doon't forget that I knows him better nor you, because I'se bin in this house for a good many years. Now I'm agooing to tell you summat that you must keep to yourself. Does you promise me to do that?'

Emma was both intrigued and impressed by the seriousness with which the other woman was now speaking and she agreed readily. 'I promise, Mrs Elwood. I'll not breathe a word to anybody about what you tell me.'

The other woman stared intently at her, then nodded as if satisfied, and went on, 'The old man has always bin fond o' slipping his hand up young girls' skirts. It aren't only come about since his yed's started to goo funny. The bugger's always bin the same. But when his missus was alive, he had to keep himself in order, because she was a real Tartar, and it was she who had the money, and the property.'

She paused, and Emma urged, 'Goo on then.'

'All right!' the cook snapped impatiently. 'I'm only drawing a breath. Anyway, it's in my mind, that old Hector aren't as bloody daft as he makes himself out to be. I reckon he uses his bloody yampy-yeddedness as an excuse to do what he does with the servant girls. Charlotte and the rest on 'um used to tell me all about the tricks he got up to, but they was all frightened of him, they didn't know how to handle him like you does. I reckon that you could get him to do anything that you wanted him to. If you gets my meaning.'

She pursed her lips with a knowing expression on her fat face, and nodded at Emma.

Emma considered what she had heard, then grinned mischievously, and questioned mockingly, 'Does you reckon I could get him to marry me, Mrs Elwood?'

The older woman frowned as if annoyed by Emma's levity, and answered sharply, 'That's exactly what I does reckon, my wench. I'se watched the way he is with you, and the way he looks at you. The old fool's besotted with you girl. He'd do anything you wanted him to, iffen it meant he could get you into his bed.'

Her instant repulsion at the very thought of being sexually intimate with Hector Josceleyne caused Emma to shake her head and exclaim, 'Bugger that for a game of soldiers!'

She grimaced laughingly, twisting her mouth and shaking her head as if she had tasted something foul. 'Could you just imagine what he'd feel like on top of you. It 'ud be worse than being shagged by a bloody snake.'

She suddenly thought of Johnny Purvis's muscular body and couldn't help but tell the other woman, 'Now if it was Johnny Purvis you was talking about, then that 'ud be a different kettle of fish altogether.'

Mrs Elwood laughed and made salacious movements with her fingers. 'Well, my duck, you could always close your eyes and try to imagine it was Johnny Purvis on top of you while it was gooing on, couldn't you?' Another thought

177

made her screw up her eyes in merriment and gasp out, 'Mind you, it 'udden't goo on for very long 'ud it? I reckon if you gave one bounce of your arse and a quick squeeze wi' your legs then the old sod 'ud drop dead with a heart attack.'

Emma laughed also, and shook her head. 'No, I reckon I'd sooner wait and see if I can get Johnny Purvis to marry me.'

Beneath the girl's laughter Mrs Elwood detected a note of yearning, and she narrowed her eyes and stared shrewdly, then said quietly, 'Men like Johnny Purvis doon't marry penniless servant girls, my wench, no matter how pretty them girls might be. Men like Johnny Purvis, who from what I'se bin told 'as made his fortune, marries women who's got a bit of money and property to offer as well.'

She noted the change in Emma Farr's expression, and pressed on. 'Men like Johnny Purvis marries rich widows, not poor maids.'

Emma answered with apparent lighthearted indifference, 'Well then, it looks as if I'll just have to forget all about him, doon't it?'

Mrs Elwood was not fooled by that outward show. She chuckled and shook her head, 'Not if you was a rich widow, you needn't, my wench. Why, I reckon if you was a rich young widow, then Johnny Purvis 'ud be hammering on your door day and night.'

Emma gestured dismissively, as though she had lost interest in this conversation. 'Come and help me give the old man his bath. I can't spend all day talking nonsense.'

Her companion nodded agreeably. 'All right, my duck. Let me just goo and check me pots, and then I'll come up to you.'

Emma slowly mounted the stairs, and despite all attempts to wipe Mrs Elwood's words from her mind, found that she could not.

'Men like Johnny Purvis marries rich widows, not poor maids . . . Men like Johnny Purvis marries rich widows, not poor maids . . . Men like Johnny Purvis marries rich widows, not poor maids . . .'

Emma frowned as the thought reverberated in her head over and over and over again.

Chapter Twenty-Two

It was some minutes past noon when Johnny Purvis reached the Unicorn Inn. The news about the wager made beween him and Arthur Dolton had spread widely throughout the town, and the taproom was filled with curious onlookers. As Johnny entered the low-beamed room a hush fell and he remembered the day of his homecoming as once more his footsteps were all that broke the silence as he walked towards the bar-counter. The shirt-sleeved, aproned landlord, Thomas Hyde, asked him, 'What's your pleasure, Mr Purvis?'

'I'll take a glass of ale, please,' Johnny told him, then turned to face Arthur Dolton who was standing at the end of the bar flanked by his drinking cronies and other hangers on.

'I was beginning to think that you'd welshed on our bet, soldier boy,' the butcher said jeeringly. 'I thought the time agreed for settling up was twelve sharp.'

His meaty face was flushed and sweaty, and he stood with his customary arrogant attitude, his straw hat pushed onto the back of his sandy hair, his great belly bulging out the front of his waistcoat and hanging down over the top of his trousers.

Johnny Purvis regarded the man openly with cold distaste. He made no reply, only pulled out a small, well-filled, soft leather pouch from his pocket and tossed it onto the bar in front of Dolton, then turned away from the man and lifted the glass of ale to his lips.

The dark frothy liquid tasted good and Johnny gusted a sigh of satisfaction as he finished the drink and replaced the empty glass on the counter.

Thomas Hyde took the glass and refilled it, then placed it in front of Johnny. 'Here, Mr Purvis. This one's on me.'

When Johnny stared questioningly at him, the landlord grinned and nodded, 'I appreciates a man who can take his lumps without whining. Because from what I'se heard about that race, you should have won it by rights.'

A chorus of agreement sounded throughout the room, and hearing it Arthur Dolton scowled, 'My man was fust across the winning line, Tommy Hyde. That's good enough for me.'

His sycophants loudly supported him, glaring threateningly at those men in the room who voiced their protests at the butcher's statement.

Johnny Purvis had no wish to be the cause of trouble erupting, and he said evenly, 'I've no complaint to make about the result. What happened to me and young Barclay could have just as easily happened to Ozzie Clarke. As far as I'm concerned, Ozzie Clarke won; he crossed the line first. There's no more to be said about it.'

He drained the fresh glass in one long continuous swallow and set it down with a word of thanks to Thomas Hyde. He would have left at that point, but Arthur Dolton jeered loudly, 'Any time you fancies making another bet wi' me, soldier boy, then just say the word. I doubt you'll have the guts for it, 'ull you? I reckon you'se bin put fair and square into your place, aren't you.'

Again Johnny Purvis turned to face the other man. As he met Dolton's bloodshot eyes, he mentally saw again the bruises on Cleopatra Dolton's face. He knew with absolute certainty that it was Arthur Dolton's fists that had inflicted those bruises and for her sake he wanted to give this man a taste of his own brutal medicine.

In his mind he asked her wonderingly, 'How in hell's name could you ever have married a pig like this, Cleopatra Dolton?' He felt a confusing *mélange* of widely differing emotions seething within him. Angry disgust for Arthur Dolton and angry disgust directed at Cleopatra Dolton for having been willing to become the man's wife; jealousy that Dolton should possess such a beautiful woman; a poignant yearning for her and angry chagrin with himself for experiencing that yearning; but, above all else, one other emotion that with every passing moment became increasingly dominant: a fast burgeoning hatred for Arthur Dolton.

The butcher stared into Purvis's eyes and a sudden wariness caused him to clench his fists. With that wariness came a pulse of fear. He could see murder in Purvis's eyes and at this moment in time he blessed the fact that he was surrounded by his cronies and sycophants who could be relied upon to join in on his side should the other man assault him physically.

Johnny Purvis's lust to do just that was tearing at him with a ferocious savagery that he was hard put to keep in check. Here his past experience of life stood him in good stead. He realised that if he struck Dolton then he would be immediately swamped by the other man's cronies and, tough and strong though he was, Johnny knew that he would stand no chance against such overwhelming odds. Nevertheless, despite all those odds ranged against him, he was still determined to humiliate Dolton here and now. So he grinned ferociously and took a single step towards the group; his action caused them to stiffen and tense visibly. 'Yes, Dolton, I'm willing to make another bet with you.' Johnny Purvis deliberately raised his voice so that everyone in the room could hear him. 'Only this time I want to make a match directly beween us, that we can bet on. Directly between you and me, Dolton, not between me and your hired help.' He paused so that the listeners would appreciate the emphasis of his next words. 'Have you got the guts to try and match me man to man, Dolton? Shall we say for two hundred sovereigns a side? Or is that too rich for your blood?'

'No it aren't!' Dolton blustered. 'I'll put two hundred sovereigns down on the table any time.'

'That's good.' Johnny felt a savage satisfaction and from the inside pocket of his jacket he pulled out another small soft leather pouch, which bulged with the heavy gold coins. 'There's two hundred sovereigns in here.' He held the pouch high so that all could see it, then slammed it down on the counter. 'I'm challenging you in front of all these chaps to make a match against me, man to man.'

Dolton's thick liver lips parted slightly, and his coated tongue licked nervously against them. 'What sort o' match?' he questioned uncertainly. 'Doing what?'

Johnny Purvis deliberately scoffed. 'Why, doing anything that you think you might be capable of beating me in.' He pointed to the butcher's overhanging belly. 'I doubt you'll manage to run any distance carrying that, will you, and if you wanted to make a horseback race against me, then you'd need to find a horse with a backbone made from steel.' He shook his head contemptuously. 'No, Dolton, you aren't capable of matching me in any sort of race, are you? So what other sort of contest do you think you might stand a chance against me?'

'Ateing and drinking?' a wag suggested, and the crowd roared with laughter.

'Plugging a wellshaft with your bellies?'

'Blocking a railway tunnel with your arses?'

'Rolling downhill?'

'Being rendered down for the most tubs o' lard?'

Each facetious suggestion brought fresh gales of laughter and Arthur Dolton's meaty features almost purpled with rage at being made an object of mockery.

Then one of his cronies suggested, 'Why doon't you box him, Arthur?'

Immediately the rest of his party added their urgings to this suggestion. 'Yes, that's it, Arthur. Take the bugger on with your fists.'

'You'll bloody murder him, Arthur.'

'Take him on, Arthur. Yoom the hardest man in this town.'

Thomas Hyde caught Johnny Purvis's attention and raised his eyebrows in silent query. The younger man winked and nodded, and the landlord shouted loudly, 'Let's have a bit of hush! Quiet! Quiet now!'

The crowd fell silent, and the landlord, who in his youth had been a prizefighter himself, stated, 'If both parties are willing, then we'll do it proper. With a ring, timekeepers and seconds. I'll organise it all meself.'

He asked the two men, 'How about it, am you chaps

183

willing to make a boxing match between you?'

Johnny Purvis nodded readily, inwardly exalting. This was precisely what he had wanted to happen. A straight fight between them where Dolton's cronies would not be able to intervene.

Arthur Dolton agreed with a show of confidence. 'That'll do for me. The sooner the better.'

His cronies cheered and applauded him, and he swaggeringly raised his clasped fists and shook them as if in triumph. But beneath his bluster, he was more than a little fearful. Johnny Purvis was obviously fit and strong, but apart from these physical attributes there was an indefinable quality about the man which made would-be aggressors wary of crossing him. It was as if beneath the façade of pleasant good manners, there lay hidden a ruthless ferocity that, once unleashed, would exact a terrible price before it could be enchained once more.

In an effort to dispel his own fears Arthur Dolton endeavoured to put up a bold front. 'I'll make raw liver out o' this bugger,' he blustered.

Johnny Purvis smiled contemptuously and said to Thomas Hyde, 'Here's my stake money.' He placed the leather pouch on the counter in front of the landlord and turned to Dolton. 'Right then, let's do it now. Let's you and I settle it right here, man to man.'

'We'll do the thing proper,' Thomas Hyde said excitedly. 'We can have it in my yard at the back theer and I'll act as the referee and stake-holder meself. Does that suit you both?' he asked the two protagonists.

Johnny Purvis nodded, but Arthur Dolton seemed hesitant.

'Well Arthur, what about it?' Thomas Hyde pressed.

The butcher's eyes flickered furtively around the room, as if seeking a way of escape. Now that the moment had come to actually fight Johnny Purvis man to man his courage was fast deserting him. In desperation he tried to bluster his way out.

'I'd like nothing better, Tommy, but right now I can't fight this flash bugger. I hurt me back yesterday when I was shifting some sides o' beef. It'ull have to wait until I'm recovered.'

The men crowding around the bar exchanged meaningful glances. Most present silently exalting in seeing the butcher showing cowardice by avoiding this fight with such a lame excuse.

Johnny Purvis hissed in contempt and picked up his stake money.

'I'll just have to wait until a later date then, won't I?' he said quietly, and walked towards the outer door.

'I'm looking forward to trimming your lamps for you, soldier boy,' Arthur Dolton shouted after him. 'After I'm done wi' you, you'll wish you'd never come back here with all your bloody lies about what you did in South Africa. Youm gooing to find out what a real fight is like.'

Johnny could not restrain himself. He swung about and gritted from between his clenched teeth, 'And so are you, fat man. It won't be like hammering your poor wife. You won't be beating a defenceless woman. You'll be getting a taste of your own medicine.'

Arthur Dolton's features became livid. 'What's you saying about my missus?' he growled.

'I'm saying nothing against her,' Johnny gritted out. 'I'm telling you that I'm going to give you a taste of what you give her.'

'How does you know what happens beween me and my missus?' the butcher demanded.

'I've seen the bruises on her face,' Johnny told him. 'The bruises that you've put there.'

'Is that what her says?' Dolton's expression was murderous. 'Is that what her tells you? That I'm giving her bruises?'

'She doesn't need to tell me,' Johnny hissed. 'I can see plainly enough. So don't think you've managed to wriggle your way out of fighting me, Dolton. Because I intend to have you one way or another. And it'll be as much for her sake, as for my own. I don't like cowards who batter defenceless women. And I don't like you in particular, you gutless bastard.'

He swung around and walked from the room leaving a buzzing, seething excited crowd behind him.

Chapter Twenty-Three

The massive ox carcass slowly revolved and the juices exuding from the flesh dripped down onto the glowing bed of coals exploding in tiny gouts of smoke and flame. The heavy succulent scents of roasting meat hung on the warm air, and spread across the field where the crowds wandered amid the stalls and roundabouts of the fair. A steam organ pumped out gay waltzes and polkas and the raucous-voiced showmen grew hoarse as they shouted in competition against each other and the loud music.

'Hoop-la! Hoop-la! Hoop-la! Finest prizes in the land. Hoop-la! Hoop-la! Hoop-la!'

'Coconuts, three balls a penny! Coconuts, three balls a penny!'

'Try your luck now! Try your luck on Fortune's Wheel! Come on sir, come on ma'am, try your luck now! Try your luck!'

'Who can knock orf Kruger's yed? Who can knock orf Kruger's yed? A golden sovereign to be won, my lords, ladies and gentlemen! A golden sovereign to the fust one to knock orf Kruger's yed!'

Miriam Josceleyne wandered through the fairground, holding a bag of ginger snaps in her hands, from which she took crinkly crisp oily golden pieces and crunched them between her sharp teeth, revelling in their hot sweet flavour. She stopped by a small carousel of garishly painted wooden horses with fierce glass eyes and flying manes, and chuckled to see the delighted shrieking children riding round and round and round, while the sweating showman's head bobbed up and down as he turned the wheel that powered their steeds.

Beyond the carousel the shining pipes of the steam organ towered skywards and on an open stretch of grass before it young girls and boys danced and skipped to the strains of a polka. When the polka gave place to a waltz, older women and men took their partners and swung and circled as gaily and gracefully as any citizens of old Vienna.

Miriam moved across to watch the dancers with a smile of pleasure, mentally super-imposing splendid uniforms and ball-gowns upon the suits and blouses, skirts and blazers, the flat flowered hats, the bowlers, boaters and caps. She found her neat-booted feet beginning to tap in rhythm with the music and she wished with all her heart that she could be one of these dancers.

'Pardon me, miss.' A tall, rosy-cheeked, young countryman in a belted Norfolk jacket, baggy flat cap and high stiff collar, touched his cap peak politely. 'Would you dance with me please?'

Miriam stared at him in shock, and he grinned at her engagingly, showing widespaced white teeth.

'I'm not meaning to be forward, miss, or disrespectful, but all me mates have got partners, and I've been practising me dancing for months now, and aren't had a chance to try me steps out.'

She still stared at him with wide eyes and he coaxed, 'Come on, miss. Please give me just one dance. Arter all this is the Coronation Fair, aren't it? And that doon't come around very often, does it?'

Recovering from her initial surprise, Miriam's instinctive reaction was to refuse him indignantly. But then, to her own amazement, she allowed impulse to rule her, and smiled and nodded acceptance.

Still clasping her brown paper bag of ginger snaps, she allowed him to lead her onto the open space, and let herself be swept into the dance.

The young man moved confidently and well, and Miriam, after a brief initial stiffness, suddenly relaxed, allowing her long-suppressed natural talent as a dancer to reassert itself and the sheer enjoyment of the swirling rhythm to dominate her completely.

She closed her eyes and existed solely in a world of

187

music and movement. Polka followed waltz and waltz followed polka. Miriam lost all sense of time and in her mind was once again the gay, lighthearted young girl she once had been.

At length the sheer weariness engendered by such sustained unaccustomed exercise forced her back to the present; she came to a reluctant halt and told the young man, 'Thank you very much, sir, for partnering me. I must leave now.'

His face was shiny with heat and perspiration as he grinned at her. 'Can't you stay and keep me company for a while longer, miss? I'll take you on the swingboats and the roundabouts if you like. Me name's Joe Harper. What's your name?'

It took several seconds for Miriam to realise the full import of what the young man had said to her. She did not know whether she was flattered or offended by his invitation.

'It's all right, miss.' He saw the doubt in her expression and hastened to reassure her. 'I'm a respectable chap, with a steady job. I aren't a loose living sort at all. Only I saw you watching the dancers, and I thought how pretty you looked, so I wanted to get to know you. I hopes you aren't offended by me telling you so.'

Miriam could only continue to stand and stare at him in silence, while in her mind she struggled to understand her own reactions to his words. 'If he had said this to me yesterday, I would have been mortally offended,' she marvelled silently. 'Yet here I am, feeling somehow pleased and flattered that this working man who must be much younger than I and is a complete stranger has shown such lack of respect for my position, that he has dared to invite me to accompany him as if I were some silly little servant girl. Dear God, I've gone mad! I really must have gone mad!'

She blushed in confusion and rising embarrassment, and the young man could only stare at her in puzzlement.

'Youm not offended, am you?' he questioned with some anxiety. 'Believe me, I warn't meaning you any insult. I can see that youm a ladylike sort of girl, and I respect you for that. Truly I does. You'll be safe wi' me. I won't try and take any liberties wi' you. I swear to that.'

Miriam drew a long breath, and exerted all her willpower to re-establish control over her rampaging emotions. She shook her head. 'I don't doubt but that I would be safe with you, Mr Harper. I am grateful to you for your kind invitation, but I'm sorry, I must refuse it. I have to go now.'

His rosy face showed disappointment, and for a fleeting second she was tempted to accept his invitation to accompany him around the fair, but then she ruthlessly called a halt to her own wayward impulses, and with a muttered farewell, hurried away from him.

As she threaded through the crowds she felt her cheeks burning hotly, embarrassment mortified her as she thought how she had so shamelessly danced with a stranger in front of so many onlookers.

'God help me, but I've been behaving as loosely as any factory girl. What must people have thought of me?'

But even as she asked the question her sense of mortified embarrassment was rapidly ebbing and being overlayed by the recollection of how much she had enjoyed dancing with the young man. And her rediscovered, rebellious self-assertiveness flooded back. 'I don't really care what anyone thought of me. Besides, they were all strangers to me anyway, so what does it matter? For once in my life I've thoroughly enjoyed myself. So damn them all!'

By the time she was walking the road back towards Redditch, some three miles distant, she was pleasurably recalling how the young man had admired her, and wanted to come to know her better. In her mind she triumphantly told her brother, 'There now, Franklin. I'm not such a dried-up old maid, after all. That young man was quite presentable. All right, he was low class, I admit, but he was still very presentable and gentlemanly despite that.'

She smiled happily to herself. 'He thought I was pretty, didn't he?' The recollection encompassed her like a warm comforting embrace. 'That young man thought I was very pretty.'

She found that she was still clutching the paper bag of ginger snaps and with immense gusto she started to crunch the last remaining delicious golden pieces.

It was twilight when Miriam Josceleyne reached the town centre. Again Church Green and the main streets were ablaze with coloured lights and festive crowds promenaded. Although she was now weary and footsore, Miriam was still in a state of elated excitement from her adventures of the day and could not bear the thought of going straight to her home. Instead she joined the crowds and wandered slowly along Evesham Street to view the various displays. She was honest enough to admit to herself that the main reason for her present wanderings was the hope that she might encounter Johnny Purvis, and with her new-found confidence she knew that for once she would be able to greet him without any diffidence or self-consciousness.

At the end of Evesham Street on the bottom slope of Front Hill she halted to admire the rival illuminations of the gas and electric companies. All around her people mingled, exchanging greetings and jokes and laughter, and Miriam felt a sudden sense of acute loneliness. It seemed that in all this crowd, only she was solitary. Sadness touched her and she turned to retrace her steps towards Church Green. In front of her a young couple walked with entwined hands, and smiled lovingly at each other as they snatched a brief kiss. Miriam envied them their happiness and experienced a poignant painful yearning for such a relationship of loving closeness. Her eyes brimmed with tears as she thought of her own desolate life.

Then she felt a touch on her shoulder and for a brief instant she imagined it was Johnny Purvis who had touched her. She turned with a radiant smile that faltered and stilled when she saw that it was another man who had come behind her.

'Why Miss Josceleyne, thith ith a pleasant thurprise.' James Whitehead's ill-fitting false teeth had momentarily slipped as he greeted her, causing him to lisp and cover his mouth with his bowler hat, shuffling his feet in embarrassment.

190

Intensely disappointed though she was, Miriam Joscel-eyne could still pity the man, and sought to put him at his ease. 'Good evening, Mr Whitehead,' she forced herself to greet him pleasantly. 'They make a fine show, do they not?' She indicated the various displays and decorations, deliber-ately staring at the lights to give him opportunity to adjust his dentures.

Behind his hat he had managed to do this and now he agreed eagerly, 'Indeed they do, Miss Josceleyne. I've never seen anything to match such a brilliance in all my life.'

They stood facing each other in an uncomfortable silence for several seconds, and then Miriam told him, 'I'm return-ing to my home, Mr Whitehead, so I'll bid you goodnight.'

His own disappointment showed clearly in his expres-sion, and almost desperately he asked, 'Might I accompany you, Miss Josceleyne? I'm going home myself, and we must walk in the same direction, must we not.'

'Ah well, it seems that I am now back to reality,' Miriam thought sadly, dismissing her hopes of meeting John Purvis. Aloud she accepted, 'Very well, Mr Whitehead. We can walk homewards together.'

His plump clean-shaven features beamed with pleasure, and as they walked side by side along Evesham Street he talked garrulously in a vain effort to entertain her.

Only half listening to his long-winded accounts of his attendances at the Band of Hope, and the St Stephen's Temperance Society, Miriam felt all her earlier elation and excitement inexorably drain away and the customary mind-deadening boredom that this man evoked in her began to wrap its crushing tentacles around her spirits.

Inwardly she ruefully comforted herself, 'It's only a few hundred yards to walk. I'll soon be free.'

Then a tiny voice jeered in her mind, 'Free to do what, Miriam? Sit by yourself in a silent dreary room? Sit in your usual solitude? That's what you'll be free to do, isn't it? Sit by yourself and be lonely and miserable. That's what you'll be free to do.'

Chapter Twenty-Four

The pale gaslight bathed Cleopatra Dolton's naked body as she unpinned her hair and let it fall about her face and shoulders like a dark cloud. She stared at her reflection in the dressing table mirror as she drew the brush through the long glossy strands, and whispered, 'Why do you look as you do?'

Her physical appearance had always been a subject that had fascinated her. Always she had wondered about her ancestry. From whom had she inherited her dark, sultry beauty? Her father had been of blue-eyed, fair-skinned Saxon stock, as had her mother. Cleopatra had heard sufficient about her mother from the older people in Silver Street to be certain that she was her father's child, and had not come from the loins of some casual lover her mother had taken into her bed.

'Perhaps you're a changeling? An elf-child left by the fairies,' she accused her reflection, and smiled at the fanciful thought, remembering how when she was only a small child an elderly neighbour had once accused her of being that very same thing.

Her thoughts now turned to her own children and she frowned unhappily. All three of them had inherited her own physical colourings. The dark hair and eyes and swarthy complexion. Sadly, they had not inherited her robust health and native toughness, but were all three of them prone to illness and of weakly physique. These were attributes which their father bitterly resented, as if it were an aspersion on his own manliness, just as he resented their timidity and their gentle natures.

Cleopatra's frown deepened. Arthur Dolton had wanted

sons made in his own image: big, blustering, brutal bullies.

The clock on the wall behind her whirred and chimed and she counted the hours.

' . . . eight, nine, ten, eleven. He'll be home soon.' Her full lips drew back in an ugly snarl. 'The drunken pig will be back. I just hope that he won't want me tonight.'

A shudder of repulsion passed through her as she visualised his gross body and slobbering lips.

'I wish he'd find himself a woman, so that he wouldn't want me any more.' Again the ugly snarl disfigured her mouth. 'Or better yet, that he'd die, then I could be sure that I'd never again have to suffer him on top of me.'

She went on brushing her long hair; the rhythmic action slowly soothed her strained nerves and enabled her to think more rationally. Cleopatra Dolton possessed the capacity to be ruthlessly honest with herself, and now, in a calmer mood, she could accept the fact that in some measure she had contributed towards the present abysmal state of her marital relationship.

'I'm a victim,' she told herself now, 'but in a sense, Arthur Dolton is a victim also.'

Arthur Dolton's family had been respectable tradespeople with an established business, and he had been expected by them to marry someone from his own class. She knew that he had married her despite the virulent opposition of his family to the match. She knew also that he had been the subject of ridicule and sneering contempt among his own peer group for marrying a girl from the slums, who had borne an illegitimate child.

She smiled mirthlessly. 'In a way, I could almost feel sorry for him.'

She remembered how slavishly besotted with her he had once been, and how she had so perversely teased and tormented him, glorying in the power she wielded over him.

'I suppose that if I had wanted to, I could have ensured that our marriage was bearable enough. We could have moved away to another town, where no one knew about my background and he wouldn't have had to put up with all the aggravation of knowing that people were laughing and sneering at him behind his back for having wed me. He wanted to move, didn't he, but I wouldn't have it.'

A fleeting sense of guilt assailed her at the thought of that refusal. Then she angrily thrust it from her. 'Why should I have to move to escape from what people said about me? It wasn't my fault that my own father was such an animal, was it? It wasn't my fault that I was born in a slum. I've never shown him up since we've been married. I've always conducted myself like a lady.'

Her anger redirected itself towards Arthur Dolton. 'It's his fault that he wasn't strong enough to accept what had happened to me before I knew him. I told him that I'd had a child and he said that it didn't matter to him. He still wanted to wed me. I was always honest with him.'

'Oh no! You weren't always honest with him,' another side of her mind flatly contradicted. 'Do you remember how you told him that you loved him, when all the time you saw him as a way out of Silver Street, a way out of poverty, a way to be respectable?'

She tugged at a knot of hair in sudden irritation, then mentally shrugged. 'All right then, I lied to him about being in love with him, but I liked him well enough when he was courting me. When we were first married I went to his bed willingly enough, didn't I?'

Again her memories spanned the years. Arthur Dolton had not been so fat and gross then. Although he was a crude and rough lover, she had been able to accept his physical intimacy and even at times to respond to and enjoy his body. But after the birth of her second son, James, she had begun to feel a repulsion for sexual contact and had tried to reject her husband's demands, eventually to the extent of sleeping in a separate room. Because she had never felt more than a casual liking for Arthur Dolton, she had no reservoir of love to draw from, which would have enabled her to tolerate his need of her, or to soften his resentment of rejection by showing him tenderness in other ways. Arthur Dolton himself had been baffled and angered by his wife's rejection, her refusal of what he considered to be his rightful demands upon her body. All the brutish tendencies in his nature, which in his early marriage he had tried to keep hidden, were now brought to the surface because of his sexual frustration. He had begun to drink more heavily and in drink to assert his sexual demands by force. So the situation between them had inevitably worsened at an ever-accelerating pace.

The front door opened and then slammed shut with force enough to cause the gaslight to waver momentarily. Cleopatra Dolton experienced a fast mounting dread as she heard the sound of a heavy body colliding with the hallway table and sending the silver tray that stood upon it clanging on to the floor.

'He's drunk.' She rose from her dressing table and snatched up a long robe to cover her nakedness. For a brief moment she debated whether to turn off the gaslight, and lie in bed as if she were asleep. But even as she thought of this, almost simultaneously she dismissed it, knowing how futile it would prove if Arthur Dolton was hungry for her body.

She sat down on the dressing table stool facing the door and steeled herself for what was to come. 'I'll not argue with him or try to prevent him, and then it will be over quicker,' she decided, amazed at herself for how calmly she was able to face the prospect of sexual union with this man that she hated and despised.

She heard his footsteps passing along the passageway that led to the kitchen, and a wild hope that he might sit at the table there and fall asleep sprang up in her.

Then she grimaced. 'That would be too much to hope for, wouldn't it?' She waited resignedly for the heavy footsteps to come thumping erratically up the stairs, as she had waited so many times before through the long years.

Her thoughts began to wander haphazardly. Suddenly she visualised the face of Johnny Purvis and recollected the effect of the moments they had spent in close proximity to each other outside the Royal Hotel.

Despite the present despondency of her mood, she was able to smile grimly to herself, 'Now if Johnny Purvis was coming up the stairs towards me, I'd have the door open ready for him.'

Then the flash of gallows humour fled as quickly as it

had come, as she heard Arthur Dolton come back from the kitchen and begin to mount the stairs. Her previous calm resignation threatened to desert her and she shivered slightly as a tremor of nervous dread struck her. But she fought it down and mustered her courage, so that when her bedroom door finally swung open and Arthur Dolton entered, she was able to meet him with steady eyes.

He stood glowering at her, breathing harshly through his open mouth and saying nothing, until she felt an increasing nervousness and was impelled to ask him, 'What's the matter, Arthur? Why do you look at me so?'

'What's the matter? Why do you look at me so?' He broke his silence to savagely mimic her. 'What's the matter, Arthur?'

He was behaving in a manner that she had never witnessed before, and its very novelty was unnerving to her.

His head moved from side to side and when he spoke it was as if he were addressing an invisible audience. 'Just listen to this fuckin' cow, 'ull you! What's the matter, Arthur? What's the matter, Arthur? Just listen to her! What's the matter, Arthur? What's the matter?'

Her nervousness became actual fear and she rose and stood tensed, while her heart thudded frantically.

'You'se found yourself a fancy man,' he accused hoarsely, and she stared at him in complete bewilderment.

'Oh yes, I knows all about it.' He grinned ferociously and nodded his head rapidly. 'I knows about it. Oh yes, I knows all right!'

Cleopatra's own head shook in denial. 'No! That's not true!'

'Just listen to her, 'ull you!' Again it was as if he was demanding the attention of an invisible audience. 'Can you hear her? No, she says! No, it aren't the truth! She aren't got a bloody fancy man!'

His bloodshot eyes locked onto her face and he growled menacingly, 'I knows it's the truth, you fuckin' whore! Because he's as good as told me to me face that he's your fancy man.'

She shook her head wildly, 'Who's told you? Who's told you such a thing? It's not true! It's not true!'

'Oh yes it is. He's showed me up in front of the whole fuckin' town, so he has! Blaggardin' me in public for beating you! As if a man's got no right to give his own missus a smack in the chops when her deserves it. And by Christ, you deserves it often enough, doon't you, you fuckin' cow!' His voice rose to a roar, 'You dirty fuckin' whore!'

Despite her fear, Cleopatra could still remember her children, and be fearful for the effect this scene would be having on them, should they be awake. 'Please, Arthur, don't wake the kids!' she begged him. 'Don't scare them!'

'Why? Aren't they got the rights to know what a dirty fuckin' whore their own mam is?' he demanded to know, but his voice was quieter now, as though her pleas had taken effect.

She drew a shuddering breath, and asked, 'Who is it? Who is this fancy man you're accusing me of having?'

'It's that fuckin' toy soldier, aren't it. That fuckin' Johnny Purvis!' Saliva sprayed from Dolton's liver lips as he stepped towards her and, gripping her shoulders with brutal hands, began to shake her violently. 'It's him, aren't it? It's that fucker?'

'No! It's not true! I haven't got any fancy man!' Still fearful for her children, Cleopatra choked the words out as loudly as she dared.

'I'm gooing to teach you a real lesson this time!' Arthur Dolton's face was maniacal with hatred as he snarled like some rabid animal.

He wrapped one hand in her long loose hair, so that she was powerless to move her head, and then tore the long gown from her body with his other hand. With a brutal tug that threatened to tear the hair from its roots he forced her to her knees, then with his free hand he unbuckled the thick leather belt he wore around his great belly.

Still grasping her hair to keep her trapped he whirled the belt high above his head and then brought it slashing down across the tender flesh of her back. The heavy metal buckle bit deep into her soft skin and blood instantly welled from the cut. The pain was like a white-hot iron

197

tearing into Cleopatra, and she screamed out, then thinking of her children, she snatched the robe from the floor and crammed it into her mouth, to muffle her cries as the belt whirled high and slashed down, whirled and slashed down again and again and again and again.

Chapter Twenty-Five

Johnny Purvis spent a restless night, drifting in and out of shallow sleep, troubled by strange eerie dreams in which he continually heard a woman's piercing screams and cries for help, but, struggle as he might, was powerless to break out from a dark mist that enveloped him, and so could not find her or go to her aid.

When he finally awoke, the grey light of early dawn was penetrating through the gap in the curtains of his room at the Plough and Harrow Hotel, and he lay on his back staring up at the ceiling, trying to understand why he should be gripped by a mood of anxious foreboding.

Johnny Purvis was a sensitive and intelligent man; he had experienced and witnessed too many strange happenings in his life to carelessly dismiss such unaccountable sensations of foreboding as being of no import, or caused merely by something he had eaten or drunk.

Getting out of bed he pulled on a dressing gown and went to the bathroom further along the landing. While the bath filled with hot water from the foul-smelling, loud-hissing gas geyser, he brushed his teeth and shaved with his old army issue cut-throat razor. Then, while soaking in the steaming bathwater, he thought carefully about the possible reasons for his strange dreams and strong sense of foreboding.

'I wonder if Cleopatra Dolton is all right? Could it have been her screaming in my dreams? Has her husband been beating her again?'

A loud knocking sounded on the bathroom door, and a woman's voice called, 'Who's that in theer?'

'It's Johnny Purvis, Mary,' Johnny recognised the voice

as belonging to one of the hotel servants.

''Ull you be wanting a full breakfast when youm finished in theer?'

'No thank you, Mary. Just a pot of coffee in my room, please.'

'All right, my duck. I'll goo and fetch it up for you now.'

The woman went away and Johnny grinned to himself at her use of the endearment. He had known the middle-aged woman, Mary Phelan, when he had been a young boy and he realised that despite his present affluence, and his status as a guest renting the hotel's finest rooms, to her he would always be the young Johnny Purvis of Izods Yard.

He towelled himself briskly, enjoying the tingling in his skin and the feeling of being refreshed and energised that his bath had given him. His earlier sense of foreboding was fast receding and he had a busy day ahead of him. But he still promised himself that he would make discreet enquiries as to Cleopatra Dolton's well-being. It had been a woman who had been screaming and crying in his dreams, and he gave sufficient credence to such dreams to feel concern for her.

The jug of coffee was in his room when he returned there, together with a bowl of lump sugar and a smaller jug of cream. Johnny poured and stirred his first cupful and sipped it slowly, savouring its strong hot sweetness. Then he lit up a thin cheroot, drew the fragrant smoke deep into his lungs, and for a time sat in perfect contentment, alternately sipping his coffee and taking pulls on the cheroot.

During his absence the previous afternoon, several parcels of clothing had been delivered by Billy Bunegar and after his breakfast of coffee and tobacco, Johnny unwrapped the parcels and examined the various articles they had contained. For some time he tried on his new clothes in front of the large wall mirror, and mentally gave the Bunegars full credit for their tailoring skills.

He dressed in a dark-green tweed lounge jacket, waistcoat and trousers, high collar and cravat, highly polished bootees, with a wide brimmed soft black felt hat on his close-cropped head, and took a light whangee cane in his kid-gloved hand when he left his rooms.

On the stairs leading to the front door of the hotel he met Mary, the middle-aged servant, and she stared at him admiringly. 'Youm looking like a real toff, my duck. A bit different from when you was living in Izods Yard.'

He laughed with genuine amusement, and teased her, 'You really ought to be calling me Mr Purvis, Mary, not addressing me as my duck.'

She grinned, displaying her blackened stubs of teeth, and good-naturedly scoffed, 'Gerroff wi' you. I tanned your arse too many times when you was a nipper, to start calling you mister now.'

He held up his hands in mock surrender. 'All right, Mary. I give in.'

'Am you coming back for your dinner today. Or 'ull you be gallivanting round the town instead?'

'I'll be gallivanting, Mary,' he smiled and touched the brim of his hat with his cane. 'I bid you good day, ma'am.'

'Gerroff wi' you, you young varmint! Or I'll lay that bloody cane across your arse, big as you am!' She pretended to cuff him, and laughing they parted.

In Izods Yard Johnny found his father up and dressed, and immediately he entered the tiny living room the older man angrily berated him, 'What's this I hear about you and Arthur Dolton gooing to fight? Why am you still behaving like a hooligan? Aren't you got any sense at all in your yed? Youm acting like a town scruff. It's time you started to act like a grown man deserving of respect. You aren't in the army now, you know. It might be all right for redcoats to brawl and kick up a ruction, but it aren't fitting for a respectable man to do such.'

Johnny mentally acknowledged the continued efficiency of the town's bush telegraph. It was an old adage in Redditch, if a man on one edge of the town had bacon and eggs for breakfast, then before he had finished eating them another man living on the opposite edge of the town would be able to say which pig and which hen that bacon and eggs had originated from.

He sat patiently until the older man's tirade had come to

an end, then said quietly, 'I had no real choice in the matter, Dad. Arthur Dolton has been insulting me ever since I came back home. I'm going to give him the hiding he deserves. From all accounts he should have had it years ago. He's one of the town's bullies, isn't he?'

Old Ezra grudgingly admitted the truth of this statement, and Johnny pressed his advantage. 'Well then, Dad, what would you have me do? Would you think better of me if I'd have turned my collar to him? Can you truthfully tell me that you'd want me to act the coward?'

'O' course I 'udden't,' the old man gestured impatiently, then hesitated for a couple of seconds, before saying with obvious concern, 'Listen, son, it's not the fact o' gooing to fight wi' Arthur Dolton that's giving me cause for worry. God only knows, I'se used me fists a few times meself when I was a younger man. It aren't that that's moithering me at all. It's the reason that youm gooing to fight wi' him that's troubling me.'

Johnny shook his head in puzzlement. 'I really don't understand what you're talking about, Dad.'

Ezra Purvis showed a flash of anger. 'Doon't you come the innocent wi' me, boy!'

Johnny frowned and told him emphatically, 'I'm not trying to come anything with you, Dad. But you'll have to speak plain and make your meaning clear, if you want me to understand you.'

'It's as plain as a pikestaff, boy,' his father snorted. 'As plain as a pikestaff! The good Book tells us, "Thou shalt not covet thy neighbour's wife!" doon't it?'

Dismay flooded through Johnny Purvis as he realised the implications of what his father had just said to him. Frowning, he demanded, 'What exactly are people saying, Dad? Come on now, I want the full account.'

In his turn his father frowned unhappily, and told him quietly, 'People am saying that you and Arthur Dolton am gooing to fight because youm his wife's fancy man.'

Johnny sighed disgustedly and slowly shook his head. 'That's nonsense, Dad. I've hardly exchanged more than a dozen words with the woman, and even those words have been spoken when other people were present. It's absolute nonsense.'

Ezra Purvis stared hard at his son for several seconds, then satisfied, he told him, 'I believe you son, but you know what this town's like for gossip and bad mouthing, doon't you? It was Mrs Hicks who come running to tell me what was being said and that was yesterday afternoon, so God only knows what they'm saying about you by now.'

Again John Purvis sighed heavily. Then he shrugged his broad shoulders.

'Whatever they might say about me, Dad, can't do me any real harm, can it? I'm beholden to nobody in this town for anything. Eventually people will come to know that it's only false gossip anyway. What worries me is the effect it might have for that poor woman. Arthur Dolton gives her a terrible time already, from all accounts, and I've seen the bruises on her face myself that he's given her.'

'A man's got a right to chastise his own wife,' Ezra Purvis stated positively. 'And Arthur Dolton's wife comes from bad stock. It nigh on killed his old dad and mam when he got wed to her. She'd already had one bastard. I doon't doubt but that she deserves whatever her gets from him.'

Although Johnny totally disagreed with what his father was saying concerning a man's right to beat his wife, he didn't make any attempt to argue the point. He knew that the old man was merely voicing a widely held conviction, a conviction deeply entrenched in the minds of many men from all ranks of society, and, hard to credit though it might be, also shared by many women.

Realising that at this time he was powerless to do anything to aid Cleopatra Dolton, Johnny could only silently pray that things might not get too hard for her. To change the subject, he asked his father, 'Have you thought any more about what I asked you, Dad. About coming to live with me in Grange House?'

'I have, son, and the answer is no,' the old man told him, then explained, 'I want to end my days in this house, son. Where I was happy with your Mam for so many years. It's filled with my memories you see. If I moved to Grange House, then I'd be leaving my memories behind, wouldn't I? And I couldn't bear to do that. They'm all

I'se got left to me now.'

'You would still have your memories, Dad,' Johnny argued gently. 'And I'd be there for company when you needed it. You'd have your own rooms for when you wanted privacy. I'm going to have both the gas and electric fitted there, and have the place modernised so that you can be really comfortable. I'm sure that once you've made the move, then you'll be happy.'

Old Ezra shook his head. 'No, boy. I knows you means well and I thank you for it, but I wants to stay here. It aren't only memories, you know, son. Theer's times when your mam comes here to be with me. She'd never do that again iffen I was to move up to Grange House. She could never abide big houses you know.' He chuckled hoarsely and his rheumed eyes were tender. 'Her always said that it was when her was in service wi' the Windsor-Clives up at Hewell theer, that her began to hate big houses. She always told me that on the day her left that house to marry me, she swore a solemn oath that she'd never agen step foot inside a big house.' He smiled broadly at the younger man. 'And does you know, son, her never did, not from that day on. Never once. So it stands to reason that her aren't about to change her mind now, is her?' He shook his head again. 'No son, thank you all the same, but I'm agoing to stay here, wi' your mam.'

A lump had risen in John Purvis's throat as his father told him the story, and his eyes blurred with tears. He swallowed hard, then stood up and patted the old man's fragile bony shoulder. 'All right, Dad. I'll not press you to do anything you don't want to do. I'll have to go now because I've a lot of matters to attend to. So I'll come and see you tomorrow.'

When he left the small terraced cottage Johnny Purvis called in at another cottage some distance further along the yard.

A rosy-cheeked, motherly looking woman answered to his knock and invited him in. Ever since his return home Johnny had been paying her well to keep an unobtrusive watch on the old man and to see to those domestic matters that Ezra could not manage himself. Knowing his father's fierce pride and virulent hatred of what he considered to be demeaning charity, Johnny had been forced to arrange matters secretly, so that his father did not suspect that he was being cared for in this way.

After a short conversation Johnny handed the woman, Mrs Bint, some money, and went on his way.

As he strolled along Evesham Street Ozzie Clarke came out from the butcher's shop to accost him. 'How bist, John?' He was grinning broadly, and Johnny could not help but return the grin.

'I'm fine, Ozzie, and you?'

'In the pink, mate, in the pink. I hear that you and my boss had a little set to the other day.'

It was more statement than query, and Johnny asked, 'What else have you been hearing, Ozzie?'

A look of envy came into the young man's face. 'Well, they do say as how you and the Queen of Egypt am real close friends – if you get my meaning.'

Johnny grimaced and shook his head. 'Do you know, I'd all but forgotten just how bad this town is for gossip. Believe me, there's no truth in what they say. I've only ever spoken to the woman on a couple of occasions.' He frowned thoughtfully. 'Tell me, does Arthur Dolton know of what's being said?'

The other man shrugged. 'I dunno, mate. But one thing's certain sure, if he doon't know now, then he wunt be long in hearing it.'

Johnny Purvis's frown deepened. 'I think I'll go and see him myself and tell him that there's no truth in it.'

Ozzie Clarke shook his head. 'I 'udden't bother if I was you. Let the bastard stew in it!'

'No, it's not for his sake that I'm going to see him, Ozzie, but for his wife's. He gives her a bad enough time as it is. I wouldn't like to think that by leaving matters as they are, I was making it harder for her.'

Ozzie Clarke grinned knowingly. 'Got a soft spot for her has you, John?'

A surge of irritation caused Johnny Purvis to scowl as he shook his head. But in his mind he was forced to acknowledge that it was the inherent truth in Ozzie

Clarke's words that had caused his momentary flash of resentment. Aloud he asked, 'Where can I find Arthur Dolton?'

'That's hard to say, the bugger might still be at home. It depends how drunk he was last night. Does you know wheer his house is?'

'Is it that big place next to the Huins down Red Lane?' Johnny sought confirmation, and when Ozzie Clarke nodded, added, 'I'll go down there now, and see if he's in.'

'Watch out that he aren't got a gun in his hands when he opens the door to you, John,' Ozzie Clarke joked.

As Johnny Purvis walked away, Walter Spires came out from the shop to stand with Ozzie Clarke and asked curiously, 'What did he say about him and the Queen of Egypt then?'

Ozzie Clark shook his head. 'He denied that theer was anything between 'um. He's gooing down to see Arthur Dolton now, to tell him the same.'

'Gawd Strewth!' the other man exclaimed. 'I'd like to be theer when they meets.'

'Me as well, Walter,' Ozzie Clarke grinned. 'Me as well.'

Chapter Twenty-Six

Cleopatra Dolton hissed with pain as Mrs Danks sponged the dried crusted blood from the wounds on her back.

The cook grimaced angrily as her fingers traced the swollen weals that Arthur Dolton's belt had left upon her mistress's soft flesh.

'He oughta be flogged himself, the wicked bastard!' she exclaimed, and told the younger woman, 'You oughta leave him, you know. Gawd knows what he'll end up doing to you. He could bloody well kill you one o' these nights.'

'I'd like nothing better than to leave him, but where would I go with the kids?' Cleopatra Dolton said with hopelessness in her heart.

'You listen to me, my wench, you'se got to start thinking of yourself first. If I was you then I'd goo from this house this very day. I'd leave the kids here.'

'How can you even think that?' Cleopatra protested forcefully. 'I could never leave my kids for that pig to ill-treat as he pleased. You know as well as I do that he would ill-treat them if he hadn't got me here to take his temper out on.'

'That's as maybe,' the other woman said grimly, 'but once you'd got yourself set up somewheer, then perhaps you could come and get the kids away from him.'

'Don't talk so soft,' Cleopatra told her irritably. 'He'd never let me have the kids, and well you know it.'

'Well I knows that if you doon't leave the bastard, he'll end up putting you into your bloody grave, my wench. You wunt be the fust poor cratur whose man has bate her 'til he finally killed her. It happened to me own sister, God have mercy on her soul! The bugger her was wed to bate her black and blue for years and she ended up in her coffin because of it. Now he's wed another poor cratur, and he's giving her the same bloody treatment.'

Cleopatra shook her head despairingly. 'I don't know what to do, Mrs Danks. I just don't know what I can do.'

The older woman gently squeezed Cleopatra's shoulder and said pityingly, 'Try and make up your mind to leave him, my wench. Before it's too late, and you ends up crippled or dead.'

'Did Simon or James hear what was happening?' Cleopatra asked anxiously.

'I doon't think so,' Mrs Danks told her reassuringly. 'I give 'um their breakfast and sent 'um off to school. They both seemed all right. Simon wanted to know wheer you was, but I told him that you was sleeping late. I'se sent Milly out to take Andrew for a long walk.'

'Where's their father?'

'I'm buggered if I knows wheer he's gone to. He went out early. I hope he gets knocked over and killed by a wagon, the wicked bastard!' Mrs Danks wished fervently.

Both women heard the front door bell jangling and, when Doll opened it, the sounds of muffled voices. Then Doll came hurrying up the stairs and knocked at the bedroom door.

'Cover my back,' Cleopatra instructed in a whisper. 'I don't want her to see what he did to me.'

Mrs Danks obeyed and then went to the door.

'Theer's a man who wants to see Mr Dolton.' The young maidservant's eyes were bright with excited curiosity as she peered into the room. 'Here's his card.'

The cook brought the slip of pasteboard to her mistress and Cleopatra Dolton's breath caught in her throat as she read the name printed on it. 'Oh my God!'

'What shall I tell the gentleman, Mrs Dolton?' Doll wanted to know. 'Only I told him already that Mr Dolton was out, but then he said that he wanted to speak with you and that it was urgent.'

Cleopatra Dolton's initial impulse was to tell the maid to send John Purvis away and she opened her mouth to instruct her to do just that, then suddenly altered her mind.

'Show the gentleman into the drawing room, Dolly. Tell him that I'll come and speak with him in a few minutes.'

When the maid had scurried away, Mrs Danks stared at the younger woman in bafflement. 'What does you think youm doing?' she demanded incredulously. 'Has you gone bloody well mad? What 'ull Arthur Dolton do if he finds out that you'se bin talking to John Purvis in this house?'

Cleopatra's own mind was filled with bafflement because she truly could not understand herself why she was taking such a terrible risk. She shook her head in bewilderment, then instructed the other woman, 'Quick, put the dressing on my back.'

Tutting with her lips to show her disapproval, the cook lifted the prepared sheet of ointment plaster and gently covered the wounds. Then helped Cleopatra to get dressed in a dark blue day-gown. The younger woman drew breath sharply as the cook tugged and arranged the leg of mutton sleeves and the tight-fitting bodice, sending lances of pain across her back.

'Youm mad to do this, my wench,' she told her mistress. 'God knows what your husband 'ull do when he hears about it. Why must you do it?'

'I don't know,' Cleopatra replied in genuine puzzlement. 'I just feel that I must, that's all.'

She held her body stiffly as she entered the drawing room and a look of concern came on John Purvis's features as he saw her pale, drawn face, and the great purple shadows beneath her dark eyes.

They shook hands. Cleopatra could not help but wince slightly as the movement sent pain shooting across her back.

Johnny Purvis frowned, realising instinctively that his purpose in coming here had already been invalidated.

She looked at him searchingly, as if hoping to discover in his face the reason why she had agreed to speak with him. As before, his proximity was creating disturbing frissons of mixed emotions to course through her, but she could think of nothing to say to him and they faced each other in an awkward silence for several long moments.

John Purvis was experiencing the same mix of emotions

and sense of constraint, but in his case it was laced with a rapidly burgeoning anger against Arthur Dolton. It was this anger which caused him to cast aside any attempt to voice polite formalities and instead to say bluntly, 'I came to see your husband because of the malicious gossip that is being spread throughout the town concerning you and myself.' He frowned. 'I fear that I'm come too late to save you from its ill effects.'

She replied with an equal blunt honesty, 'Yes, Mr Purvis. You've come too late.' She smiled with mirthless bitterness. 'My husband is convinced that you're my fancy man.'

Johnny Purvis, impelled by an irresistible compulsion, told her, 'At this moment I could wish that I was just that, Mrs Dolton, because then I'd take you from this house and out of your husband's reach, where he could no longer treat you like he does.'

As she heard his words Cleopatra Dolton's thoughts and emotions became a maelstrom and she feared that she was really becoming insane. A part of her being clamoured to throw herself at this comparative stranger; to plead with him to take her and her children out of this house. Simultaneously another part of her being was filled with self-disgust that she should even entertain such thoughts. She clenched her teeth so that she would not open her mouth and voice what she was feeling.

Johnny Purvis was being wracked and torn by a similar dichotomy. He, in his turn, was afraid that if he opened his mouth he would say things which might well cause both of them an everlasting regret. He was suddenly overwhelmed by the need to escape from her presence, to get away and be alone so that he could marshal his rampant thoughts and emotions that were veering dangerously near to being completely out of his control.

It was the woman who was first able to find the strength to reassert some degree of control and tell him, 'I'm very grateful to you for your concern, Mr Purvis, but there is no need to involve yourself any further in my affairs. I am well able to manage them myself.'

She spoke with a coolness that at first caused John Purvis to wonder if he had made a terrible mistake, but then he saw in her dark eyes an expression of yearning which belied her tone. He told her quietly, 'I've taken rooms at the Plough and Harrow Hotel, Mrs Dolton. If you should ever have need of me, if there is anything at all you want of me, anything, then a message sent there will always find me.'

She nodded a silent acknowledgement, then abruptly turned and walked out of the room.

Johnny Purvis left the house and walked slowly back towards the town, tormented by the fear that in coming to speak with Cleopatra Dolton he might well have caused her further trouble.

From behind the net curtains of her bedroom Cleopatra Dolton watched his tall figure recede into the distance and asked herself wonderingly, 'What is it that draws me so strongly towards that man? I hardly know him and yet somehow I feel that we have known each other for countless years. I feel that in some way we are bonded together. But why should that be? Why should I feel this? Why?'

Chapter Twenty-Seven

More than a week had passed since the day of the Studley Fair and during that week Miriam Josceleyne had not ventured out from Cotswold House. For most of the time she had remained in her room, refusing to accept any visitors, making the excuse that she was unwell when the Reverend Mosse MacDonald and several of her lady acquaintances had called to see her.

Her moods had fluctuated wildly, from elation to depression, from hopeful expectation to hopeless despair, and now as the fourth day of July dawned Miriam Josceleyne awoke with the realisation that she could not continue to remain in this self-imposed seclusion. It was with relief that she greeted her present mood of calm clarity of thought. The wild swings of her emotions during the previous days had not been a pleasant experience for her.

For more than an hour she remained lying in her bed, gazing up at the ceiling, relishing her present certainty of purpose. When she heard Emma's footsteps in the corridor she called to the girl, 'Emma, come here please.'

The girl was wearing her working dress of checked gingham, floppy mob-cap and canvas apron.

'Good morning, Miss Miriam. Are you feeling better today?' It was not solely a polite formality that Emma voiced. She genuinely liked her kindly, timid mistress, and did not enjoy seeing her troubled in health and spirits.

'I'm very well, thank you, Emma.' The older woman pushed herself upright in the bed and smiled at the maid. 'Could you prepare a bath for me please?'

Emma frowned doubtfully. The house had never been

modernised, and to prepare a bath entailed heating the water downstairs and carrying it in buckets to the bathroom on the first floor.

'I'll do it and gladly, Miss Miriam, but it'll take a bit of time. I've not had a chance to light the copper yet and Mrs Elwood aren't due in for another hour.'

'No matter,' Miriam Josceleyne smiled at a sudden sense of lighthearted well-being swept through her. Pushing aside her bedclothes she got up and reached for a long gown to cover her flannel nightdress. 'I shall come down and make the tea for us, and you can light the copper. The water will heat very nicely while we're having our breakfasts in the kitchen.'

The girl's black eyes widened in surprise at this statement. Ladies did not make tea for their servants, nor sit in kitchens eating breakfasts.

Miriam Josceleyne giggled and tossed her long thick plait of hair, and at that moment looked like a mischievous young girl.

'Don't look so shocked, Emma. I'm not suggesting anything improper, am I?'

Emma Farr grinned cheekily. 'That 'ud depend on who might hear it, Miss Miriam. I aren't never worked for a lady before who'd offer to make me my tea and have breakfast with me in the kitchen.'

'Times are changing, Emma,' her employer gaily informed her. 'This is the modern age. We are living in 1902 not 1802.'

'All right, Miss Miriam, I'll just look in on Mr Hector, then I'll goo down and get the copper filled and lit.'

She went to the old man's room and quietly opened the door to peep in. He was lying on his back, propped up by big pillows, tasselled nightcap pulled low on his head, his toothless jaws gaping wide and snoring loudly.

Emma tiptoed into the room and stood for some moments staring down at the sleeping man. His grey-stubbled face and throat, wax-like in the pale light of dawn, reminded Emma of her grandfather's corpse that she had seen lying just like this on his deathbed.

Mrs Elwood's assertion that Hector Josceleyne would be

213

prepared to marry her had been in Emma's mind constantly during the intervening days. 'Could I stand being wed to the old bugger?' she wondered yet again, looking at his claw-like, black-veined hands lying on the outside of the coverlet, visualising how they would feel moving upon her body, clawing greedily at her flesh.

The familiar shiver of disgust coursed through her. 'It 'ud be like being shagged by a bloody snake,' she told herself, but then giggled as she remembered the cook's other gibe about the old man. How one bout of lovemaking with a vigorous woman would possibly kill him.

The gleam of speculation entered her black eyes. 'I can handle him easy enough now when I'm only the maidservant, surely I'd be able to handle him a bloody sight easier if I was wed to the old sod. Once it was all signed and sealed then I needn't do anything with him that I didn't want to do.'

He snorted and coughed weakly, saliva dribbling from the corner of his slack mouth, but did not wake up.

'He's standing at death's door now, aren't he?' Emma told herself. 'I reckon I'd be a widow in next to no time. A rich widow. Men like Johnny Purvis 'ud look at me a bit different then, 'udden't they? I'd be a fine catch then if I was a rich widow, and not just a bloody serving girl who aren't got above two ha'pennies to rub together.'

Her sense of mischievous humour caused her to giggle to herself. 'Mind you, looking at the state of the old sod now, I reckon I'd better make me mind up bloody sharp, or he'll die before I can get him into the bloody church to sign the register.'

She winked at the sleeping man, and whispered, 'See you later, my lover.' Then she went downstairs to the scullery and busied herself with filling the big wash-copper with fresh water.

In the meanwhile Miriam Josceleyne brewed a pot of tea, fried slices of ham and fresh eggs, and cut and buttered thick chunks of crusty bread. The two women sat in a companionable silence, eating heartily, and Miriam Josceleyne found that she was relishing plain wholesome food with a gusto she had not known for many long years.

Emma sneaked covert curious glances at her mistress. She still did not know where Miriam Josceleyne had disappeared to on the day following the Coronation celebrations. She had speculated in concert with Mrs Elwood about the reason for her mistress's self-imposed seclusion since that day.

A flurry of knocking on the back door sent Emma scurrying to answer it. A hefty-bodied middle-aged woman, wrapped in a man's ragged overcoat, with a man's cap on her frizzled grey hair and a huge apron fashioned from sacking tied round her ample girth, handed an empty wooden bucket to Emma.

She was the step-girl who called at the house once a week to wash, scrub and hearthstone the flight of front doorsteps and the paving fronting the house.

Emma filled the bucket with clean water and when she gave it back to the step-girl the woman jerked her head conspiratorially and whispered hoarsely, 'Theer's a young chap wants a word wiv you, missy.'

'Who?' Emma asked, having already guessed the young man's identity.

The woman leered, displaying multi-coloured mis-shapen teeth. 'Well he says he's your fiancé.'

'Well, you can tell him from me to bugger off from here,' Emma told her tartly, 'because I aren't got any fiancé.'

Albert Bott poked his head around the corner of the wall, and pleaded, 'Doon't send me off without a word, Emma.'

He was dressed in soiled overalls with a small peaked cap on his head, a muffler tied around his neck to cover his collarless shirt and carrying his canvas tool bag slung across his back.

Emma scowled angrily and glanced back over her shoulder for fear her mistress might be able to overhear what was taking place.

Albert Bott came up to the back door, and the step-girl stood with her full bucket in her hands, gazing with avid interest.

'I wants to talk with you, Emma.' The young man was at

the same time both stubborn and hangdog. 'I knows it aren't convenient, but I aren't gooing from here until I'se talked with you.'

'Well I doon't want to talk with you, Albert Bott,' Emma hissed furiously. 'You'll lose me my place here if you stays pestering me. My mistress is in the kitchen.'

A mulish expression came on his round pink face. 'Then you'll just have to lose your place, my girl. I aren't going until you'se spoke with me.'

'That's it, kid, you tell her,' the step-girl applauded.

'You just sod off and get on with your work!' Emma rounded angrily on her. 'He could lose me my place coming here like this.'

'Emma? Emma?' Miriam Josceleyne's voice sounded from the kitchen. Emma swung on the young man.

'Theer now, Albert Bott, just look what you'se bin and gone and done now. Just gerroff 'ull you!'

'No, I wunt!' he shook his head positively and, folding his arms, leaned against the doorpost. 'I'm staying here until you agrees to meet me somewheer and have a talk.'

'That's it kid, you tell her.' Again the step-girl applauded and again Emma angrily rounded on her.

'Will you sod off and mind your own business?'

Now the other woman took umbrage. 'Doon't you use that tone to me, you cheeky little cow.'

Emma's fiery temper flared. 'Doon't you goo becalling me, you old bitch!'

'What did you call me?' the woman shrieked, and Emma lost control. 'An old bitch! That's what I called you and that's what you am. Now sod off and do the work youm paid to do.'

The step-girl shrieked a curse and without any hesitation hurled the contents of her bucket over Emma.

Emma took the force of the cold water full in her face, and for a moment could only stand gasping for breath and wiping her streaming eyes. Then, as the step-girl laughed jeeringly, Emma growled an oath and hurled herself upon the bigger woman.

The impact of her body sent the step-girl toppling backwards, but as she fell her hand hooked into Emma's

216

hair, and she pulled the girl down with her. They rolled over and over across the back yard, scratching, biting, tugging hair, pummelling and kicking, while Albert Bott stood staring down at them in open-mouthed amazement.

The commotion brought Miriam Josceleyne hurrying to the back door, and the sight of the fighting women shocked her so badly that she could only stand in the yard wringing her hands, weakly imploring them to stop, and begging Albert Bott, 'Do something! Do something!'

Albert Bott had never been a violent man and, although fights between women were a regular occurrence in the slums of the town, he personally had rarely witnessed one. Spurred on by Miriam Josceleyne's pleas he made an ineffectual attempt to separate the two women, only to be sent reeling, clasping his damaged testicles as the step-girl's heavy iron-shod boot caught him with a savage kick between the legs.

He almost collided with Mrs Elwood who had arrived for work. The big fat woman did not hesitate. Emma had by now managed to get astride of her opponent and was punching savagely at the woman's face. Mrs Elwood bent and grasped the girl around the waist and by sheer bodily strength dragged her off and propelled her, still struggling and cursing, through the back door, which Mrs Elwood then slammed shut and held fast against the girl's efforts to tug it back open.

The step-girl staggered to her feet. Her face bloodied, her hair a wild tangled mass.

'I'm fetching a copper to that fuckin' cow!' she gasped out, and left in a shambling run.

'Oh my God!' Miriam Josceleyne's face blanched. 'What will Franklin say? What will he say? Oh my God!'

All her earlier calm confidence and sense of well-being had disappeared and she was once again the familiar timid, nerve-wracked woman of old.

Albert Bott, still clutching between his legs, took up his tool bag and followed the step-girl.

'Now you just quieten down, Emma,' Mrs Elwood bawled through the door. 'They'se both gone.'

She let go the door handle and Emma burst out into the

217

yard. The girl's gutter-devil was in full arousal; her black eyes alight with the fury of combat. Her dress had been badly ripped in the struggle and her face was bloody. She impatiently tossed back her long wet hair which had come unpinned.

'I'll swing for that bloody bitch! I take me oath on it, I'll swing for the bugger!'

Face still blanched, hands twining and tugging at each other, Miriam Josceleyne went silently back into the house. Mrs Elwood frowned worriedly, then snapped at Emma, 'What the bloody hell has you done here, girl? Miss Miriam looks as if it's made her real poorly.'

Emma calmed a little when she heard this. 'I didn't mean to cause Miss Miriam any upset. That bloody cow started it.'

'Well my wench, if her's gone to the police, it 'ull be them who finishes it, that's a fact. You might well goo to jail for this. And one thing's certain sure – you'se lost your place here. Mr Franklin 'ull goo bloody mad when he hears about this little lot. He'll have you out o' the house so fast that your feet won't touch the ground.'

Enough gutter-devil was still raging in Emma to cause her to scoff at this threat. 'Let him. I doon't give a bugger!'

'You 'ull when youm walking the streets with no character, my girl. You'll give a bugger then all right,' the older woman sniffed.

'Theer's work in the factories,' Emma countered.

'Oh yes, theer's work in the factories all right,' Mrs Elwood agreed sneeringly. 'Theer's plenty of work theer for them who doon't mind being called common as muck. But that won't suit you, my lady, and well you knows it.'

She paused, then softened a little. 'You'd best goo and get yourself claned up, my wench. I'll goo and see if Miss Miriam's all right. When youm claned up, then you'd best apologise to Miss Miriam for upsetting her and beg humble pardon for what you'se done.'

Emma tossed her head defiantly, but after a moment's reflection, did as she was bid and went to the scullery to wash herself.

As she used the rough flannel to clean the blood and

dirt from her face and hands, her adrenaline-charged muscles gradually relaxed and her excitement cooled. She felt a twinge of apprehension, which intensified to a gnawing anxiety as she thought of the possible consequences of the fight with the step-girl. Quite apart from the prospect of legal punishment, if she lost this position then she would find herself in real difficulties. She knew that her father would not take her back in his house to live this time, and she had no money with which to rent a room, or pay for food until she might find other work. Her mother would be willing but unable to help her, her father would make sure of that.

'He'll cool down eventually.' She tried to draw comfort from that thought, but then realised, 'We parted on bad terms, didn't we? The miserable old bugger 'ull want to see me suffer before he softens towards me. Even then I'll have to beg and plead with him for him to take me back home to live.'

Her fierce pride rebelled at that prospect. 'Bugger him, I'll not plead to goo back to that bloody slum.'

Later, wearing a clean dress and apron, her hair brushed and pinned up beneath her cap, she knocked at the door of Miriam Josceleyne's room.

'Come,' the woman called, and when the girl entered sat staring at her with troubled eyes.

Long red weeping scratches covered Emma's face and neck, and there was an angry puffy swelling already discolouring her eye, while the knuckles of both hands were skinned and raw.

'Oh Emma, what are we to do?' Miriam Josceleyne's eyes filled with tears and she wrung her hands miserably. 'If my brother comes to hear of this, he will insist that I discharge you from our service.'

'But it wasn't me who started it, Miss Miriam,' Emma protested. 'It was that old bitch!'

'Franklin will not care who was the cause of the disturbance, Emma. He does not tolerate any misbehaviour by servants.'

'It wasn't my fault, Miss Miriam,' Emma repeated, and a hint of impatience entered her voice. 'You doon't want me

219

to have to goo, does you, Miss Miriam? Surely it's up to you whether or not I loses my place here?'

'No Emma, I confess I do not wish to lose you. But I have no power in this matter.' Miriam Josceleyne was almost self-pitying. 'My brother is the head of the family and I am duty bound to accept whatever he decides to do in this matter. I have no other choice but to obey him.'

Contempt flashed in Emma's black eyes, and she thought scornfully, 'What a bloody weakling you am, Miriam Josceleyne.'

The older woman sighed raggedly. 'Go on about your duties, Emma. Let us just pray that my brother will not come to hear of this unhappy occurrence.'

'All right, Miss Miriam.' Emma bobbed her head and went out into the corridor. Outside the door she stood for some moments, her smooth forehead deeply furrowed as she thought hard.

The dull thumping of a stick being pounded on the floor came from Hector Josceleyne's room. Emma suddenly grinned mirthlessly and tapped Miriam Josceleyne's door, calling, 'It's all right, Miss Miriam, I'll goo and see what Mr Hector wants.'

Then she hurried into the old man's room.

'Where have you been?' he whined querulously. 'I've been awake for hours and no one has troubled themselves to come near me.'

Emma forced herself to smile warmly at him, then slowly walked towards the bed, deliberately thrusting out her high pert breasts.

'There, Mr Hector,' she told him huskily, 'I'm here to look after you now, aren't I?'

Chapter Twenty-Eight

By early afternoon Miriam Josceleyne had recovered somewhat from the shocks of the morning and, much to her relief, her brother Franklin had not come roaring into the house to dismiss Emma Farr. Miriam dreaded the prospect of losing the girl. Since she had entered their service the burden of caring for Hector Josceleyne had been lifted completely from Miriam's own shoulders; she had gratefully relinquished it to Emma Farr and the thought of having to reassume that burden filled her with dismay.

Faced with the prospect of her brother's imminent arrival, Miriam Josceleyne had desperately tried to summon back her newly acquired mood of calmness and certainty of purpose, but she had been forced to accept the unpalatable fact that she had once more reverted to being the timid nerve-wracked old maid. She knew that if her brother came to her in a fury, she would quail before him and supinely agree to whatever he might demand of her.

To avoid the possibility of an afternoon confrontation with Franklin, she sought in her mind for an excuse to be absent from the house and remembered with thankfulness that today it was the turn of Mrs Ida Huins to be 'at home' to her select coterie.

She dressed in a sombre dark grey gown and long coat and pinned a low-crowned, broad-brimmed hat on her severely bunned hair. Then, after leaving instructions with Mrs Elwood for the evening meal, she left the house. As she closed the front door behind her, Miriam Josceleyne could have sworn that she heard the sound of Emma Farr's laughter coming from the upper floor of the house, and she frowned to herself. 'How can that girl be so lighthearted when there's every likelihood that she might shortly be dismissed from her place?'

The sun was high and hot, but a soft breeze rustled the leaves of the great trees that shaded Church Green, and in the recreation garden the flowerbeds were colourful and sweetly scented. Miriam Josceleyne's spirits rose slightly.

'Perhaps all will be well. After all, if Franklin had been informed of what happened this morning, surely he would have come to see me before now.'

Drawing comfort from that wishful hope, Miriam Josceleyne began to feel almost cheerful. She crossed Church Green and went on down Unicorn Hill. The usual knot of loungers were sitting and standing around the stone steps that led up to the Unicorn Inn's taproom and Miriam kept her head averted and quickened her pace as she passed them. It was not unknown for respectable ladies to be offered greetings and insulting familiarities by the low-class ruffians who patronised that establishment.

As she descended the steep slope of the hill a train was crossing beneath the roadway bridge, pumping out thick clouds of smoke and creating a din of clanging metal and hissing steam. By the time she had reached the entrance drive to the station itself the passengers from the newly arrived train were already coming out onto the roadway.

'Good afternoon, Miss Josceleyne.' From among the oncoming passengers Johnny Purvis stepped out in front of her, lifting his soft black felt hat in greeting. 'This is a pleasant surprise.'

Miriam was forced to halt, since the man showed no sign of stepping aside for her. To her mortification she felt the hot flush spread upwards from her throat to her cheeks, yet despite that she was forced to admit to herself that she was pleased to see him.

She coughed nervously, and managed to return his greeting. 'Good afternoon, Mr Purvis.'

'You're walking to Red Lane, Miss Josceleyne.' It was more statement than question, and after a moment's hesitation she nodded stiffly. 'I am, Mr Purvis, but only to Mrs Huins' house.'

'Then please allow me to accompany you for that distance. I'd greatly like to talk with you about the history of Grange House,' Johnny Purvis requested, smiling.

Miriam Josceleyne thought how charming his manner was and how manly and attractive he looked in his dark green tweed suit and the raffish hat he wore with such a dashing air.

Again she nodded stiffly, pleasure and embarrassment battling for domination within her.

They walked slowly onwards, side by side, and he began eagerly, 'Tell me, Miss Josceleyne, did you know that there is an account in the Birmingham City archives that tells of Royalist troops being quartered at Grange House some weeks previous to the Battle of Worcester?'

Her interest sparked immediately and her sense of constriction in his company began to slip away as she told him, 'No, I did not know, Mr Purvis, but can you tell me more of this?'

By the time they had travelled the few score yards that brought them to the Huins' house, they were talking with the ease of old friends and when they arrived outside the front gate of the house Miriam Josceleyne felt an acute reluctance to part from him.

As if he sensed this emotion, Johnny Purvis looked keenly at her, and then said almost diffidently, 'I've had workmen digging trenches for water pipes up at the Grange these last few days, Miss Josceleyne. Yesterday morning they uncovered a rather curious artifact that I'd greatly like to show you.' He smiled apologetically. 'Unfortunately it's too large and heavy for me to carry to your home, so perhaps you might like to come up to the Grange and view it.'

After only a moment of hesitation, Miriam Josceleyne smiled and nodded firmly. 'I would enjoy doing so, Mr Purvis.'

'Good!' he beamed delightedly at her. 'Shall we say tomorrow? I shall be there all day, so any time you wish to state will be convenient.'

'I'll come in the morning,' she returned his smile, 'at about eleven o'clock.'

'Good! I'll look forward to our meeting.'

They shook hands warmly. Then he lifted his hat in farewell and walked onwards up the slope of Red Lane.

She remained by the gate watching him, a smile curving her lips as she drew intense pleasure from the prospect that she would so soon be in his company again, then abruptly realised that other curious eyes might be on her and in a fluster of embarrassment hurried up the gravelled driveway which curved around the wide tree-shaded front lawn.

Her embarrassment would have been too much for her to have borne had she known that curious eyes had indeed been watching her and her companion.

Mrs Ida Huins' lips quirked in malicious pleasure as she let the corner of the net curtain fall and went downstairs from her front bedroom to rejoin her guests. Ida Huins' delight in seeing Miriam Josceleyne standing at her gate with Johnny Purvis was slightly marred by the impossibility of being able to impart that tasty piece of gossip to her other guests before the advent of Miriam Josceleyne to their circle. But then, the woman's pleasure returned in full measure as, on second thoughts, she realised how she could so deliciously slide a verbal stiletto into Miriam Josceleyne's feelings.

Ida Huins was very peeved with the Josceleyne family at this moment in time. Her husband, George Huins, was one of the town's leading businessmen, but recently a series of bad investments had left him temporarily embarrassed for ready cash. Only the previous week he had been summoned to the premises of the Metropolitan Bank and forced to endure a humiliating lecture from his bank manager, Franklin Josceleyne.

Ida Huins gloated now with keen anticipation, promising herself that she would extract a very full payment of revenge from that insufferably arrogant little prig's sister for his humiliation of her husband. 'It's Miss Miriam Josceleyne, if you please, mum,' the maid announced.

'Why Miss Josceleyne, how good of you to call.'

Ida Huins smiled radiantly and rose in gushing

welcome. 'I trust you are fully recovered from your indisposition, my dear. Please, take this chair, won't you. I was saying only this moment to the other ladies how sadly we have been missing you from our little gatherings of late.'

A chorus of agreement sounded from the other women present and Miriam Josceleyne's eyes moved to each in turn as she acknowledged their greetings. Mrs Amanda Allcock, Miss Julia Playfair, Mrs Beatrice Kendrick and Mrs Violet Milward were all present, as well as a recent addition to the charmed circle, Mrs Gertrude Eadie, whose husband was the manufacturer of the famous eponymous bicycle gears.

Their sumptuous clothing and large ornately decked hats made Miriam feel very dull and dowdy in comparison and she mentally steeled herself to endure yet another tedious afternoon in their pampered, over-dressed, self-satisfied company.

Ida Huins prided herself upon her 'at homes'. Instead of one maid to wait upon the guests she always deployed two, looking very trim and smart in their black dresses, snowy white high-bibbed aprons and long-streamered caps. The salvers, triple-tiered cake-stands, water, milk and cream jugs, teapots, sugar basins, tongs, knives, forks and spoons were all fine examples of the silversmith's art. Her guests could choose from several expensive brands of both China and Indian teas and gorge themselves on extra thin slices of brown, white or wholemeal breads with salted or unsalted butters. The cream cakes, fruit tarts, chocolate eclairs, biscuits and plain cakes were in abundant supply and always freshly made that very day, and the cups, saucers and tiny plates were of the most delicate porcelain china.

'Shall we take some refreshment, ladies?' Ida Huins invited, and the familiar ritual began. While the maids brought in silver teapots and placed them before their mistress, the other women removed their gloves and those with veils lifted the filmy whisps of gauze up over the brims of their hats. Mrs Violet Milward, the youngest and most fashionable lady present, favoured the very latest style of long gloves, so instead of removing them, she unbuttoned the backs and turned the hands back over her wrists.

'China or Indian, Mrs Allcock?' Ida Huins enquired each of her guests' preference as she poured the tea. 'One lump or two, Miss Playfair?' There is demerara should you prefer it, Mrs Kendrick.'

The maids brought the delicate cups and saucers to the guests, who held the cups high, curling their little fingers fashionably as they drank. The maids also brought round the eatables. The conversation was disjointed and uneven as the women ate heartily, balancing the tiny plates on their knees.

As Ida Huins sipped her tea, her eyes peeped covertly over the rim of the cup towards Miriam Josceleyne who was nibbling abstractedly at a slice of bread and butter. Unknown to her guests, Ida Huins was a close confidante of the Reverend Mosse MacDonald and earlier in the week he had told her in the strictest confidence of his intentions regarding Miriam Josceleyne. Sharing as she did the cleric's antipathy towards Franklin Josceleyne, Ida Huins had applauded his decision to ask for Miriam Josceleyne's hand in marriage, knowing that to lose control over his sister's finances would cause the bank manager considerable anguish.

Now Ida Huins wondered how much progress the Reverend MacDonald had made towards achieving his aim. He had told her that he had called at Cotswold House twice, only to be turned away at the door because of Miriam Josceleyne's indisposition. She had expected MacDonald to be here today and was puzzled by his absence. It was most unlike the man to miss any opportunity to indulge his appetites at her expense.

A feeling of grudging admiration for Miriam Josceleyne fleeted through Ida Huins' mind. 'What a sly cat you really are!' she thought. 'There you sit looking like the proverbial church mouse, yet all the time you are playing with two men. Mosse MacDonald wants to marry you – only for your money of course. Nevertheless he's a fine figure of a man and is not a match to be sniffed at by any means. And at the same time you are carrying on a relationship with that Purvis man.'

A frisson of sexual appreciation shivered through Ida Huins' corpulent body as she visualised Johnny Purvis's hard-looking features and lean, muscular physique, and a spasm of envy struck her momentarily.

'What can such an attractive man possibly see in a dried-up stick like you, Miriam Josceleyne? It must be your money. After all, he was born and bred in a slum, wasn't he? Perhaps he thinks that by having a relationship with you, he is rising up from his class.' She attempted to draw spiteful satisfaction from that thought, but then remembered, 'From all accounts he's come back from the war a very rich man indeed. He became an officer did he not, and is now quite the gentleman from what people tell me. So perhaps it's not money or social position that he wants from you.'

Ida Huins' eyes narrowed in puzzlement as she studied Miriam Josceleyne's physical fragility, and she was forced to mentally shake her head in bewilderment. 'God might know what John Purvis sees in you, my girl, but I most certainly do not.'

The last cup of tea was drunk and the final cream cake chewed and swallowed. The maids cleared away the debris and the ladies settled themselves for an exchange of gossip.

Today it was Mrs Beatrice Kendrick who offered the first titbit. One of her neighbour's maids had been discovered to be pregnant and consequently had been discharged and packed off back to her home in a nearby village.

The ladies deplored the low state of morals among the lower classes. Then Amanda Allcock enquired eagerly, 'Did she name the father, Mrs Kendrick?'

'Oh yes,' Beatrice Kendrick's lips pursed as if she was relishing some dainty morsel and her eyes sparkled. 'She had the gall to claim that it was the eldest son, Richard. She said that he had promised to marry her and so she had permitted him to have his way with her.'

A chorus of shocked yet delighted exclamations sounded from her audience, then Amanda Allcock tutted indignantly. 'I should hope that she was soundly thrashed for telling such wicked lies. I know Richard Bennet personally, and he's a fine Christian young man.'

'Yes, indeed he is,' Ida Huins murmured agreement. 'There have lately been too many cases where a serving girl has got herself pregnant and then tried to lay the blame for it on the menfolk of the very family who have been kindly enough to give her employment.'

There was now displayed a complete concord among the ladies as to the wicked ingratitude shown towards their employers by servants in general and maidservants in particular.

Miriam Josceleyne sat listening to the conversation with a burgeoning sense of uneasy guilt. She had the example of her own father's treatment of his maidservants directly before her, and at last she felt constrained to say, 'But surely there have been cases where the unfortunate girls have been speaking the truth. I do not know Richard Bennet personally, but how can we be so certain that he is indeed innocent?'

Her statement was greeted with expressions of pained surprise, and disapproving murmurs, then Ida Huins told her with an acid smile, 'I can be certain because Richard Bennet is a young gentleman and a true Christian, my dear Miss Josceleyne, and his family have always been of the very highest repute. I just cannot believe that he would tell a lie.'

Miriam Josceleyne flushed at being the focus of disapproval but doggedly argued, 'Perhaps the girl's family and friends think as highly of her and cannot believe that she is lying. After all, not all those who claim to be gentlemen act as such, do they, and even the most reputable families can produce black sheep, can they not?'

Ida Huins inwardly crowed with satisfaction. The opening she had been hoping for had just been presented to her.

'Indeed they can, Miss Josceleyne,' she agreed warmly. 'You are speaking very truly when you say that.' She paused, and smiled, and those who knew her well realised that she was about to impart one of those juicy pieces of scandalous information for which she was so renowned. An almost tangible air of expectancy descended upon the group, and their eyes glistened greedily.

'Why, only next door we have a prime example of a black sheep . . .'

Ida Huins' listeners mentally hugged themselves. The Dolton's were invariably a meaty subject.

'On the day after the Coronation celebrations, according to what my housekeeper has told me, Arthur Dolton came home in the evening in his usual beastly state of drunkenness, and actually tore the nightshift from his wife's body and then proceeded to flog her with a leather belt, apparently inflicting very severe injuries. My housekeeper says that there were bloodstains all over the carpet and the bed.'

Audible gasps of delighted horror sounded in Ida Huins' ears and she preened visibly, taunting silently, 'Match that, if you can, Beatrice Kendrick.'

Then she continued aloud, 'Horrible man though Arthur Dolton is, yet in this case there might be a certain amount of justification for what he did.'

Miriam Josceleyne was still feeling irritated with her companions for their attitude towards the pregnant servant girl, and now she felt impelled to protest, 'How can there ever be any justification for a brutal man to treat any woman so wickedly?'

Ida Huins smiled condescendingly at her, then glanced at the other women and shrugged as if to entreat their mutual forbearance towards this unworldly old maid, before going on, 'Apparently, that very day, Arthur Dolton had discovered that his wife was indulging in an illicit affair with another man.'

Breathing stilled and bodies unconsciously leaned towards their hostess.

'It seems that Arthur Dolton was drinking in that awful Unicorn Inn in company with his fellow ruffians, when the other man came in, and threatened Arthur Dolton, warning him that if he hurt Cleopatra Dolton in any way, then he, the other man, would kill him. Apparently blows were struck, then the men intervened to drag Arthur

229

Dolton and his wife's paramour apart. The paramour then challenged Dolton to fight him for two hundred sovereigns.'

The narrator fell silent, waiting for the eager urgings of her audience.

'Pray do continue, Mrs Huins.'

'Yes, do go on!'

'It's so exciting. Just like one of those Penny Dreadfuls!'

Ida Huins smirked triumphantly. Basking in the knowledge that she had so effortlessly reasserted her position above any possible challenger as the supreme purveyor of sensational scandal.

'Arthur Dolton accepted the challenge, and they are going to fight within the next few days.'

'Who is the other man, Mrs Huins?' Mrs Violet Milward's pretty face was feral with her hunger to know.

'Yes, do tell us. Do tell us.' Julia Playfair beseeched.

Ida Huins' eyes switched direction to dwell briefly on Miriam Josceleyne and Miriam experienced a sudden uneasy dread as she saw the gloating malice in the other woman's expression.

'There is something more to be told, before I give his name,' Ida Huins informed. 'And frankly, if I had not seen it with my own eyes, I would never have believed it possible.'

'On the day following his challenge to Arthur Dolton, the other man actually had the audacity to call at Arthur Dolton's house and to remain closeted alone with Cleopatra Dolton for some considerable time. I saw him go up the pathway to the front door and enter it myself. Quite by chance, I happened to be looking out of my bedroom window to study the condition of my lawn, when he came back out of the house. Walking out of the front door as bold as brass.' She nodded emphatically. 'As bold as brass!'

Mrs Violet Milward could not restrain her impatience any longer.

'Do tell us who he is, Mrs Huins, I beg you. Who is Cleopatra Dolton's fancy man?'

Ida Huins smirked with triumphant malice at Miriam

230

Josceleyne.

'He's just returned from the war, Mrs Milward, his name is John Purvis.'

Miriam felt as if she had been struck a physical blow, she could actually feel the blood draining from her face. Sudden nausea invaded her and she drew breath sharply. Shame flooded through her at the awareness that all the other women were staring at her; she could sense their spiteful delight in witnessing her immediate involuntary reaction to what Ida Huins had said. Her next reaction was disbelief. Refusal to accept what she had heard. Then, from deep within her a terrible anger boiled upwards and that anger brought with it a fierce self-pride and a rejection of her own sense of shame.

Ida Huins was staring avidly at her, displaying an open malicious satisfaction.

Miriam drew a long breath, filling and expanding her lungs until her flat chest strained against the tight bodice of her dress. She rose to her feet and told Ida Huins with utter loathing, 'You are nothing other than a wicked mischief-maker, Mrs Huins, and the rest of you are almost as bad. You remind me of a coven of spiteful witches and I want nothing more to do with any of you.'

With that she walked with a quiet dignity out of the room and from the house leaving a stunned silence behind her.

Chapter Twenty-Nine

Cleopatra Dolton had seen little of her husband following the terrible thrashing he had inflicted upon her. He went out early in the morning and returned late at night, only to go to his own room and sleep. For her part she felt only relief that he was deliberately avoiding her, but during the last couple of days a fresh concern had arisen to torment her.

Simon and James Dolton were pupils of the Redditch Grammar School, a small private establishment claiming to educate the sons of gentlemen. The principals and proprietors of the school, Mr and Mrs J.E. Bryant publicly prided themselves upon the quality of their teaching and the select nature of their clientele. Although in private they admitted to each other that there were in fact very few sons of actual gentlemen among their pupils. The eighty-odd boys who attended came mostly from the families of local shopkeepers, clerks, and factory foremen, with a scattering of the sons of skilled artisans.

Simon and James had always seemed content at the school and although they were both shy and timid boys, had appeared to be on friendly terms with the majority of their fellow pupils. However two days previously Simon had returned with swollen bleeding lips, his clothes torn and dirtied, while James's eyes had been reddened and puffed with weeping.

Both boys had at first stubbornly refused to tell her the reason for their appearances until after long questioning Simon had told her that both of them, when on their way home, had been set upon by a group of boys from the National School.

Cleopatra, although distressed, had been able to accept that boys would be boys and that such fights were common enough between the different schools. The National School was a school for the children of the poor, and a traditional enmity existed between the youth who attended private and non-private schools. The uniform of the Grammar School was a livid green, purple and yellow striped cap and tie and this combination of colours seemed to act as a goad upon the ragamuffins from the National School.

Yesterday, however, the same thing had occurred, only this time both of them had borne the contusions of harsh treatment on their faces, bodies and clothing. Once more both had maintained that it was again a fight with National School boys who had been waiting to ambush them as they came home.

Now, at three o'clock in the afternoon, Cleopatra Dolton sat in her drawing room, trying to concentrate on reading a book but unable to do so because of her worries about her two eldest sons. Yesterday she had threatened to go up to the National School which was on the northern side of the town centre and complain personally to the headmaster there, but that threat had so distressed both of them that she had not had the heart to carry it out. Now, however, she was wishing she had done so and was dreading what might have happened to them; her vivid imagination was creating frightening images in her mind.

At last, unable to contain herself, Cleopatra put on her outdoor clothing and left the house. The Grammar School was in Park Road, which sloped westwards from the bottom of Front Hill where the Council Offices stood. As she walked slowly towards the railway station, Cleopatra Dolton suddenly began to wonder about the truth of what her sons had told her. She found it increasingly hard to credit that boys from the National School should come all the way across the town centre two days in succession in the hopes of catching pupils from the Grammar School, whose classes finished a good half an hour earlier than their own. Particularly since her sons' route home was only a comparatively short one through respectable streets and

233

there were many other Grammar School pupils whose routes homewards took them much nearer to the National School's environs.

She crossed the railway bridge and the entrance driveway to the station and turned south up the long slope of Oakley Road which paralleled Evesham Street and Front Hill. Several connecting streets and pathways traversed the slope which stretched between the two thoroughfares and Park Road was one of these. As she neared its corner Cleopatra heard a loud chanting of many youthful voices and she smiled. It was good to hear young people enjoying themselves with such obvious gusto.

She slowed and halted when she came to the turning into Park Road and peeped round the corner of a tall garden wall to see what the chanting was all about. There was a large crowd of boys dressed in the Grammar School caps and ties only yards from her. They were all screaming and chanting at the tops of their voices, all clustered around the wall, their faces focused on something in their midst. Cleopatra smiled and listened carefully to the chant, recognising the tune as being 'For he's a jolly good fellow'. Then her smile froze as she managed to distinguish the words.

'Your mother's got a fancy man! Your mother's got a fancy man! Your mother's got a fancy man, and so say all of us! And so say all of us! And so say all of us! Your mother's got a fancy man. Your mother's got a fancy man. Your mother's got a fancy man, and so say all of us!'

Then the crowd eddied and swirled and voices shrieked excitedly. Cleopatra's hands went to her mouth as she saw Simon locked in savage combat with a much bigger boy and James on the floor with another boy on top of him pummelling wildly with his fists at James's head and face.

For a moment or two Cleopatra could only stand and stare with horrified eyes, her body seemingly powerless to move. She saw Simon almost wrestle the bigger boy to the ground and then two other boys leapt on Simon enabling his first opponent to smash him a heavy blow in his face. Blood gouted from Simon's nose, and the sight of that scarlet stream galvanised Cleopatra into mindless fury and she ran forwards screaming, 'Leave him alone, you bastards! You fuckin' bastards! I'll kill you! I'll fuckin' kill you!' Once more she was a gutter-devil of the slums, battling with all the ferocity of a wildcat in defence of her young.

The boys scattered before her, some shocked and frightened, others cat-calling and laughing wildly. Simon was still battling with his opponents and Cleopatra's clenched fists swung into faces and bodies, and her fingers hooked and clawed. Then suddenly there was only herself and her two children against that tall wall and the other boys were fleeing in all directions as a tall bearded man clad in a college-gown and mortar board came hurrying from higher up the roadway, wielding a long whippy cane which slashed into boys' backs and buttocks as they ducked to escape him.

'What happened here, Mrs Dolton?' James Bryant asked in anxious puzzlement.

Cleopatra's mindless fury was now fast receding and she became aware of the curious faces that the commotion had attracted to the windows of the adjacent houses.

'Did the boys attack you, ma'am?' the schoolteacher questioned. 'What on earth has been happening?'

She shook her head. 'No, no one attacked me, Mr Bryant.' An ironic smile briefly touched the corners of her mouth. 'In actual fact it was I who attacked them.'

The man frowned and she went on to explain, 'I saw a group of boys fighting with my sons and I intervened to stop them.'

Bryant's frown deepened, as he stared uncertainly at her. Then he looked towards the nearest houses and saw the curious faces peering through the windows. His frown became one of dismay. 'This could reflect very badly on my school, ma'am,' he stated unhappily.

Cleopatra was wiping the blood from Simon's face, and simultaneously telling the weeping James, 'Come now, darling, dry your eyes. It's all over now. It's all over.'

Once more the schoolmaster repeated worriedly, 'This

incident could reflect badly on the good name of my school, ma'am.'

She looked at him in silence, and after a moment he invited, 'Perhaps you would care to accompany me back to the house, Mrs Dolton, where we can discuss this unhappy event in privacy.' He looked meaningfully at the surrounding houses. 'People are watching us.'

'I'm well aware of that fact, Mr Bryant,' she answered with a touch of asperity. 'And I expect those same people were watching when my sons were set upon three times in successive days. It's a pity that they cannot find better things to do with their time.'

Over the years Cleopatra Dolton had become inured to critical stares, learning to ignore them and keep her head high and proud.

The man spread his hands supplicatingly, 'Nevertheless, Mrs Dolton, i' would be best if we went back to the house to discuss this matter.'

Cleopatra glanced at her sons' faces and saw the distress and embarrassment in their expressions. Her heart was torn for them. She smiled and told them, 'Run on home, you two. I'll follow.'

'But I have to question them, ma'am,' Bryant objected.

'No, there's no need for that,' she told him firmly, and gestured to the boys. 'Go now. Go home.'

They hurried away and she waited until they had rounded the corner then turned to the schoolmaster.

'Let us go to your house then, Mr Bryant.'

His school premises were contained in a large old house standing towards the top of the sloping Park Road, facing the town's fire brigade station. A couple of the firemen were standing at the station's entrance, and they stared appreciatively at Cleopatra Dolton as she neared them.

'Theer's the Queen of Egypt coming,' one of them muttered, and grinned salaciously. 'I wish her was coming to visit me.'

'It's a pity your name aren't Purvis, her might be then,' his companion gibed.

As she and Bryant entered the school house Mrs Bryant came hurrying to them, but her husband frowned and ushered her away, then led Cleopatra into his office.

He invited her to sit on the straight-backed chair in front of his large desk, then stood before her, his hands clasped behind his back, his head tilted forwards so that the tassel on his mortar board fell to the front.

'This is a painfully delicate matter for me to have to broach, ma'am,' he began, and hesitated as if waiting for her to make a comment.

Cleopatra instantly intuited what he was referring to, but perversely declined to spare him any embarrassment and made no answer.

He coughed nervously, covering his mouth with ink-stained fingers, then clasped his hands behind his back again. He moved to stand staring out of the window as if not wishing to look directly at her, and began again, 'This is a most painfully delicate matter, ma'am, yet broach it, I must. I am aware of the fact that your sons have been badgered by their fellow pupils during these latter days and I am aware of the reason for that badgering. Needless to say, I do not condone such a course of conduct by the boys. However, I was reluctant to intervene, fearing that by doing so I should only worsen Simon and James's unhappy situation.'

He paused, and now she spoke. 'Let us both speak plainly, Mr Bryant. We both know the reason for the boys' conduct. There is, at present, a malicious and completely unfounded rumour being spread around this town concerning the relationship between myself and a certain gentleman. We are innocent of any wrongdoing but, unhappily, slanderous gossip has never paid any attention to truth, has it?'

The man turned to look directly at her and his expression mirrored his unhappiness and unease. 'Nevertheless, Mrs Dolton, this gossip is doing much harm, is it not? I tell you frankly, that although I personally do not believe a single word of what is being said about yourself and the gentleman in question, nevertheless I cannot afford to have the good name of my school threatened by it.'

'But it is nothing to do with your school's good name, is it, Mr Bryant?' Cleopatra argued.

'Unhappily, Mrs Dolton, you have witnessed what is

happening. I just cannot afford to risk a repetition of the scene which occurred today. Therefore I must ask you to withdraw your sons from my school.'

Her initial reaction was a quick anger at the injustice being done to her boys. Then a fearful dread of what their father's reaction would be when he heard of this shivered through her, and she almost pleaded with Bryant, 'Is this really necessary, Mr Bryant? Why must my boys be penalised for something which has no foundation, and for which they are not responsible? It is unjust.'

He sighed unhappily. 'I am truly sorry, Mrs Dolton. I have no choice in the matter.'

'Of course you have a choice!' her voice rose in angry protest. 'You can choose not to be influenced by wicked lies.'

His sense of guilt caused him to react irritably and his own voice rose indignantly. 'I can only choose to defend the best interests of my school, Mrs Dolton. I will not jeopardise its well-being for the sake of any individual pupils. If this means that I must appear to be acting unjustly, then so be it. I have nothing further to say to you, ma'am, except to bid you good day.'

Cleopatra's own fierce pride prevented her from arguing further. 'Good day to you, Mr Bryant.'

'I shall of course reimburse this term's fees in full, ma'am,' he told her, as he escorted her to the door.

'There is no need for full reimbursement, Mr Bryant,' she said acidly. 'I would not wish to be a recipient of your charity. I insist on paying for the time of my sons' attendance here.'

She walked down Park Road with her back straight and her head held high. The faces in the windows watched her pass and thought her pride to be arrogance.

When she reached her home she found the two maids and the cook fussing around the boys in the kitchen.

'Those scruffs oughta be sent to jail!' Mrs Danks stated angrily. 'It's disgusting when decent respectable boys can't walk the streets in safety. You should goo up to that National School and give that headmaster a piece o' your mind, Mrs Dolton.'

238

Cleopatra shook her head. 'It wasn't boys from the National School who did this, Mrs Danks. It was the boys from the Grammar School.'

The woman looked shocked. 'But they'm supposed to be young gentlemen.'

'They are boys, Mrs Danks, and all boys have the capacity for cruelty,' Cleopatra told her, and then spoke gently to her two sons.

'Simon, James, I want you to come up to my room now.'

Upstairs she seated herself on the chair before her dressing table and drew the two boys close with her arms around their waists. She felt near to tears as she looked at their cut and bruised faces, and saw her own apprehension and distress reflected in their dark eyes. She swallowed hard, and asked them gently, 'Do you both understand what people mean when they talk about fancy men or fancy women?'

It was Simon who answered her question. He nodded and faltered out, 'They mean wicked men and women, don't they Mother?'

She smiled sadly and shook her head. 'No, my dear, it doesn't really mean that.' She hesitated, trying to find the right words to describe the term, then continued haltingly, 'I think the best way to describe a fancy man or woman is to say that they are the objects of forbidden love. A sweetheart that the world frowns upon.'

The boy's brows furrowed in puzzlement, while his younger brother could only stare blankly at her.

Cleopatra felt impatient with herself for not being able to make the boys understand her clearly, then decided to abandon the attempt, knowing that she could well confuse them both even further.

'Well anyway, I want both of you to know, that when those boys were chanting that I had a fancy man, they were lying.'

'I know that already, Mother,' Simon answered gravely, his eyes shining with trust. 'I know that you're not wicked.'

Now tears did fall and Cleopatra was forced to release the boys and use her handkerchief to hide those tears.

'Why are you crying, Mother?' James questioned in

239

alarm. 'Did the boys hurt you as well?'

She fought for control and was able to force a smile. 'It's nothing, honey. Go on downstairs now and ask Mrs Danks to give you your tea.'

When they seemed loath to leave her, she urged gently, 'Go on now. I'll come down myself in a little while.'

After they had gone she sat staring at her reflection in the dressing table mirror and for a few brief moments let the full flood of her misery overwhelm her. Tears fell freely and her cheeks glistened with their moisture, but she made no attempt to dry them.

'I wish he was my fancy man.' The realisation came without warning and a sudden yearning to see Johnny Purvis swept over her. 'What am I to do?' she asked her reflection. 'What am I to do?'

But her reflection could give her no answer.

Chapter Thirty

'I reckon youm the luckiest cratur I'se ever come across, my wench,' Mrs Elwood grinned. 'With Mr Franklin getting sent for to goo to London on the bank's business like that. My bloke's very friendly wi' Sergeant Brunton and he told my bloke what happened. Ethel Fletcher went to the police station to report you for giving her what for and the Superintendent, Alf Hayes, happened to be theer. Well, he's a big mate of Mr Franklin's aren't he, so he told her he'd deal with the matter and he went round to have a word wi' Mr Franklin. But when he got to the bank Mr Franklin had had a telegram come to say that he'd got to goo to London immediate, and he'd already left. So, he aren't bin told yet about what happened, and that gives you time to get things sorted for yourself, doon't it. Mr Franklin might not be back for a week or more.'

It was evening and Emma and Mrs Elwood were sitting in the kitchen of Cotswold House, convivially sharing a bottle of gin.

Emma sipped the fiery clear liquid and gusted a sigh of satisfaction, then returned the other woman's grin. 'There's nothing to beat a drop of "Oh be Joyful", is there, Mrs Elwood?'

'Nothing!' the older woman agreed emphatically, then cackled with laughter. 'It's bin my ruin, as well as me mother's. I reckon Miss Miriam could do wi' a couple o' glasses o' this. It 'ud cheer her up a bit.'

Their mistress had returned from her visit to Ida Huins' house looking very depressed, and had gone early to her bed, telling Emma that she did not wish to be disturbed.

The gin was beginning to affect Emma, and now she chuckled a little tipsily, 'I reckon it needs more than a drop o' this to cheer the poor cow up. I reckon what she needs more than anything else is a good man between her legs. That might tickle her enough to make her laugh.'

Mrs Elwood cackled with laughter. 'I could do wi' a good man between me own legs, my duck. Old Elwood aren't a lot o' use these days. He carn't get it up at all lately.' She peered slyly at the young woman, and asked, 'How about you, my duck? Am you getting any lately?'

Emma Farr was not totally inexperienced in sexual matters. During her life she had permitted an occasional youth to caress her intimately, and had twice had full sexual intercourse with a handsome travelling pedlar who had stayed in the Silver Street lodging house for some weeks. But she had never been promiscuous and as she grew older had become increasingly fastidious about potential sexual partners.

The cook pressed pruriently, 'Did you let Albert Bott have a bit?'

Emma shook her head. 'No fear!'

She smiled and stretched her arms wide, pushing her firm breasts against her bodice. 'I reckon what I'se got to offer deserves a bit better than Albert Bott, Mrs Elwood. I reckon I deserves somebody like Johnny Purvis. He's a real man, not a boy like Albert is.'

The older woman's eyes were envious as she stared at the beautiful girl. She nodded, 'Youm a bonny looking cratur, right enough. Theer's nobody can deny that.'

Then the slyness came into her face again, as she asked, 'Has you give any more thought to what I said to you? About doing yourself a bit o' good here?'

'With old Hector, do you mean?' Emma asked.

'That's right,' Mrs Elwood nodded. 'You keep in mind what I told you, my wench: men like John Purvis doon't marry penniless maids, they marries women who'se got a bit o' cash or property to offer.'

'I believe you,' Emma concurred readily enough, but then her smooth forehead creased as she sought for words. 'Does you know what I'se bin thinking these last

242

days though, Mrs Elwood? I'se bin thinking how sick I am of being at other people's beck and call all the time. I'se bin thinking how tired I am of being beholden to other people and of being at their mercy.'

'We all thinks like that, my duck,' the cook stated. 'But theer's precious little that folks of our class can do about it, is there? We'em born into the wrong station in life, aren't we, to be able to do anything to change things for ourselves. We just has to make the best o' things. That's all we can do.' She paused and took a swig from her glass, then belched resoundingly, and went on, 'You'll be all right, my duck. With your looks you'll have no trouble finding yourself a good steady husband when you wants to.'

Emma frowned and shook her head. 'That's just it though Mrs Elwood. I'm starting to think that I doon't really want to get wed and become a servant to a man for the rest o' me life. Even if I marries a good steady chap, then I'm still his bloody servant, aren't I?

'I wants to be me own woman, Mrs Elwood and be independent of everybody. Then if I wants a chap like John Purvis, I can have him, and still be independent. If I had me own money and property, then I wouldn't be under any man's thumb, 'ud I? I'd be his equal and we'd be real lovers if we was equal, not master and servant.'

The cook's fat face screwed up in puzzlement. 'Youm too deep for me to understand, my wench. I can't grasp what youm about.' She abruptly cackled with laughter. 'Even if youm equal lovers the man still lies on top o' you, doon't he? A woman still has to be beneath a man, doon't her?'

Emma didn't answer, but only sipped from her glass of gin and stared into the glowing ashes of the fire.

The clock in the hallway whirred and struck the hour, and throughout the house other clocks added their echoing chimes.

'Bugger me, it's bloody ten o'clock already. My old man 'ull goo bloody mad if I aren't got his supper on the table for when he gets in from the pub.' The cook rose and swayed, then cackled wih laughter. 'Heyup theer. Steady

243

past your granny's, girl. I'll see you tomorrow, my duck,' she told Emma, and went unsteadily from the room.

Emma nodded absently as her friend left, and remained staring into the fire. Her mind was a swirl of random thoughts and images: memories came and went, faces appeared and disappeared, voices sounded and fell silent. One train of thought dominated.

'I'm sick to death of being at the bottom of the muckheap. It's time I was doing a bit of crowing from the top of it. But when bloody Franklin Josceleyne gets back from London he's bound sure to give me the sack and what sort of a mess 'ull I be in then?'

She grimaced angrily to herself. 'It aren't my fault this time, is it? That's what makes me mad! God Strewth! I wish I was rich!'

A thumping sound came to her ears, muffled by the intervening doors and she scowled. 'Hark at that old bastard. Let him hammer on the bloody floor all night for all I cares.'

She took another long gulp of her gin. Then came to a sudden decision.

'I'll just goo up now, and see if theer's any truth in what Mrs Elwood has bin saying.'

She went quickly upstairs carrying the bottle of gin and her glass with her and went into Hector Josceleyne's room.

'What's you making all this racket for?' she demanded.

The room was dimly lit by a low gaslight, and the old man was sitting upright in the bed. He scowled petulantly at her. 'You said that you'd come in and settle me comfortably for the night. Where have you been?'

Emma shrugged carelessly and put the bottle and glass on the great chest of drawers that dominated one wall of the room.

'What's that you've got there?' Hector Josceleyne demanded querulously. 'Have you been drinking?'

Emma pouted sulkily and then lifted her glass and drained it. She grinned cheekily at his shocked face and refilled the glass. Then invited, 'Would you like a drink yourself, Mr Hector?'

His toothless jaw gaped in shock and she giggled drunkenly.

244

Alcohol made Emma uncaring and reckless and under its influence she was able to overcome her innate distastes and act without scruple.

She smiled at the old man, and asked him huskily, 'Do you still want me to be nice to you, Mr Hector?'

She leaned back against the tall chest of drawers, and very slowly removed her high-bibbed white apron. Then, equally slowly, her fingers unbuttoned the top of her bodice.

The old man's earlier shocked expression now became overlayed with quickening lust. 'Come here, girl. Come here to me,' he ordered hoarsely, but she smiled and shook her head.

'Not yet, Mr Hector.'

Beneath her dress she wore only a thin shift, and now she opened further buttons, and pulled her bodice open so that he could see the rounded tops of her smooth firm breasts, and the deep shadowed cleft between them. His breathing became harsh and ragged and he begged, 'Come closer, girl! Come closer! I'll give you money! Lots of it!'

Emma stared at him with calculating eyes. 'You must keep your voice low, Mr Hector. You doon't want to wake Miss Miriam up, do you?'

'I'll be quiet,' he promised feverishly. 'I won't make any noise. Only come close will you.'

He tried to get out of the bed, but his stiff joints were too painful and he groaned in mingled agony and frustration. Then cursed hoarsely, 'God damn and blast you, you little bitch! Come here to me, will you?'

Resentment at his tone caused Emma to scowl and she hissed venomously, 'Doon't you start becalling me, you old bastard, or you'll get nothing. I'll goo from here right now.'

She made as if to rebutton her bodice, and he protested in quick panic, 'No, don't do that! Don't leave! I'm sorry if I spoke harshly, Emma. I'm sorry for it.'

She held her silence while he stared at her with beseeching eyes, and, once satisfied that she had gained dominance, she relented and let her bodice fall open once more. She moved slowly towards the bed, and whispered, 'If you doon't hurt me, Mr Hector, then I'll let you touch me. I'll let you kiss me here,' she indicated her hard nipples thrusting out the thin cloth of her shift.

Hector Josceleyne was all but slavering, and he nodded eagerly, 'Yes. Yes. I'll do as you say, girl. I won't hurt you, I promise.'

Emma slipped her dress back from her shoulders and then lowered her shift so that her breasts jutted free and proud in the pale light.

She took Hector Josceleyne's hands in hers and placed them on the warm smooth pulsing globes of flesh.

He groaned aloud and she pressed his face against her breasts and whimpering he sucked at the hard erect nipples, drawing breath in noisy choking gasps. Emma's right hand went beneath the bedclothes and sought for his manhood. She felt a shock of repulsion as she found its hard throbbing length, but steeled herself to finish what she had begun.

By now Hector Josceleyne was so wildly excited that his fingers and lips and toothless gums were ravenous upon her flesh and he climaxed within seconds as she stroked him. He vented a long drawn-out wailing cry. Emma freed herself from him and quickly rearranged her clothing. Stepping back to the chest of drawers she drank directly from the gin bottle, gasping and coughing as the fiery spirit burned its way down her throat. Then she moved back to the bedside and stared down at the old man, now lying back against his pillows.

'You're a good girl, Emma,' he panted hoarsely. 'You'll not lose by this, that I promise you. I'll pay you well.'

She made no reply, only remained staring ambiguously at him, and he asked, 'Are you all right, girl?'

She nodded silently.

When his rasping breath had eased, he bared his toothless gums in a smile, and told her, 'Next time, Emma, I want you to take off all your clothes. I want us to do it properly.'

She could not help but smile mirthlessly. 'How can you manage to do it properly, Mr Hector, with your rheumatics?'

He licked his lips and his eyes gleamed with lust. 'You'll have to do it on top of me in that case, won't you, girl?'

Now Emma slowly shook her head and she watched the dismay spread across his features. 'There won't be a next time, Mr Hector. You won't have me laying naked in your bed unless you meets certain conditions of mine.'

He gestured irritably. 'I've already told you that I'll pay you well, haven't I?'

'Oh yes, you've told me that all right,' she agreed, an ironic smile playing around her lips.

'Well then?' he became impatient. 'What's wrong with you? You know that you can trust me to pay you, don't you?'

Emma nodded.

Hector Josceleyne licked his lips and his eyes roamed over her body. 'Come into bed now, girl. Stay with me tonight.'

Emma shook her head, and then said coolly, 'The next time I do this sort of thing with you, Mr Hector, then I want to be your lawful wedded wife.'

He stared at her as if he could not believe what he had heard. 'My lawful wedded wife?' he gasped incredulously. 'My wife?'

Emma nodded calmly. 'That's right, Mr Hector. If you wants me in your bed, then you must wed me. Otherwise, you get nothing at all from me.'

She deliberately ran her hands down over her body. 'Just imagine how I'd look and how I'd feel lying naked in your bed, Mr Hector. Just imagine the things you could do to me then.'

His initial disbelief became outrage. 'Marry you?' he jeered the words. 'A Josceleyne marrying a servant girl? You must be mad even to think of such a thing.'

Emma grinned and told him, 'Well, Mr Hector, them's my terms. Take 'um or leave 'um.'

She lifted her bottle and glass from the chest of drawers and quietly went out of the bedroom, leaving the old man staring wildly after her.

Downstairs once more, nausea suddenly assailed her. She rushed out to the scullery and, bending over the stone sink, vomited uncontrollably.

When her retching had ceased and her aching stomach was empty, she rinsed her mouth and throat with cold fresh water and washed her clammy face and neck. Standing in the darkness of the scullery she battled to come to terms with her sense of self-disgust. Slowly her determination steeled until she knew with complete certainty that, no matter what price might be demanded of her flesh, she would be capable of paying it to gain her objective.

'I'm going to be my own mistress!' she thought certainly. 'I'm going to become rich, and when I am, no man or woman is ever again going to dominate me. Never ever again.'

Chapter Thirty-One

After a restless night beset by troubled dreams, Miriam Josceleyne awoke before dawn and lay in her dark room reflecting on the events of the previous day. With some surprise she found that she was able to view her rupture with Ida Huins' coterie with comparative indifference. Indeed with a sense of relief in fact, that she would no longer have to endure the tedious round of visits and 'at homes'.

'In future I shall choose whom I associate with,' she decided firmly. 'And whoever that might be, it will most certainly not be Ida Huins or any of her cronies.'

Her thoughts turned to the rumoured relationship between Johnny Purvis and Cleopatra Dolton. By now she had reluctantly accepted the fact that she was emotionally enthralled by Johnny Purvis. 'I know I'm behaving like a stupid lovesick fool, but I can't help myself.'

She was experiencing a curious mixture of happiness and pain and a snatch of poetry came into her mind, which she repeated aloud, "The sweet melancholy of love". Yes, that describes how I feel about him,' she decided, and decided also that she would treat the rumours concerning him and Cleopatra Dolton as being only malicious slander.

Arriving at that conclusion cheered her immensely and her spirits were further raised by the knowledge that this very morning she was going to visit his home at his invitation.

'Surely he would not seek my company unless he held some regard for me,' she thought hopefully.

Concentrating on this notion, she happily drifted into sleep once more.

When she next awoke it was daylight and although her restless night had left her body feeling tired and sluggish, mentally she felt happily alert.

She ate breakfast in the drawing room and noted that Emma seemed morosely preoccupied as she brought in the tea and toast and boiled eggs.

'How selfish of me,' Miriam Josceleyne chided herself. 'The poor girl is obviously worried as to what is going to happen to her when Franklin returns from London.'

In her present mood Miriam felt quite capable of defying her brother and of defending her maid. 'She shan't go from my service.' Miriam felt very determined. 'I don't care how much Franklin may rant and rave, I shall not permit him to dismiss Emma. If the girl wishes to remain with me, then she shall, no matter what Franklin or anyone else may want.'

When the girl came in to clear away the breakfast dishes, Miriam asked her, 'Emma, do you wish to remain in my service?'

The girl's eyes were wary and her expression guarded. 'Have you heard anything from Mr Franklin then, Miss Miriam?'

Miriam smiled. 'How could I have heard anything from Mr Franklin, Emma? He's in London.'

The girl appeared to be very tense. 'Oh I know that, Miss Miriam, but, but I just thought . . . That is, I wondered . . .'

'Enough, Emma,' Miriam held up her hands to silence the girl. 'All I want you to tell me is whether or not you wish to remain in my service?'

Still with wary eyes, Emma nodded. 'Yes, Miss Miriam.'

'Very well,' Miriam nodded, and smiled, then gestured. 'Please, finish clearing these things will you, my dear.'

Emma's mind was racing as she carried the dirty dishes back to the scullery. 'What's she asking me that for if she aren't heard anything from her brother yet?' she wondered. 'Surely she never heard me and that old bastard last night, did she?'

She stacked the dishes in the sink, remembering the previous night. She had not yet gone in to see the old man

250

this morning, but she was confident that she would get what she wanted from him, given sufficient time. She allowed herself no regrets or recriminations for what she had done with Hector Josceleyne, remaining coldly determined to succeed. Then the thought struck her that the reason for Miss Miriam asking her those questions just now was perhaps because her mistress had decided that no matter what Mr Franklin might say, she was going to retain Emma in her service.

The girl smiled at the thought. 'That'll do me just right, that 'ull, if she keeps me here with her. I'll have the old bugger in church within a bloody month if she does.'

The front door bell jangled, and since Mrs Elwood had not yet come into work, Emma hurried to answer it, drying her hands on her apron as she did so.

'Is Miss Josceleyne at home, girl?'

It was the Reverend Mosse MacDonald.

'I'll just goo and see if she's receiving visitors, sir,' Emma told him, but he halted her with an imperious wave of his hand, and instructed, 'Tell your mistress that it is imperative that I speak with her. Imperative!'

'Very good, sir. I'll tell her.' Emma was not impressed by the cleric's masterful attitude. 'But I doon't reckon she is receiving any visitors.'

Leaving MacDonald scowling at her back she went into the drawing room. 'If you please, Miss Miriam, it's the Reverend MacDonald, and he says it's imperative that he sees you straight away.'

Miriam grimaced unhappily, and then reluctantly consented to receive the man.

Emma took his top hat and gloves from him and placed them on the hall table, then when he had entered the drawing room, she pressed her ear to the closed door and listened intently.

'My dear Miss Josceleyne, what can I say?' With an expression of concern upon his pink plump features Mosse MacDonald advanced to the seated woman and took her hand between his own.

Miriam Josceleyne regarded him with some surprise.

251

'Say? Say about what, Reverend MacDonald?'

She pulled her hand free and gestured towards a chair. 'Please, won't you be seated.'

For a moment he reacted with an uncertain stare, then recovered himself, and after sitting down leaned towards her. 'I called at Mrs Huins' house yesterday afternoon, Miss Josceleyne, only to find that you had left there some time previously.'

She nodded. 'Oh, I see.'

Still with a concerned air, the man told her, 'Mrs Huins and the other ladies were deeply distressed, my dear Miss Josceleyne. They feared that you had taken offence at something that was said, but all confessed to having not the slightest notion why you should have done so. Mrs Huins in particular voiced her utmost concern, and told me that she felt both hurt and deeply saddened that you should have departed in such a manner from her house.'

'I'm sure she was,' Miriam answered with irony. 'The lady in question is noted for her extreme sensitivity is she not?'

The cleric looked doubtfully at her. This was not the timid, uncertain, flustering creature he knew as Miriam Josceleyne. This woman appeared to possess hitherto unsuspected attributes of acerbic confidence.

'Upon your next visit to Mrs Huins, you may inform her that I have no intention of ever returning to her house and that she is no longer welcome to call upon me here. That fact also applies to the other members of Mrs Huins' inner circle of confidantes.'

Mosse MacDonald was completely nonplussed, and after a moment of speechlessness could only splutter, 'But they are all very amiable and estimable ladies, Miss Josceleyne.'

'They are all malicious gossip-mongers, Reverend MacDonald,' Miriam informed him tartly. 'And to my mind resemble a veritable coven of witches.'

She rose to her feet and moving to the bell-rope at the side of the fireplace tugged sharply on it.

'You must excuse me now, Reverend,' she told him politely. 'But I have a pressing matter to attend to.'

Shocked out of his usual complacency as he had been,

the Reverend Mosse MacDonald allowed himself to be ushered out of the house without making any attempt to prolong his visit, and found himself standing outside on the roadway wondering what had happened to the timid, down-trodden woman he had seriously intended making his wife.

He drew a long long breath, and adjusted his top hat, then paced away with a ponderous dignity.

'Perhaps I've been too hasty in considering Miriam Josceleyne to be a suitable wife for myself,' he told himself. 'I believe the woman is becoming deranged.' His lips pursed in a spiteful pout. 'But then, mental derangement runs through that family, does it not? Just look at her father and brother.' His eyes swept briefly upwards and he murmured. 'Thank you Lord for saving me from my own foolishness, and in your infinite mercy, showing me the error of my ways. I'll seek a wife elsewhere.'

Miriam stood staring through the net curtains, watching the cleric depart, and chuckled to herself. 'There now, Reverend, that's given you and the other cats something more to miaow about, I'll bet.'

From overhead sounded the thumping of Hector Josceleyne's stick upon the floor. Miriam moved out into the hallway and as Emma came from the rear of the house, told the girl, 'It's all right, my dear, I'll go and see to my father.'

'I can goo, Miss Miriam.'

Emma appeared nervous and edgy, and Miriam frowned puzzledly.

'Are you all right, Emma?'

'Yes, ma'am, why do you ask me that?' the girl challenged defensively, and the older woman misunderstanding the reason for the girl's behaviour, told her, 'Listen Emma, if you are worried about losing your place here when my brother returns from London, then you have no need to be so. Because I intend to keep you in my service.'

Before the girl could reply the rear door bell jangled furiously and Miriam said, 'That will be Mrs Elwood, the back door must still be locked. Go and let her in, Emma.'

With a sullen reluctant air the girl moved away from the foot of the stairs and went into the rear of the house. Miriam Josceleyne shook her head in bafflement at Emma's attitude, so unlike her normal lighthearted demeanour, and went on upstairs to Hector Josceleyne's room.

The old man was sitting up in bed and when Miriam entered the room he frowned and questioned anxiously, 'Where's the girl? Where's Emma? She hasn't gone, has she?'

Miriam Josceleyne's sense of bemusement deepened even more. First Emma, and now her father, behaving so strangely.

'No, she's busy in the kitchen,' she told him, and he suddenly scowled angrily and shouted, 'Get out and send Emma to me. I want her to look after me, not you. Get out, damm you!'

Miriam's precarious sense of self-confidence momentarily wavered, then recovered, and she replied tartly, 'Don't shout so, Father. I'll send Emma to you, only don't shout so.'

'I'll shout as much as I want!' the old man stormed. 'It's my house. I'm the master here. If you don't like me shouting, then get out from my house.'

Knowing the futility of arguing with him in his present mood, Miriam went down to the kitchen and told Emma, 'My father wants you to attend him, Emma. He's in one of his bad moods this morning, I'm afraid.' She smiled at the girl's sullen features, hoping to see some indication of a change of temper. 'But you'll be able to cope with him well enough, I'm sure. You always do.'

'All right ma'am,' Emma muttered, and with her face averted, brushed past her mistress.

'What is the matter with the girl, Mrs Elwood?' Miriam asked the cook, who only shrugged her meaty shoulders and replied, 'T'is probably her time o' the month, Miss Miriam, if you gets my meaning. It affects some worser than others, doon't it?'

Miriam was quick to seize on this comforting explanation. She did not enjoy seeing the girl so miserable.

'Yes, I'm sure you must be right, Mrs Elwood. It must be as you say.'

'Come here girl, and close the door. I've no wish to be overheard,' Hector Josceleyne instructed.

Emma obeyed, and came to stand a couple of yards distant from the bedside.

The old man smiled toothlessly and pointed his stick at the great chest of drawers. 'Open that bottom drawer, girl. You'll find a cashbox in the right-hand corner. Bring it over here to me.'

Again Emma silently obeyed him, and carried the small but heavy metal box to the bed.

From under his pillows the old man produced a key with which he unlocked the box.

'Look Emma.' He showed her its contents, and she could not restrain a hiss of surprise when she saw the stacked piles of sovereigns that completely filled its interior.

'Here, girl, these are for you, for being nice to me last night.'

He lifted a couple of the coins between his long-nailed finger and thumb and offered them to Emma.

She shook her head, and told him contemptuously, 'You can shove them up your arse. I want none on 'um.'

He scowled angrily and challenged, 'How much do you want then, you little bitch?'

He snatched up several more coins. 'Here, take these as well.'

'Didn't you hear me before, you old bastard?' she questioned venomously. 'Didn't you hear me say I want none on 'um? I'm leaving this place and I want nothing from you.'

Hector Josceleyne reacted to this with a show of anger. 'You will not leave my employment, girl.'

'Doon't you try telling me what I can or can't do. I'm gooing and that's that!'

Emma tore the floppy mob-cap from her head and hurled it to the floor. Thick strands of her long hair came loose and she tossed them back from her face. The old man's throat dried suddenly as he saw her beauty. All the show of anger left him and he seemed to crumple bodily.

'Don't go, Emma. Please! Stay here with me. I need you, Emma. I need you!'

'Am you gooing to marry me then?' she demanded to know.

After a long moment of hesitation, he slowly nodded. 'Yes, girl. I'll marry you, if that's what you want.'

'When? When 'ull you marry me?' she pressed.

'Well, it is not easy to set a date,' he prevaricated.

Deliberately she drew a long deep breath, and saw his eyes move to her thrusting breasts and his tongue flicker out across his lipless mouth.

She moved closer to him and his hands came greedily seeking her breasts and thighs. For a moment or two she allowed him to maul her flesh, then stepped back and told him, 'I want the banns called this Sunday'.

'This Sunday?' he protested querulously.

She nodded firmly and again moved close to him, this time taking his hand in hers and pressing it tightly between the apex of her thighs.

'In three weeks' time we could be wed, Mr Hector. Then you'll be able to do whatever you want with me, won't you?' she whispered huskily. 'I'll be in your bed laying naked next to you every night when we'em wed. You knows how much you'll like that, doon't you?'

He groaned softly and tried to pull her against him and his fingers dug fiercely up between her legs, causing her to hiss in pain. She broke free, and demanded, 'Well then? Am you gooing to send for the parson and tell him to call the banns next Sunday?'

Enslaved by his lusts and driven by his frustration, Hector Josceleyne nodded irritably. 'Oh, very well then girl, I'll do that.'

Emma grinned in triumph, but her shrewd brain realised that although she had apparently so easily gained her wish, there could still be obstacles raised to foil her purpose.

'Doon't say anything about this to anybody else just yet, Mr Hector. Let it stay our secret until the parson's called the first lot of banns.' He nodded impatiently, and

256

pleaded, 'Just let me touch you now, girl. Just come here to me.'

She shook her head firmly. 'No, youm gooing to have to wait until we'em wed.'

When he persisted in his pleas, Emma displayed a flash of anger.

'No, I said! Be told, 'ull you? When we'em wed, and not before.' She seemed to soften, and added, 'Just be a good boy and in a few weeks you'll get all that you wants.'

Grudgingly, he acquiesced.

Smiling happily to herself Emma told him, 'I'll get you your breakfast now, Mr Hector, and after you'se ate it, I'll bring you pen and paper so you can write a note to the parson.'

Chapter Thirty-Two

'Steady now, lads. That's it. Set it down there,' Johnny Purvis directed, and the four workmen carrying the litter lowered their heavy load to the ground at the side of the great front door.

For a little while all five men stood staring curiously down at the statue, which had been carved from a single massive block of sandstone. It was the effigy of a man clad in a monastic gown and cowl, with sandalled feet and tonsured hair. One arm was outstretched as if bestowing a blessing and the other held a long staff.

'Who does you reckon he was Mr Purvis?' one of the workmen asked.

Johnny shook his head. 'I can't say for certain, Harry. I think it's probably one of the early Abbots of Bordesley. This used to be a grange of the Abbey didn't it?'

'But why 'ud they fetch a great heavy thing like this all the way up here?' another of the workmen wondered. 'I'd have thought they'd have kept it down in Bordesley theer.'

'Perhaps when the Abbey was broke up some of the monks brought it up here so the King's men couldn't take it,' another of the workmen suggested.

'I can't really believe that Henry VIII would have had much use for it,' John Purvis grinned, then offered, 'Perhaps it's always been here at this grange. Maybe one of the monks that worked here was a sculptor and he carved it during his free time.'

'But why should it have been buried so deep, Mr Purvis?' the man questioned.

Johnny shrugged. 'There's a story that in the Civil War Royalist troops were quartered here for a time. It could be that they buried it to save it being smashed by Cromwell's Ironsides because it was a representation of a Papist. The Ironside troopers were pretty active in these parts for a while. They sacked and burned Beoley Hall and attacked Coughton Court, didn't they?'

'Ahr, so they did,' the first man put in. 'My old dad took me one day and showed he wheer Oliver Cromwell placed his cannons on Beoley Hill to bombard the Abbey. That's how the town got its name, you know. When Cromwell bombarded the Abbey he killed so many people that the ditches ran red wi' blood.'

Johnny Purvis smiled inwardly as he heard the old legend repeated yet again. But he forbore to contradict the man, knowing that for centuries the apocryphal story had been a tenet of belief in his native town.

'Can you help me get this old bloke onto his feet, lads?' he requested. 'I want him facing out across the valley. I think he deserves a decent view after being below ground for so long.'

Grunting and straining, they jointly raised the statue upright onto its plinth, then admired it once more.

It stood a good seven feet in height; the figure was that of a very big and powerful man.

'I shouldn't ha' liked to meet that bugger on a dark night, if he was as big as that,' one workman joked.

'I dunno how you can say that, Charlie, when you looks at the size of your old 'ooman. Her's broader across the beam than this old bugger is and her uses a thicker stick when her sets about you,' another man gibed, and there was a general laugh.

'Many thanks, lads.' Johnny handed their foreman some coins, 'Here, have a drink for your trouble.'

'Thank you, Mr Purvis.'

'Thank you kindly.'

The men touched their caps and went back to the long deep trench they were digging for the water mains to be laid in.

Johnny Purvis went to fetch a bucket of water from the pump, and with a scrubbing brush began cleaning away the thick clay that layered the statue.

As the lumps of earth were cleared, details of the sculpture were revealed which he had not been able to see previously. He increasingly admired the skill and quality of the workmanship and wished that he knew the identity of the man who had created this piece. His vivid imagination took wing and his mind filled with dreams of past centuries when monks had dwelt in this house.

'It's wonderful, Mr Purvis.' Miriam Josceleyne's voice caused him to turn in surprise, and she apologised, 'I'm sorry, I did not intend to startle you.'

'No matter,' he smiled, and realised that he was very pleased to see her. Then glanced ruefully at his wet dirty hands and arms, and his rough clothing. 'Excuse my appearance, Miss Josceleyne. I wasn't expecting you until eleven o'clock.'

'It is eleven o'clock, Mr Purvis,' she told him gently, then stepped forwards and touched the carved rope belt of the statue.

'This is superb workmanship, Mr Purvis. One could almost believe that this was real rope.'

'It is superb, isn't it,' he agreed enthusiastically. 'Do you know, Miss Josceleyne, until I began to clean it up, I never realised myself just how fine a piece it is.'

She stood staring with a rapt expression at the statue and he glanced covertly at her.

She was dressed very simply in a black dress and long coat, with a plain straw boater hat upon her bunned hair. Johnny noted with concern how pale and tired she looked with dark shadows beneath her faded green eyes. Again the protective instinct stirred within him, and he asked himself wonderingly, 'What is it I feel for this woman? Why does she arouse such a feeling of concern in me?'

'Have you any theories to offer about who it is, Miss Josceleyne?' he asked aloud, and she started to shake her head, then stopped, and offered smilingly, 'Could it be John de Acton, I wonder?'

He laughed delightedly, 'If it is, then perhaps the Saracen Witch will make her appearance next.'

Then he frowned slightly as the disconcerting visual

260

image of Cleopatra Dolton suddenly came into his mind. To hide his momentary discomfiture he turned back to the statue and scrubbed at the clay embedded in the lower folds of its gown.

She watched him in silence, content to be near him, allowing herself to imagine that this was her husband, and this was their home, and that shortly they would enter the house together and spend the evening at their own fireside, talking, sharing thoughts, sharing dreams. Her imagination dared to enter forbidden realms and she pictured the coming of nightfall, the shared bed in which their bodies would meet and merge in ecstatic union of the flesh. The mental images came so strongly that she felt her heart quicken and her breath catch, and when Johnny Purvis looked up at her and smiled, she blushed as if he had penetrated her mind and read her innermost thoughts.

'There, that will do for the present.' He straightened his body and regarded his handiwork with satisfaction. 'What do you think to him now?'

'As I said before, Mr Purvis, I think him to be wonderful,' Miriam smiled back, and was suddenly uncaring that her cheeks were still flushed, and that her secret thoughts had been so boldly shameless.

'She looks really pretty, almost like a young girl,' Johnny Purvis thought as he saw her green eyes lucent and glowing, and the fresh colour that had come to her sallow cheeks. Affection for her goodness and simplicity surged through him; he felt a sudden urge to take her in his arms, to draw her close to him.

Miriam Josceleyne's lips parted slightly and unconsciously her body swayed towards him. She wanted to be in his arms, she hungered for his mouth on hers. All the mores, all the strictures, all the puritanical inhibitions engrained upon her mind from childhood were fast slipping away, and for the first time in her life she found herself experiencing lust for a man without guilt and shame wracking her.

Then a handcart pushed by two workmen came noisily crunching across the gravel and the mutual absorption that had enfolded the man and woman was abruptly shattered.

Johnny Purvis looked at the handcart and grimaced ruefully, 'It's the gas fitters, Miss Josceleyne.'

Miriam, jolted into awareness of other eyes upon them, was momentarily flustered. She blushed furiously, and her hands twined and tugged at each other.

With a real regret Johnny Purvis told her, 'I'll have to give them their instructions, Miss Josceleyne. It may take quite a while.'

On impulse, he laid his hand over hers and asked her, 'Miss Josceleyne, I need advice on some aspects of furnishing this place. Could I ask you to help me?'

'Well,' still flustered, she stared confusedly at him. 'Well, Mr Purvis, I don't really know if I am the most suitable person to advise you.'

He smiled and told her firmly, 'Yes you are, Miss Josceleyne. With your permission I shall call on you later this week, shall we say Friday? Yes, Friday afternoon, and discuss it further.'

After a brief hesitation, she nodded, and gulped out, 'Friday afternoon then, Mr Purvis.'

Then, with happiness bubbling within her, she hurried away.

Chapter Thirty-Three

'Mam, Mam, it's our Emma coming!' The grubby-faced urchin raced excitedly homewards bawling at the top of his voice, and Amy Farr, sitting with her neighbours in the alley outside their front doors, grimaced anxiously. 'Oh God, I hope she aren't got the bloody sack again. Her feyther 'ull bloody well kill her if her 'as.'

'Well, her aren't carrying any bundles, Amy,' one of the neighbours observed. 'So it doon't look as if her's expecting to stay.'

'Doon't her look posh!' another woman exclaimed admiringly. 'Her's as pretty as a pitcher, aren't her?'

The women were sitting on a row of assorted broken-backed chairs and three-legged stools, enjoying the warmth of the evening. Thankful to escape the cramped confines of their homes and enjoy each other's company, while their menfolk were mostly in the public houses.

Amy Farr smiled proudly at her approaching daughter. In the mean fetid alleyway, Emma Farr was a rare example of fresh young beauty. Now, dressed in a white dress and a flowered veiled hat, with a parasol over her slender shoulder, she drew envious stares from all who saw her.

Her younger sisters and brothers and their friends were clamouring around Emma, who smiled down at their dirty faces and unkempt hair as she distributed sweets from a large brown paper bag.

'Her's a good-hearted little wench, bless her!' Amy's next door neighbour told her. 'You'se got a good daughter theer, Amy Farr.'

'I knows it,' Amy declared proudly. 'But her dad gets

very riled with her at times.'

'That's only natural, aren't it?' another woman put in. 'All feythers gets riled wi' their kids sometimes. I know my bleedin' man does.'

'This is the last one.' Emma handed out the final sweet, and told the crowd of urchins, 'Get off and play now. I wants to see me mam.'

She came smiling to the row of seated women. 'Hello Mrs Green, hello Mrs Walton, hello Mrs Heath, hello Mary, Chrissie, Hello Mam.'

They chorused their greetings, complimenting her on her appearance, then her mother asked worriedly, 'What's you doing here on a Thursday night, our Emma? It aren't your normal night off, is it?'

'No, but I worked most of Wednesday night, so Miss Josceleyne gave me tonight off instead.'

'You'se got a good mistress theer, my wench,' Heather Walton told her.

Emma nodded agreement, then told her mother, 'I wants to have a bit of a talk with you, Mam. Is me dad gone out?'

Amy Farr's broken, gapped teeth bared in a mirthless grin. 'What does you think, my duck? The bugger's wheer he always is, down at the bloody pub theer.'

Emma frowned. 'It's a pity he can't spend more time at home and give you the money he swills down his neck.'

There was a rumbling of agreement from the other women, who all knew what it was to go short of money while their husbands drank their wages away.

Her mother led the way into the house and invited, 'Does you want a cup o' tay, our Emma?'

The girl shook her head, then told the older woman, 'Listen Mam, this is for you and the kids, not for me dad.' She pushed some coins into her mother's hand.

Amy Farr stared down at the coins, her worn haggard features mirroring her shock.

'Theer's five sovereigns here, our Emma!' she gasped. 'Wheer's you got this lot from?'

Emma grinned, and winked mischeviously. 'Never you mind, Mam. Theer's plenty more wheer that come from.'

'Oh Emma, what's you bin and gone and done now?' Amy Farr's expression was alarmed. 'Wheer's you got all this money from?'

Emma felt a touch of impatience at her mother's anxious reaction to this gift.

'It's come by honestly, Mam. I haven't pinched it!' she snapped shortly.

Amy Farr shook her head bemusedly. Five sovereigns represented a huge sum to her, she had never in her life held such an amount in her hand. 'How did you get it, our Emma?' she persisted plaintively.

Emma smiled fondly at her mother, and hugged her. 'You'll find out soon enough, Mam. But it's nothing to worry about, that I can promise you.'

'When? When 'ull I find out wheer it's come from?' Her mother's worn haggard features were pitiful in their worry, and Emma softened. 'Listen Mam, I'm gooing to tell you summat, but until after next Sunday morning it's got to stay a secret between you and me. After then it doon't matter who knows of it.'

Curiosity overlaid anxiety and Amy Farr begged, 'Tell me, my duck! Tell me!'

'All right then, but you must swear on the babies' grave that you'll not breathe a word on it to anybody. Anybody at all.'

'I swear,' Amy Farr whispered solemnly.

'I'm getting wed, Mam,' Emma said gravely. 'I'm getting wed to old Hector Josceleyne. Parson MacDonald is gooing to call the first set of banns on Sunday morning. I'se sworn him to secrecy as well and he took his oath that he 'udden't breathe a word on it until then.'

Amy Farr's lower jaw dropped in complete amazement and she could only stare speechlessly at her daughter. It was several seconds before she recovered sufficiently to blurt out in protest, 'But he's an old man, our Emma! And they say he's bloody mental as well! You can't marry him!'

Emma frowned and nodded vigorously. 'Oh yes I can marry him, our mam, and I'm gooing to. I know he's old, but he aren't really mental. He's just a bit dolally-tap sometimes.'

'But why doon't you marry a young chap if you wants to get wed?' her mother beseeched plaintively. 'Theer's young Albert Bott, aren't there? He's a good steady chap and in regular work. He'd be good to you as well. Why must you marry an old man like Hector Josceleyne? He aren't your class anyway. He's gentry aren't he?'

Emma chuckled bitterly. 'He's a dirty old bastard whose hungry enough for me body to marry me for it, Mam. And he's rich! When he dies, which God willing won't be too far from now, then I'll get his money and his property.'

'Oh our Emma, how can you do such a thing?' the older woman's disapproval and incredulity that her daughter could behave in such a way was plain to see. 'It aren't right, our Emma. It aren't right.'

Emma's patience snapped. 'What is right then, our Mam?' she demanded angrily. 'Is it right for me to marry a bloke like me dad and suffer the sort of life you'se had to suffer. Living in this stinkin' slum, without the money to feed and clothe the kids or yourself proper. Another babby in your belly every year. Treated like dirt, and given fist pie and boot pudding for your supper every time that bastard comes home drunk from the pub and takes his badness out on you.'

Her black eyes flashed with fury and her cheeks glowed with angry colour.

'Well bugger that for a game o' soldiers! I'se got a chance to become rich. I'se got a chance to change me life so that I'll never have to crawl to nobody ever again and I'm gooing to take that chance, our Mam, no matter what you or anybody else says against it.'

Her mother, a little alarmed by this display of temper from her normally affectionate daughter, hastened to mollify her. 'All right then, our Emma. All right, if that's what you wants to do. All right then.'

Emma was calming rapidly, and now she smiled a trifle sheepishly, and hugged her mother again. 'I'm sorry I shouted at you, our Mam. But I'se had a lot on me plate lately and I'm a bit moithered at present.'

She closed her mother's fingers firmly around the five golden sovereigns.

'Now no more arguing, Mam. They'm yourn. And theer'll be plenty more to follow from now on. You'll not goo short of food or clothes again, I'll see to that.'

Tears brimmed in Amy Farr's tired eyes. 'But 'ull you be all right, my duck? 'Ull you be all right when youm wed to Hector Josceleyne?'

Emma forced a smile and answered with assumed lightheartedness. 'When I'm Mrs Hector Josceleyne I'll be more than just all right, our mam. I'll be the bloody Queen of Redditch, you just wait and see if I won't.'

'God I hopes so, my duck. I truly hopes so,' the older woman prayed with heartfelt emotion.

Chapter Thirty-Four

It was Friday morning and Arthur Dolton groaned and stirred, then broke wind loudly. The foul smell issuing from under the blankets caused him to grimace in disgust, even though it was a product of his own body, and he cursed and rolled out from the bed. The hands of the wall-clock pointed to half past six and the man stood for a moment bleanfy squinting at the black Roman numerals, as if he had difficulty in deciphering their meaning. Then he belched and his liver lips twisted when nauseous bile filled his throat. He stumbled to the wash-stand and retched noisily into the large crock washing basin, almost filling it with sour smelling vomit.

He was still dressed in his outdoor clothing, having been too drunk to discard his jacket, trousers and boots when he had returned home the night before. Staring at his reflection in the wall mirror he ruefully examined his dishevelled appearance.

'Youm going to have to get a grip on yourself, Arthur, my lad,' he told his reflection. 'Today's Bromsgrove market, aren't it?'

The market was a cattle and sheep mart and Arthur Dolton bought much of his stock from there. He was a shrewd buyer, but he knew that to successfully barter with the farmers and stockmen he would need a clear head. On the chest of drawers there was a half-filled bottle of brandy and he looked speculatively at it. His head was pounding and his lungs were wheezy from the effects of excessive intakes of alcohol and tobacco, while his stomach churned queasily.

'Now the question is, Arthur, does you take a drop to steady yourself?'

He gave the question some consideration, knowing with his appetite for alcohol that one drop might well become two or three or four and then the whole contents of the bottle.

'You can't afford to be drunk at Bromsgrove Market, Arthur, else one of those fly bastards that gets theer could well get one over on you.'

On the other hand, in his present condition he doubted that he was capable of even reaching Bromsgrove Market, let alone doing business there.

'Bugger it. I needs it.' He reached for the bottle and uncorking it, gulped the fiery spirit. He coughed and gagged, but managed to hold it down. The heat spread through his stomach and chest and after a couple more gulps of the brandy he began to feel decidedly better.

He went out onto the landing. The house was still and silent, and he cursed inwardly, 'Them lazy bastards must still be stinking in their bloody pits.'

Then, from below, there came the sounds of people moving around, and the rattle of iron implements as one of the maids raked ashes from the firegrates.

'Good job for them that they'm up or theer'd ha' bin trouble for 'um,' he thought sourly.

He passed his wife's bedroom door and for a moment toyed with the idea of going into her. Although he had deliberately avoided her these last days, Arthur Dolton retained his obsession with his wife in full measure. He knew that she despised and hated him, yet his desire for her body was still as all-powerful as it had been when he had first met her. He did not love her, yet he was besotted with her. He felt no tenderness toward her, yet he needed to feel her naked body crushed beneath him. There were times when he actively hated her, yet above all else he wanted her and needed to possess her. He preferred to spend his days and nights drinking with his cronies, yet he was obsessively jealous of her, and insisted that she account for every hour of her day. She obeyed his commands, yet he felt that he had never mastered her. He could not live with her, yet could not live without her.

For some moments he stood outside the bedroom door,

his hand resting on the brass door knob, then he visualised his wife's expression should he enter and wake her, and he thought of the last terrible beating he had inflicted upon her, and turned away.

It was Milly who was clearing the ashes from the grate in the dining room, and when he entered she looked at him with wary eyes, fearful of his uncertain early morning moods.

'Leave that and fetch me a cup o' tay,' he ordered brusquely, and she immediately scurried away.

Arthur Dolton slumped down at the darkly gleaming table and tried to clear his fuddled brain. Ozzie Clarke was to call and collect him at eight o'clock and they would travel to Bromsgrove using the firm's horse and cart, which would be utilised to carry any animal carcasses he might purchase at the mart. Mostly he bought his meat on the hoof, enjoying doing his own slaughtering.

Milly brought in a laden tray and laid it before him, and he growled at her, 'Goo up and clean my wash-stand and when I'se drunk this I wants some hot water took up to me room.'

'Yes, Mr Dolton.' She bobbed her head nervously, being mortally afraid of her employer. 'If you please, Mr Dolton, Mrs Danks wants to know what you'd like for your breakfuss?'

'I want nothing,' he grunted.

A hour later, washed, shaven and changed he sat waiting in the drawing room for Ozzie Clarke to come.

He could hear his sons going through to the kitchen for their breakfast, but ignored them. They were a disappointment to him, and he was impatient of their timidity and weakly physiques.

Glancing out of the front window he saw the blue uniform and peaked shako of the postman coming up the driveway and he rang the bell for the maid.

'Bring the post into me.'

There was only a single envelope, addressed to his wife.

'Who the fuck is writing to her?' Suspicious jealously instantly stirred and without hesitation he broke the seal and opened the flap.

The letterhead was that of the Redditch Grammar School. Arthur Dolton scanned the lines of fine copperplate handwriting, then scowled at the banker's draft pinned to the sheet of notepaper.

His face was thunderous as he stamped upstairs and stormed into his wife's bedroom.

Cleopatra had just finished dressing, and she was coiling and pinning her long thick hair around her head. She swung to face him and alarm showed in her eyes as he brandished the letter and banker's draft in front of her eyes and bellowed, 'What the fuck is this then? Why have the boys bin chucked out of bloody school? Why warn't I told about it? Why didn't you tell me?'

The woman's face blanched and her breath caught in her throat. She had been living in dread of this moment, hoping against hope that her husband by some miracle would not discover that his sons had been expelled from their school, but knowing all along that inevitably the moment of truth would arrive. Flustered, she tried to formulate an explanation that might avert her husband's fury, and faltered, 'They were having trouble there, Arthur . . .'

'Trouble? What sort of fuckin' trouble?' he broke in brutally. 'I'm gooing up theer meself, right this minute, and I'll see bloody Bryant about why they'se bin chucked out. If that bastard thinks he can do that to my kids without so much as a by-your-leave, then he'd best think again.'

Cleopatra's heart quailed within her, but knowing that if her husband was told the reason for her boys' expulsion by anyone else then it would only be the worse for her, she screwed up her courage.

'Mr Bryant wanted them withdrawn from the school because of the lies that are being told about me.'

The man's first reaction to her words was a stare of blank incomprehension then, as understanding dawned, a murderous fury reddened his eyes, and Cleopatra's mouth became dry with fear and she could not even swallow to dispel the lump that came heavy in her throat.

271

'What lies?' he gritted out from between clenched teeth. 'What lies are people telling about you, that causes my sons to be kicked out o' their school?'

With an enormous effort of will she managed to gasp out, 'Lies about John Purvis being my fancy man.'

Arthur Dolton's face purpled and he vented an animal howl as he struck her. His fist smashed into her face, blood gouted from her nose, and she screamed as she fell backwards.

He hurled himself onto her howling maniacally, 'I'll kill you! I'll kill you, you fuckin' whore!'

Choking on her own blood, her breath crushed from her by his bulk, the woman felt the clutch of his hands around her throat, and her sight was veiled with scarlet-flashed blackness as she drowned in a raging sea of pain.

'Theer, my duck. You'll be all right. You'll be all right.'

Cleopatra could hear the voice and slowly the swirling blackness receded and light came and she opened her eyes to see the chalk-white, frightened faces of Mrs Danks and Doll staring down at her. With consciousness, terror and pain returned, and she started wildly, her eyes seeking Arthur Dolton.

'He aren't here, my duck. He's gone. You'll be all right now. Just stay quiet for a bit. Stay quiet.'

Mrs Danks hands pushed her gently back, and Cleopatra moaned as the agony of her broken nose throbbed through her. But even in her agony she pleaded anxiously, 'The boys? Where are the boys?'

The words came out in a broken hoarse utterance and her throat felt as if it had been ripped raw internally.

'Milly's took 'um out for a walk, my duck,' Mrs Danks reassured. 'Lie still now, while I clanes your face up for the doctor to see it.'

While the woman carefully sponged the blood away, Cleopatra's senses returned fully. She became aware that she was lying in her bed, and the elderly, frock-coated Dr Pierce came into her field of vision.

'Drink this, Mrs Dolton.'

While Mrs Danks lifted her head from the pillows he held a glass of liquid to her lips and she drank it obediently. After a while the throbbing pain in her face and head slowly eased and a feeling of drowsiness crept over her. Once more she slipped into darkness.

Awareness seeped back and the darkness gave way to light.

'There now, Mrs Dolton, remember you must not touch your nose, and try to avoid disarranging the dressing in any way.'

Still woozy-headed from the effects of the laudanum draught Cleopatra nodded and Dr Pierce smiled and told her briskly, 'In a few weeks you'll be as good as new, Mrs Dolton. Don't be alarmed by the swelling and discoloration around your eyes, it's the natural accompaniment to a broken nose. I've reset it very carefully, so that when it's healed there should be no crookedness. Your throat will feel sore and it will pain you to swallow for some time I fear, but there is no lasting harm done there either.'

He frowned with concern as another thought struck him, and asked her, 'Do you have any relatives or friends with whom you might stay for a time, Mrs Dolton?'

She started to shake her head, and hissed as the movement caused her swollen face to pain her.

The man's frown of concern deepened and he told the two servants, 'Wait outside for a moment, will you.'

When he was alone with Cleopatra, he said in a low voice, 'Mrs Dolton, your servants have intimated that these injuries you have suffered were not come by accidentally. Yet when I pressed them to explain more fully they were loath to do so, they appear frightened. Perhaps you might care to tell me how you received these injuries?'

Cleopatra lay silent, her eyes closed. A part of her wanted to tell the world what Arthur Dolton had done to her, wanted to shout from the rooftops that he was a vile bully, a vicious animal, a brute. But another part of her was experiencing a terrible sense of shame and degradation. All the filthy abuses inflicted upon her during her early life came back now to torture her with their memories. She had battled all her life to overcome

273

the mental and physical effects left by those abuses; to rise above her beginnings and to become a woman who could be worthy of respect, who could walk the streets of this town with her head held high and unashamed, who could walk with pride and know in her heart that that pride was well earned and well deserved.

Her courage and her pride had enabled her to endure the ill-treatment from Arthur Dolton and to continue to respect herself up to this moment in time. But now, with this last assault, something seemed to have broken within her spirit. She was feeling, for the first time in her married life, exactly as she had felt after she had borne her father's child: soiled, degraded, worthless, a creature of no value, a thing that could only be regarded with disgust and repulsion. She felt now that she would sooner be lying dead in her grave than have the world come to know how Arthur Dolton had abused her. At this moment she had no courage, no pride, no hope left in her.

The elderly doctor was a man of vast experience, and he could surmise accurately enough what had transpired in this room. He could also sense something of what this woman was feeling and suffering, and he pitied her and forbore to press her further. Shaking his head sadly, he told her, 'I'll leave you to rest now, Mrs Dolton. I'll call on you in a couple of days and see how you are progressing.'

The tears were running down Cleopatra Dolton's cheeks as she wept soundlessly. Doctor Pierce, with a last pitying look, quietly left her to her sorrows and ushered the servants away with him.

Chapter Thirty-Five

'I wonder who her visitor's going to be?' Mrs Elwood was puzzled. 'I thought you said that her had fallen out with Ida Huins and that crowd?'

'Well, that's what I heard her tell the parson when he came to see her that time.' Emma was equally mystified. 'Whoever it is, she's gooing to a lot of trouble. She seems really excited.'

'Her's never got me to get out all this lot afore anyway. All the best stuff, this is. Normally her only fetches out the second best silver.'

The two women were facing each other across the kitchen table, which was strewn with the family silverware. Emma gave a final polish to a beautifully fashioned Apostle spoon and examined it critically. She smiled to herself as she savoured the secret knowledge that soon all this fine silverware would belong to her.

'Is there only one coming, Mrs Elwood?'

'That's what her told me.' The cook grinned slyly. 'I reckon it's somebody her's got a powerful fancy for, you know, Emma. In fact, I 'udden't be at all surprised if it aren't her fancy man coming.'

Covertly she watched for the younger woman's reaction, and was delighted to see Emma's sudden frown.

'Who do you mean?'

'Why it's got to be Johnny Purvis, aren't it? Her was up at his house a couple of days since, warn't her? And her came back here looking as pleased as a pig in shit.'

Jealousy lanced through Emma's mind and she snapped, 'I can't see that Johnny Purvis 'ud be interested in an old maid.'

Mrs Elwood could not resist turning the verbal blade, because, although she liked the younger woman, she was naturally envious of her youth and beauty.

'Oh I wouldn't think it's what's between her legs that he's interested in, my duck. But like I'se said afore, a man like him wants a woman whose got a bit o' money and property to offer, doon't he?'

For a brief instant Emma flared unguardedly, 'She won't have a lot of either to offer in a few weeks.'

She could have bitten out her own tongue when she saw the expression on the cook's fat face.

Mrs Elwood's eyes widened and gleamed, and she gusted out, 'Bugger me! You'se done it aren't you, you sly little cat! You'se got Mr Hector to agree to wed you, aren't you?'

'Doon't talk so sarft!' Emma denied forcefully, but Mrs Elwood refused to accept that denial.

'You can't kid me on, my wench. I'm too long in the tooth to be kidded on. You'se done it, aren't you?' She waggled her head admiringly. 'Does you know, I thought summat had happened like that, when you 'udden't let me near the old bugger yesterday, but insisted on bathing him by yourself. I thought then that summat was gooing on. Well bugger me, Emma, if you aren't the slyest little cat I'se ever come across.'

Emma, dismayed though she was, realised the futility of further denial, and begged the older woman, 'Doon't say anything to anybody 'ull you, Mrs Elwood. I wants to keep it a secret until Sunday morning. The parson's agreed to keep quiet until then as well.'

The other woman nodded sagely. 'Yes, that'll be when the fust banns am called, won't it? Does you know, I wondered why Reverend MacDonald come here the other day to see the old man, and then had a couple o' words wi' you in private. O' course, I can see why now. That's when you arranged for the banns to be called, warn't it?'

She sought confirmation and Emma nodded. The cook's eyes narrowed and she started to piece the jigsaw of the situation together.

'O' course it stands to reason that the parson 'ud not say

anything about it to Miss Miriam, doon't it? He's very thick with Ida Huins, aren't he, so when Miss Miriam fell out with that old cat, then he was bound to take sides against her, warn't he? That's why he's kept it a secret for you, aren't it?'

Again Emma nodded confirmation.

'Him and Mr Franklin doon't like each other either, does they, so the parson 'udden't tell him anything either.' The cook threw up her hands and cackled with laughter. 'Bugger me, but youm a case, you am, Emma Farr. Youm a real case if ever I met one, and that's as true as I'm sitting here, that is!'

'You won't say anything to anybody, 'ull you, Mrs Elwood?' Emma pleaded, and the older woman delightedly assured her, 'Not me, my duck. Cross me heart and hope to die if I breathes a word on it to anybody. Wellll . . .' Her jowls quivered as she shook her head in complete admiration. 'You sly little cat! Youm a case, you am, Emma Farr! A real case!'

Despite the plaudits of the older woman, Emma sought for more. 'Does you think I'm doing the right thing, Mrs Elwood? Marrying the old bastard?'

'Bugger me, yes!' the cook stated emphatically. 'He can't last much longer, can he, and then you'll be the mistress here.'

She blew out her fat cheeks. 'Gawd Strewth! I wish I'd had the same chance when I was your age, I'll tell you. Believe me girl, it's the only way any wench from our class can ever better herself in this world. You marry the old sod, then get him buried as quick as you can. Wear the bugger out in bed, my duck!' She laughed uproariously. 'Like I told you before, one good squeeze wi' your legs and a couple o' bumps wi' your arse, and it'll be all up with old Hector. He'll be pushing up the bloody daisies in next to no time.'

Emma frowned unhappily. 'I'm not looking forward to sharing his bed, Mrs Elwood.'

The cook regarded her sympathetically. 'I doon't expect you am, my duck. But have a drop o' gin afore you beds him, then it won't seem so bad. You must just keep your eyes closed while he's shagging you and try to put your mind on other things.'

Emma grinned sardonically. 'Try to think of England, must I, Mrs Elwood?'

The older woman chuckled throatily, then leaned over the table and patted the girl's hand with her own. Becoming suddenly very serious, she told her, 'Listen to me, girl, I know it's easy for me to say it, and it's you who's got to do it, but you'll find that you can get used to anything in this life. Theer aren't many of us women who finds any lasting joy in our beds. I knows many and many a poor cratur who's only ever met lifelong misery theer. At least youm doing it for a purpose, aren't you. Youm doing it to gain your independence, and you can look forwards to that every time he wants to climb on top of you.

'He's an old man, my duck, he aren't long for this world, so whatever it's like, it aren't gooing to last for ever, is it? Then, when it's all over, you'll have money and property. You'll be able to choose to do whatever you wants to do, and nobody 'ull be able to deny you. Remember what I say. Whatever it feels like being in bed wi' old Hector, in the long run it'll be worth it for you.'

She paused, then winked lewdly. 'With any luck at all, it 'ull only be a very short run anyway.'

She began to collect the polished cutlery together. 'Come on now, you goo up and get started on laying the table, then you can come and give me a hand down here.'

In the drawing room Emma prepared the table for afternoon tea. Miriam Josceleyne was upstairs soaking in a hot bath, Hector Josceleyne was sleeping, so all was quiet in the house.

Despite Emma's doubts about her forthcoming marriage to Hector Josceleyne, she was still determined to carry it through. Her insistence on secrecy was engendered by instinctive shrewdness. She did not want to risk having the old man dissuaded from the marriage by his relatives.

The first banns called in the church would stand as incontrovertible proof that he had promised to marry her. She would be in a position to threaten a legal suit for

278

breach of promise and damages should those relatives then influence the old man to refuse to marry her.

Mrs Elwood's assertion that anyone could become used to anything came back to her mind, and she was forced to acknowledge the inherent truth of the statement. When she had bathed the old man yesterday she had allowed him to fondle and kiss her breasts and mouth and had again masturbated him. Although she had felt repulsion, she had done it sober this time, without the aid of gin.

'I'll be able to stand being wed to him,' she thought with certainty, and drew added comfort from the knowledge that it could not possibly last for too long, with him being so old and in such precarious health.

She allowed herself to daydream of a future when she would be a young and rich widow, and her lips curled in a smile. 'Will I encourage your attentions, John Purvis? Or will I fancy another man by then?'

Early that afternoon Miriam Josceleyne came down into the kitchen where the two servants were arranging the sandwiches and cakes on the silver salvers. She was wearing a pastel shaded silk day-gown, and her hair was swept back into a chignon. Her green eyes glowed, and her sallow cheeks were rosy with excitement.

Both women regarded her with a sense of wonder. Their normally faded, dowdy mistress looked remarkably youthful and pretty, and Emma's jealousy flared again as she thought, 'By Christ, you aren't looking so bad at all, Miriam Josceleyne. Theer's a few chaps who could fancy you at this minute, I'll be bound . . . Maybe even John Purvis?'

'I shall entertain my visitor by myself, Mrs Elwood, Emma,' Miriam Josceleyne informed them smilingly. 'It's a lovely day outside, so you may have the rest of it free. I shan't be needing you again today.'

Emma's eyes narrowed suspiciously as her thoughts raced to wild extremes. 'But what about Mr Hector, Miss Miriam?' she questioned.

'I shall see to his needs, Emma,' her mistress smiled. 'Just bring the tea things up to the drawing room and leave a couple of kettles on the boil so that I can use the water for the tea. Then you may both go.'

Normally both servants would have reacted with delight to this extra holiday, but on this particular afternoon they were both loath to leave without knowing for certain who the mysterious visitor was to be. Emma in particular was reluctant. 'But you'll need help to serve the tea, Miss Miriam,' she protested, and the woman smiled fondly at her.

'You're a good girl, Emma, to think of me so. But I assure you that I am quite able to serve tea by myself. You must go out and enjoy a holiday this afternoon, and if you waste more time in argument, then the holiday will be wasted also, won't it?'

'Very well, Miss Miriam, thank you very much,' Emma accepted with as much good grace as she could muster. She decided that her holiday jaunt would take her only as far as a bench in the recreation garden, from where she would be able to monitor all visitors to Cotswold House.

Chapter Thirty-Six

From her vantage point on a bench in the recreation garden, Emma was able to command a view of both Church Green East and West. Although she had been sitting here in the hot sunshine for what seemed to be an interminable time no one had yet called at Cotswold House. The girl was becoming bored by her vigil, but was still determined to maintain it. She felt driven to know for certain if Miriam Josceleyne's expected visitor was indeed Johnny Purvis.

Emma could not really rationalise her feelings for Johnny Purvis. Sexually, he excited her, and he represented a focal point for her romantic longings. She was realist enough to accept that at this moment in her life he was unattainable for her. Nevertheless she did not want him to marry or fall in love with any other woman until such time as she, Emma, might have lost her own interest in him.

Little had happened to divert her during her sojourn in the garden. An occasional delivery cart or pedestrian had passed, but most people were at work, and the shoppers in the town centre were few. The somnolent warmth of the afternoon and the restful quietness of the garden imperceptibly pervaded Emma's senses and a pleasant languor spread through her body. Her eyelids grew heavy and she allowed them to close over her eyes while she indulged her fancies with daydreams of what she would do when she became a rich woman. Her breathing slowed and deepened and her daydreams merged with and became the dreams of sleep.

Johnny Purvis walked along the pathway between the churchyard and garden and did not notice the girl sitting asleep on a bench half hidden by flowering shrubs. His eyes were centred on Cotswold House, and his thoughts on the woman awaiting him inside its walls. He found himself surprised by his own eagerness to see and talk with Miriam Josceleyne once more, and his lips twitched in a rueful smile as he mentally acknowledged the attraction that this frail timid woman exerted upon him.

Crossing the roadway he drew deep breaths to steady the sudden increase in his heartbeats, and his smile broadened as he thought, 'I must be falling in love with her. I feel like a nervous boy at the prospect of being with her again.'

Before he grasped the shiny brass bell-pull he glanced down at his formal clothing, noting with satisfaction the immaculate appearance of the dark frock-coat and trousers, grey waistcoat, pristine white linen and highly polished spatted bootees. His kid-gloved hand went momentarily to his shiny top hat and then he tugged the brass handle vigorously, sending the jangles of the bell echoing through the house.

On the other side of the dark oak door Miriam Josceleyne experienced a sensation of pure panic, and her heart pounded and her hands shook. Then she caught sight of herself in the tall wall mirror and stood transfixed in wonderment at what she saw.

The sunlight pouring through the tinted glass panels of the entrance hall windows bathed her in a soft radiance of shimmering gold, softening the harshness of the years, causing her to appear the young and beautiful girl she once had been. She smiled in innocent delight at her reflection and all panic stilled, so that she was able to open the door and smile in welcome, 'Please do come in, Mr Purvis.'

Johnny Purvis's eyes widened at the sight of her, hardly able to believe what they saw. The faded, sallow, dowdy old maid had been transformed into a beautiful and eminently desirable woman.

Miriam took his hat, gloves and cane from him and laid them on the hall table. She thought that he looked impressively distinguished in his formal clothing, but in her heart of hearts was forced to admit that romantically she wanted him always to be wearing the dashing uniform in which she had first seen him.

She led him into the drawing room, and, as he dutifully followed, he realised that he had yet to speak a single word to her. At the table, laden with its opulent display she turned and indicated one of the two chairs placed ready to receive them.

'Will you be seated, Mr Purvis?'

Now a faint tremor of nervousness struck through her as she noted the slight frown on his face, and sensed a constraint in his manner, and she felt herself tensing in abrupt apprehension.

'Thank you, Miss Josceleyne.'

Johnny Purvis was uncomfortably aware of the tension that had so suddenly arisen between them, but at this moment his own emotions were in such turmoil that he could do nothing to dispel it. He had come expecting to find the mousy little creature who aroused such strong feelings of protective tenderness within him. Instead he had been confronted by this beautiful woman whom he knew instantly could arouse within him passion and desire as urgent and powerful as he had ever experienced. Desperately he fought to clarify his turbulent jumbled thoughts.

She seated herself on the other chair facing him across the table and asked diffidently, 'Do you prefer Indian or China, Mr Purvis?'

'Whatever,' he answered vaguely.

She flushed, made nervous and confused by his vagueness of manner. Johnny Purvis saw the wave of colour rising from her slender throat and up into her cheeks and a poignant tenderness swept over him. He smiled and all constraint fell away.

'Forgive me, Miriam, if I speak bluntly, but speak I will. I think that you look truly beautiful, and I have to tell you that I care deeply for you.'

Her flush deepened and she stared down at her entwined fingers twisting and turning upon her lap.

He studied her, and within his mind exalted in happy

283

wonderment. 'I'm in love with this woman! I really am in love with her!'

He hungered to go to her and raise her up and crush her to him, but something within him held him back from doing so.

'I must go gently,' he realised. 'So very very gently.'

Aloud he said softly, 'Please, don't be offended by my words, Miriam. I say them with honesty.'

Miriam Josceleyne was drawing long ragged breaths; tears suddenly brimmed and fell from her eyes.

Johnny Purvis saw those tears and frowned with dismay. 'Jesus Christ, what sort of bloody fool have I made of myself now?' he silently asked himself.

He shook his head in a gesture of self-disgust and rose to his feet.

'I do apologise most sincerely for having distressed you in this way. Believe me, I did not intend to do such. I meant no offence.' He spoke stumblingly, inwardly cursing himself for what he now perceived to be his own crass stupidity.

'I should have known that a gentlewoman like her would be mortally offended that a ruffian like me should talk of loving her,' he thought.

'Please, don't distress yourself, Miss Joscelyne. I'll leave now. And again I sincerely apologise for have spoken so.'

He stared miserably at her downcast head for a moment longer, and then turned away.

Miriam swallowed hard, and gulped, 'Don't leave me, John. Don't turn away from me.'

He swung back to face her, then moved to kneel at the side of her chair and very gently stroked her tear-wet cheek with his fingers and turned her face towards him.

He smiled tenderly at her, and whispered hoarsely, 'I could never turn away from or leave the woman I'm in love with.'

Hesitantly he touched his lips to hers, then as heart-wrenching sobs shook her slender frailty he gently cradled her in his arms and rocked her soothingly for long long minutes, until her sobs eased and the shudderings of her body stilled. Still on his knees he again sought for and

284

found her mouth; this time her lips parted to his and her arms came around his neck.

Miriam Josceleyne's body ached for his loving, all scruples, all moralities, all engrained strictures, all fears were swept away by the terrible fierceness of her need. She crushed against the man's hard muscularity as he rose to his feet lifting her with him as if she were weightless. Johnny Purvis pulled back his head to stare into her face and she nodded in answer to his questing stare and her mouth sought greedily for his. Her breath caught in her throat as she felt his warm hard hands move within her clothing to cup and fondle and caress her naked flesh. His breathing was a harsh panting in her ears and she became aware of a soft continuous moaning, and with a start of surprise realised that it was her own voice venting its cries of wanting. They sank together upon the soft hearth rug before the silken fire screen and the air felt cool to her heated skin as the man began to undress her, gently but firmly pushing aside her hands when they sought to obstruct him, and silencing her muttered protests with kisses.

Momentarily he pulled away and tore his own clothes off and she lay watching him, almost unbearably excited at the revelation of his lean hard body, spreading her slender thighs in instinctive invitation. She gasped as he came on top of her, his mouth crushing upon hers, his hands stroking, fondling, seeking, demanding, and she gloried in accepting, in giving. She felt his thighs parting her own, and opened herself eagerly to receive him, crying out as he entered her, feeling a sharp pain as his long throbbing maleness violated her virgin flesh, then moaning in delight as the fiercely urgent thrusting of his hips invoked ripples of pleasure which intensified to waves of breathtaking ecstasy. His thrusts quickened and she felt his hands cupping her small rounded buttocks, lifting them so that he could drive deeper and deeper and deeper into her and she lost all control and jerked upwards to meet his thrusting maleness, wanting him deeper and deeper within her, wanting to engulf and absorb him completely, wanting to merge into one flesh, one being, one entity.

Together they climaxed, crying out in unison, and then

285

they were still and spent. It was Miriam who now cradled his shuddering panting body against her breasts, stroked his sweat-sheened shoulders, gently kissed and nuzzled his throat and cheeks and lips.

As the thudding of her heart eased, and her straining lungs drew breath more easily, she began to explore her own feelings, and found only a delighted satisfaction. Momentarily she was shocked at the absence of shame, of guilt, of regret, but then chuckled throatily and gloried in those absences. She felt the man withdraw from her and a pang of loss struck through her being. Then he hugged her warmly and kissed her throat and lips, and murmured words of love, and that sensation of loss was replaced by a sure knowledge of possession.

'This is my man,' she told herself, glowing with pride. 'This is my man.'

Emma Farr started bodily, her head jerked up and she came to wakefulness. She blinked hard and stared blearily around her as she struggled to re-orientate herself. The sun was low and red in the western sky and the young girl's lips twisted in a petulant grimace as she realised the lateness of the hour. A glance at the clock on the church tower confirmed that realisation.

Half past seven. Emma felt aggrieved. 'If it was Johnny Purvis that Miss Miriam was expecting, then he'll be long gone by now. How the bloody hell did I manage to fall asleep sitting on this bloody seat?'

The great clock chirred and chimed to mark the half hour, and Emma scowled up at the gold numerals and stuck her tongue out at them.

'No need to put your bloody oar in, I knows what time it is,' she mock scolded.

She was fully awake by now and sat for a few moments considering how to spend the remainder of the evening. 'I suppose I could goo for a walk, or goo and see me mam, or even visit with Mrs Elwood and have a drop o' gin with her.'

Even as each thought occurred she almost instantly dismissed it. Her overwhelming need was to satisfy her curiosity.

'I'll goo back and see if Miss Miriam is all right. She might need a hand to get the old man settled in for the night.'

Emma grinned to herself. 'Doon't talk so bleedin' false, Emma,' she mentally chided. 'Admit it, why doon't you? Youm dying to know what happened this afternoon; if Miss Miriam had a visitor . . . and if that visitor was who you think it might be.'

Humming happily to herself the young girl rose from the bench and went quickly towards Cotswold House.

Emma unlocked the rear door and went through into the kitchen. The room was gloomy in the fading evening light and she used a lucifer-match to light the gas mantle. Beneath its harsh hissing glare she opened the inner door and went quietly out into the passage, listening hard for any sound. The house was still and silent, but not empty. Emma could sense the presence of others somewhere within the sombre shadows. She moved on into the hallway and called softly, 'Miss Miriam. Miss Miriam, are you here?'

'Yes Emma, I'm in here.'

Her mistress's soft voice came from the drawing room, and Emma opened its door and stared into the shadowed interior. She saw the dark outline of her mistress half lying in one of the armchairs that flanked the silk-screened fireplace.

'Am you all right, Miss Miriam?' Emma asked. 'Why am you sitting here in the dark?'

Her curious eyes saw that the tea table so carefully prepared had not been disturbed. The sandwiches, cakes, tea things were untouched.

'Why Miss Miriam, you haven't even had your tea, have you? Didn't your visitor come then?'

'Oh yes, Emma. My visitor came.' Miriam Josceleyne's voice held a note of dreamy contentment. Emma looked sharply at her, striving to see the older woman's features clearly in the room made gloomy and dark by the heavy net curtains.

'Is Mr Hector all right, Miss Miriam?' Emma was puzzled by her mistress's languorous manner.

A soft chuckle sounded from the shadowed figure. 'I assume he is, Emma. He's been quiet enough these last hours. Perhaps you might look in on him before you go to your bed.'

The young woman stared in open amazement, wondering silently at this change in the older woman.

Miriam Josceleyne yawned audibly, and rose to her feet. 'I'm going to my bed, Emma. Will you clear these things for me please? Goodnight, my dear.'

She walked past Emma, and the long skirts of her gown brushed against the girl's skirts. Emma's keen sense of smell detected the scents of lavender and rosewater, but mingled with these were other scents, heavier and more fecund. The young girl frowned in puzzlement. 'What have you bin up too, I wonder?' she silently asked the older woman as she disappeared from the room. 'Something's happened here this afternoon, something that's altered you, Miriam Josceleyne. What was it, I wonder?'

She stared down at the laden tea table and hunger assailed her. She sat down on one of the tall straight-backed chairs and began to eat voraciously, her mind still filled with her mistress's changed manner. Traces of the strange fecund scent still persisted in her nostrils and she tried to identify it, but could not.

When Emma had satisfied her hunger she began to clear the table, stacking the unused saucers and plates and cups in readiness for a tray. The gloom of the room began to irritate her and she lit the gaslight wall-bracketed at the side of the large fireplace. She had held the lucifer-match high up on its shaft and the flame licked her fingers. With a sharp cry she dropped it, then instantly knelt to pick it up once more. It was then that she saw the stain on the light-coloured hearth rug.

'Bugger it, I'll needs to clean that off now. She must have spilled something on it. I hope she doon't try blaming it on me. Is it tea or coffee she spilled?'

Emma's fingers traced the stain, finding it still damp and sticky to her touch. Then she wondered, 'How could it be tea or coffee, when she aren't touched the tea things?'

On sudden impulse she bent over until her nose was

288

only inches from the small discoloured patch, and sniffed curiously. The fecund scent filled her nostrils, and now Emma recognised it for what it was.

'Bugger me! Nooo, it can't be! It can't be!'

She could not believe the evidence of her own senses. She lit another lucifer-match and made a careful examination of the stain, even smearing some of it upon her fingers and staring at it closely, sniffing long and thoughtfully at it. Her mind went back across the years to that moment when she had first known a man's loving and she remembered the stains upon the grimy lodging house sheets. Stains created by her and the pedlar's congress.

Emma sat back upon her heels, and emitted a long sigh of acceptance. 'She aren't an old maid any longer, that's for sure. She's had a man shaggin' her on this bloody rug.'

Jealousy shafted through her. 'Was it Johnny Purvis who shagged her? How could he? How could a fine looking bloke like him bring himself to shag a dry old stick like her?

Then recollection of how attractive Miriam Josceleyne had appeared that day caused Emma to reluctantly accept, 'She looked really nice today. Pretty enough to tempt any bloke.'

Her jealousy intensified. 'It aren't fair though. An old maid like her to have a chap like Johnny Purvis. It aren't fair.'

Emma tried to assuage her chagrin at that thought.

'Perhaps it warn't him as shagged her? Jesus Christ! Why did I have to bloody well fall asleep and miss seeing who come here? It aren't bloody fair. It just aren't fair!'

Upstairs Miriam Josceleyne lay naked in her bed, her mind still filled with the events of that afternoon, still filled with wonderment at the ecstasies she had experienced. Her hands moved to stroke and cup her breasts, her belly, her thighs, and the slight mound of her womanhood, as she vividly recalled the feel of Johnny Purvis's hands, lips and tongue upon her flesh, and the sensation of his surging manhood filling the achingly empty void within her. Fresh desire rose and her lips parted as her fingers penetrated the warm moistness between her legs.

Her mind filled with the memories of Johnny Purvis's potent loving, and her hand moved in short savage jerky thrusts as she became unheeding of anything other than her hunger for his body, and her need for satiation.

Chapter Thirty-Seven

Miriam Josceleyne ate her breakfast with gusto, and then informed Emma, 'I'm going to see my brother.'

'What time will you be wanting luncheon, Miss Miriam?' Emma enquired politely.

The older woman smiled and shrugged. 'I'm not sure just how long I shall be away, my dear. Don't bother about preparing anything for me.'

'Very well, miss.' Emma bobbed a curtsey, her eyes studying the other woman curiously.

Miriam Josceleyne was looking young and fresh and radiating an air of contented happiness. Her hair was dressed in the loose chignon, and, although she was wearing her normally muted grey day-gown, she wore a brightly coloured shawl around her shoulders to relieve its drabness. Long golden earrings shimmered as she moved her head, and a golden necklace shone against the high ruffled collar at her throat.

When Miriam Josceleyne left the house twirling an opened parasol above the small beribboned boater perched saucily on her head Emma stood at the window of the front bedroom watching.

She went down to the kitchen and told Mrs Elwood, 'I've never seen such a change in a woman.'

'What woman's that?' Mrs Elwood, intent on peeling potatoes grunted absently.

'Why Miss Miriam, o' course.'

The fat face grinned knowingly, but vouchsafed no reply.

Irritation tinged Emma's voice. 'Just gone swanning off and doon't even know when she's coming back, or so she says, anyway.'

The cook's grin broadened, and laying aside the knife and half-peeled potato she turned to face the young woman.

'Come on then. Let's be hearing the full story. I knows that youm bostin' to tell me summat.'

Piqued, Emma tossed her head. 'I don't know as if I should be telling you.'

Mrs Elwood chuckled wheezily, then shrugged with an exaggerated display of unconcern, and turned to pick up the knife and potato once more.

'Oh all right then,' Emma snapped petulantly. 'But pay attention, 'ull you?'

Again the fat woman emitted a wheezy chuckle. 'Let's have a cup o' tay, shall us? And then you can tell me everything.'

Once they were settled facing each other across the white-scrubbed expanse of the table, steaming cups of tea before them, Mrs Elwood urged, 'Come on then, girl. Let's be hearing it.'

Emma drew a long breath, and then began, 'Well, when I come back here last night, the mistress was laying in the drawing room in the dark, and I . . .' As she told the story her voice rose excitedly, and the words came in a voluble stream.

In the manager's office of the Metropolitan Bank of England and Wales, Franklin Josceleyne regarded his sister with an expression of stupefaction.

'You want how much?' he demanded.

'Two hundred pounds,' Miriam Josceleyne informed him agreeably. 'That should be enough to begin with.'

'To begin with?' Her brother's voice sounded as if he could not believe what he was hearing.

'Yes,' Miriam answered brightly. 'I shall be needing more later when I buy my winter wardrobe.'

'Winter wardrobe?'

'Yes, Brother. Winter wardrobe,' Miriam confirmed, and smiled at the man's expression. 'I don't know why you are scowling at me so, Franklin. After all, I am in need of new clothes, and it is my own money that I wish to spend, is it not?'

The reasonableness of her tone acted as a goad to his quick temper.

'It is family money that you are proposing to waste, Sister!' His face reddened dully as his blood pressure rose. 'Two hundred pounds to be thrown away on useless fripperies and geegaws! You must be mad even to think of doing such. Why does an old maid need to deck herself like some silly, empty-headed girl? You are proposing to make yourself look ridiculous in the eyes of the world. For the sake of our family's good name and standing I cannot permit you to do such. It is arrant nonsense!'

For a brief instant she wavered. The long years of subservience to her parents' and then her brother's dictates could not be easily thrust aside. Then the visual image of Johnny Purvis's face came sharply into her mind, and the sure knowledge that he loved and wanted her, that she was a woman able to inspire and command the love of such a man brought strength and determination flooding through her. Her lips firmed, and her voice hardened, 'I've no wish to quarrel with you, Franklin, but I will tell you now, that if you seek to thwart me in this, I shall withdraw all my money from this bank, and place it elsewhere.'

His jaw sagged in astonishment.

'Have you gone mad?' He leaned across his desk and stared at her with bulging eyes as if seeking evidence of insanity in her face.

Miriam marvelled at her own feeling of steely confidence and inwardly she acknowledged, 'Johnny Purvis, you have indeed changed me.'

Then she herself leaned forward to meet and hold her brother's angry glare, and she gritted out, 'If you do not give me what I ask for this instant, then I shall withdraw all my money from this bank and place it elsewhere.'

'You cannot do that!' he blustered.

'Oh yes I can!' she retorted, and suddenly stood up. 'And I shall do it this very instant.'

She turned and walked with resolute steps to the door and had her hand on the brass door knob when she heard her brother's strangled voice.

'No! Wait! Come back here, Miriam. Let us try and

discuss this matter calmly.'

A smile of triumph curved her lips and, still facing the door, she challenged, 'Are you going to give me what I ask for? Or must I go to the teller for it.'

To add emphasis to the words she turned the knob and started to pull the door open.

He thought of the clerks listening avidly, thought of how they would mock and gibe behind his back if his sister carried out her threat, and came catapulting from behind his desk to slam the door closed, words tumbling from his mouth as he did so. 'Yes, yes! Very well! I'll shall give you the money. I merely wish you to act wisely, Sister. To let me advise you in these matters.'

Miriam discovered a streak of spiteful cruelty in her nature that she had long suspected she possessed, yet had never been capable of utilising until this moment.

'I wish to draw the full amount now, Brother Franklin. At some date in the future I may well be amenable to listening to your advice. At present I've neither the time, nor the desire to do so.'

He swallowed hard, and, despite the temper rampaging through him, was able to inject a note of mollification into his tone. 'Very well, my dear. As you please. But do try to take care and spend this money wisely, won't you?'

She nodded, now magnanimous in victory. 'Oh I will, Franklin. Be assured I will spend it wisely . . .'

Afterwards, when Miriam Josceleyne had gone from the bank with two hundred golden sovereigns in her purse, Franklin Josceleyne slumped down at his desk and tried to marshal his bewildered thoughts.

'What in Heaven's name has got into the fool?' he pondered miserably. 'I've never known her to behave in such a way before. Where did she acquire such aggression, such confidence? Is she indeed going mad?'

He shook his head in sadly unaccustomed doubt. 'Will I be able to reassert control over her, I wonder?'

Humming merrily beneath her breath Miriam Josceleyne sauntered along Evesham Street, picturing the new clothes she intended buying, planning how she would look for her next assignation with Johnny Purvis.

Chapter Thirty-Eight

Sunday morning services at St Stephen's church were normally well attended, it being considered something of a social event as well as the dutiful attendance upon the Lord God. The womenfolk took the opportunity to display their newest and finest clothes, the menfolk to exchange pleasantries and useful information during the general mingling after the service.

The Reverend Mosse MacDonald M.A., was normally relegated to the sparsely attended afternoon services, his temporal master, the Reverend Canon Horace Newton, preferring to conduct the morning services himself, but this morning owing to the Canon's indisposition Mosse MacDonald had been elevated to the pulpit.

As the curate listened to the reading of the second lesson his eyes roamed constantly across the serried pews before him, and he savoured the prospect of the sensation which he would shortly create among his congregation. His gaze centred on the features of Franklin Josceleyne sitting in his pew with his mountainous wife and daughters beside him, his pompous expression irritating in its smugness.

MacDonald hugged himself figuratively. 'I'll be wiping that self-satisfied smirk off your face in a moment or two, Josceleyne. What a pity that old maid of a sister isn't with you. I would have loved to have seen her reaction.'

The curate's gaze flickered further along the serried pews, seeking and finding the faces of his female coterie, Ida Huins, Amanda Allcock, Julia Playfair, Beatrice Kendrick, Violet Milward, all sumptuously dressed, all betraying signs of impatience.

MacDonald smiled inwardly with satisfaction. He had hinted to them that he would have something of a sensational announcement to make on this Sunday morning, but had adamantly refused to enlarge upon that hint.

The reading droned to an end and Mosse MacDonald rose majestically and intoned, 'There are banns to be called.' He paused to allow the rustling and fidgeting to come to an end, then staring down into the face of Franklin Josceleyne he announced loudly and clearly, 'I publish the banns of marriage between Hector Josceleyne of Cotswold House, Redditch in the Parish of Tardebigge and Emma Farr of Silver Street, Redditch in the Parish of Tardebigge. If any of you know cause or just impediment why these two persons should not be joined together in Holy matrimony, ye are to declare it. This is the first time of asking.'

The curate beamed down at Franklin Josceleyne's stupefied expression; the sudden buzzing of shock and excited comment which erupted throughout the congregation was music to his ears.

Now Franklin Josceleyne's wife and daughters were leaning towards their worldly master, eager questions tumbling from their lips, but Franklin Josceleyne made no answer, only sat staring straight ahead, his eyes bulged with shocked disbelief at what he had heard.

As MacDonald went on to call further banns the bank manager started to shake his head from side to side in denial, and then abruptly jumped to his feet and with pinched lips, staring eyes and flaming face scurried up the centre aisle and out of the building, leaving behind him an excited buzzing.

Once outside, Josceleyne began to pace wildly up and down the churchyard among the tombs of the departed, muttering to himself, shaking his head, clenching and unclenching his fists, periodically throwing back his head to glare up at the heavens, as if demanding an answer from the Lord God.

While the bank manager paced wildly backwards and forwards, the fat figure of Mrs Elwood went from the rearmost pew of the church and panted towards Cotswold House. She hurried around to the back of the house and slammed through the door and into the kitchen. Emma Farr was sitting at the large table, hands clasped hard before her in tension. When the other woman entered and came to stand leaning over the table with her hands slapping upon its scrubbed top and her lips moving soundlessly, the young girl went pale and demanded anxiously, 'Well?'

The fat woman suddenly shrieked with excited laughter and nodded vigorously, then jerked out, 'He's done it, Emma. He's done it! He's called the banns!'

Emma paled and swallowed hard. Then shook her head. Her lips curved and her white teeth glinted, then she threw back her head and laughter pealed from her.

Mrs Elwood's hands were visibly shaking as she lifted a bottle of gin from a cupboard and poured two generous measures into cups. She handed one of the cups to Emma and gulped down the contents of her own.

'Aggghhh!' she exhaled a great gust of air, then grinned at Emma with admiring awe, and babbled, 'You'se done it, girl. You'se bin and gone and done it! What a fuckin' upset this is going to create. You'se really put the cat among the pigeons this time. Youm a caution, you am, Emma Farr. Youm a real fuckin' caution, I'll take me oath on that. Youm a real proper case, you am!'

Emma took a long gulp of her own gin and in her turn exhaled a noisy gust of satisfaction. Then chuckled richly, 'I'se got the old bugger tied now, aren't I, Mrs Elwood? He won't be able to wriggle out o' this 'un, 'ull he? I'm going to be a rich woman.' Her eyes danced and shone with glee. 'I'm going to be a rich woman and no bugger 'ull ever be able to domineer over me agen, not as long as I lives they won't.'

Her eyes glittered.

'I'm going to be my own woman, Mrs Elwood. My own woman . . . and fuck 'um all!'

Chapter Thirty-Nine

At three o'clock on Sunday afternoon Cleopatra Dolton set her teeth against the aching of her battered body and left her bed.

She sat at her dressing table and examined her face in the mirror, tentatively exploring the thick plaster covering her nose and the bandages around her throat. Her eyes were mere slits in swollen purpled flesh and her head throbbed with pain.

Mrs Danks had told her what had occurred after Arthur Dolton had throttled her into unconsciousness. While he was attacking her, Ozzie Clarke had arrived with the horse and cart. Hearing Cleopatra's screams and Arthur Dolton's frenzied bellowings he and the cook herself had rushed upstairs and into the bedroom.

'It took both on us to drag him off you, my duck!' The cook's face had been white and strained with the memory. 'Thank God that Ozzie Clarke is a strong chap, or Arthur Dolton would have done for you, that's certain sure that is. I hadn't got the strength to get him off you by meself . . .'

Now, while Cleopatra still recalled those words, Mrs Danks came bustling into the room. With worried eyes she asked, 'What's you doing out o' bed? The doctor said you was to stay still until he give you word to get up.'

Cleopatra tried to speak, and grimaced at the pain of her damaged throat. Hoarsely she whispered, 'I couldn't bear to lie there any longer, Mrs Danks.'

But now that she had arisen she realised just how badly shaken and physically damaged she was. That realisation served to render her both fearful and depressed.

'Where are the boys?' she wanted to know.

'Up at their Granny Dolton's. It's Sunday aren't it?' the cook scolded. 'Did that bastard knock your senses out of you, that you'se forgot they always goes up to see her on a Sunday?'

Then her voice softened as she regarded Cleopatra's misshapen features. 'I aren't told them what happened to you, my duck. I'se only said that you aren't feeling too good.'

Cleopatra nodded her gratitude, then enquired hesitantly, 'Where is he?'

She somehow could not bring herself to voice her husband's name.

Mrs Danks scowled ferociously. 'Gawd knows. The bad bugger aren't bin back here since Friday. Good riddance to him! I hope he never comes back, the evil wicked bastard!'

She paused for a moment, her face hot with anger, then burted out, 'You should have told the doctor what that bastard did to you.'

'What good would that have done?' Cleopatra answered dispiritedly, and the cook, after a moment's reflection, was forced to shrug her shoulders.

'Not a lot, I suppose. Anyway, the doctor could see for himself what had happened, couldn't he?'

She hissed vindictively as she studied the younger woman's features. 'That Arthur Dolton oughta be hanged! I had a few hammerings from my old man, but he never served me so bad as that bastard is serving you. Youm gooing to have to leave him this time, you know, because he'll end up bloody killing you.'

Fear shivered through Cleopatra as she whispered, 'I think you might be right, Mrs Danks, but where can I go? I've no family, no friends, and I've no money. Where can I go with three children?'

The older woman sighed heavily. 'I aren't got a home o' me own, my duck, so I can't offer you shelter. But no shelter at all is better than being kicked to death.'

Cleopatra shuddered as chill struck through her, and Mrs Danks put gentle hands on her, urging, 'Come on, it's back into bed for you, right this minute. You aren't well enough to be up and about as yet.'

Cleopatra momentarily resisted. 'But what if he comes back and I'm lying helpless in my bed?'

The other woman's thin features set in a mask of grim determination. 'I'se got a big knife down in the kitchen theer. I'll shove it through the bastard if he should lay hands on you again, my duck. I swears to that on me kids' graves.'

Cleopatra shook her head weakly. 'No, Mrs Danks, I don't want to involve you in my troubles. I don't want that.'

'Come on now, into bed wi' you,' the cook pressured, and Cleopatra, feeling sick and giddy, allowed herself to be led back and put into the bed once more.

'That's better.' The cook smiled sadly down at her. 'Now you rest easy while I goes and makes you a nice dish o' broth. And don't you worry about that bastard. I'll not let him touch you whiles I'm about.'

She bustled from the room and Cleopatra thankfully sagged back against the pillows. Although she felt utterly spent and wearied she could not sleep, her mind was filled by forebodings, and she sought desperately to formulate some plan of escape from this house and this marriage.

'I need money,' she told herself. 'Enough money to get a long way from here, and to look after the children with.'

Her restless gaze fell upon the trinket box on her dressing table. In the early days of their marriage Arthur Dolton had delighted in adorning his wife with expensive jewellery and there were several pieces in the box for which she knew she could get a good price. But it might take some time to arrange their sale, and to pawn them locally would be difficult since they were very costly items. Questions would be asked which might lead to Arthur Dolton finding out what she was doing.

'What would he do to me if he found out I was pawning the jewellery he gave me?' she thought fearfully. Even in the midst of that fear a flash of gallows humour lanced through, and she chuckled wryly. 'He couldn't do much worse than he's done already, that's for sure.'

She lay pondering her dilemma, her thoughts roving widely, and then the memory of her last encounter with Johnny Purvis came to her. In her mind she heard his voice telling her, 'If you should ever have need of me . . . . If you should ever have need of me . . . . If you should ever have need of me . . .'

A sensation of relief suddenly burgeoned and served to calm her inner turmoil.

'I've need of you now, John Purvis. I've sore need of you now. And as soon as I'm fit to stir, then I'll ask you for your help.'

Comforted by this resolution Cleopatra felt herself relaxing, and settled back into the pillows. When Mrs Danks came into the room carrying the bowl of chicken broth she found her mistress sleeping peacefully.

For a brief while the cook stood staring down at the sleeping woman, then shaking her head sadly she turned and went silently from the room.

Chapter Forty

In the small cottage in Izods Yard, Johnny Purvis and his father sat facing each other on different sides of the minute firegrate. For the most part they sat in silence, only occasionally exchanging brief sentences, yet there was a tangible atmosphere of contented companionship, neither man would have wished to be in any other place, or with any other person during these quiet hours they shared in the early evening of the Sabbath day.

Both men were smoking short clay pipes and the strong smelling wreaths of smoke hung heavy in the low-ceilinged room. A big iron kettle bubbled on the hob and steam jetted from its long curved spout.

'Does you want a cup o' tay, our John?' the old man asked, and Johnny Purvis nodded, then offered, 'Shall I make it, Dad? That'll save you disturbing yourself?'

A gleam of indignation showed momentarily in the old man's eyes and he growled, 'I'm only old and stiff, my lad. I aren't lost the use o' me arms and legs yet awhile.'

Johnny smiled with fond amusement, and bantered, 'Or your cantankerousness either.'

The old man glared, then snorted with laughter. 'No, that's a fact, that is. I doon't reckon I'll ever lose that.'

He pushed himself laboriously from his wooden armchair and busied himself in brewing a pot of tea and in laying out cups and saucers, milk and sugar.

Johnny sat comfortably watching the old man. He felt a quiet happiness that at long last he was achieving the sort of comradeship with his father that he had always hungered for. A fleeting sadness touched him, as he thought, 'What a pity you can't be here to see how well me and me dad get on now, Mam.'

When the tea had been poured into the cups, and milk and sugar added Johnny drew a silver hip flask from his inner pocket, and tipped a generous measure of rum from it into his own cup. He could not resist teasing his father.

'I know you're strict temperance, Dad, so I'll not invite you to share this.'

The old man chuckled huskily. 'I give up temperance when I give up ranting and raving from the pulpit, my buck.'

Johnny laughed and topped up his father's tea with the rich dark rum.

While they sipped the hot fragrant drinks, Johnny Purvis searched for words with which to broach his new plans to his father. At length he decided to take the bull by the horns. 'I'm thinking of getting wed, Dad.'

The rheumy blue eyes regarded him keenly over the rim of the cup. 'About time you did, my lad. You aren't a young rooster any longer. It aren't good for a man to live without a mate all his days.'

Then old Ezra fell silent, his eyes fixed on the flickering flames in the firegrate.

Johnny frowned puzzledly. 'Don't you want to know who the woman is?' he asked, with a suggestion of pique at his father's apparent lack of interest, then grinned ruefully as he saw the twinkling in the old man's eyes.

'You'll tell me when youm ready to, John, I'm sure o' that.'

'It's Miriam Josceleyne,' Johnny stated bluntly.

'Who?' The old man's shocked stare brought a smile to Johnny's lips.

'Miriam Josceleyne. Old Hector Josceleyne's daughter.'

'But her's gentry, our John,' the old man protested. 'You carn't be wedding her.'

A flicker of annoyance caused Johnny to speak more sharply than he intended. 'Why not? We're as good as any gentry aren't we?'

'Oh ahr, and better nor most on 'um as far as I'm concerned,' the old man asserted firmly. 'But think on, our John. We'em as good as them in our eyes, but it's their eyes that you'se got to reckon with. In their eyes we'll never be as good as 'um. We'll always be reckoned to be beneath 'um.'

'That might have been the case in the past, Dad,' Johnny argued impatiently, 'but this is 1902. It's a modern age we're living in now. The old differences between the classes are disappearing.'

'Am they now?' Ezra Purvis challenged. 'Am they now? Well I carn't spake for how it is in foreign parts, my buck, but I can tell you that here in Redditch it's still a case of tipping your cap to the needle masters and the factory owners. Theer's nobody from Izods Yard gets invited to dinner with the Milwards and the Hemmings and the Chillingworths. Oh no.' The old head shook in vigorous denial. 'In this parish it's still the Squire o' Bentley in his mansion and the peasant at the gate, and doon't you try telling me any different, because I knows well enough that it's as I says it is.'

The younger man frowned grimly. 'I didn't fight the Empire's wars to come back here and tip my hat to any needle master or factory owner, Dad, nor to any local squire either.

'The only thing that any of them have ever had over me was the fact that they were rich, and I was poor. But things have altered in that respect. I'm as rich as any of them now, and I'll not stand at any man's gate at his beck and call.'

A look of worried concern came on the old man's face, and he said quietly, 'I don't preach any more, boy, but I still believe that theer's a deal o' truth to be found in the good Book. One truth is the warning to beware o' the sin o' pride. You bear that in mind, our John. Pride has brought better men nor you and me tumbling down into the gutter.'

Recognising the futility of arguing further against his father's entrenched, life-long mores Johnny Purvis forced a smile and said quietly, 'I don't want to fall out with you, Dad. We'll just agree to differ about this particular matter, shall we?'

'All right,' the old man accepted, then went on stubbornly, 'but you mind what I say, John. If you intends to wed this Josceleyne girl, then remember that being gentry she aren't bin brought up to work and serve, but only to lay about and to be served. She'll never be a helpmate to you, but only a burden.'

Johnny sighed resignedly, as he faced once more the futility of trying to convince his father that a woman such as Miriam Josceleyne might have known her own hardships and drudgeries.

'All right, Dad. I'll remember your words.'

Sudden anger sparked in Ezra's rheumed eyes. 'Yes, you'll remember all right, my buck. But you wunt take any heed on what I'm atelling you, 'ull you?'

Johnny Purvis could not help but laugh fondly at his father's irate expression. He shook his head and could not resist teasing, 'No, in this particular case I won't heed your words, Dad, but I promise I will remember them.'

He drained his cup, and urged, 'Come on, let's put this matter aside, and have another cup of tea. There's plenty of rum left in the flask.'

After a few moments grumbling the old man chuckled wryly himself, and drained his own cup.

Some time later Johnny Purvis left the cramped terraced cottage and went out onto Front Hill. Feeling a need for some exercise and fresh air he decided to walk for a while before returning to his rooms at the Plough and Harrow.

The evening was dark and still, and the pools of light shed by the gas lamps only served to emphasise the emptiness of the roadway. Johnny passed by the lighted windows of the public houses and taverns and heard the sounds of laughter and voices coming from within but felt no desire to enter in search of company. He was content to walk slowly in company with his own thoughts. Those thoughts centred mainly on Miriam Josceleyne, and he marvelled afresh at how his emotions towards her had so dramatically changed.

He grinned wryly to himself. Although he had told his father that he intended to marry Miriam Josceleyne, he had not yet imparted that information to the lady herself. He had no doubts concerning her reaction to his proposal.

305

In his heart he was sure that she would become his bride, and he savoured the prospect of their shared lifetime in Grange House.

Her eager reciprocation of his passion had both surprised and delighted him. Now he eagerly anticipated their assignation on the morrow. She had agreed to meet him at Grange House on Monday afternoon and he intended to ask her to marry him then. The fact that they had known each other so briefly did not worry him. He was in some respects a fatalist and held more than a passing conviction that men and women followed a predestined path through their lives. Now he accepted that he and Miriam Josceleyne had been pre-ordained to meet and join in union. If that were not the case, then how else could his complete surety concerning his feelings towards her be explained?

By now he had reached the northern apex of Church Green, and he smiled and chided himself, 'You only came here so that you could look at Cotswold House and hopefully catch a glimpse of Miriam. You're nothing else but lovesick, you bloody fool.'

Still smiling to himself he turned and retraced his footsteps. At the crossroads by the church he suddenly decided that he would enjoy a glass of ale as a nightcap, and turned towards the Unicorn Inn.

A little way along Evesham Street stood a small public house, the Royal George. Its bar was filled with Sunday night drinkers, crowded together, talking and laughing, but at one end of the bar was a small space where one man leaned against the counter, immersed in his own morose silence, being given as wide a berth as the cramped confines of the room permitted.

Arthur Dolton was unkempt and unshaven, his eyes bleared with continuous drinking, his mind filled with self-pity, the lust for violence simmering beneath the layers of that self-pity.

On Friday, instead of going to the market with Ozzie Clarke, he had taken the train to Birmingham and there had plunged into a debauch of drunken whoring. This morning he had woken in a stinking room to find his companion of the night had departed, taking with her his money, his watch and chain, his gold cuff-links and stickpin. He had been forced to go to the house of a business acquaintance to borrow his train fare back to Redditch. Strangely reluctant to return to his own home, he had gone to his brother's house to obtain more drinking money.

Now he glowered about him, red-eyed and stench-breathed. The other men in the bar studiously ignored him.

The watchful landlord was loath to offend such a good customer as Arthur Dolton, but knew that in his present mood the butcher was creating a palpable tension and unease among his other customers, some of whom had already drunk up and gone to other public houses to avoid any possible confrontation.

The butcher slurped down his ale, the liquid overflowing to run down his chin and splash his soiled collar and shirtfront.

'Give us a refill,' Dolton shouted, and slammed his pot down onto the wet counter.

The landlord moved to confront him across the counter. 'I reckon you'se had enough, aren't you, Arthur?' he questioned, smiling in mollification. 'Why don't you goo and get some sleep now. You looks all done up.'

Dolton blinked hard, and glared challengingly at the other man. 'I wants another drink,' he growled.

For a few brief moments the landlord debated with himself, then decided discretion to be the better part of valour, and reluctantly took the crock quart-pot and refilled it.

As he took Arthur Dolton's money, inner resentment at his own surrender caused the landlord to say, 'But this is the last one you gets here tonight, Arthur.'

Dolton's wet liver lips were slack as he hard-stared the other man.

'The last I gets here, is that what youm telling me, Jimmy?'

The landlord screwed up his courage, aware that by now the other customers were taking a keen interest in the exchange.

'Yes Arthur, the last you gets tonight. Youm very

307

welcome to come back tomorrow and drink all you wants. But you'se had too much tonight, Arthur. I has to think about my licence, you know. I can't afford any upsets in my pub.'

'Does you know what you can do with your fuckin' licence, Jimmy?' Dolton growled threateningly. 'You can shove it up your arse. And you can shove this up your arse as well.'

He lifted the refilled pot and hurled the contents into the landlord's face, then smashed the pot itself upon the counter, shattering it into a score of pieces.

Grinning triumphantly he swaggered out of the room, using his bulk to buffet his way through the crowd.

As he passed through the door and into the street Arthur Dolton's grin died, and a wave of maudlin self-pity swept over him. 'Even my mates am turning against me.' He felt close to tears. 'I'se always bin a good bloke, and free with me money. Me life was all right until I met that fuckin' whore I'm wed to. It's all her fault, this is. Turning people against me, that's what she's doing. Telling lies about me all over the fuckin' place. I'se give that poxy slum-bitch everything, and how does she repay me? She's makes me a fuckin' laughing stock, that's how she repays me. Gallivanting off with that fuckin' fancy man her's got. That bastard toy soldier! I'll swing for both on 'um! I'll teach 'um to laugh about me and make a cunt out of me! I'll learn 'um the lesson, just wait and see if I doon't.'

He glared about him as if seeking an opponent, then moved unsteadily towards the Church Green crossroads, mumbling aggressively to himself.

'I'm going home. It's my house, my property. Everything in it is my property as well. I'll give that fuckin' whore a right seeing to when I gets home. It's all her fuckin' fault that I got robbed up in Brummagem. If she warn't such a fuckin' bitch, then I 'udden't have gone up theer in the first place. Well I'll teach her a lesson when I gets home. I'll put her in her rightful place. She wunt stop skriking for a fuckin' week after I gets through with her tonight.'

He came to a swaying standstill beneath the garish sign of the Unicorn Inn and peered blearily up at it.

'I'll just call in and get another sup of ale. Tommy Hyde's a good bloke. He'll serve me all right.' He scowled savagely. 'The bugger had better serve me, if he knows what's good for him.'

Dolton stumbled up the flight of stone steps, banged the door open and lurched through the low doorway of the taproom.

The noisy entrance brought all eyes swinging to the door. Standing with a line of drinkers at the bar counter Johnny Purvis turned and his lips twitched in disgust at the sight of the drunken Arthur Dolton.

Behind the counter Thomas Hyde also stared with disgust at this new arrival. His shrewd eyes instantly recognising the man's condition, past experience telling him that this presaged inevitable trouble.

Dolton's bleared gaze fixed on Johnny Purvis, and made brave by drink he spat out, 'Well, look who's here. Just the fucker I wanted to see.'

He swayed up to the bar counter and stood face to face with Johnny Purvis, whose body imperceptibly balanced and tensed.

'Well, well, well, if it aren't the fuckin' toy soldier himself?' Dolton sneered.

'Leave it alone, Dolton. You're drunk,' Johnny Purvis told him evenly.

The butcher's reddened eyes opened owlishly in mock surprise. 'Leave what alone, toy soldier?'

'Leave me alone,' Purvis answered. 'I'm not looking for trouble with you tonight.'

'Oh aren't you now?' The butcher swayed visibly as he sneered. 'You was ready enough for trouble with me when I'd hurt me back and was fuckin' well crippled by it, warn't you?'

Now a madness was beginning to seethe in Arthur Dolton's brain, a mental image of his wife lying naked and spread beneath the naked body of Johnny Purvis suddenly imposed itself upon his vision, and that seething madness boiled over and erupted.

'Bastard! Fuckin' bastard!' he howled, and his fists balled and swung, and met only empty space, as Johnny

Purvis ducked and side-stepped.

'Leave it alone, Dolton!' Purvis shouted, but the butcher was in the grip of a blind lust to destroy and words could not penetrate his consciousness. Again his fists swung wildly, again Purvis easily evaded the blows. Then realising that Dolton was beyond all reason, Purvis blocked the next blow with his left arm and pistoned his right fist into the bulging overhanging belly of the other man.

The air exploded from Dolton's gaping mouth, his face purpled and he dropped to his knees, doubled over so that his forehead was pressing against the floor.

Johnny Purvis stared briefly down at his attacker, then told Thomas Hyde, 'I'm sorry about this, Mr Hyde, but there was nothing else to be done with him.'

The landlord nodded agreement, then advised, 'You'd best be off. It'll save any more trouble.' A grin quirked his mouth as he looked down at the retching, groaning Arthur Dolton.

'Not that he'll be able to give you any, that's a fact. But if the police comes to hear about there being a fight here, then they'll only come nosing around, and that can only cause you more aggravation, can't it? You're always more than welcome to call again, Mr Purvis.'

Johnny could appreciate this sound advice, and with a final glance at his helpless opponent, he left the taproom.

Thomas Hyde scowled down at the pool of evil-smelling vomit in which Arthur Dolton was lying, and he instructed his potman, 'Lug that bastard down to the stables and leave him on the straw heap. Let him sleep it of theer. He aren't able to walk home tonight, that's for sure.'

As he made his way to his lodging, Johnny Purvis felt like cursing the impulse that had taken him into the Unicorn Inn. Now, with all his new plans, and the sudden blossoming of his relationship with Miriam Josceleyne, the last thing Johnny Purvis wanted was trouble of any sort. Particularly trouble involving other men's wives.

'I just hope that Miriam doesn't come to hear of tonight's happenings,' he wished fervently, but glumly accepted that in this particular town with its highly developed bush telegraph, that fervent wish was almost certainly doomed.

Chapter Forty-One

Franklin Josceleyne locked himself into his office and remained there alone through all the hours of Sunday afternoon and early evening. For many of those hours he pored through his family documents and financial and property records. He studied the wills of his mother, his grandparents and great grandparents. Then he rechecked the records of his own financial affairs. Then at last he accepted that there was nothing in these sheaves and rolls of ribbon-bound documents that could serve him.

His body slumped disconsolately and for a long, long period he sat with his face buried in his hands and allowed despair to overwhelm him. Periodically waves of fury would shudder through him and he would vent curses and execrations. Even as he mouthed the vilest epithets that his mind could conjure, deep within him he knew that fury and execration would avail him nothing. Cunning was needed now.

'I must move very very carefully here, if I'm to remain in control of this family. Roaring at that senile old fool and my half-wit of a sister will achieve nothing.

'I wonder if that slum-rat can be bought off?'

Much calmer now, Franklin Josceleyne spent a further hour in pondering various plans of action. Then he decided that the primary necessity was to ascertain just what the present situation was at Cotswold House.

He crammed his top hat on his over-large head and without bothering to take up either gloves or walking cane hurried across Church Green and rang the bell at Cotswold House.

It was the fat Mrs Elwood who answered the door, and

he questioned, 'Why does the maid not come to the door, Mrs Elwood?'

The cook's eyes held a gleam of derisive satisfaction.

'Because her's upstairs tending to Mr Hector, sir.'

Franklin Josceleyne had noted that gleam, and he stared hard at the woman, almost daring her to openly deride him.

'Miss Miriam is in the drawing room, sir,' the cook informed. 'Shall I announce you?'

'No need,' the bank manager snapped curtly. 'I know my own family well enough not to need be announced to them, Elwood.'

'As you please, sir.' The woman bobbed a submissive curtsey, but still Franklin Josceleyne was irritatingly aware of that gleam of mocking laughter in her eyes.

Miriam Josceleyne was sitting reading, her hair hanging in loose waves around her slender face and throat, a voluminous, richly hued velvet dressing gown falling in graceful folds to her feet.

The man felt irritated at seeing her so informally dressed, but he bit hard on the scathing comment that arose to his lips, and instead forced a stiff smile.

'Good evening, Sister. I trust I find you well?'

She looked at him guardedly, then replied quietly, 'Very well, I thank you, Brother Franklin.'

She made no attempt to enlarge upon her reply, and Franklin Josceleyne found himself marvelling yet again at this sudden and dramatic metamorphosis in his sister. Even physically she had changed, her green eyes were lucent, her skin looked fresh and vibrant. Above all else she radiated an aura of strength and confidence instead of the weakness and timidity to which he had so long been accustomed.

Despite his intentions, the bank manager could not restrain the hectoring note in his voice when he demanded, 'What is all this nonsense concerning our father and your maidservant?'

She regarded him coolly and for a brief moment he could have sworn that the same gleam of mocking laughter that he had detected in the cook's eyes were in hers. Then she shrugged casually. 'You had best ask them, Franklin. It is their personal business, after all.'

His jaw gaped. Of all possible replies she could have made to his demand, this was the last he would have expected. For a few seconds his lips moved soundlessly, and then he burst out, 'Is that all you can say? Don't you care about the fact that he is bringing our family name into disrepute? That he is making himself, and us as well, a laughing stock in the eyes of the town? Were you not shocked when you heard that the banns had been called for them?'

Miriam frowned slightly. 'Please don't shout so, Brother. I have a slight headache.' She hesitated, then went on, 'Yes, I admit it was something of a shock to be told that the banns had been called. But called they have been, and there's naught to be done about it.'

He brushed aside her answer with an impatient sweep of his arm, and demanded with loud incredulity, 'What has happened to you? Why are you so uncaring about this sad matter? Do you not realise the gravity of it? Do you not realise that if father marries this damned slum-rat she will become his heiress? She will inherit this family's money and property. Don't you care about that?'

Miriam sat silently considering these points for some length of time, while her brother snorted and vented breathy exclamations of impatience. She deliberately prolonged her silence, drawing spiteful pleasure from her brother's reactions. In all truth, she knew that she really did not care what happened to the family's money or property. Her life had been transformed beyond her wildest dreams and fantasies by the advent of Johnny Purvis. He was the focus of her thoughts, her desire, her ambitions, to the exclusion of all else. She was utterly besotted by him and gloried in that fact.

When she judged that her brother's nerves could stand no further strain, she smiled at him with a gentle malice, and told him sweetly, 'Do you know, Brother Franklin, now I've given the matter some thought, I find that I really do not care one jot what happens to the family money and property.'

'But we'll all be ruined!' he almost wailed the words.

Again she smiled with gentle malice. 'Oh no, Brother Franklin. I shall not be ruined. I have other prospects.'

'What?' His forehead creased interrogatively. 'What's that you say? Other prospects? And what might they be, pray tell me?'

She chuckled huskily. 'All in good time, Franklin, my dear. I shall tell you all in good time.'

He began to strut up and down the room in his agitation, muttering wildly to himself, and she sat smiling amusedly at him, mystified at how she had allowed this ridiculous little man to dominate and tyrannise her for so many long and bitter years.

At length he halted in front of her, scowling down into her smiling face. 'I see that it is pointless to continue this discussion with you, Sister. All you can do is to sit grinning at me like a half-wit. I shall take the matter up with Father.'

She nodded agreeably. 'Yes, Franklin. You do that. I'm quite sure that Father will listen eagerly to your comments.'

He glared at her, then stamped from the room.

In the hallway he turned towards the flight of stairs leading upwards and had actually placed his foot on the first riser, when another thought brought him to a standstill.

He knew well enough that there was little love lost between himself and his father. He realised that in his present mood of anger and agitation he might well voice words that would precipitate a complete schism between them. Struggling to regain control over his rampant mood, Franklin Josceleyne drew a series of long deep breaths, which served to calm him a little and enable him to begin to think more rationally.

'I'll leave this until tomorrow,' he decided. 'And consider carefully about what's best to do.'

With that resolution he snatched his hat from the hall stand and slammed out of the house.

In the drawing room Miriam heard the slamming of the door and began to giggle. Those giggles became pealing laughter, and she laughed and laughed and laughed until her sides ached and her eyes streamed with tears of joy.

When at last her laughter died away, she sat staring blankly at the page open before her, but was not seeing the printed words, only the face of Johnny Purvis. She sighed contentedly and murmured his name aloud over and over again.

A tapping at the door disturbed her reverie and she called, 'Enter.'

Emma Farr slipped into the room, looking unaccustomedly ill at ease.

Miriam smiled at her. 'Come in, Emma, and sit down. We have much to talk about.'

The girl did as she was bid, and sat stiffly perched on the edge of the deep armchair, her fingers tugging against each other.

'Are you vexed with me, Miss Miriam?' she asked nervously.

This was the first time that Miriam had either seen or spoken to the girl since earlier that afternoon Mrs Elwood had told her of the banns being called.

'No, my dear, of course I'm not vexed with you.' Miriam regarded the beautiful young face with something akin to pity. She was imaginative enough to have some understanding of the degree of the desperation that could force poverty-stricken young girls into marrying rich old men.

'But tell me, Emma, do you really believe that you will be able to bear being married to such an old man? Have you considered what marriage entails? The depths of intimacy that you will have to participate in as my father's lawful wife?'

A sudden repulsion surged through Miriam as she visualised this young fresh beauty in sexual congress with the withered flesh of Hector Josceleyne. A raging disgust at her father brought the constriction of anger to her throat.

'It is not right for you to do this, Emma,' she spoke more curtly than she intended, and the young girl's mouth instantly pouted in resentment.

'It's for me to judge what's right for meself, miss,' Emma retorted defiantly. 'Me and Mr Hector will do well enough, I'm sure.'

'But he is so old, and ugly, and unclean in his ways,

315

Emma. I confess that I am disgusted with him for forcing you into such a union,' Miriam protested heatedly. 'I do not blame you for it. I can understand how poverty can drive women to acts of sheer desperation. But I cannot believe that you will find happiness in marrying my father. I can only believe that you will find nothing but misery and bitter regrets.'

The girl's fresh complexion flamed with her resentment, all trace of nervousness and diffidence fell from her, and she spoke with a voluble fierceness. 'I was born and bred in Silver Street, miss. You can have no idea what my life theer was like. You're telling me that I'll only find misery and bitter regrets if I marries your dad. What does you think my mam ever found? What does every woman born into poverty ever find? I'll tell you, shall I? They finds misery and torment and suffering all the days of their lives. A babby in their belly every year, and when they'se nearly died birthing it, more often than not it goes and dies. Their husbands drinks the housekeeping money away, and if the woman makes complaint, they batters and kicks her until she's near dead. You know what a Silver Street kid gets to fill its empty belly, Miss Miriam? I'll tell you, shall I? It gets fist pie and boot pudding. Do you know what it gets when it's perishing wi' the cold? More fist pie and boot pudding to warm its blood for it. Well, no kid o' mine is ever gooing to suffer what I've suffered in me life. I'm gooing to make sure o' that.'

'Emma?' Miriam tried to cut short the flow of words, but the young girl would not be silenced.

'I'm telling you now, Miss Miriam, that I'm going to wed your dad. It doon't matter a damn what you or anybody else thinks or says about it. I'm gooing to wed him, and that's that.'

She rose to her feet, bobbed a curtsey, and went out of the room.

Miriam sat thoughtfully listening to the sharp clicking of the girl's boot heels receding into the rear of the house. As the last faint clicks died away she sighed heavily, and shook her head. 'I hope you come through it all, Emma. I really do.'

Now the almost farcical incongruousness of the present situation suddenly struck home.

'If they do get wed, then young Emma will become my stepmother. She will be the mistress here. What exactly is the position now, with her having become the acknowledged betrothed of my father? She cannot continue to work as my maidservant.'

For the first time Miriam Josceleyne felt a stirring of sympathy for her brother. 'Emma will also be Franklin's stepmother. How embarrassing it must be for him. How will he be able to continue in this town, knowing that so many people will be sneering at our family for what father intends doing? I don't care for myself, not now I've found Johnny, but I can't help feeling somewhat sorry for Franklin, pompous prig though he may be.'

She smiled fondly. 'What will Johnny think about what's happened, I wonder? I'll find that out soon enough, at any rate.'

With a keen anticipation Miriam Josceleyne turned her thoughts to the morrow, and her assignation at Grange House with Johnny Purvis.

Emma Farr sat scowling at the kitchen table, her fingers toying with the glass tumbler of gin.

'Now then, my duck, what's upset you? You looks like you'se lost a pound and found a penny.' Mrs Elwood grinned at the young girl and lifted her own tumbler of gin in a toast.

'Here's to the bride. May she prosper and grow fat wi' good living.'

'Don't make mock o' me!' Emma snapped angrily. All her earlier elation about the banns being called had left her. Now she was experiencing increasing doubts about the wisdom of what she was going to do.

The older woman regarded the young girl with a shrewd appreciation of what was troubling her.

'Getting cold feet about wedding the old sod, am you, Emmy?'

The girl nodded slowly. 'It aren't something to look forward to, is it, Mrs Elwood?'

'No it aren't,' the older woman stated bluntly. 'But

317

you'se got to concentrate your mind on why youm adoing it, my duck. The old sod aren't long for this world, and in the long run it's going to be worth whatever aggravation you has to put up wi' for the next few months.'

Emma's lips twisted with irritation. 'I knows that well enough, Mrs Elwood. Me mind is made up to wed the old bugger. But I can't help thinking how unfair it all is. There's that old maid setting her cap for Johnny Purvis, and here's me going to wed her bloody dad.'

'So that's wheer the land lies,' Mrs Elwood thought. 'Youm jealous o' Miss Miriam because her's got John Purvis. You'd like him for yourself, 'udden't you, girl?'

Spitefully she could not resist figuratively turning the knife, and said aloud, 'He's certainly made a change in Miss Miriam, that John Purvis has. Why her's looking as young and pretty as her ever did look.' She winked salaciously. 'It just goes to show what a bloody stallion he must be. Her's looking like the cat who's swallowed the cream. He must have given her a real good seeing to on that bloody rug in the drawing room.'

Emma scowled and slammed her own glass down so hard that the gin sloshed over and spilled.

'How does you know for certain that it was John Purvis who was in the drawing room with her?' she challenged furiously.

The older woman nodded positively. 'It was him all right, and you knows that well enough yourself, girl.'

Emma glared, then jumped to her feet and ran from the room.

In her own bleak attic she threw herself face downwards upon the narrow bed, and suddenly burst into bitter tears.

'It aren't fair! It aren't fair that that old maid should have Johnny Purvis. He should belong to me, not to her. He should be mine.'

Chapter Forty-Two

Cleopatra Dolton rose early on Monday morning and made a cautious and apprehensive exploration of the silent house. To her relief there was no sign of Arthur Dolton, his bed had not been slept in, his razors and toilet articles had not been used.

Curiosity as to his whereabouts mingled with her relief at his absence, and she prayed fervently that he would not return to the house before she was able to leave it.

Back in her own room she regarded her reflection in the dressing table mirror and felt a terrible anger at the sight of her swollen, bruised features. Lust for revenge burgeoned and expanded and her hatred for Arthur Dolton burned with uncontrollable passion. Overtaken by her emotions she sat staring at herself and lost all track of time.

Mrs Danks came into the room and looked with worried eyes at her motionless mistress.

'Am you feeling all right to be out o' bed?' she demanded anxiously.

The sound of the woman's voice dragged Cleopatra from her violent reverie, and she grimaced. 'It's not important how I'm feeling, Mrs Danks. I have to go out.'

'Where to?' Mrs Danks wanted to know.

Unconsciously, Cleopatra's fingers moved to touch the trinket box.

'I've business to attend to.'

Mrs Danks noted her mistress's fingers lingering on the ornately patterned box and understanding brought a thankful smile to her lips.

'Youm agoing to leave him, aren't you,' she declared, and Cleopatra nodded slowly.

'Yes, I'm leaving him. I'm going to sell my jewellery and

use the money to take the kids far away from here, to where that bastard will never be able to find us.'

Mrs Danks' thin face radiated relief. 'I'll be sorry to see you goo, my duck, but I'm glad that youm gooing for your and the kids' sakes. You'll be all right. I knows you 'ull.'

She helped her mistress to make her toilette and to dress.

Cleopatra experimented with various combinations of veils to enable her to cover her disfigurations while still retaining vision.

Mrs Danks snorted indignantly. 'You should goo out without a veil, my wench; let the world see bloody Arthur Dolton's shame!'

Cleopatra shook her head and murmured miserably, 'It's my shame as well, Mrs Danks.'

By now the maids were up and bustling around the house. Cleopatra could hear her sons' voices as they trooped downstairs for breakfast.

Not wanting her children to see her injuries, Cleopatra remained in her room, and instructed Mrs Danks, 'I want you to send the boys for a walk with one of the girls, Mrs Danks.'

When, an hour later, she heard the boys trooping out of the front door, she wrapped the trinket box in brown paper and slipped it into a small reticule. Waiting to give the boys time to be clear of the house, she slipped out of the front door. To avoid embarrassing encounters with people she might know she took the backstreet route to the Plough and Harrow Hotel. She climbed steep footpaths to come out on Mount Pleasant where Front and Back Hills converged with the Plough and Harrow standing at their confluence.

She glanced around her to check that no one was watching where she went. There was no one in sight except for a horse-drawn baker's delivery van coming down Mount Pleasant towards her. Cleopatra hurried across the roadway and entered the front doors of the large square building.

In the hallway a small handbell was lying on a table and Cleopatra lifted and swung it, flinching as the clapper rang out with a preternatural resonance. A middle-aged serving woman appeared and stared curiously at the thick veil shielding Cleopatra's face.

320

'Yes, Ma'am. Can I help you?'

For a moment Cleopatra wanted to turn and run, but she mastered that impulse and asked, 'Is Mr Purvis in, please? Mr John Purvis?'

She felt embarrassment as the woman's expression became avidly curious.

'I'll goo and see for you, Ma'am. What name is it?' Mary Phelan knew well enough what this elegant woman's name was.

Cleopatra swallowed hard, and gulped out, 'Tell him that it's Mrs Dolton.'

Mary Phelan's eyes gleamed, but her face was impassive as she answered, 'Just wait theer, if you please, Ma'am.'

Going upstairs she told herself, 'It's bloody true then, what they'se all bin saying. He is her bloody fancy man arter all.' She smiled with a grudging affection. 'You aren't changed has you, Johnny Purvis, youm still a wild reckless bugger.'

Johnny Purvis had just finished eating his late breakfast and was sitting at the table, contentedly puffing on a cheroot, his thoughts pleasantly dwelling on the afternoon to come, when he would meet Miriam Josceleyne up at Grange House. He was wearing only a long dressing gown covering his undervest and trousers when the maidservant knocked.

'Come in,' he called.

When Mary Phelan told him who his visitor was he frowned in surprise, and, seeing the knowing expression on the servant's face, told her sharply, 'It's not what you think it is, Mary.'

'How does you know what I thinks, Johnny Purvis?' she demanded with a great show of indignation, and snapped, 'Well? Does you want me to show her up, or what?'

Irritably he nodded. 'Oh very well then.'

And Mary Phelan smiled even more knowingly just to annoy him, then flounced away leaving him scowling impotently at the doorway.

He rose and went to the door and saw Cleopatra Dolton coming along the corridor. The sight of the lush lines of her body in the tight-fitting bolero jacket and hip-hugging skirt sent frissons of differing emotions shivering through him. This woman possessed a power to excite and disturb him

321

which he had never known before in any other woman.

She reached him, and even through the dark veiling he could see the plaster on her face. He frowned as he ushered her into his room. As soon as the door was closed he burst out, 'Your husband's been knocking you about again, hasn't he?' Guilt assailed him as he remembered the encounter of the previous night. He wondered if his clash with Dolton had provoked the man into inflicting this fresh injury upon his wife. Reaching out Johnny gently loosened her veil, then lifted it from her face while she stood passively.

He drew in his breath with a sharp hiss when he saw what Arthur Dolton had done to her and a murderous anger shuddered through him.

'When did he do this?' he demanded to know. 'Was it last night?'

'No, he did this on Friday morning.' Her voice was little more than a hoarse croak. 'You once told me that I could ask for your help if ever I needed to?'

'I did,' John Purvis confirmed with a brusque nod.

'Well I need your help now, Mr Purvis.'

Again he nodded brusquely. 'You shall have it, Mrs Dolton. Just tell me what it is you want of me.'

She took the paper-wrapped parcel from her reticule and held it towards him. 'There are some good pieces of jewellery in there, Mr Purvis. I want you to dispose of them for me.'

Arthur Dolton coughed and stirred, broke wind loudly, and became painfully aware of the chilled stiffness of his body. The straw rustled as he pushed himself to a sitting position and blinked blearily around him. He could vaguely recall the events of the previous night and now he scowled around the stables, inwardly cursing his aching head, foul-tasting mouth and general drink-induced malaise.

An old man carrying a big yard broom came into the stable and grinned toothlessly when he saw the dishevelled man sprawled upon the straw heap.

'How bist, master? Had a good night, has you?'

Dolton scowled at him, fumbled for his watch, then remembered that it had been stolen.

'What's the time?' he growled.

'Just gone eleven,' the old man informed.

'Fuck it!' The butcher, painfully clambered to his feet, wincing as his movements sent sharp throbbing pains lancing through his skull.

'I'll have to goo home and get cleaned up,' he decided.

His tongue moved over his sticky lips and his throat was sore with dryness.

'I'll have a livener first though.'

In the taproom Thomas Hyde greeted Dolton guardedly, recognising the morose surliness that could erupt into savage violence.

He served Dolton with a flagon of ale and a large tot of whisky, then moved further along the bar busying himself with unnecessary tasks, wishing that his unwelcome customer would drink up and take his leave.

Two other men entered, but seeing Arthur Dolton's glowering face took their stance at the far end of the bar and deliberately kept their eyes averted from him, knowing him well enough to fear that in his present mood he would try to pick a quarrel with them.

A baker's delivery-man came through the door carrying a large cottage loaf which he handed to the landlord. The delivery-man knew Arthur Dolton, and he grinned cheerily at him.

'Mornin' Mr Dolton, I thought you was in the Plough and Harrow.'

Dolton glared at him. 'Why? Why should you think that?'

The man grinned nervously as he recognised the other's mood and to mollify him said quickly, 'It's only that I thought I saw your good lady gooing in theer when I was coming down Mount Pleasant.'

'What d'you say?' Arthur Dolton stepped up to the baker's man and gripped the front of his white jacket. 'What's that youm saying about my missus?'

'Nothin' wrong, Mr Dolton. I just thought I'd seen her going into the Plough and Harrow, that's all. I doon't mean anything wrong!'

Dolton's foul breath gusted hoarsely through his slack beer-wet lips as his drink-fuddled brain sought for remembrance. Then, when remembrance came he cursed aloud and pushed the baker's man roughly from him. He slammed out through the door, and as the other men stared wonderingly after him, Thomas Hyde grunted, 'Thank Christ he's buggered off! I hates him coming in here when he's in that sort o' mood. He'll end up killing some poor bugger one day when he's like that.'

'From what I hears it won't be Johnny Purvis he kills though, 'ull it, Tommy?' one man quipped. 'It'll be the other way round if he picks on Johnny Purvis again. Dolton 'ull be the one who gets killed.'

There was a round of appreciative laughter and the talk turned to other matters.

Panting heavily Arthur Dolton went hurrying along Evesham Street towards Front Hill.

'That bastard is staying theer, aren't he? Fuckin' John Purvis! Her fuckin' fancy man! That's why her's gone in theer. To meet that bastard!'

He was muttering his raging thoughts aloud as he mounted the hill towards the tall square building, and in the heat of the day the sweat was pouring down his red face and saturating his body.

Mary Phelan was in the entrance hall when Dolton stormed in.

'Wheer is she? Wheer's my fuckin' wife?'

His aggression caused the woman to hesitate before answering, and he growled out a foul oath and grabbed her arm, brandishing his clenched fist before her face in threat.

'Wheer is the cow? You'd best tell me straight away if you knows what's good for you, you old bitch.'

Frightened, she gasped out, 'Her's upstairs. Room five!'

He hurled her from him and she cannoned back against the wall. Then as the man went stamping up the flight of stairs, she came behind him and screamed, 'Johnny! Johnny! Look out!'

In room five Johnny Purvis and Cleopatra Dolton were sitting closely facing each other, the trinket box open on Johnny's knees, when Mary Phelan's screams sounded, and it was Cleopatra Dolton who was the first to intuit what was happening.

324

'My husband!' she exclaimed. 'He's here!' Her hands went to her mouth and she physically cringed.

The next instant the door crashed open and the butcher burst into the room. His bloodshot eyes saw Johnny Purvis and his wife sitting close together and registered the fact that Purvis was wearing a dressing gown.

'Getting ready to shag her, am you, you bastard?' he bawled, and his face was that of a madman. 'I'll fuckin' kill the pair on you!'

Insane with rage he hurled himself at Johnny Purvis, who came to his feet. Reacting instinctively Purvis slipped the wild punches Arthur Dolton threw at him, then hooked his own fists into the fat belly, and as the breath exploded from Dolton's body and he doubled in agony, Purvis brought his knee up into the other man's face with explosive strength, simultaneously bringing his clubbed hands down onto the back of the fat neck with a terrible force.

The snap of breaking bone was clearly audible, and Arthur Dolton slumped face downwards to the floor, blood pooling instantly beneath his head. He twitched, gurgled once, and was still.

Johnny Purvis's breath rasped in his throat as he stared down at the sprawled body. He knelt and felt for the carotid arteries with his fingers, then for the heartbeat.

Mary Phelan was standing in the doorway, her face chalk white and strained, while Cleopatra Dolton was by the window, her gaze fixed on her husband, her full lips slightly parted, her full breasts rising and falling with her heavy breathing.

Johnny Purvis sighed, and told Mary Phelan quietly, 'You'd better send for the police and the ambulance, Mary. He's dead.'

The woman emitted a low moaning sound, and then ran down the hallway shouting for the landlord.

Johnny Purvis rose and came to Cleopatra Dolton. He spread his hands helplessly and could only mutter, 'I'm so sorry, Mrs Dolton. I'm so sorry.'

Her eyes glowed as they dwelt on the fallen man. Without looking at Johnny Purvis she uttered, 'Don't be sorry. I'm not. I'm glad he's dead!'

325

Chapter Forty-Three

'Let me, Emma. Let me!' Hector Josceleyne begged wheezily, but the girl easily evaded his clutching hands and laughed.

'You bitch!' he shouted angrily, and now cruelty sparked in her black eyes, and she spat at him, 'You'll wait 'til we'em wed, you old sod. If you keeps on playing me up, why I'll walk out of this house right this minute.'

He sulkily surrendered, and whined, 'You treat me very badly, Emma.'

She accepted his surrender graciously and came to plump up his pillows and settle him more comfortably in his bed.

'Now just be patient, Hector,' she told him quietly. 'We can be wedded by this time next month, then you'll get all you want.'

Petulantly he puffed out his shrunken cheeks and she patted the side of his face, smiling down at him with a certain fondness.

'You be a good boy now and stay here nice and quiet. I'se got to goo out for a bit.'

'You'll come back, won't you, Emma?' he questioned apprehensively.

She chuckled. 'O' course I'll come back, you silly old bleeder.'

His watery red-rimmed eyes were slavish as they followed her trim figure around the room. Emma was fully aware of his gaze and equally aware that she held him completely in her thrall.

She tripped lightly down the stairs and went through to the kitchen where Mrs Elwood was angrily muttering as she examined a piece of meat.

'What's up?' Emma asked.

'This veal's turned,' the woman explained. 'I knowed it warn't as fresh as that bloody Ozzie Clarke told me it were.'

'Wrap it up and I'll take it back to the shop,' Emma offered. 'I'se got to goo out to see Mr Franklin anyway.'

Early that morning a note addressed to Emma had been pushed through the letterbox. The note had been sent by Franklin Josceleyne asking her to come to his office later that morning.

'Has you told Miss Miriam that Mr Franklin wants to see you?' Mrs Elwood enquired.

'No,' Emma shook her head. 'It's nothing to do with her, is it? Anyway, I know what it is he wants to see me about. It's bloody obvious, aren't it?'

The cook nodded. 'He'll be trying to talk you out o' marrying Mr Hector, no doubt about that.' She stared speculatively at the younger woman. 'What if he offers you money to call off the wedding? What'll you tell him?'

'To sod off!' Emma retorted shortly, and her full lips compressed into a hard thin line, matching the determination in her eyes.

'He might offer you a lot o' money, Emmy,' the cook persisted.

'He'll never be able to offer me as much as this wedding can earn me, Mrs Elwood.'

'That's it, girl, you stick to your guns,' the cook applauded, and Emma nodded. 'Oh, I 'ull, Mrs Elwood. Don't you doubt it. I 'ull stick to me guns.'

'Miss Miriam's late ringing for her breakfast,' the cook observed.

'I'll goo and see if her's ready to ate,' Emma offered, and the other woman chuckled throatily, 'It must be queer for her, you know, Emmy. Here's you, her maid, and youm gooing to be her stepmother. She must be feeling really queer about it.'

Emma's tenseness eased and she giggled mischievously. 'If Miss Miriam's feeling queer about it, then how does you reckon Mr Franklin's feeling?'

The cook's fat face reddened as she roared with

327

laughter, and choked, 'Am you gooing to make him call you mother, Emmy?'

Emma laughed also, and nodded. 'I might just do that, Mrs Elwood. Just for badness, I might just do that.'

She returned upstairs and knocked at Miriam Josceleyne's bedroom door.

'Come in,' Miriam Josceleyne was standing in front of the full length mirror dressed in a fashionable bolero jacket and slender-hipped skirt, turning slowly, craning her head to study her appearance.

Emma studied her mistress briefly, grudgingly acknowledging how youthful and pretty the woman appeared and how well the new clothes became her.

'Do you want breakfast, Miss Miriam?' Emma enquired, and could not help feeling stiff and constrained.

In an attempt to lighten the strained atmosphere that had lately arisen between them, Miriam smiled, and indicated her new clothes, 'Well, Emma, what do you think to them? Do they suit me?'

'Yes miss. You look very nice,' Emma muttered. A pang of jealousy striking her as she thought, 'Youm dressing up for Johnny Purvis, aren't you?'

Miriam Josceleyne stood looking into the young girl's face, and spoke hesitantly, 'Listen, Emma, I have accepted the fact that you are to wed with my father. Naturally, it came as a great shock to me. But since you appear to be determined on this match, then so be it. We can at least be friends, can we not?'

A note of pleading had entered her tone as she voiced the final sentence, and the sincerity underlying her words was patent.

Emma stood uncertainly for some moments. Then said tentatively, 'It's awkward for both on us, miss, I appreciates that. But I'm of the same mind as before. I'm gooing to wed with Mr Hector, and that's that.'

Miriam smiled and nodded. 'I've already said that I accept that fact, Emma. Why, just between you and I, I may tell you that I could well be getting married myself in the not too distant future.'

'Oh yes, miss.' Emma did not want to hear any more

about her mistress's wedding plans. A torment of jealousy was now gnawing at her as she visualised this woman and Johnny Purvis as man and wife. But just as a child is driven to deliberately agitate its own aching tooth, so Emma was constrained to ask, 'Is it Mr Purvis youm getting wed to?'

The older woman's green eyes glowed and her lips wreathed in a smile of pure happiness. 'Yes Emma, I hope so.'

Emma's lips twisted as she bit sharply upon their soft inners, and then she gritted out, 'Will you be wanting your breakfast, miss?'

Miriam Josceleyne's thoughts were now dwelling on her forthcoming meeting with John Purvis; food held no attraction for her. She shook her head. 'No, thank you, my dear. I'll not be wanting any breakfast, or luncheon either. I shall be going out for the day.'

'Very well, miss.' Emma bobbed a curtsey and turned to leave, but her mistress detained her.

'Wait a moment, Emma.' She paused, searching for the right words to approach this delicate matter. 'I don't think it fitting that you should continue as my maid now, Emma, not in view of the changed circumstance of our relationship. I shall engage another girl to replace you in that capacity. If you wish to continue caring for my father until such time as you are wed to him, then so be it. But I think that you should change your present quarters. The rear bedroom is unused at present and will be much more comfortable for you.'

This display of kindness and consideration caused Emma to soften momentarily towards the other woman. She answered with some warmth, 'Thank you very much, Miss Miriam. But I don't mind continuing as we are. There'll be time enough to change and get another girl in when I'm wed to Mr Hector.'

Miriam smiled and nodded understandingly. 'Very well, Emma. Whichever you prefer. I leave it entirely to your choice.'

'Yes miss.' The girl left and Miriam Josceleyne turned once again to the mirror.

329

*

Franklin Josceleyne had given much thought to this interview. Despite his inbred contempt for those who were socially beneath him, he did not make the mistake of underestimating Emma Farr's intelligence or her capacity for cunning.

When Emma Farr arrived at his office he greeted her courteously and invited her to be seated on the chair in front of his desk. He was forced to admit to himself that she was a creature of rare beauty in her pristine white dress with the small boater perched on her piled chestnut hair.

Emma sat with demurely downcast eyes, her hands clasped upon her lap. Despite her ever-present gutter-devil and defiant air, she had in the past always felt a certain unease and lack of confidence in face-to-face confrontations with the gentry. The calling of the banns however had instilled in her an immense self-confidence, and now she waited for the bank manager to speak with a sense of almost gleeful anticipation.

'So, Emma, you are going to marry my father,' Franklin Josceleyne began pleasantly. 'Do you really believe that you will find happiness and fulfilment in such a match?'

The girl's black eyes fixed boldly upon his and she told him bluntly, 'I'm not seeking happiness, Mr Franklin. I'm seeking security and position.'

He could not mask the surprise that this answer gave him.

Seeing his expression Emma nodded. 'Oh yes, Mr Franklin, you'll find that I speaks what's in my mind. Now I think that you've brought me here to try and talk me out of marrying your dad.' She slowly shook her shapely head. 'You'll not be able to do that, Mr Franklin. I'm getting wed to Mr Hector, and that's final.'

His eyes narrowed and anger threatened to explode, but he drew a long deep breath, fighting to remain calm and in control of himself.

Emma intuited his inner conflict and her sharp wits guided her now. She smiled sweetly at the little man, and told him, 'Listen to me for a minute, Mr Franklin. Theer's nothing to be gained by me and you falling out over this, is there? You knows that theer's nothing you can do or say to change Mr Hector's mind about marrying me. He's set on it.'

She decided to launch an oblique assault.

'Let's lay all the cards on the table, shall we? You might try and get Mr Hector declared unfit in his mind and stop the wedding by having him committed to the loony bin, but that 'ud be really messy and create a deal of nasty talk in the town. I don't believe it 'ud work anyway, because you and me both knows that Mr Hector aren't as daft as he makes himself out to be.'

She paused, seeking to evaluate the effect of her words. Emboldened by what she saw in Franklin Josceleyne's face, she smiled bleakly and went on, 'Miss Miriam's just told me this very morning that she intends getting wed herself.'

This was a bombshell to Franklin Josceleyne, and his eyes widened and he snorted disbelievingly. Emma nodded emphatically.

'Oh yes, Mr Franklin. It's the truth. She intends getting wed to Johnny Purvis.'

Again the man snorted and his eyes bulged. He would have spoken, but the girl held up her white gloved hands, and instructed, 'No, doon't say anything yet. Let me finish.'

Scowling he nodded agreement.

'Now Mr Franklin, it's my belief that you deals with all financial matters for the family? That you decides what's done with the money and property of Miss Miriam and Mr Hector?'

She waited expectantly until he nodded confirmation, then nodded her own satisfaction with that confirmation.

'If Miss Miriam weds, then John Purvis 'ull most likely take control of her money, won't he?'

This time Franklin Josceleyne grunted sourly, 'That is what I would expect him to do, girl.'

He was beginning to regard this young girl with considerable respect. He also sensed that she was building up to a proposition and his own shrewdness directed him to give due consideration to whatever she might offer.

331

'Of course you'll be wondering if I'd try to persuade Mr Hector to take charge of his own financial affairs?' She paused again and Franklin Josceleyne was wise enough merely to nod.

'Well, Mr Franklin, wheer I was brought up we always used to say that if you scratch my back, then I'll scratch yours. If you gets my meaning?'

For Franklin Josceleyne this last statement was like sudden light glimpsed at the end of a long and dark tunnel. He took the continuing silence of the girl to be an invitation for him to speak. He cleared his throat gutturally, then forced a smile. 'I would of course be prepared to continue my administration of my father's money and properties when you become his wife.'

She smiled brilliantly. 'I'm prepared to let you goo on administering Mr Hector's money and properties after I'm wed to him, just so long as it was mutually satisfactory to both on us, o' course.'

Relief coursed through the bank manager's mind.

'To our mutual satisfaction, of course, girl.'

Her smile hardened, and her voice had a sharp edge as she told him, 'I doon't really like being called, girl. Now that we'em going to be all one big happy family, you may call me, Emma, and I shall call you, Franklin.'

Sullen resentment instantly flooded through him, but he kept his expression neutral and agreed. 'Very well, it shall be so . . . Emma.'

She chuckled with deep satisfaction and rose to her feet, staring pointedly at the paper-wrapped parcel of veal that she had put on his desk previously.

'I'll have to be getting along. I'se got to take that stale meat back to the butchers.'

The man also rose and lifted the packet to hand it to her.

'I'll talk to you about the wedding expenses when me and Mr Hector have fixed the date for it,' she informed, and beamed at her future stepson, while mischief danced in her black eyes.

'It'll be a bit strange for me at first, having you for a stepson, but I expect I'll soon get used to it, won't I,

Franklin?'

With that she went, leaving the bank manager glowering sourly after her.

On the bank steps she halted and drew a long deep breath of the warm morning air, savouring the feeling of her lungs expanding. Intense satisfaction filled her mind and she hummed happily to herself as she began to walk towards Evesham Street. The town centre looked comparatively deserted with only a couple of delivery carts parked at the roadside, and the occasional pedestrian or shopper. So when she reached the crossroads opposite the church and the police inspector and sergeant came cantering past her on horseback, to be followed some moments later by a sweating trio of constables running on foot, her interest was immediately aroused.

She watched their dark blue-clad figures distancing her along Evesham Street and speculated what event might have happened.

A clattering of hooves and the crunch of iron-rimmed wheels brought her head turning; she watched the horse-drawn ambulance from Smallwood Hospital pass her also as it travelled at a fast pace along the street towards Front Hill.

The passage of police and ambulance had brought the shopkeepers out from their premises to stare after them, and Emma could hear their excited questions and comments as she walked by.

At the shop of the Redditch Meat Company, Ozzie Clarke and Walter Spires, clad in their striped aprons, their straw boaters on their heads, were standing staring after the ambulance as it went round the curve of Front Hill.

Ozzie Clarke turned to the girl as she neared him and grinned. 'Well now, if it aren't the lovely Miss Emma Farr coming honouring our humble abode.'

Emma knew and liked the personable young butcher, and she grinned and told him, 'This aren't a social call, Ozzie Clarke. I'se got a bone to pick with you.'

He bowed mockingly. 'Miss Farr, I counts it a privilege

to pick a bone wi' you. The smaller the bone, the closer I could be to you, and the better I'd like it.'

'This meat's gone off, and Mrs Elwood reckons you knew it was stale when you sent it.'

The man opened the parcel and sniffed, then shrugged casually. 'Youm right, it's turned. I'll change it for you, me duck.'

All three of them stepped back inside the shop, and, as Ozzie Clarke cut and shaped a fresh piece of veal, Emma wondered aloud, 'What's happened to bring the police and ambulance charging about?'

Walter Spires had remained staring out of the window, and suddenly he exclaimed, 'Bugger me! Come and see this!'

The mounted inspector and the three foot constables were returning down Front Hill with an excited group of other people surrounding them.

Emma cried out faintly in shock as she recognised Johnny Purvis. Bareheaded, a jacket covering his collarless shirt, his hands secured behind him with iron cuffs, he marched grim-faced, his head held high and proud between two constables, with the mounted inspector leading. Behind Purvis, a heavily veiled woman was walking by the side of the third constable. Emma recognised her full lush figure and dark hair.

'Jesus Christ!' Ozzie Clarke ejaculated as he came to stand by the other two. 'It's Cleopatra Dolton!'

He hurried out of the shop to join the rapidly increasing clamorous crowd eddying around the small procession.

Emma followed, all thoughts of veal forgotten.

As the procession passed along the roadway, it was continually augmented by new arrivals and by the time it had reached the police station at the far end of Church Road it numbered hundreds. The police and prisoners disappeared inside the building and scant minutes later the horse-drawn ambulance came clattering to the station to enter its yard, which was immediately sealed by the massive gates being locked and bolted. Several constables came out to stand guard along the front of the building and to keep back the crowd.

The constables stood dourly silent, refusing to answer any of the questions hurled at them from the seething mass of people, which was being continually swelled by fresh arrivals.

Emma saw a young man that she knew standing in the front of the crowd, and pushed through to his side.

'What's happened, Eric? What's they done?' she questioned, and the young man told her in thrilled tones, 'They'se murdered her old man, Arthur Dolton! They'se just cut his bleedin' froat for him up at the Plough and Harrow theer!'

'That's bollocks that is!' Another man swung round and scoffed. 'It just goes to show how bloody thick-yedded you am, Jonesy. Arthur Dolton's throat weren't cut at all. His neck's bin broke by Johnny Purvis.'

'But why?' Emma demanded to know, and the new speaker winked broadly.

'Well Arthur Dolton caught his missus and Johnny Purvis in bed, didn't he? They was having a bit, warn't they? And he had a goo at 'um. But Johnny Purvis got ahold of him and broke his bleedin' neck!'

Emma felt suddenly faint and nauseated and she desperately fought her way clear of the clamorous crowd. Once clear she stood for a moment confused and very badly shaken by what she had been told. Then, impelled by instinct, she hurried back towards Cotswold House.

Miriam Josceleyne was putting the final touches to her appearance when she heard the slamming of the rear door echoing through the house.

Moments later there sounded the clattering of hurried footsteps upon the stairs and along the corridor, then her own bedroom door was thrust open and a wild-eyed Emma Farr rushed into the room.

'Emma? What is it? What's the matter?' Miriam Josceleyne demanded as an intense sensation of foreboding unaccountably engulfed her.

'Is it Johnny Purvis youm gooing to meet today?' the girl questioned breathlessly.

For a few moments Miriam could only stare, she was both puzzled and somewhat annoyed by the girl's rude intrusion upon her privacy, and by this personal question. Then she asked, 'Why do you wish to know that, Emma?'

'Tell me, is it him?' the girl demanded with open aggressive impatience.

Although the girl's tone was now hardening her own annoyance, Miriam Josceleyne slowly nodded. 'Yes, I am meeting with Mr Purvis.'

Emma shook her head, and a strange *mélange* of fleeting emotions passed across her features. There was both pain and triumph, distress and satisfaction. The older woman could only stare in mystification.

'What is it, Emma? Why are you behaving so strangely?'

The earlier foreboding now dominated all other feelings in Miriam Josceleyne's mind; a rapidly increasing constriction of dread tightened around her throat and chest causing her to breathe hard and rapidly.

'Has something happened to Johnny?' she questioned fearfully.

Emma's face twisted as if in angry grief and she hurled the words from her trembling lips.

'That fuckin' whore Cleopatra Dolton is what's happened to him. Her husband's just copped the pair on 'um in bed together, and Johnny Purvis has killed him.'

Miriam Josceleyne's brain and body seemed to become numb, her green eyes were huge and darkened. She shook her head and her lips moved, but no sound came from them.

'Can't you understand what I'se told you?' Emma Farr advanced. Grasping her mistress's upper arms she physically shook the other woman, and screeched at her hysterically, 'Doon't you hear me? Johnny Purvis had just killed Arthur Dolton. He's just broke the bugger's neck. Johnny Purvis has been shagging Cleopatra Dolton. All the time he was making eyes at me, and courting you, he's bin shagging Cleopatra Dolton. He's bin shagging that bloody whore ever since he come back to this town!'

Even as the girl screeched, Miriam Josceleyne began to shake her own head and to deny frantically, 'No! No! No! No! No!'

'Yes! Yes! Yes! Yes! Yes!' Emma Farr screamed.

'Stop it! Stop it, the pair on you!' Mrs Elwood stormed

into the room and her big hands whiplashed backwards and forwards across both of the hysterically shrieking faces, then she grappled and tore them apart, and sent Emma Farr reeling towards the door.

'You get down them bloody stairs, girl!'

Emma was weeping wildly now and she stumbled through the doorway with her hands covering her face and disappeared from view.

Miriam Josceleyne's colour was a sickly grey. She stared with haunted eyes into Mrs Elwood's fat red face and pleaded brokenly, 'It's not true, is it, Mrs Elwood? Tell me it's not true. Emma's lying about Johnny and the Dolton woman, isn't she? He hasn't done anything to Arthur Dolton, has he?'

The cook's heart welled with pity for the tragic woman before her, and she could only tell her sadly, 'It's true, Miss Miriam. All on it. Youm gooing to have to be very brave, my duck.'

She heard the harsh gasping of Miriam Josceleyne's breathing. Her own breath exhaled sharply in pity as she saw the agony in Miriam Josceleyne's grey features, saw the slender shoulders sag dejectedly, saw the light flee from the green eyes. She could have wept herself as the faded, ageing, defeated old maid re-emerged from the fragile cocoon of recent hope and happiness.

'Am you all right, Miss Miriam?' the cook asked anxiously, as her grey-faced mistress slumped down into a chair, her hands knotted, writhing and twisting together on her lap, her tortured eyes staring down at the floor.

'Leave me, Mrs Elwood. Leave me alone.' Miriam Josceleyne's voice was a weak thready whisper.

'''Ull you be all right, my duck?' the older woman entreated, and Miriam Josceleyne nodded jerkily.

'Please, just go. I need to be by myself,' Miriam Josceleyne pleaded, and reluctantly the fat cook shuffled from the room and quietly closed the door behind her.

As her heavy footsteps receded down the stairs, Miriam Josceleyne again shook her head as if in disbelief, then she vented a choking cry and harsh sobs began to judder her frail figure.

Chapter Forty-Four

The sound of bolts being withdrawn and a key rattling in the lock caused Johnny Purvis to open his eyes. He came to a sitting position on the wooden sleeping bench in his cell as its heavy iron-studded door was opened.

The tall bulky-bodied Police Sergeant Brunton entered the gloomy confines. He regarded the prisoner with sympathetic eyes.

'How are you feeling, Johnny?'

'Well enough, thanks, Sergeant.' Johnny felt no animosity or resentment towards his captors. He appreciated the fact that they had treated him as well as they could do, considering the circumstances.

'What's happening to Mrs Dolton?' he asked anxiously. 'Is she all right?'

'Oh yes, she's as right as ninepins.' The sergeant's lips pursed under his full beer-stained moustache, as if he was doubtful about speaking further. Then he added, 'As a matter of fact she's been released days since.'

'She's not to be charged then?' Johnny sought assurance.

The sergeant again pursed his lips, and for a moment appeared reluctant to answer. Then he said, 'Well, just between you and me, your statement exonerates her of any offence, doon't it? Then there's Mary Phelan's statement as well. No, she'll not be charged with anything. She'll have to appear as a witness, o' course.'

'It's good to hear she'll not be charged with anything. She's suffered enough,' Johnny said sincerely.

The sergeant's broad features assumed an ambiguous expression, but he made no comment on that point. Instead he informed, 'Your friend's arrived to see you – Mr Saul Shibco.'

Johnny nodded his satisfaction, and the other man went on, 'I'm going to let you talk to him in our charge room. I'll have to have a man there to keep an eye on you, naturally, but you can talk freely enough.'

'Thank you very much,' Johnny grinned wryly. 'This room isn't really fit to receive visitors in, is it?'

The policeman returned the grin, and then jerked his head. 'Come on then, I'll take you along.'

Saul Shibco rose to greet Johnny as he entered the small austere room and his face mirrored his troubled concern.

A middle-aged constable came to stand against the door, and the sergeant left them.

They were seated on the straight-backed wooden chairs that, together with a battered table, comprised the sole furnishings of the room. Shibco began to volubly express his regrets and sorrow at finding Johnny in such straits, but Johnny quickly moved to cut off the flow of words. 'What's happened has happened, Saul. I've just got to soldier on now.'

Johnny had been in custody for several days, and had appeared before the examining Justices to be committed for trial at the next Worcester Assizes on a charge of man-slaughter.

'You're taking it very coolly, my friend,' Shibco observed with mingled surprise and admiration. 'If I were in your shoes I'd be frightened half to death, and cursing my evil fortune.'

Johnny shrugged. 'I'm a fatalist, Saul. Naturally I'm scared, naturally I'm feeling sick at heart at my luck, but it's no good my giving in to such feelings, is it? After all, I've faced worse than the prospect in front of me now and survived it. Better men than me have suffered more grievous fates.'

The big blond head nodded sadly. Then Shibco made an obvious attempt to speak more cheerfully and confidently. 'Well at any rate you've no need to worry about your affairs. If the worst should happen, I'll see to your new house and all the other matters. You will have nothing to concern yourself about on that score, I swear on my dear brother's memory to that.'

'I've no wish to put you to such trouble, Saul,' Johnny protested, but the other man brushed aside the protest.

'It's no trouble to me at all. In fact I regard it as a privilege, and it would give me grievous offence if you did not permit me to do it.'

Johnny nodded. 'I'm very grateful to you.'

'Now, is there anything more that I can do to help you?' Saul Shibco pressed. 'Anything? Anything at all? Please, Johnny, if there is I beg you to tell me.'

Johnny hesitated, glancing at the silent constable, who pretended to be very interested in the stained, cracked plaster of the ceiling.

'Come now, my friend. If there is any service I can render, then I beg of you to allow me to do it,' Saul Shibco pressed.

Still Johnny was hesitant. Ever since his arrest, the thought of Miriam Josceleyne had tormented him almost unbearably. He longed to see her, or to receive some message from her, and dreaded what effect these violent and tragic happenings had had on her. She had made no attempt to contact him while he had been here in the police station, and his reluctance to involve her in anything that might cause her pain or embarrassment had prevented him from having made any attempt to contact her. Yet he yearned for her both physically and mentally. The thought that he might now have lost her he found almost unbearable.

The sergeant had allowed him to buy envelopes, notepaper, pen and ink, and slowly and painfully he had composed a long letter to Miriam Josceleyne expressing his love for her, and his bitter regrets for what had occurred. In the letter he had also pleaded with her not to dismiss him from her life.

Again Johnny glanced at the constable, who still appeared to be engrossed in contemplation of the ceiling. Then he spoke in a low voice, 'There's one great service you could do for me, Saul. You could deliver this to Miss Miriam Josceleyne of Cotswold House, Church Green East, and try to obtain an answer to it from her.'

Now he surreptitiously took the letter from his inside jacket pocket and slipped it into Saul Shibco's ready hand. It disappeared instantly and Shibco winked slyly, then

340

asked aloud, 'How much longer do you remain here?'

'I'm being transferred to Worcester jail this afternoon. The Assizes take place next week.'

'You've engaged lawyers?'

'Yes. All that's been arranged. I've got a good barrister to defend me.'

'Right then,' Saul Shibco lowered his voice to a whisper. 'I'll do this little errand for you and I'll be back directly with her answer.'

He waited until Johnny Purvis had been escorted from the room then went to find the police sergeant who readily gave permission for him to return for another brief visit before Johnny Purvis's transfer to Worcester that afternoon.

The day was warm and sunny and as Saul Shibco crossed Church Green he could smell the scents of the flowerbeds and hear birds singing and chirruping in the trees and bushes.

Cotswold House was at variance with the brightness of the day, its windows dark with drawn curtains. Saul Shibco rang the bell and waited. Then rang again. Then again. Then again.

For almost fifteen minutes he stayed on the front porch, fruitlessly ringing the bell, at last deciding that there was no one at home and he walked away, intending to call back later. As he turned to shut the outer gate behind him, he saw the heavy dark drape of the right-hand ground floor window move aside and switch back rapidly, and he frowned.

'There is someone at home. Well I'll be dammed if I'll let them ignore my ringing.' He was well aware that Johnny Purvis placed great importance in this letter, and he was determined to deliver it, and to obtain some sort of reply for his friend as well.

He quickly crossed to the front porch once more, and this time kept up a constant furious jangling on the bell.

At last the door opened, and a beautiful chestnut-haired girl scowled angrily at him. 'What does you think youm doing, mister? Disturbing folks who doon't want to be disturbed.'

'I must speak with Miss Miriam Josceleyne. It's very urgent that I do so. My name is Saul Shibco.' He took his

341

expensively embossed calling card from the inner pocket of his dove-grey frock-coat and handed it to Emma Farr.

She scanned the card then examined him curiously, noting his prosperous appearance and gentlemanly manner.

'Miss Josceleyne is unwell,' she told him. 'What business have you got with her?'

'It is a private matter of considerable delicacy. I really must insist upon seeing Miss Josceleyne personally.'

Saul Shibco was puzzled by this beautiful young woman, who spoke with the accents of the lower classes, yet was wearing an expensive gown, and bore the appearance of a gentlewoman.

'Might I enquire if you are related to Miss Josceleyne, ma'am?' he asked politely, raising his top hat briefly.

Emma Farr could not restrain an impish grin. 'I'm shortly gooing to be very close related to her, mister.'

This news coupled with his mounting frustration, caused Saul Shibco to throw his customary caution to the winds.

'That being the case, then I will speak frankly, ma'am. I am acting on behalf of my close friend, Mr John Purvis, who is, as I expect you already know, at present experiencing some considerable personal difficulties.'

Emma Farr's black eyes widened slightly, and her shrewd brain raced.

'Mr Purvis has entrusted me with a personal letter for Miss Miriam Josceleyne, and entreats her to grant him an immediate reply to it. I shall act as the bearer of any such reply.'

Emma came to an instant decision, and now she told him charmingly, 'Well, Mister Shibco, like I told you already, Miss Miriam is unwell at the moment, and the doctor thinks it could be catching. So it's best that you doon't come into the house. But if you'd like to wait here then I'll take the letter to her, and get her reply.'

The man smiled in relieved gratitude. 'That is most kind of you, ma'am.'

'Not at all,' Emma smiled brilliantly.

The door closed behind her and Saul Shibco waited patiently upon the porch.

In the hallway Emma Farr examined the envelope and found it to be unsealed. Quickly she pulled out the contents and read them. Her eyes glinting with jealousy as she scanned the tender impassioned words. Once she had read it she replaced the letter in the envelope, then leaned back against the wall. She thought with a scathing contempt of Miriam Josceleyne, now lying ill with grief upon her bed.

'That weak cow 'ull never be any good to you, Johnny Purvis. Any trouble and she collapses. It's a woman like me that you needs. I can be a real mate for you.'

The prospect of Johnny Purvis being sent to prison and the subsequent slur on his name did not bother Emma Farr. The respectability so treasured by those above her in the social scale was a matter of no importance whatsoever in her life.

'From what folks say, he'll not get above five years for what he's done. I'll have old Hector long dead and buried by then. I'll be a rich widow, all footloose and fancy free. Just ready to comfort a good-looking man like you, Johnny Purvis, when you gets out o' the nick. You'll soon get over Miriam Josceleyne. I'll write to you while youm inside.'

She tore the envelope and its contents neatly in two, then placed the pieces on the silver salver from the hall table. Assuming a regretful expression she opened the door and said with dismay in her voice, 'Oh Mr Shibco, I'm ever so sorry, but this is what Miss Miriam did. She 'udden't even read it when she knew who it come from. She's told me to give you the message that she wants nothing more to do wi' Mr Purvis. Not ever, she doon't. She realises now that he is not a gentleman, and 'ull never be such.' Emma shook her head sadly. 'There's nothing to be done about it, Mr Shibco. Miss Miriam's mind is made up, and she's a very stubborn woman. She says to tell John Purvis that he doon't exist for her and that she's bitterly ashamed that she ever was friendly with him.'

Back in the police cells, Johnny Purvis heard Saul Shibco's account with grimly impassive features, while inwardly his heart was weeping. Then he summoned his own stubborn pride and courage, and nodded decisively.

343

'Well, Saul, if that is what the lady desires, then that is what she will get. I'll not trouble her further.'

Back in his cell he slumped down upon the wooden sleeping bench and sadly considered his life. Thoughts and random images came and went in aimless succession. At times a lump came to his throat, and tears brimmed in his eyes as he thought of his father, and the terrible shame the old man must be feeling at his son's disgrace.

Johnny did not blame Cleopatra Dolton for what had happened. He felt that she had been mercilessly driven to come seeking his aid.

Thoughts of Miriam Josceleyne he tried to thrust from his mind, but without success, and at last he was forced to let his grief at losing her overwhelm him, and allow his tears to fall freely.

The release of his feelings slowly assuaged the keenest edges of his mental sufferings. Eventually he was able to summon his courage and his resolution once more, and to face his uncertain future with proud resolve. 'I'll not let it destroy me. Whatever might happen, I'll face it as a man, not as a snivelling coward. What's done is done and over with. I've just got to soldier on now and bite on the bullet when the pain gets too hard to bear.'

He thought of the dead man, Arthur Dolton, and grimaced. 'I'll not be a hypocrite and claim that I mourn your death, Dolton. You were a worthless hound as far as I'm concerned, and you remain so wherever you might be now. But I really did not intend to kill you, and that is the truth.'

Again his thoughts turned to Miriam Josceleyne. 'I'm truly sorry for any pain this has caused you Miriam, my love. I'll respect your wishes now. You'll never hear from me again, I swear to that. I only hope that you will someday find happiness.'

He lay back on the hard narrow bench and gazed up at the white-washed ceiling of the cell, and smiled grimly to himself.

'Now just soldier on, Purvis, and bite hard on the bullet . . .'

Chapter Forty-Five

'Man that is born of a woman hath but a short time to live and is full of misery. He cometh up, and is cut down, like a flower. He fleeth as it were a shadow, and never continueth in one life . . .'

The sonorous tones of the Reverend Mosse MacDonald M.A., were taken by the gentle breeze and carried across the graves and tombstones of the cemetery. They could be heard clearly even by those who were at the extreme edges of the large crowd of spectators gathered in the hilly cemetery to witness the burial of Arthur Dolton.

At the open grave itself were the family mourners, friends and some business acquaintances of the deceased. They stood tightly clustered at one side of the grave, at the head of which Mosse MacDonald was thoroughly enjoying his officiation at this widely publicised funeral.

'In the midst of life we are in death. Of whom may we seek for succour but of thee, O Lord, who for our sins are justly displeased.'

The curate emphasised this last sentence, and a murmurous ripple of approval sounded from the Dolton family, as their eyes glared across the deep black hole to where on the opposite side, standing completely isolated, Cleopatra Dolton stood proud and erect, her head held high.

The burial men were busy with their ropes, preparing the coffin for lowering into the grave and now as Mosse MacDonald's voice boomed on, they moved to take centre stage and began to lower the coffin into its final resting place, a process which the females of the Dolton family greeted with sobs and wails of grief, while their menfolk endeavoured to maintain a stern manly demeanour of suffering being nobly borne.

Cleopatra watched the coffin disappearing into the cold yellow-red clay and behind her thick dark face-veil her full lips curved into a smile of pure satisfaction.

The coffin reached its floor and the burial men respectfully moved away from the graveside to allow the casting of earth while Mosse MacDonald exerted all his histrionic arts.

'Forasmuch as it hath pleased Almighty God of his great mercy to take unto himself the soul of our dear brother here departed, we therefore commit his body to the ground. Earth to earth. Ashes to ashes. Dust to dust . . .'

The cleric's eyes moved questioningly towards the widow. She was supposed to be the first person to take up a handful of earth and to let it slowly dribble down with all due reverence upon the coffin lid in token of her grieving renunciation of her beloved husband's fleshly body to the earth to which all flesh must eventually return.

Mosse MacDonald always appreciated the theatrical gesture, and savoured this part of the service above all else.

He nodded meaningfully at the widow, and continued. '. . . In sure and certain hope of the Resurrection to eternal life through Our Lord Jesus Christ . . .'

Among the clustered mourners facing Cleopatra Dolton, angry scowls were now being directed at her still figure, swathed in its funereal finery. They too were eager to take centre stage momentarily and cast their individual handfuls of earth.

'. . . who shall change our vile body, that it may be like unto His glorious body, according to the mighty working whereby He is able to subdue all things to Himself.'

Mosse MacDonald was frowning for all to see as he came to the end of this address, and he openly stared with reproach at the widow.

As if suddenly cognisant of her own remiss behaviour, Cleopatra crouched, her black-gloved fingers hovered above the heaped soil taken from the grave. Then, quite deliberately, she selected a large heavy clump of clay and

346

stone. She advanced to the edge of the grave and with gesture that radiated contempt she pitched the big clump down onto the coffin, its impact thumping loudly enough to be heard by the nearest of the casual spectators.

A concerted gasp of outrage sounded from the Doltons, and Mosse MacDonald was so disconcerted that he stumbled over the next part of the address.

'I,I,I errr, I heard, I heard a voice, err, a voice from heaven saying unto me . . .'

Cleopatra turned and walked away from the grave, and the crowd of spectators eddied back to give her passage. She looked neither right nor left, and although later many of those present claimed that she had been laughing, in all truth her thick black veils rendered her features indistinguishable.

She passed through the cemetery gates to where her closed carriage was waiting. She had ridden alone to the church, had sat alone and isolated during the service there, now she left the cemetery to return alone to the house in Red Lane where her children and servants waited for her.

During the short trip Cleopatra Dolton sat smiling happily. She had already been informed by her husband's solicitors that she would inherit all his money, businesses and properties, and now she gloatingly savoured her new future.

'I can be alone whenever I choose to be. Alone, with no man to abuse or hurt me. For the rest of my life I can be safe from men . . . and alone with my own peace.'

Final Chapter

The summer had ended. The autumn wind skittered the fallen leaves across Church Green in an erratic swirling dance.

In the small cottage in Izods Yard, Ezra Purvis sat at the table laboriously writing a letter to his son. Because of his trembling hands, the penmanship was wide-scrawled and spidery, and he breathed a silent prayer of thanks as he reached the end of his task. He folded the sheet of notepaper and slipped it into the envelope. A knock came on the door and he called, 'Is that you, Mrs Bint?'

The rosy cheeked woman poked her head into the room.

'Have you finished your letter to Johnny, Mr Purvis? I'll take it down wi' me now and post it for you.'

'Thank you.' He handed the envelope to her, and she saw the sadness in his face, and comforted him.

'Theer now, Mr Purvis. He'll be home in four years, wunt he.'

'I'm feared I'll not be alive to see him though, Mrs Bint.'

'You 'ull, Mr Purvis. I'm sure on it.' She smiled warmly, and taking the letter with her, left the old man sitting silently gazing into the flickering flames of the fire.

The front door of Cotswold House opened and a frail slender figure came down the steps and into the roadway. The dowdily dressed woman hurried with bent head along the pavement past the row of shops at the end of Church Green East.

'Miss Josceleyne?' James Whitehead came from his shop doorway to accost her.

Her faded green eyes regarded him without enthusiasm, and he smiled nervously, displaying his ill-fitting false teeth.

'I didn't see you at church last Sunday, Miss Josceleyne, and I feared you might still be feeling unwell.'

Her hands entwined and twisted and tugged. 'No, I'm very well, I thank you, Mr Whitehead.'

'And your father and his lady wife, I trust they are well?' the man persisted, trying to detain her with him.

She frowned slightly, and her eyes flicked from side to side as if seeking a way of escape. 'Yes, they are well, Mr Whitehead.'

'Will I see you in church this Sunday?' the man asked, with a pleading note in his voice.

'Well, I don't know, as yet, Mr Whitehead.' Miriam Josceleyne's voice was strained and her manner tense and ill at ease. 'I really must go, Mr Whitehead. My brother Franklin is expecting me.'

Reluctantly he stood aside and raised his bowler hat politely.

'I'll bid you good day then, Miss Josceleyne.'

'Good day, Mr Whitehead.' Miriam Josceleyne scurried onwards, her posture reminiscent of some small frightened creature seeking shelter from the dangers of open spaces, and the man stood wistfully staring after her.

In the kitchen of Cotswold House Emma Josceleyne and Mrs Elwood sat at the table sharing a bottle of gin, talking and laughing. From somewhere overhead there sounded the faint thumping of a stick upon the floorboards, and the older woman grinned.

'Your lord and master wants you, my duck, by the sounds on it.'

Emma chuckled. 'He'll just have to goo on wanting then, won't he?' She lifted her glass to her lips and took a long slow swallow, then expelled a loud gust of satisfaction. 'This is a drop o' good, aren't it, Mrs Elwood?'

The other woman agreed vehemently. 'It is that, Emma. Mind you, theer's bin quite a few good things that's come out o' your wedding aren't theer?'

349

Emma returned her grin, then looked with satisfied complacency at her expensive fashionable gown, and the profusion of costly jewellery that adorned her. 'Yes, I can afford the best stuff now, carn't I?'

The thumping stick increased its tempo, and both women could hear the faint shouts that accompanied it.

Emma chuckled, and again looked with satisfaction at her expensive gown. 'If that old sod thinks I'm gooing to goo up theer and let him paw me while I'm wearing this, then he's sadly mistaken.' She winked at her friend. 'I forgot to tell you, Mrs Elwood, I went to the agency this morning and I've engaged two maids.' Her eyes danced with devilment. 'They'm both likely girls, if you gets my meaning. Very free and easy. They'll help keep the old sod happy.'

Mrs Elwood threw up her hands and cackled with admiring laughter. 'Youm a case, you am, Emma. Youm a real case.' She sipped from her own glass, and smacked her lips with relish. Then questioned, 'Has Miss Miriam said any more about getting her own place to live?'

Emma shook her head, and her eyes softened. 'No, I think I've managed to persuade her to stay on here. I'm very fond of her, and I 'udden't like to think that I'd driven her from here by marrying her dad. She'll be all right.' She grinned mischievously. 'At least her knows now that I doon't expect her to call me mother.'

'And you'll be all right when your fancy man gets out o' jail, my wench.' The fat cook's features wore a sly expression. 'I saw that letter you know. It was laying on the hall table.'

Emma scowled with quick resentment, then shrugged her shapely shoulders and chuckled, 'I wrote to John Purvis as a friend, Mrs Elwood, and he wrote back to me as the same. That's all we are. Friends.'

'You still fancies him though doon't you, my wench?' The fat woman challenged.

Emma again shrugged. 'I'm not sure really. Still four years is a long time, aren't it? A lot can happen before he gets released. I'm expecting to be a widow by then. We'll just have to wait and see, won't we?'

From above the thumping stick suddenly stilled, and Emma laughed uproariously when Mrs Elwood quipped, 'You might be a widow right now, my duck. He's gone very quiet all of a sudden, aren't he?'

Walter Spires arranged the tray of meat in the window of the shop and then looked down the street and called back over his shoulder, 'Here's the boss coming, Ozzie.'

Ozzie Clarke came to stand by his workmate and stare at the oncoming woman. He made a faint sucking sound with his teeth.

'She's looking very toothsome today, aren't her, Walter?'

Cleopatra Dolton came along Evesham Street, dressed in black widow's weeds, a demure toque with a whispy veil and a black silk parasol over her shoulder.

Walter Spires cupped his genitals with his hand and groaned jokingly. 'What udden't I give for a night with the Queen of Egypt! I'll tell you what, Ozzie, I reckon Johnny Purvis had a bargain theer, doon't you? Four years for bloody manslaughter, and then when he gets out I reckon he'll have the next four years in bed with her. I knows I 'ud.'

'Chance 'ud be a fine thing, Walter. Who know's what might happen before Johnny Purvis gets out o' nick. Besides, him and her denied that theer was anything between 'um, didn't they?'

Ozzie Clarke's brown eyes were thoughtful. He pursed his lips, then said, 'Come on, we doon't want her to catch us standing doing nothing, does we. Or else she might sack us like she did Tommy Thomas last week.

'Ahrr!' his companion agreed. 'Her's turned out to be a real Tartar to work for, aren't her. I reckon we was better of wi' Arthur. He was too bloody drunk to care what we was doing half the time, warn't he.'

When Cleopatra Dolton came into the shop both men were working at the great wooden chopping block.

'Hello Mrs Dolton. I never saw you coming,' Ozzie Clarke grinned and came towards her, his eyes appreciatively dwelling on her shapely body, displayed to its best advantage in her tight-fitting black silks.

'Hello Mr Clarke.' Cleopatra Dolton's features bore little trace of the damage inflicted by her husband's fists; only a hardly discernible thickening of the bridge of her fine nose, and a faint hairline scar above one eyebrow.

She smiled invitingly at the handsome young man. 'I'd like some fresh beefsteaks, please Mr Clarke. Could they be delivered before six o'clock do you think?'

'But o' course they can, Mrs Dolton. Youm the boss.' He grinned at her and his eyes were speculative, as he thought, 'I wonder now? I wonder if her's feeling hungry for a man? Should I chance me arm, or what?'

She laid her gloved hand upon his arm and squeezed gently. 'Many thanks to you, Mr Clarke. I'll expect delivery before six o'clock then.'

The pressure of her fingers, and the warm smile curving her moist full lips caused Ozzie Clarke to cast caution aside.

'Shall I bring them down meself then, Mrs Dolton?' he asked in a low coaxing tone, then inwardly cursed as he saw her lips set in a hard line, and behind the wisp of veil her eyes fix coldly upon him.

'Do we still employ a delivery boy, Mr Clarke?'

'Yes, Ma'am,' he sighed with simultaneous dejection and disgust that he could have allowed himself yet again to misread the signs.

'Then let him deliver the meat, Mr Clarke.' Cleopatra Dolton's voice was as cold as her eyes.

'Very well, Ma'am,' he accepted meekly.

Cleopatra turned and walked slowly away, and both men stared after her with open lust. She passed the shop windows that lined Evesham Street, conscious that from behind the panes of glass many eyes watched her. She walked with a pride that those who saw her thought to be arrogance, and she walked alone . . .